PRAISE FOR THE NOVELS
OF JESSE HAYWORTH

HARVEST AT MUSTANG RIDGE

"Jesse Hayworth writes delightful tales that will wrap themselves around readers' hearts. With breezy, light-hearted writing and plenty of laughter, charm, and emotion, Jesse Hayworth gifts her readers with a book that will keep them turning the pages and rooting for these wonderful characters."

—*New York Times* bestselling author Jill Gregory

WINTER AT MUSTANG RIDGE

"Jenny and her love interest, Nick, are endearing with their playful banter, and their natural chemistry resonates. With lyrical storytelling and genuine characters, Hayworth has created a love story that will wrap itself around any reader's heart."—*RT Book Reviews* (4½ stars)

SUMMER AT MUSTANG RIDGE

"A superb read: a gorgeous setting and a beautiful love story."

—*New York Times* bestselling author
Catherine Anderson

"Warm, witty, and with a great deal of heart, *Summer at Mustang Ridge* is an instant classic."
  —*New York Times* bestselling author Kristan Higgins

"The Wyoming backdrop is beautiful, watching a foal being born is miraculous, ranch life sounds like a lot of fun, and Foster and Shelby are sweet and tender with each other."   —*Publishers Weekly*

continued . . .

"Hayworth paints the setting so beautifully, you won't want to leave. The romance is slow and subtle but with enough encouragement to keep you reading all night. I can't think of a better recommendation for a sweet romance: horses, scenery, and working cowboys."

—*Kirkus Reviews*

"A beautiful love story expressed in simple, elegant language. . . .With a solid plot and a host of sympathetic, genuine characters, Hayworth takes her time in weaving a tale of love and healing, all set against the beautiful rural backdrop of the Wyoming mountains. This heartwarming story is a keeper." —*RT Book Reviews*

"Hayworth does a wonderful job creating realistic and great characters . . . a wonderful book to read. . . . If you are looking for a fun and wonderful romance, look no further than *Summer at Mustang Ridge*."

—The Reading Cafe

"Jesse Hayworth let Shelby's and Foster's feelings and emotions take the lead. *That* is ROMANCE! Romance where hearts heal, love, and then soar."

—Once Upon a Romance

"An enjoyable book, providing interesting characters and a sweet love story with just enough unexpected special touches to keep the reader turning pages. . . . *Summer at Mustang Ridge* is exactly what sweet romance lovers crave, creating anticipation for what promises to be an enjoyable Western contemporary series. A tender love story, told in a unique voice, sure to please any romance lover." —Romance Junkies

HARVEST *at* MUSTANG RIDGE

JESSE HAYWORTH

A SIGNET ECLIPSE BOOK

SIGNET ECLIPSE
Published by the Penguin Group
Penguin Group (USA) LLC, 375 Hudson Street,
New York, New York 10014

USA | Canada | UK | Ireland | Australia | New Zealand | India | South Africa | China
penguin.com
A Penguin Random House Company

First published by Signet Eclipse, an imprint of New American Library,
a division of Penguin Group (USA) LLC

First Printing, August 2014

SIGNET ECLIPSE and logo are trademarks of Penguin Group (USA) LLC.

ISBN 978-0-451-41916-3

Printed in the United States of America
10 9 8 7 6 5 4 3 2 1

To Jennifer Fusco for being a voice in the industry. To my writer-friends at CTRWA for always being there with a hug, a critique, or a cute cat video to keep the juices flowing. And to my readers for sharing the Skye family with me. There would be no Mustang Ridge without you.

Dear Reader,

Once upon a time, one of the girls at the barn where I worked sidled up to me and whispered, "Tim likes you. He wants to know if you like him back." And so began my first relationship—he was my first kiss, my first "I love you," and my first a whole lot of other things. And for a splendid year, everything was perfect. We planned our futures, named our kids, and did all the things you do when you think there's no way that something so great won't last forever. But then I went off to college, and he stayed home to work in the family restaurant, and even though we promised nothing would change, everything did. He started making excuses, I started clinging, and things went downhill from there. And eventually, he became another first for me: my first heartbreak.

Maybe that's why I love reunion romances . . . not because I want to get back together with Tim—who I hope is happily married with a restaurant of his own and a bunch of kids—but because I adore the idea of two people much like us finding each other years down the road, when they've had time to grow into their own skins.

Take Krista Skye and Wyatt Webb, for example. They loved each other utterly in college, but when Wyatt betrayed her—betrayed them—the pain almost destroyed her. Now, years later, she's the heart and brains of Mustang Ridge Dude Ranch in the beautiful Wyoming hills . . . and she needs his help. So let's saddle up, grab some of Gran's famous biscuits, and join Krista and Wyatt for a wild ride!

Love,
Jesse

1

"Knock, knock?" Krista cracked the sliding barn door and stuck her head through to scan the interior. "Anyone home?"

Horses moved in the stalls that lined both sides of the concrete aisle, offering her a couple of snorts and an optimistic whinny, which she interpreted as *Got carrots?* There was no answer of the human variety, though.

Stepping out of the summer heat, she scanned the stall doors. "Claire? Are you in here, honey? Your mom is looking for you."

Instinct had Krista heading for the last stall on the right, where a small sparkly purple halter hung beside a nylon stall guard, which was only a couple of feet off the ground but was chest high on the fuzzy gray pony within. And, sure enough, she saw the toe of a small pink sneaker peeking out from a corner.

"Hey, Marshmallow," Krista said. "I don't suppose you've seen Claire, have you? You have? Where— Oh!" she said as the sneakers moved and a dark-haired girl eased into view. "There you are!" *Phew.* "Did you come to give Marshmallow another hug and tell him you'll see him soon?"

The little lower lip went into quiver mode, and Claire's big brown eyes filled as she whispered, "Next summer isn't soon."

Krista fought a small smile, knowing it wouldn't help the situation right now. But as far as she was concerned, the response deserved something along the lines of trumpet fanfare, a big *TA-DAAA* and a standing ovation. A week ago, when the new guests had stepped off the airport shuttle, Claire had tried to make herself invisible, staying hidden behind her mother. Now she was sneaking out to the barn and talking back. Maybe that wouldn't seem like a victory to some, but Krista would totally take it. Same for Claire's mom, who had already booked a return trip for later in the season, swearing the staffers to secrecy because it was going to be a birthday surprise for the little girl.

"You'll be back here sooner than you think." Krista held out a hand. "Come on. Let's make sure your mom packed Mini Marshmallow." The stuffed toy wasn't officially part of the ranch's gift lineup yet, but she had given Claire one of the prototypes last night during the send-off campfire so she would have something more than memories to hang on to when she left.

Claire reached back to stroke the patient pony's neck. "Do you think he'll forget about me?"

Krista's heart tugged, because of course the answer was *yes*. Soon, Claire and her mom would be back on the airport shuttle, heading home to their regular lives, while the people and animals of Mustang Ridge took a precious few hours of downtime before gearing up to do it all again with a new crop of guests. And while Krista would remember the quiet little girl who had started to creep out of her shell under the big, wide-open Wyoming sky, she doubted the same could be said of the pony.

But that wasn't what Claire needed to hear. Krista sensed that she wanted—needed—to feel special. Didn't everybody?

"Hey." Krista lowered her voice to a conspiratorial whisper. "I've got an idea. Can you get me the scissors out of the tack room? They should be on the shelf beside the door."

As Claire quietly scooted off, Krista worked her fingers through the pony's mane, sectioned off some of the longer hairs and began plaiting the strands together, weaving them into an intricate four-stranded pattern. She had just reached the bottom when the little girl returned.

"Thanks." Krista took the scissors. "How attached are you to those pigtail ribbons?" They were pink to match the sneakers, and cute as the dickens with white and purple polka dots.

Claire pulled the ribbons free and handed them over, eyes going wide as Krista cut one of them in two, braided half into the lower section and used the other half to tie off the top. "Is that for me?" she whispered.

Freeing the plait with a quick snip that gave the

pony a mini-Mohawk, Krista said, "It sure is, kiddo. Hold out your wrist." The horsehair bracelet was a perfect fit, and she fastened it in place by tying the ribbon ends into a fat bow. "You can have your mom take it off for showers and such, or even for you to tuck away back home. You don't have to wear it all the time—but this way you'll still have a part of him with you."

Claire touched the bracelet, tracing her fingers over the wiry gray braid. Then she smiled, making rare eye contact. "Thank you."

How could the words sound so small, yet make Krista feel so big? Grinning, she said, "That's not all. Watch this." Taking the other ribbon, she sectioned off an inch of mane right behind the pony's furry little ears and began a second braid, this time working the ribbon in about halfway down, so the pink with the purple and white polka dots showed alongside the gray. When she reached the bottom, she tied off the braid with a bow that matched the one on the bracelet. "See? Now he won't forget you, either."

Eyes wide and round, Claire touched the braid, then leaned in to wrap her arms around Marshmallow's neck. Pressing her face into his mane, she whispered, "I'll be back. I promise."

As the little girl reluctantly pulled away, the barn doors rolled open wider, and Claire's mom, Vicki, stepped through, blinking as her eyes tried to adjust to the shadows. "Krista? Are you in here? Did you find— Aha!" Her features relaxed as she zeroed in on her daughter. "We figured you might have snuck back out here, Missy Claire. What were you doing, trying to see if you could smuggle a pony home in your suitcase?"

Krista chuckled. "I think the TSA might've noticed."

"I would've paid the overweight charge," Vicki said piously. "What have you got there?" she asked her daughter, noticing the bracelet.

As Claire crossed to her mother and held up her wrist, measured bootfalls rang from the other end of the barn, where a covered walkway connected the newer, guest-friendly structure to the older barn. Krista turned, expecting to see her head wrangler, Foster, even though he was supposed to have left half an hour ago. "Running late?" she called. "I thought— Oh." She stalled when a stocky form stumped through the doorway. As eyes the same blue as her own landed on her and narrowed, she reoriented. "Hey, Gramps. How's it going?"

Wearing jeans, a faded long-sleeve work shirt, and a layer of trail dust that said he'd gone out riding early, Big Skye didn't look much different from when Krista was Claire's age and had been his constant shadow. Back then, he had put her up in the saddle in front of him and called her his best little cowgirl. Now he just gave her a sour look and said, "Where's Foster?"

It was stupid to be disappointed. She and Big Skye were getting along better these days, with him helping her out by managing the Over the Hill Gang—a herd of retirees and rescues that had taken over the top pasture. But that didn't stop her from wishing things could go back to the way they had been between them.

Then again, Jenny always said she was the stupid optimist of the two of them. As far as Krista's twin sister was concerned, Krista either needed to challenge their gramps to a duel—boxing gloves in the bonfire pit, maybe, or seeing who could go eight seconds on Buck the Bull—or grow a thicker skin.

Doing her best to channel a tough-skinned armadillo, Krista said, "Foster is probably halfway to the water park by now. He and Shelby are chaperoning Lizzie's class trip." A few years ago, that would've sounded like the biggest whopper ever told at Mustang Ridge, but these days her alpha male head wrangler was married and fully domesticated.

"Bueno needs a shoe tacked back on," Big Skye grumbled. "Guess I can do it myself."

"Wait!" Stifling visions of herniated disks and her gramps in traction—he was *not* a good patient—she thought fast. "Nick should be dropping Jenny off any minute. He can do it."

"And charge us out the wazoo, no doubt," Big Skye said with a cattleman's typical reaction to the thought of calling the vet for something simple. Even if that vet was married to his other granddaughter and had to be reminded—repeatedly—to bill Mustang Ridge. But he tacked on, "Any minute you said?"

"They're on their way."

"Fine. Tell him to meet me by Bueno's stall." He nodded to Vicki and Claire. "Ladies." Then he thumped back the way he had come, muttering about vets thinking they knew how to shoe horses, and how when he'd run the place, he'd had a dozen cowboys working for him who could've set a nail blindfolded.

"What's that, sweetie?" Vicki asked as Big Skye's boot steps faded into the shadows of the back barn. She leaned down, listened to her daughter's whisper, and nodded. "That's right! That's the man from the videos." Straightening, she grinned at Krista. "I had been talking for a while about wanting to bring Claire to a guest ranch, and a friend sent me a link to *Mustang Ridge: The Cowboy Way*. By minute three, I was ready to book our reservation."

Krista's lips curved. "I'll be sure to tell him." Big Skye might claim he had come around to supporting the dude ranch—sort of—because of logic and profit margins, but his becoming a minor YouTube celebrity hadn't hurt the turnaround. "And my sister, Jenny. She's the filmmaker in the family. She and Gramps made *The Cowboy Way* and *The Early Years* while she was on hiatus from filming *Jungle Love*."

Vicki's eyes lit up. "The dating show on TV? How cool! Did you see last season, when Bryce showed up riding that big black horse, pulled Valerie up in front of him, and took her galloping down the beach in the moonlight?"

"I remember seeing that episode." With Jenny sitting next to her, saying stuff like, "See that cut? I bet she fell off two steps later," and "Bingo. They totally had to redo her hair."

Vicki put a hand to her chest. "Swoon! Oh, we should all be so lucky, to have a gorgeous guy like that show up and sweep us off our feet."

Pass, Krista thought wryly. She had done the swept-up thing, and it hadn't ended well. "Jenny isn't on the show anymore. She moved back home and married our vet." And thank goodness for that.

"Still, how cool that she had those experiences! I think a girl has to get out there and live a little, don't you?"

"Absolutely." Krista tipped her head toward the double doors leading out. "Are you two ready to catch the bus? Rumor has it, Gran baked chocolate chip cookies for the road."

As they headed out—with Claire sending a final wave in Marshmallow's direction—Krista fielded Vicki's questions about her twin's stint on *Jungle Love* and dished some PG-rated gossip on the contestants, amused yet again that Jenny ranked way higher on the cool scale than she did. That was just fine by her, though. She didn't need glitz, glamour, or a handsome man to sweep her off her feet. She was good at taking care of the little things.

An hour later, after the last good-bye was said and the airport shuttle gave a cheerful horn blast as it crested the hill, Jenny elbow-bumped Krista. "Okay, they're off. Now it's our turn. I hope you're feeling lucky!"

"On a day-to-day basis? Absolutely." Krista took a long, satisfying look around them—from the sprawling ranch house, barns, and guest cottages nestled in their valley, to the ridgeline and the gorgeous mountains silhouetted against the clear blue sky. Despite what Big Skye thought, she was true to her roots.

"I'm talking about the mustang lottery, and you know it."

"Yeah, but it never hurts to remember to be grateful for what you've got."

"You go ahead. I'd rather look forward to what's coming next." Jenny bounced on her toes. "This is going to be fun!"

Thanks to a progressive new mayor and some state funding, the nearby town of Three Ridges—well, nearby in backcountry Wyoming terms, at any rate—was undergoing a major renaissance, including the resurrection of the decrepit fairgrounds and the county fair that had long been an end-of-summer fixture. And with her usual flair, Mayor Tempe Tepitt—often called Tempest Teapot by those who got in her way—had added a modern twist to the old favorite by cooking up the Harvest Fair Mustang Makeover.

The premise was simple: Two-person teams would choose a training project from a group of fresh-caught wild mustangs. Six weeks later, the teams and their horses would meet at the Harvest Fair, where they would compete for prizes and bragging rights. Better yet, all the proceeds from the ticket sales would go to a local mustang preserve.

Last winter when the competition was first announced, Krista and Shelby—aka Foster's wife, Krista's

BFF next to Jenny, and goddess of all things advertising—had jumped on the idea, even coming up with a new theme week and a plan for the ranch guests to cheer for Team Mustang Ridge in the ride-off. Now, the entry fees were paid, the cabins were fully booked for Makeover Week, and it was time for Krista and Jenny to head for the fairgrounds and pick their mustang.

She's right, Krista told herself. *This is going to be fun.* Win or lose, she and Foster would be adding a new mustang to the herd. She'd be posting progress reports to the ranch's Web site and social media outlets, so their growing network of guests could stay involved. And Makeover Week was going to be a blast, whether or not she picked a horse that could be turned into a superstar. Still, she had rodeoed through her teens and won more than her share, and even though she was committed to the whole "enjoy today" thing, she had to admit that the idea of competing in front of a big crowd put a stir of excitement in her belly. Not to mention that she had a plan for the prize money—one she thought Big Skye would like.

"I hope we get a good horse," she said with a look toward the barn, where Foster and Junior had set up a quarantine pen in the riding ring.

"Too bad you're human antimatter when it comes to raffles."

"Why do you think I wanted you to come along?"

Jenny patted the camera bag slung over her shoulder. "Free advertising?"

"That, and because you're the lucky one. Maybe it's the hair."

Although they were identical twins, Krista still used braids and ponytails to corral her long, fine blond hair. Jenny, on the other hand, had gone short and brunette, partly so it wouldn't get in the way of the camera, and partly to distinguish herself from her sister. As if spending nearly a decade filming in exotic locations while Krista stayed home and transitioned Mustang Ridge from a cattle station to a dude ranch wasn't enough distinction between the two of them.

"We've got a little time if you want to hit the Lady Clairol," Jenny offered with a wicked twinkle. "I bet Mom's got some you can use."

Laughter bubbled up, followed by a guilty look toward the main house. "*Shh,*" Krista said. "She thinks nobody noticed."

"She can't possibly be that delusional. Anyway, if I'm your good luck charm, does that mean you've decided on your top picks?"

Krista patted her back pocket, with its folded-up program. "Foster and I swung by the holding pens earlier in the week and took a look. We came up with our top three choices and the bottom five, and I've got notes on the others, in case we wind up selecting in the middle of the pack." *Fingers crossed we go early, though,* she thought, because she really, really wanted a certain big gray mare.

"Well, then." Jenny hooked an arm through hers and aimed them toward the parking lot, where the horse trailer was hitched and the truck was ready to roll. "What are we waiting for? Let's go get lucky!"

2

The fairground took up a hundred or so acres of high-country prairie, with a fringe of pine in the middle distance and the mountains rising beyond, jagged against the blue summer sky. The parking lots and paths were overgrown, wildflowers sprouted around half-repaired concession stands, and the smells of fresh sawdust and new paint mingled with the scent of horses. Trucks and trailers were clustered near the livestock building like cattle jostling for water, and the two hundred or so lottery-hopefuls and hangers-on were crammed into the adjoining arena, waiting for the selection process to begin.

Thanks to a longer-than-usual line at the diner, where they had stopped for burgers and fries, Krista and Jenny had missed out on the folding chairs and wound up sitting on the three-rail fence at the back, far away from the announcer's stand, where a cylindrical wire crank-cage held several dozen Ping-Pong balls.

"They totally stole that setup from Wednesday-night bingo," Jenny said, pitching her voice to carry over the crowd noise. "What do you think we're going to be? B-8? Maybe N-31?"

"How about something in the G's, for *good-looking gray mare*?" Krista bounced her boots on the bottom rail as four people climbed up into the judges' stand. "Here comes the committee, or at least part of it."

Tempe Tepitt stepped up to the microphone. She was short and bulldoggish, with steely hair pulled up under a baseball hat that was probably intended to play down the plum-colored power suit, but instead made it look like her head and body didn't belong together. Behind her stood Marsh and Martin Lemp—a couple of sun-bleached, weathered cowboys Krista had known all her life, and who had been in charge of picking the makeover mustangs from the latest gather.

It was the fourth person in the small group that caught Krista's attention, though. "What's Sam Babcock doing up there?"

Dark-haired and dressed down in the same sort of jeans-and-a-plain-shirt routine the Lemps were rocking, the thirty-year-old rags-to-riches owner of Babcock Gems looked like he could be just another hired hand. More, he looked much as he had in college—big framed but thin to the point of gauntness, with his hands clasped behind his back to keep his fingers still.

Or maybe not. Maybe he had changed since then, just like she had.

"I guess he's on the committee," Jenny said, "or donating. Probably both. Trust me, by the time the mayor got done with Nick, he had gone from 'sure I'll sponsor one of the prizes' to doing all the health exams and gelding operations for free." She slid a look in Krista's direction. "You okay?"

"Of course. Why wouldn't I be? It's not Sam's fault that his best friend turned out to be a jerk." He had warned her, after all. "Besides, that was college. Everybody does dumb stuff in college."

"I didn't."

"Two words: naked skydiving."

"Hey!" Jenny protested, laughing. "That was in the cone of silence!"

The mayor leaned in, gave the microphone a couple of taps, and then said in a rah-rah voice, "So, what do you say, folks? Are you ready to give me a ten-count, and we can get this party started?"

That got a cheer, and the crowd chanted along with her: "Ten . . . nine . . . eight . . ." Krista and Jenny chimed in at six, and when everybody got to "One!" all four big sliding doors on the nearby livestock building rolled open, revealing the horse-filled pens. The crowd clapped and whooped, and a few of the mustangs whinnied as if to say, "What's going on out there?"

Little did they know how much their lives were about to change. And while Krista hated knowing how scared and confused the horses would be at going from open range to holding pens and now to their new homes, the wild herds were growing too quickly for the shrinking rangeland to handle, making the sales and lotteries necessary.

When the crowd noise mellowed, the mayor lifted her microphone and said, "By the power vested in me, I declare the Harvest Fair Mustang Makeover officially open!" She paused for another cheer, this one louder and longer. "Today, you'll be drawing names and choosing your mustangs. You'll have six weeks to train your horse from the ground up, and when we all get together for the final ride-off, I expect to be blown away. So choose wisely!"

Krista took another look at the catalog, wondering if the gray mare was really her best bet. At seven, she was older than most of the others, which could mean that her training would move faster . . . or she could be too set in her ways, too used to being in charge of things. The last thing Team Mustang Ridge needed was for their mustang to take one look at the screaming-kid-loaded roller coasters and Tilt-A-Whirls, decide the horsepocalypse had come, and try to round up the others and stampede them to safety.

"No second-guessing," Jenny said without looking up from her camera, where she was making the last couple of tweaks in prep for filming the lottery.

"Taking a minute for a reality check isn't the same as second-guessing."

"It is when you've got good instincts." Jenny turned on the camera and aimed it up Krista's nose. "What does your gut say?"

She batted the camera away. "That nobody wants to see my nostrils on YouTube. And knock it off. I'm being serious here."

"Go for the gray. First choice is usually right, and all that."

Boots bouncing harder on the bottom rail of the fence, Krista focused as the mayor finished reading through the rules and shifted back to her rah-rah voice to say, "In addition to helping bring attention to our part of the great state of Wyoming and getting some well-earned bragging rights, the winning team will take home cash and prizes totaling over twenty thousand dollars."

As she ran down the list of sponsors—with Babcock Gems front and center, no big surprise there—Krista craned to see into the back corner of the barn, looking for something that said she was making the right decision. Was it too much to hope for a big foam finger coming out of the sky and pointing to one of the mustangs in a cosmic moment of "Hello, Universe speaking here"?

Nada. There was never a good foam finger around when she needed one.

Inside the barn, four guys moved around the pens with the saddle-swagger she associated with lifelong horsemen. Closest to her, grizzled, crotchety old Mel Lemp—an older cousin of Marsh and Martin—was holding a clipboard and glowering like he'd rather be somewhere else. Behind him, two younger cowboys were muscling additional pipe-corral panels into place, building the loading chute they would use to chase the horses onto their new owners' rigs. And beyond them, over by the gray mare's pen—

Krista straightened, feeling like she'd grabbed on to a strand of hot wire while standing barefoot in a puddle. "Whoa. Who is *that*?"

"Where?" Jenny swung the camera toward the barn.

"Don't—" She bit off the protest, knowing she was lucky to have Jenny's help in promoting the ranch, even if the whole being-filmed thing sometimes put her on edge. Especially when she was seeing things. "In the back corner. Jeans, dark shirt, brown felt hat." Which stood out against all the summer straw and brought on a full-body shiver, followed by a whole lot of, *It's not him. It* couldn't *be*.

Except that it totally could. Sam was there, after all.

Jenny zoomed in and hummed. "Hello, he is *built*. Get a load of those guns!"

Which argued against it being Krista's one-and-only ex, who had been wiry rather than jacked. "Is he . . ." She didn't even know what she was trying to ask—couldn't think past the sudden buzzing in her ears.

"Maybe you should pick him when the mayor calls your name." Jenny dialed up the zoom. "Let me see if I can get his hip number."

"Give me the camera." She needed to get a look at his face, needed to know for sure.

"In a minute. Oh, yes. Very nice."

Krista tugged at her arm. "Give it here." Someone called her name, but she waved them off. "Hang on just a sec."

Laughter sputtered and then swelled, yanking her attention away from the barn and back to the lottery, where most everybody had twisted around to look at her. Realizing she and Jenny had missed something major, she shot out an elbow and hissed, "*Ssst!*"

Her sister swiveled around, camera and all, and did a double take. "Um. Hello?"

"Are we interrupting something?" the mayor drawled over the loudspeaker, looking at them with the oh-for-Pete's-sake expression worn at some point by every teacher who'd ever wound up with the two of them together in class.

Intensely aware of the red *blink-blink-blink* that said Jenny's camera was getting every nanosecond of this, Krista called, "I'm sorry, Mayor Teap—er, Tepitt. Please continue."

"I will . . . as soon as you pick your horse."

"I—oh!" Excitement kicked. "Is it my turn?"

The mayor gave an exaggerated eye roll. "Okay, rewinding." Holding up a Ping-Pong ball, she pantomimed taking it out of the bingo barrel and intoned, "And now, first choice in the inaugural Harvest Fair Mustang Makeover goes to"—she spun the sphere and read the name inked on it in Sharpie—"Krista Skye!"

The applause was sprinkled with laughter, and somebody yelled, "Go, Krista! Woo-hoo!"

Grinning, she shouted, "Well, then, I'll take hip number forty-one!"

A murmur ran through the crowd, along with some knowing nods and a couple of *Awww* noises that said she and Foster weren't the only ones who'd had their eyes on the gray.

"Forty-one goes to Krista Skye of Mustang Ridge Ranch," Mayor Tepitt confirmed. "Best of luck with your new horse!" There was more applause while Martin got the bingo balls bouncing again, and then the mayor stuck in a hand and grabbed one. "Next up is going to be . . . Amos Allwood!"

As a skinny young cowboy with spidery arms and legs shot to his feet, Krista turned to Jenny and whisper-squeaked, "We got the gray mare!"

"Whee!" They high-fived, hugged, and did a little seated wiggle-dance to celebrate the lottery win.

Jumping down off the fence, Krista beckoned. "Come on. Let's get her loaded and hit the road!" She turned for the barn and started for the nearest open door, but then hesitated, remembering the cowboy in the brown hat.

She didn't see him, but he was back there. Somewhere.

"Hang on. Call me stupid, but I'm just putting two and two together and getting ex-boyfriend." Jenny grabbed her arm and pulled her close. "You don't think that was—"

"No." Krista said, cutting her off before the name got out there in the universe, tempting the foam finger. "As far as I know, he's never set foot in Three Ridges. It was seeing Sam that made me think of him, that's all. The power of suggestion."

She hoped.

It didn't take them long to get the rig into position—they had both pretty much learned to drive with a trailer in tow, and the aluminum gooseneck was one of the nimblest in the Mustang Ridge fleet. It also had the bonus of being open inside, with padded walls and not too much room for the mare to hurt herself in the panic of being separated from her herd and chased into an unfamiliar metal box.

"The minute she's on board, I want you to get moving," Krista told Jenny, who was behind the wheel of the big white dually. "She'll be less likely to bounce around in there if she has to focus on her balance. Keep it slow and I'll catch up."

After swinging open the trailer gate and fastening it in position, she headed for where Mel and the two younger wranglers were gathered beside the loading chute, muttering over clipboards. As she approached, another figure stepped out of the barn—big guy, brown hat, shoulders that went on for a mile.

Krista didn't let herself slow down.

The cowboy kept his back to her as he gestured toward the horse pens. She caught a glimpse of dark brown hair that had a touch of red to it, making her think of a black horse that had bleached in the sun. Just like he-who-shall-not-be-named. This guy was taller and broader, though, his center of balance high in his chest rather than low on his hips. More like a calf wrestler than a bull rider.

Exhaling a relieved breath, she approached the huddle just as it broke up, and Mel and the two younger men headed into the barn. "Hi there," she said to the big guy's back. "I'm here for hip number forty-one."

"Figured you might be," he said, and turned.

Krista. Stopped. Breathing.

Because after all that it-couldn't-possibly-be-him, it totally was. Wyatt Webb, her one-and-only ex, was standing right there in the flesh. And the bastard looked good.

3

A thin trickle of oxygen seeped into Krista's lungs as she took in the familiar dark brown eyes, angular jaw, and the nose that carried a pronounced bump from one too many face-first landings off a bucking bull. There were those extra inches of height and breadth, though, and a layer of heavy muscle outlined beneath his work shirt. Even his hands were different, wider and thicker, with heavy calluses that didn't come from reins or ropes.

He had grown up and done it well.

Annoyed by the sudden urge to tug at her logo'd polo shirt and wish that she had gone for something more in the makeup department—she looked good, too, dang it—she forced air into her lungs and refused to give him the satisfaction of seeing her surprise. Because he had clearly been expecting her.

Jerk.

"I need hip forty-one," she repeated, forcing everything to be level and professional—her expression, her voice, her body language. "The gray mare in the far pen."

"She'll be along in a minute." He paused, searching her face. "You looked good out there." A nod to the arena, where a cheer said another name had gotten picked. "Happy."

Heat stirred at the knowledge he'd been watching her. As metal gates clanged and unshod hooves thudded into the loading chute, she said, "What do you want, Wyatt?" He had to want something. Otherwise, why even make himself known?

"I wanted to apologize to you. To . . . I don't know"—he scrubbed a hand across the back of his neck—"clear the air. I know it was a long time ago, and we've both lived our lives since then, but I wanted to say I'm sorry for how I handled things. You deserved better."

"Yes, I did." And once upon a time, she would've given anything to have him admit it. "Nice of you to make such an effort to track me down. Oh, wait. You didn't."

He shifted in his boots. "I'm staying with Sam for a couple of weeks in between jobs. He volunteered me for this, said you'd be here. I thought it would be easier this way, just running into each other."

Easier for you, that is. Though, really, there wouldn't have been a good time for this. She didn't need an apology, didn't need the mere sight of him bringing back a whole lot of memories that were better off forgotten. Didn't need *him.* Jamming her hands in her pockets—and only then realizing they had balled into fists—she stepped back. "Like you said, it was a long time ago." Behind her, the truck door slammed.

Moments later, boot steps approached, and Jenny said, "Is everything okay?" Coming up beside Krista, she fixed Wyatt with a look that said *I know who you are and what you put my sister through.* "Is this guy bothering you?"

Yes. "No. It's fine. We're done here." To Wyatt, she said, "You'll get the trailer gate when she's loaded?"

He held her eyes for a moment, then nodded. "Will do. You take care, Krista Skye." It was more of a good-bye than he had given her before.

"You, too, Wyatt," she said, if only to have the last word. She didn't let herself run, didn't let herself shake, just climbed in the truck and slammed the door.

And wanted to weep.

Jenny grabbed her arms. "Ohmigosh! That was him, wasn't it? That was—"

"Wyatt." She made herself say the name. "Yes."

"Unbelievable." Jenny craned around to look toward the barn, where he had moved to man the gates of the loading chute. "Did he . . . Did you . . ."

To Krista's relief, there was a sudden commotion in the barn, a couple of hoots and hollers, and then hoofbeats clattered on metal and the trailer rocked and rolled, making the truck shimmy and signaling that the new horse was aboard. Moments later, the trailer door banged shut and the latches clanged into place, and Wyatt's voice called, "You're all set!"

She put the truck in gear and hit the gas, not letting herself stomp down nearly as hard as she wanted to.

As they rolled past the hot dog stands, Jenny stuck

her head out the window to get a better look at the trailer. "I can see her ears through the Plexi," she reported. "You want to stop and double-check the latches?"

"No. We're good."

"You trust him?"

"To close up a trailer? Yes." She would trust him with a horse anytime, anywhere. But as for anything more than that? Forget it. She may have gotten the care-and-nurture gene from Gran, but it was balanced by the one-strike-and-you're-out attitude that came straight from Big Skye's DNA.

"Soo . . ." Jenny drew it out as they turned onto the main road and the ride smoothed out. "You want to tell me about it, or should we pretend we spent the morning shoe shopping?"

So tempting. "If we went for shoes, then where did the horse come from?"

"Get one free with every flat of annuals at Maas's Feed and Grain next door?"

Given Ernie Maas's recent "two ducklings and a shrub, one low price" ad in the local paper, it wasn't all that farfetched. Unfortunately, the charade wouldn't appease Jenny's curiosity, which on a scale of one to creepy stalker, fell somewhere around the *National Enquirer* level.

"Shoes, marigolds, and a bonus mustang," Krista said, trying to keep it light when there was suddenly a whole lot of heavy inside her. "That sounds way better than an ex who couldn't be bothered to get in touch, but wanted to do the apology thing when we ran into each other."

Jenny made a face. "Which part was he apologizing for? Stringing you along, standing you up in public, or dumping you with a crappy Dear Jane letter?"

Ouch. Trust the filmmaker to bring things down to bullet points. They were accurate, though, and eight years was long enough for the wounds to heal. "We didn't get that far. And, frankly, I don't care. I've got better things to worry about—like a ranch full of guests arriving this afternoon, and a new mustang to train."

She didn't need Wyatt Webb or his apology. She had Mustang Ridge.

Wyatt was dog-tired by the time he got back to Sam's ridiculously big house and let himself in through the kitchen. Dragging ass worked for him, though—the more tired he was, the less his brain would spin. And after his run-in with Krista, there was some serious spinning going on.

He had known she would be there today—hell, he'd had his guard up ever since arriving in Three Ridges, figuring they would cross paths at some point. He hadn't figured he'd have trouble looking away from her when they came face-to-face, though, and he hadn't expected to feel like he'd gotten caught staring at the sun. She had gleamed like the sun, too, with a white straw hat, yellow-blond hair, and tanned skin the color of pale honey. And she had looked exactly the same as he remembered, fresh and vibrant, like it had been eight days rather than eight years. Her hair was a shade or two darker beneath the sun streaks, and the coed bounce had turned to a woman's poise, but he could've picked her crazy long legs and cowgirl swagger out of a crowd. Heck, he *had* picked her out of the crowd, even before the mayor called her name.

It was no surprise that the beautiful girl had grown into a knockout of a woman. It was also no surprise that she didn't want anything to do with him. But being in Three Ridges had gotten him thinking about her, gotten him remembering. Maybe too much.

Lucky for him, he was good at moving on. He had just hoped to do it with a clearer conscience this time.

"That you, Wyatt?" Sam called from the front of the house, voice echoing through the under-furnished space.

"Yeah. Hey, hon, I'm home."

"Ha! I'm in the game room." The sounds of canned gunfire, explosions, and screams suggested he was killing zombies or something.

Wyatt followed the noises and paused with a shoulder propped on the door frame. One of the few fully furnished spaces in the whole place—along with the home theater, master bedroom, and kitchen—the game room at Casa Babcock bore a strong resemblance to the bridge of the *Enterprise*, except with a ratty sofa, a relic from their college days, facing the wall of monitors instead of captain's chairs. *Not zombies,* he noted, glancing at the screen. *Aliens.*

Sam froze the game and spun in his chair. Wearing sweats, a ripped T-shirt, and yesterday's stubble, he looked nothing like the unexpected heir to a gem-mining fortune, and everything like the guy who'd made it through his last year of college by volunteering for any medical study that would pay him a few bucks. "Well? I saw you talking to her. How'd it go?"

"About how you'd expect."

Sam lifted the controller. "You want in on this game? Blow some stuff up? Might make you feel better."

Wyatt wasn't big into gaming but appreciated the offer of mayhem rather than touchy-feely. "Maybe in a minute. I'm going to call my sister first. It's her birthday." And he was already riled up. Might as well call the fam.

"Tell Ashley I said hey. Oh, and when you come back, bring my blue water bottle with you."

"Sure. Where is it?"

"Ask Klepto," Sam said darkly.

"Right." Wyatt smothered a snort and headed for the kitchen.

He hadn't figured out where his scruffy gray mutt was hiding his stash in the huge house, but when he did, it would be a heck of a pile. He should probably feel bad, but as far as he was concerned, Sam's life needed some shaking up. Besides, he and Klepto had an understanding: He didn't try to stop his dog from "appropriating" the occasional sock or shiny thing, and Klepto acquiesced to act housebroken.

As Wyatt rounded the corner to the kitchen, he was

just in time to see the tip of a gray, wirehaired tail disappear around the corner of the fridge. He considered following but figured that finding Klepto's stash would entertain Sam when they'd left. So instead, he grabbed the landline handset—cells were seriously unreliable out in the high country—and punched in his mother's number, doing his damnedest to get Krista out of his head. *Case closed, moving on.*

His mom picked up on the third ring. "It looks like a Wyoming number," she said, her voice muffled like she was relaying the info. "I think it must be Wyatt." Then, voice becoming clearer, she said, "Wyatt? Is that you?"

He scrubbed a hand across the back of his neck. "Hey, Ma. Yeah, it's me."

"It's Wyatt," she called, like that was news to anyone in her immediate vicinity. "How are you, sweetie? How did the lottery go?"

"It was . . . interesting."

"How so?"

"Lots of horses, lots of people."

"Did you see anything that you liked?"

About five three, one ten, blond, and blue-eyed, with a swagger that makes a man want to do something stupid. So much for getting her out of his head. He cleared his throat. "I wouldn't have kicked any of them out of the barn. Why, you in the market?" As far as he knew, she hadn't been on a horse in thirty years. Back in the day, though, she had been a rodeo queen—it was how she'd met his old man.

"Not on your life. How are your sketches going?"

"They're going." And by that, he meant he'd thought about unpacking his pencils the other day. "How is Jack? Did that new chiro help any?" His mother's husband had come along too late to be a father figure, but Wyatt would always be grateful to Jack for giving him his life back.

"He's good. He said to say hello."

They spent a few more minutes catching up, keeping to surface things because they did best that way. Then Wyatt said, "Is Ash around? I want to wish her a happy birthday."

There was a beat of silence before his mom said, "She went back to Los Angeles last week. Didn't she call you?"

"She—" He bit off a few choice words. "No. She didn't. I take it she's back with Kenny?"

Kenny was his younger sister's deadbeat ex-boyfriend . . . or he had been, the last time Wyatt checked. After two years of on-again, off-again, she had finally moved back home, got a waitressing job, and started saving the money she wasn't paying in rent to attend community college in the fall.

At least that had been the plan the last time Wyatt had talked to her.

"You shouldn't be so hard on him," his mother chided.

"I didn't say anything."

"There was a tone."

"Maybe we should change the subject. How is your garden coming?"

"You just don't understand how women think."

So much for changing the subject. "The guy is a loser, and he drags her down with him." The drummer for a band that booked just enough gigs for its members to convince themselves that they didn't need real jobs, Kenny was a self-absorbed, self-important dope who, when Ash had spiked a temp of one oh four with the flu on a night he was supposed to play, had loaded her in a cab and told the driver to take her to the ER, leaving her to figure out how to pay for the ride and the meds.

"He's young," his mother said. "They both are. They'll figure it out as they go along."

Like you did? Or like he had? His mother's marriage to Jack—her only marriage, mind you, as Ash and Wyatt's old man hadn't ever quite made it to the altar—was the exception to the otherwise ironclad rule that both sides of his family sucked at relationships, and that was because Jack had the perseverance of a limpet. "I'd rather see Ashley figure out things for herself," Wyatt added. "Once that starts happening, ten bucks says she'll go for a different kind of guy." Like one with a job. Maybe even a retirement plan. *Hey, there's a thought.*

"She doesn't want another guy. She's in love with Kenny."

"She'll get over it."

"You don't get to choose when to love someone," she said tartly. "It's all or nothing."

Which was ironic, really, given how many times she

had fallen in and out of love with his old man. "I'm just saying I'd rather see her stay with you guys and go back to school. Maybe while she's doing that, Kenny will pull himself together."

"You could help him with that, you know. You've got connections."

Not as many as she liked to think, but still. "I tried." Several times, in fact, allowing Ashley's pretty-please eyes to overrule his common sense. "I got him a sit-down with Nigel at Studio 101. He never showed."

"He was having car trouble, remember?"

"Yeah, I remember." It had been his car that time, the flu the time before, and a hangover the time before that. Always an excuse, just like he'd heard from his mother all through childhood. *Your father didn't mean it; he's just tired; he's changed; you should give him another chance. . . .*

"You should give him another chance." Her voice merged with the memory, sparking a burn of frustration in his gut. "Ashley loves him. And she loves you, too. You should call her. Tell her you're not mad."

"I thought I *was* calling her." But where the first few minutes on the phone with his mom had been fine, now he just wanted to hang up.

"She's got a new cell. Let me get you the number."

"Just tell her to call me when she gets a chance, okay?"

"Are you coming for a visit soon? The side gutter is overflowing again, and with Jack's back bothering him . . ."

"I'm not sure. I'll let you know in a few days." He

ducked a few more questions and finally said, "I've gotta go, Ma. I love you." Which was true—he loved them both, her and Ashley. But he had long ago learned that loving someone wasn't the same as wanting to be with them, or even having much in common.

Hanging up the phone with more force than necessary, he grabbed a couple of beers out of the fridge and headed for the game room. Suddenly, he was in the mood to kill the heck out of some aliens.

4

The next morning, when the alarm went off, Krista woke fuzzy-headed and fuddled from dreams that had involved lots of prancing hooves and a cherub wearing fringed chaps and wielding squirt guns.

"Ohhh-kay, then," she said, and sat up in bed, rubbing her eyes as things came into focus around her—mercifully without the kid.

A few months ago, her mom had insisted that the room needed a facelift, and in a two-week orgy of paint chips and fabric swatches, the rodeo-princess-turned-businesswoman décor had given way to a rustic, homey blend of earth tones and comfortable fabrics. The centerpiece was a hand-carved bureau that had a herd of galloping mustangs flowing around three sides, with the same movement picked up in the swirling pattern of the bedspread and a wall collage made from Krista's favorite prize ribbons.

Her mom had described it as "equine eclectic with a modern Italian touch." Krista didn't know about that,

but she figured it said, "You've come a long way, baby."
And she liked that.

After dressing for the day, she headed downstairs
and followed her nose to the big commercial kitchen
that took up the back of the main house. There, exposed
beams and potted herbs provided homey touches, baking racks bulged with muffins and sourdough rolls,
and she could practically feast on the yeasty air.

"Morning, sweetheart," Gran caroled as she bustled
between the ovens and the pantry. Wearing jeans and a
mock tee under a bright yellow apron decorated with
singing peppers, she looked far younger than her years,
even with the wispy white of her hair escaping from
beneath a denim ball cap.

At the butcher-block end of the long counter, her
round-cheeked assistant cook, Dory, said, "Hey, Krista,"
and waved a jalapeno. Then she went back to her pile,
coring the small peppers and sticking them upright on
a custom-made rack. Over the course of the day, the
peppers would be roasted, skinned, and turned into
Gran's famous green chili, which had its own page on
the Web site, its popularity second only to her sourdough starter, fondly called Herman. Who had his own
Twitter account.

Krista may not've had *pretend to be bread dough online*
on her life list, but she figured that you never knew
what the fans would glom on to—and when they did,
you had to run with it. Given that Herman had more
followers than the official Mustang Ridge account, she

had gotten pretty good at sharing ranch tidbits from a biscuit's point of view.

"Good morning, you two." She headed for the coffeepot, thinking maybe she should start an account for Marshmallow, too, so kids like Claire could keep in touch with their favorite pony. "How were things yesterday?"

"Your mom and I did just fine with the guests and vice versa," Gran assured her. "No problems to report." Which a couple of years ago would've seemed like a miracle. But just as Big Skye had found himself a new purpose in managing the ragtag herd of rescued horses and cattle that had accumulated because Krista couldn't say no to protruding ribs or a hard-luck story, Gran and Rose Skye had made peace at long last, agreeing to a cease-fire that left Gran in control of the kitchen and Rose in charge of special guest services and events.

"Is there anyone I should keep an eye on?" she asked. It was Reunion Week, with a full booking of twenty-four guests split up into families, friends, and couples, all looking to reconnect with one another.

Gran pursed her lips. "Maybe the McConnells."

Krista flipped through her mental "Who's Who This Week" file. "Married couple, looking to put the spark back into things?"

"Looks more like Mr. McConnell and a new, much younger girlfriend."

Krista hissed out a breath. "Well, that's just . . ."

"Totally not what Reunion Week is for?" Dory suggested.

"We'll go with that." Krista took a swig of her coffee, feeling the rich, thick sludge—which was how the old-timers had made it and how her Gran preferred it still—hit the back of her throat. "I guess things must've changed since he booked the trip. Oh, well, most of the getting-to-know-you activities are carryovers from Singles Week. Hopefully, they'll still have a good time."

"You haven't met her yet," Gran warned. "I'll bet you a biscuit she's going to kick up a fuss about something. If not the cabin or the food, then how she stepped in manure or broke a nail. Maybe all of the above."

And Gran's radar was good like that. Krista nodded. "Gotcha. I'll keep an eye on her. How about the Nixons? Father and teenage son trying to patch things up." Before putting down his deposit, Bradley Nixon had quizzed her up, down, and sideways, wanting her to guarantee that a week of trail riding would make him and his son best buddies in the wake of a rough-sounding divorce. That had earned him a yellow flag in the reservation database: *potentially high maintenance.*

"They didn't set off any real warning bells," Gran said. "Randy doesn't seem like he wants much to do with his dad, but he's polite enough. He asked if it was okay for him to throw his baseball up on the roof for some practice. I told him he needed to stay away from the horses and the main house, but it was fine for him to use their cabin or your father's shop."

Krista grinned. "You mad at Dad for something?"

"No, I just figured it wouldn't hurt to mess with his

bubble. He's too much like his father for his own good, and your Gramps has been in a mood this past week."

"I noticed. Is Betty Crocker giving him grief again?" The brown-and-white spotted cow had come to Mustang Ridge after being found abandoned on state land, seemingly shuffled off because she was too old to produce milk anymore. As soon as she'd gotten some food into her, though, and perked up, it became obvious that she was a devil in cow clothes. Someone had raised her as a pet and taught her to come into the kitchen for treats, and now she did it for sport—sneaking away from the Over the Hill Gang, finding her way through the fence, and making a beeline for Gran's kitchen. Which, given the whole guest-ranch thing, was a big problem.

"He hasn't mentioned Betty in particular, but I wouldn't be surprised if something like that hasn't gotten under his saddle." Gran patted Krista's hand. "He'll settle down. He always does."

"Or maybe," Dory put in slyly, "he's planning something supersecret for your big anniversary. When is it again?"

When Gran pinkened and flapped her towel at them, Krista answered for her. "December tenth. The big five oh. You're coming to the party. Right, Dory?"

"Wouldn't miss it for the world! Especially if Arthur has something up his sleeve."

Gran touched her hair with a sweet smile. "Maybe. I hadn't thought of that."

Note to self, Krista thought. *Make sure Big Skye comes*

through with something special. She'd get Jenny to help lean on him. "Is there anything on your wish list?"

Her grandmother's eyes went dreamy. "Breakfast in Paris, dinner in Venice. You know, the usual. Oh, and the opportunity to kick bug-eyed Billy Bollinger in the nuts for kissing Mindy Cassidy when I was wearing his letter jacket back in tenth grade."

"Gran! You did not just say *nuts.*"

"What, you'd prefer a synonym? Well how about—"

"No! Please." Krista put her hands over her ears, laughing. "I don't want to know what you call them."

"I've got lots of names for them. How else do you think your grandfather and I made it to forty-nine years and counting?" Gran grinned as she tweaked an oven timer. But then her voice got more serious. "Speaking of exes we'd like to kick in the tender bits . . ."

It took a second for that to sink in, another for Krista to mostly smother the wince. "Jenny told you what happened yesterday." She had been trying not to think about her run-in with Wyatt. It was too pretty a day to start off with a cloud over her head.

"She wanted me to make sure you're okay."

"I'm fine." At Gran's narrow look, she put up both hands. "Seriously, I'm good. Sure, I was surprised to see him again, but it really wasn't that big a deal." *Over and done with, nothing to see here, move along.* A decent night's sleep—weird dreams notwithstanding—had put things into better perspective, leaving only a residual ache that she figured would disappear once she got into her groove with the guests.

"I don't know how you can be so calm about it. When I remember"—Gran pressed her lips together, no doubt thinking back to the night of Krista's college graduation party—"it makes me so mad that he did that to my girl."

"I was barely out of my teens, Gran. If I've learned anything from the guests, it's that teenage girls do most everything with their emotional volume cranked to ten." Maybe twenty. "You haven't seen me like that since then, have you?"

"No, but I also haven't seen you get serious about anybody else," Gran pointed out, then lifted her apron to pantomime a kick. It was more shin-high than crotch-level, but it got the point across.

"I've been busy." It sounded weak, even to Krista. "And, hello, I've dated." A little, anyway. "In case you haven't noticed, the pickings are a little slim in Three Ridges." It was the sort of place young singles escaped from and retirees escaped to.

"In case you haven't noticed," Gran parroted, "you've got guys parading through here—a fresh crop each week."

Dory nodded. "If you count out the families, single women, and guys who are too young, too old, taken and/or gay, there are probably, what, two or three dozen legitimate candidates per season? Even if you figure ninety percent of them aren't a good match, that still leaves a couple of datable guys coming through Mustang Ridge per year."

Krista blinked at the math. But while she'd certainly

had a handful of male guests who ranked up there on the good scenery scale—not to mention ten times that many hookup offers ranging from charming to "eww"—she'd never been tempted. "Sorry, ladies. Besides the whole 'holy unprofessional behavior, Batman,' it takes longer than a week for me to get interested in a guy."

"I'd say it depends on the guy," Dory said.

She'd had her whirlwind. It hadn't ended well. "I'm not dating a guest. Period."

"Fine." Gran nodded like Krista had made her point for her. "You'll go on one of those Web sites."

"Hang on. I didn't mean—"

"If the local dating pool is too small, then it's a woman's God-given right to widen it. At least that's what Ruth says." At the thought of Nick's administrative assistant, Gran brightened. "In fact, you should ask her to help you! Before she met Nick's father, she was an online dating pro."

Ruth was also seventy-something, purple-haired, and hadn't been all that picky. Or maybe it was fairer to say that after losing her husband, she had been ever hopeful that the next first date would turn out to be her new Mr. Right. But whereas Ruth had seemed to enjoy the process, the thought made Krista want to stick her head in one of the commercial ovens. "I don't know, Gran. I don't think the online thing is for me."

"Promise me you'll think about it?"

"I promise." Which wasn't at all the same as promising she would think about it in any sort of positive light. Krista lifted her mug in a salute. "Thanks for the pep talk, ladies, but I need to get going. I told Foster I'd meet him to check out the new horse before things get started for the day."

"You'll take him a muffin," Gran said. "And one for yourself."

"Thanks." Krista snagged the muffins and kissed her gran's soft, sweet-smelling cheek. "You're the best." Which went without saying but was still worth saying now and then.

"Poosh." Gran waved her off. "Go on and see to your horse. Keep an eye on the clock, though."

"What, me lose track? Never." Well, hardly ever.

"And call Ruth."

"I said I'd think about it, okay? But, and this is just a word to the wise"—Krista fixed her gran with a look—"if I find out you and Ruth put your heads together to make me a profile and chat up random guys on my behalf, I'll . . ." Okay, she didn't actually know what she would do—she'd never had to threaten Gran before. She snapped her fingers. "Got it. I'll post your cookie recipes on the Web site."

Dory gasped, and Gran's eyes narrowed to slits. "You wouldn't."

No, but when she was twelve, Big Skye had taught her how to win at poker. "If I start getting e-mails like '*Roses r red, violets r blu, I saw ur profile, and I want to do u*'? Count on it." As Gran and Dory whooped, she waved her way out the door. "Catch you guys later."

Outside, it was shaping up to be a gorgeous summer

day, perfect for a picnic ride up to one of the high lakes with a new crop of dudes. Excited to see the gray mare—she was toying with "Jupiter" as a name—and talk to Foster about a training plan, she jogged down the steps from the kitchen door and headed for the barn. Halfway there, her phone let rip with the *Lone Ranger* theme, and she grinned and took the call. "Hey, Foster. Sorry. I got caught up with Gran. I've got muffins, though, which should make up for it. I'll be there in a sec."

"Actually, it's Shelby."

Krista stopped dead at the sound of choked-back tears in her best friend's voice. "What's wrong? Where are you?"

"I'm at the hospital."

Her stomach plummeted. "*Shelby!* What happened?"

"Foster fell under one of the horses. It's his knee, and it's bad. But when it first happened, I thought . . ." She didn't finish.

"I can be there in forty minutes." A tangle of half-formed thoughts whipped through her head—*Mom can handle the opening remarks. Is the trailer unhitched? Doesn't matter. I'll take one of the cars.*

"Krista, no! You've got guests."

"If it was me, would you stay home?"

Shelby's voice strengthened. "No, but I don't have one less wrangler than I was expecting for Reunion Week."

The bad thing about doing business with friends was that your friends knew your business. "I don't care,"

Krista said stubbornly, even though Shelby was right, dang it. She had gotten away with being shorthanded all summer—what with Ty going on the road with a country band, and Stace part-timing it while she finished her thesis—but now her inability to find more riders to add to Team Mustang Ridge was poised to bite her in the butt. "Damn. I wish I could be there for you."

"You are." Shelby's sigh echoed down the line. "It looks bad, Krissy. Like surgery and major-time-off bad. We'll know more after the X-rays and probably an MRI, but . . ." Emotion thickened her voice once more. "One second he and Pardner were pushing the cows back up toward the high pasture, and the next thing, *boom*. Pardner tripped, did a somersault, and went right over on top of Foster. He was scrambling to get up when I got there. The horse was, I mean. Foster . . . he wasn't moving. I couldn't even tell if he was breathing." She sob-hiccupped.

"God, Shelby." Krista cradled the phone to her cheek, like that would do anything to bring her friend closer. "Seriously, forty minutes. Or at least let me call Jenny."

"I already did. She's on her way."

"Good. That's good." It didn't make Krista feel any better about not being there, though. "You'll call me with updates? I don't care when, how often, or what I'm doing when the phone rings, I want you to call me. Promise?"

"I will. I promise. But"—another hiccup—"you're going need to make some other calls, you know."

Krista could've sworn her stomach had already sunk as low as it could go. "Don't say it. Not yet."

"Sorry, kiddo, but sometimes the truth sucks. And the truth is, you're going to have to find a new head wrangler to finish out the season."

5

By the time the weekend rolled around, Krista had proof positive of something she had long suspected: Foster was irreplaceable.

Granted, he could be crabby with the guests, but he had been her go-to guy since about five minutes after she'd taken her first reservation. Now, she was leading the rides herself with Junior bringing up the rear and both of them trying not to blink—because when you mixed horses, greenhorns, and the great wide open, the craziest things had a way of happening. Like when Art Finkle overbalanced in the saddle during a river crossing, made a panicked grab for his estranged wife, and took them both down with a big, messy splash. Or when the Miller family tied their horses to one another rather than the hitching rail in Keyhole Canyon, and Sassy—a chestnut mare who more than lived up to her name—made a high-speed beeline for the green grass of the upper pasture, dragging the other three along for the getaway.

"Smile, sweetie." Her mom nudged her with an elbow. "It was a good week."

In the office, maybe. But Krista plastered on a smile as several sets of guests headed for where she and Rose stood with Gran near the shuttle bus, which was packed and ready to go.

"Thank you!" Mandy, a single mom to a pair of sulky preteens who had softened considerably over the course of the week, gave Krista a fervent hug. "This was . . . You're amazing. All of you. We'll be back next year, and I'm telling all my friends about Mustang Ridge."

Krista returned the hug, feeling her smile turn genuine. "I'm so glad you had fun. You've got great kids and you're doing an amazing job with them. I'll look forward to seeing all of you next summer!"

Even better, she got smiles and hugs from Mandy's daughters, Bria and Kyle, who had been full of eye rolls and *whatever*s when they arrived.

"Tell Jenny we said bye," Kyle ordered. "She's the coolest."

"I'll do that," Krista promised. "Have a safe trip home and don't forget to double-check your cinch before you mount up."

Bria looked mournful. "I don't think we'll be able to ride much in Chicago."

"It's a metaphor," Kyle said with lofty scorn, then added, "Duh."

"I knew that," Bria shot back. "I was being ironic."

"You were not."

"Was so."

"Annnd, they're off." Mandy came around her

daughters and herded them up the shuttle steps. "See you!"

Next in line was a rawboned teen, all hands and feet and hair that fell in his eyes. "Hey, Randy!" Krista offered a fist bump and got one in return. "I see you've got your rope."

"You know it." He patted the coil she had given him, which he wore slung over one shoulder in fine cowboy style. "I'm going to practice every day back home."

"Not on your brothers or any family pets, okay?"

"How about my stepfather?"

She shot him a narrow look at that one, but Bradley Nixon—who had quickly graduated from *potentially high maintenance* to *type A but a good guy*—stepped up and slung an arm across his son's shoulders. "Actually, Randy and I are going to keep riding. I did some research, and there's a barn not far from my house that offers lessons."

"They've got team penning, calf roping, and even cowboy-mounted shooting!" Randy put in.

"No guns," his father said immediately, but then qualified it with, "at least not at first. Let's get our riding solid, and we can go from there."

They were going to be okay, Krista thought as they headed for the shuttle. It was nice knowing she had played some part in opening the lines of communication . . . though the horses and the high country should get most of the credit there.

After the Nixons, there were more hugs, more gratitude and promises to return, until the bus filled up and the line wore down to the final two: Art and Amy Finkle, who stood with their fingers twined together, wearing matching smiles.

Krista blinked. "Well. Look at you two!"

"Hard to believe, isn't it?" Amy reached up and patted Art's vacation-stubbled cheek. "That dunking in the river got us laughing together for the first time in— God, I don't know how long. Then we talked a little, and a little more, and, well . . ." She blushed.

"The next thing we knew," Art said with an eyebrow wiggle, "we were sitting out behind our cabin with a couple of empty wine bottles, watching the sun come up over the mountains." He kissed Amy's temple. "It was a pretty perfect moment."

And so is this, Krista thought. Maybe Reunion Week hadn't been as much of a disaster as she had thought. "I hope we see you again."

"Count on it," Amy promised.

They exchanged final hugs and good-byes, and Krista watched as the Finkles climbed onto the shuttle, with Art keeping a hand on the small of his wife's back like he didn't want to let go, even for a second. Then the shuttle door accordioned shut, signaling the end of another week.

As the bus lumbered off, Krista gave one last wave, then turned back to her mom and Gran with a sigh. "One week down, seven more to go before the end of the summer season. I hate feeling that way, but there it is. On the upside, I don't think the guests suffered."

"Are you kidding?" Gran said. "That was our best

Reunion Week yet. As long as there are horses to ride and cookies in the saddlebags, we can fudge the rest."

Rose made a face. "I'd rather not have to fudge for too much longer. I'm beat, Eddie is hiding in his workshop, I haven't seen Big Skye in days, and no offense, Krissy, but you look like death."

"Wow, Mom, way to rock the tact." Not to mention reminding her that she had spent most of last night trying to catch up in the office and prep for the new guests.

"You should take a nap."

"Can't. Too much to do."

"Like hire someone to fill in for Foster?"

"Gee, why didn't I think of that?" Krista tipped her head back and stared up at a fluffy white cloud that was shaped like a sledgehammer. "I feel like Goldilocks." She pitched her voice to a girly falsetto. "This one can't ride her way out of a paper bag. This one has the people skills of a lima bean. And this one is just ri—whoops, never mind. He's staring at my chest." Dropping her voice back to normal, she added, "I'm not finding a 'just right,' or even an 'I can live with this for a couple of months.' Foster and I have called in all the favors we can think of, but nobody good enough to do the job wants it. I even tracked Ty down and offered him twice his old pay to come back for a couple of months, but I guess his band is doing really well."

Gran shook her head. "Bummer. I mean, good for Tyler, but that would have been an easy solution."

"Who needs easy? At this point, I'd settle for complicated if it would get the job done." Saying it brought a pang, though, because there was one very complicated option that Krista had been doing her best to ignore ever since it snuck its way into her head in an annoyingly chirpy little chorus that started with *Wyatt's in town* and went through several variations of *He'd be perfect for the job.*

Ugh. Unfortunately, her inner ranch boss had a point—he'd had a part-time job leading trail rides when they met in college, and even the rankest of beginners had swaggered like cowboys when they climbed off at the end of a ride with him.

"You'll figure something out." Gran patted her hand. "You always do."

"From your lips, Gran. In the meantime, I'm going to hit the office and see if I can knock a few things off the to-do list." Like confirming the hair and makeup people Jenny had found for Makeover Week and taking a crack at the growing digital mountain in her e-mail in-box. Maybe a message from the perfect fill-in would be waiting for her.

But instead of an "I heard you were looking for a temporary dude wrangler, here are my awesome creds" message, there were thirty other new e-mails since that morning—inquiries from potential guests, order info from suppliers, and a few offers to make parts of her anatomy bigger or smaller, depending.

Those could be deleted. The others she would have to deal with. Thing was, she couldn't settle into a productive rhythm. Her eyes drifted to the window, her fingers tapped on the desk, and her toes beat a pattern on the floor. *Just do it*, she told herself. *Just call him.* She surged to her feet and paced the small space, resisting the urge to kick a box of logo-embroidered towels out of the way. It wasn't their fault she kept coming back around to the seemingly perfect solution that made her want to stick a Bic in her eye.

Make the call. What's the worst that could happen?

He could say no.

Or, worse, he could say yes.

Gah!

She already had the number—she had gotten it from the mayor, along with the go-ahead for him to compete in the mustang contest, even though he'd worked behind the scenes for a day. Which was putting the chuck wagon ahead of its team, but whatever.

"Just do it!" She snatched up the phone and dialed before she could talk herself out of it again. Then, listening to it ring, she crossed her fingers. *Please be voice mail, please be voice mail, please be—*

Click. "Hello?"

Not voice mail. Bracing herself against the sound of his mellow baritone, she said, "Wyatt. It's Krista. Which you probably figured, if you've got caller ID." *Don't babble. Be professional.* "I, ah, wanted to talk to you."

"Oh?" he said, inflectionless.

Tightening her grip on the handset and telling herself to pretend this was just another stranger who'd been recommended for the job, she said, "I don't know if you heard, but my head wrangler blew out his knee over the weekend."

A beat of silence. "I caught something to that effect."

"Then you know I need to hire someone for the next couple of months."

More silence. Then: "Are you offering me a job?"

No. Yes. This is crazy. "If you're available." She hadn't been able to make herself look him up, hadn't wanted to know what he'd been doing for the past eight years. Which was irresponsible from a business perspective, but it was where the business and personal sides of the situation had locked horns. "I know it's short notice, but you mentioned being between jobs."

"You seemed like you were in a real hurry to get away from me the other day." His voice rumbled on the airwaves, stirring echoes inside her as he asked, "What changed?"

Nothing. Everything. Dang it! "I kept thinking about closure and bringing things full circle, and . . ." She pinched the bridge of her nose, unable to lie, even to him. "I'm desperate, okay? It isn't easy to find someone with the right mix of teaching ability and horse skills, and I know you've done the job before." When he didn't say anything, she launched into her sales pitch. "It'd be an eight-week contract, room and board plus salary." She named a generous figure. "You'd be in charge of training Jupiter, the gray mare I got the other day, and overseeing all the guests' interactions with the horses. Lessons, trail rides, mounted games, cutting cattle, overnight trips, the works. You'd be staying in Foster's old bunkhouse, which is mid-reno at the moment, as we're turning it into a luxury cabin. It's livable, though. It's six days a week, Saturdays off, and you can have a stall if you've got a horse to put in it."

"You want me to work for you." It wasn't a question.

"Think about it." Her heart thudded against her ribs. "Or just come out tomorrow for a trial run, and we can see how it goes."

"Okay."

"We'd need to work together some, especially on the training, but—"

"I said okay."

He had, hadn't he? She tried to swallow, but her throat had gone completely dry. "Okay you'll think about it, or okay you'll do it?"

"What time tomorrow?"

She wasn't really doing this, was she? "Breakfast starts at seven thirty, but the barn stuff doesn't really get rolling until more like nine."

"I'll aim for seven thirty. Get the lay of the land."

Holy crap, holy crap, holy crap. "Okay, I guess I'll see you then." That felt so inadequate, even over the sudden rushing in her ears, that she added, "And, Wyatt?"

"Yeah?"

"Thanks. If this works out, you'll be saving my bacon, big time. I'll owe you one."

"The way I see it, we'll be even."

Her stomach twisted. *So not going there.* "Let me give you Foster's number. You can talk to him about the specifics of the job." There, that sounded businesslike and in control, didn't it?

But when he rang off, she sat there for a second, staring at the computer screen, not feeling professional. At all.

What was she, nuts? She couldn't do this, not in a million years. She should call him back and tell him she didn't need him. She could tell him that she found somebody else. Or was moving to Belize. Anything but "see you in the morning."

Ohmigosh. He would be there tomorrow morning. At Mustang Ridge. It should've been one of those twisted reality-meets-impossibility dreams. Not her real life.

She couldn't do this.

Hands shaking, she dialed again. Twice, because she messed up the first time.

Jenny answered on the second ring. "Hey, sis. What's up?"

"I need alcohol, chocolate, and girl time," Krista announced, "and not necessarily in that order." She hesitated, then went ahead and said it out loud. "I just sort of hired Wyatt to work at Mustang Ridge."

6

"You should stay here and hang out with me." Sam pounded his hammer on a chunk of rock that looked like every other rock in the immediate vicinity. "That'd make more sense than working for Krista. Especially when you don't need the job."

When a fist-size nodule broke free, he frowned at it and then chucked it aside, letting it tumble-roll down the steep slope with a *clackity-clackity-clack* and a *sssst* of pebbles rattling in its wake.

Wyatt watched it go. "Didn't you say this was the kind of place where neighbors helped each other?"

"Volunteering for the mayor's mustang deal, sure. But not something like this. And Krista's not your neighbor—she's your ex." Sam wedged his crowbar beneath a flat rock. "Help me flip this over, will you?"

It had taken them an hour to reach the site on the ATVs, another ninety minutes to work their way up the shifting mountain face to where Sam's gut said he would find something amazing—pink emeralds, maybe, or more of the colored diamonds that had turned him from the poorest kid in town to the region's richest orphan.

It had taken Wyatt that long to mention Krista's call because he figured he'd get exactly this sort of reaction. And because he didn't have a good counterargument.

Guys like him didn't circle back around to an ex. Especially not one like her.

Angling his pick beside Sam's crowbar, he said, "On three. One, two . . ." On *three* they put their shoulders into it. The rock slab shifted, teetered momentarily on its axis, and then overbalanced and fell, bouncing down the scree—pinwheeling and starting a dozen tiny rockslides shushing down with it.

Sam didn't watch it go, focusing instead on the darkness that had been hidden behind. He hunkered down and slither-slid his top half into the pitch-black. "I can't believe she called you." His voice echoed back at Wyatt.

"Sounded like she was out of options."

"You never saw her after you disappeared. She was a wreck at graduation."

"It was a long time ago."

"Still."

And he had seen her. He had meant to be long gone, but had driven back to watch her graduate with Sam and the others. Wearing sunglasses and a baseball hat, he had lurked at the edge of the crowd, reminding himself to breathe when she walked across that stage. Then, later, seeing her surrounded by her family, he had walked away. "So what you're saying is that I owe her one."

"Yeah. Which means you should take off."

"Can't do that. She asked. I said I'd help her out. Besides, I need to get back riding. Not just dinking around on the trails near your place, but real saddle time on a good cow horse."

"There are other places where you could play cowboy." Sam backed out of the crevice holding a fist-size chunk of rock threaded through with dark crystal facets.

Wyatt leaned in. "What's that?"

"Violet iolite." Sam twisted the rock, which glittered purple, blue, and green in the sunlight.

"Is it valuable?"

"Not especially. But it's interesting to find it right now."

"Why is that?"

"According to the woo-woo people, it's supposed to help you make good decisions." He held it out. "Here. I'd say you need it more than I do right now."

When Krista reached the Double-Bar H ranch later that night, Shelby was waiting for her on the porch and Jenny was just pulling in. As Krista mounted the short flight of stairs leading up to the renovated farmhouse, she lifted a wrapped plate. "I come bearing brownies."

"And a story, I gather." Shelby searched her face. "You okay?" Wearing a sleeveless tee made of silk rather than cotton and jeans from a designer Krista had never heard of, the curvy brunette was dramatic and put together from the tips of her manicured toes to the top of her every-four-weeks haircut. But despite the city shine that still hadn't totally worn off—or maybe partly because of it—she and Krista were the best of friends.

"I'm fine," Krista assured her, going in for a quick one-armed hug and taking a moment to lean on her.

"Baloney." Shelby pulled away and gave her a little shake. "This is the Girl Zone. You don't have to be brave in the Girl Zone. It's in the bylaws."

"I'm not trying to be brave. I'm trying to be"— *reasonable, logical, rational*—"a grown-up. The ranch needs him." At least that was what she kept telling herself. The mantra had gotten her through welcoming the new guests, but now it was starting to wear off.

"Ranch, shmanch." Shelby made a rude noise. "And being a grown-up is overrated."

"Hey!" Jenny jogged up the steps with a loaded bag. "No fair starting without me. I've got Ben and Jerry's and three bottles of that nice red with the creepy baby on the label."

"Sounds like the makings of a Girl Zone to me." Shelby herded them through the front door and into the main living space, which was sleek and modern but still felt very much like a home, with soft fabrics and family photos galore. "I thought we'd set up at the breakfast bar. Foster, Lizzie, and the dog are down in the man cave watching a *Firefly* marathon, so we should have our privacy—or at least fair warning before we're interrupted."

Krista hesitated, looking toward the stairs leading down to the finished basement. "I should say hi and see how he's doing."

"He said to tell you hey and that he'd catch you later. I mentioned that we were going to be engaging in Level Five girl talk, and he bolted."

Which totally sounded like Foster. "His second surgery is next week?"

"Yep. Then rehab."

"Is he going stir-crazy yet?"

"Actually, he's doing okay. He's being stubborn about the pain meds, no surprise there. But rather than staring out the window and bitching about being stuck inside, he's signed up for a couple of online sci-fi writing classes, and he and Lizzie have been talking about collaborating on a story. I'm sure he'll get itchy before too long, and well before he's cleared to be off his crutches, but for now he's doing okay." When they reached the gleaming, open-concept kitchen, she pointed to a padded bar stool. "But enough about him. Plant it, girlfriend, and start talking. What *happened*?"

Krista sat as Jenny stuck a glass of wine in her hand and Shelby put a plate of ice cream–topped brownies in front of her. But despite having spent the afternoon alternating between thinking she had lost her mind and looking forward to hashing things out with her sister and their best friend, now she hesitated. "I don't know where to start."

"How about with 'I just sort of hired Wyatt,'" Jenny suggested. "But drink up first."

The first sip of wine fought a battle of tart and sweet on Krista's tongue, while the second loosened up the tightness in her tonsils. Reminding herself that she was the one who had called for emergency chocolate and wine, she said, "I called him. I wasn't going to, kept talking myself out of it, but after the guests left I got to chatting with Mom and Gran, and going over the to-do list in my head, and it hit me that we can't keep going on like we did last week." The third sip went down smooth and warmed her insides. "So I called him. And he said yes. Well, he said okay, but it's the same thing. He'll be at breakfast tomorrow."

"I don't know," Jenny said, shaking her head. "This is Wyatt we're talking about. Your one-and-only. There's a whole lot of worms loaded to come out of that can."

"I'm not opening any cans. I'm just hiring a wrangler."

"There's nothing 'just' about it. You were head over heels for the guy, and he took off without an explanation."

Krista stared into her wineglass for a moment. "He explained."

"He left a note. That's not the same thing."

"Hang on. Time out." Shelby made a "T" with her hands. "What note? What happened between you two? It's hard to know whether to hate him or give him a second chance when I've only got the CliffsNotes."

It was part of the Girl Code that they tried not to swap each other's secrets. Otherwise, Jenny would've undoubtedly spilled the whole cringe-inducing story. A few minutes ago, Krista might have said it didn't matter how it ended, only that it had. But wine and friendship made it easier to say, "Wyatt and I met our senior year, right after spring break. And if it wasn't love at first sight, it was darn close."

She had ridden out that day with her friend Darcy, and on the way home the conversation about their final projects—converting a multigeneration cattle station into a dude ranch for her, eco-friendly guest accommodations for Darcy—had turned to gossip about the new guy at the barn. "He's older," Darcy had revealed. "I heard that he rode bulls for five or six years between high school and college. And he's got that swagger, you know?" She made an "mmmmm" noise of approval as Krista maneuvered her horse to open the gate and let them through the perimeter fencing. "Sooo cute. And nice! Even cranky old man Briggs likes him, and he doesn't like anybody. In fact, I heard— Oh!" Darcy squeaked at the sight of a small herd in the courtyard. "There he is!"

The cowboy was still astride, guiding his horse from one student to the next as they climbed down and fumbled with their reins and cinches. He sat straight and easy in the saddle, his cues nearly invisible, reminding Krista of the hardcore, tell-a-man-by-his-horse cowboys who worked for Big Skye. *Yum,* she thought. But when he turned and looked at her from beneath the brim of his chocolate-brown Stetson, Krista saw that Darcy had been way off. There was nothing cute about his square jaw and the aggressive jut of his nose, nothing so bland as nice about the way his dark eyes locked with hers. He was gorgeous. Arresting. One hundred percent male. And the way he was staring back at her suggested that he liked what he saw.

"He asked me out the next day," she told Shelby. "We went to dinner and a movie, and he kissed me good night. Then a couple of days later, we took a long moonlit ride out to this little hidden waterfall he knew of. It was . . ." *Magical.* "Overwhelming. It was like I had designed my perfect match from the ground up, and then he turned real. I didn't tell him about Mustang Ridge right away, but when I showed him my final project, he understood what I was going for right away and had some ideas of his own. Good ones. Eventually, I told him it wasn't as much of a dream as it seemed—that I had the property in my family, just had to get the others on board. We used to stay up late, talking about what it would be like to run the guest ranch together." She hesitated. "I thought we were planning our future. So I didn't listen when his roommate tried to warn me off."

"That would be Sam Babcock?" Shelby asked.

Krista nodded. "He wasn't talking behind anybody's back—he'd said it right in front of Wyatt, how I'd better watch out because for him relationships were like bull riding, only the buzzer was set for eight weeks, not eight seconds."

Shelby winced. "Ouch."

At the time, it hadn't stung so much as annoyed her. "I liked Sam well enough, but this was Wyatt we were talking about. The man I thought I was going to spend the rest of my life with." How strange to say that, to remember what it had felt like to be twenty and so sure of everything—her man, her plan, what her life would look like five years down the road. "When I asked him about it, he said it didn't matter because I was different. That he felt more for me than he had those other girls, wanted more with me. That was the first time he told me he loved me." They had been cuddled together in his bedroll on the shore of their waterfall, drinking cheap wine from the bottle while their horses grazed nearby. "He told me that he'd never said it before, never felt it. That I was the most important thing in the world to him, and he'd do whatever it took to keep us together. And I believed him . . . for seven and a half glorious weeks."

"Here." Jenny nudged the ice cream in her direction. "Dig in."

"I'm okay. It was a long time ago." Except that talking about it put her right back there. "He started acting funny around week five or six, but I chalked it up to the stress of finals. Turned out, he was looking for his pickup rider." The cowboys who rode up, flanked the bucking bull and got the rider loose after the eight-second buzzer. "Things came to a head the day before graduation. My whole family was due in and I was dying for them to meet Wyatt. But when it came time for us to go pick Jenny up at the airport, he bailed. Said he'd meet us later at the restaurant."

She had stared at him, wondering how hard to push. "Are you nervous about meeting them?" she had asked. "Don't be. They're going to love you, I promise."

Settling his hat lower on his brow, he had brushed a kiss across her cheek. "Thanks for understanding. I'll see you later." He had headed out of her apartment, sketching a wave over his shoulder like it was no big deal, just a couple of errands like he'd said.

That was the last she'd seen of him.

Jenny dropped a hand on her shoulder. Krista covered it with one of her own, appreciating the contact as she said, "We waited an hour for him at the restaurant. By then I was past worried and headed toward frantic—he wasn't answering his cell and nobody was picking up at the apartment. I insisted that we bag the big, fancy dinner and go over there." Three generations of Skyes in their party clothes, trooping up the stairs to the dingy off-campus apartment he and Sam had shared, and watching while she let herself in with her key. "He wasn't there, though. And neither was his stuff."

"He cleared out?"

Krista nodded. "There were two notes on the kitchen table, one for me and one for Sam, with the rent money. Mine was a whole lot of *it's not you, it's me* and *I'm sorry*. There weren't any details, nothing about where he was going or what he was going to do. Just that I deserved better."

"Well, he was right about that!" Shelby said. "Jerk. You totally deserved better than that."

I didn't want better. I wanted him. But he hadn't wanted her, had he? Not enough to stay. "You're supposed to get your heart broken at least once when you're a teenager, right? Well, I guess I got mine in right after the cutoff."

"Why did he do it?"

"How should I know?"

"I thought you said he apologized the other day."

"Not in detail." Krista held up a hand before Shelby could press her on it. "And, no, I'm not going to ask him. Don't care, don't want to know. I'm just hiring him to keep the guests safe and help me finish the season with a bang at the mustang ride-off. Neither of us is interested in reconnecting."

Jenny made a humming noise and moved around the granite-topped bar to break the corner off a brownie. Nibbling thoughtfully, she said, "I wouldn't be so sure about the *neither of us is interested* thing. Did you see how he was looking at you the other day?"

"Like he was afraid I was going to turn into a human hand grenade and blow up all over him?"

"Not from where I was standing. To me, it looked more like he wanted to lean in and take a bite."

Hot and cold washed over Krista like a breeze had just blown past. "You're imagining things."

"What if I'm not? What if he's interested in starting back up with you? Or starting something new?"

"Then he's going to be disappointed." *No way, no how, not going there.*

"It could make things awkward."

"It's just a couple of months," Krista said staunchly. "I can handle anything for a couple of months. Even Wyatt."

7

From the moment Wyatt drove Old Blue through a battered wrought-iron archway, where welded horseshoes spelled out ELCOME TO MUSTAN RIDGE with gaps where the missing letters should have been, he felt like he and Klepto were traveling back in time. Not just because the high country was ageless or because the rough-hewn log structures nestled in the valley looked like they could have been a pioneer homestead on steroids, though both of those things were true. It was more that once upon a time, he had pictured himself making this drive under very different circumstances—the kind that involved promises, permanence, and people depending on him.

Ignoring the sudden ache in his molars, he rolled down the winding driveway between two lines of tensile fence, taking in the main ranch building with its two big barns, the horse- and cattle-filled holding pens, and the scatter of log cabins down by a pretty lake. With the grassy valley sweeping up to the ridgeline, and beyond that the gray-blue mountains and dawn-pinked sky, it was a hell of a view.

For a second, he almost wanted a pencil.

He parked beside the dually Krista and her sister had been driving the other day, its gleaming white paint and professionally done ranch logo making Old Blue look shabby and faded in comparison. "Come on, Klepto. And remember what I said: Behave yourself, or I'll have to shut you in a stall during the day. The way I hear it, I'm going to need to keep both of my eyes on the greenhorns."

His phone conversation with Foster had been short and to the point—either the guy wasn't the chatty sort, or he knew there was some history between him and Krista and didn't want to get in the middle of it. Still, Wyatt had come away with a good idea of the setup, along with forewarning that some of the dudettes could get pretty aggressive in their efforts to bag a cowboy. Which wouldn't be a problem for him—he had zero interest in being bagged; he was there just as a sop to his anemic excuse for a conscience.

He followed the signs pointing him to the dining hall, figuring Krista would be setting up for breakfast. When he pushed through the swinging, saloon-style doors, though, he found himself alone in the big, sweet-smelling space, which had lots of exposed wood and a double row of picnic tables set with cheerful red-and-white checkerboard linens.

"We'll take ours to go," Wyatt told Klepto, and

headed for an arched doorway, where the scents of homemade bread and bacon-in-progress got stronger, and voices carried along a wood-paneled hallway. His attention was snagged, though, by an old-timey picture that was set into a shadow box beside the doorway and lit from above, bringing the washed-out sepia tones back to life. In it, a man and a woman stood together in a dusty-looking bit of backcountry. He wore a vest and leaned on a long rifle, while she cradled a swaddled baby and had chickens pecking around the hem of her long skirt. There were log buildings in the background, along with an uncovered wagon, its metal hoops exposed to the wind and weather.

Which was cool and all . . . but what was even cooler was that he could see the same mountains through a nearby window, from what looked like the same angle. The cabins and wagon were gone, but the scooping bowl of the valley was there, as was the ridgeline beyond. As far as he could tell, the dining hall had been built right where the photographer had been standing. *Talk about some family history.*

"Amazing, isn't it?"

Wyatt turned toward the voice, saw soft white hair and a welcoming smile. And then did a double take at the sight of Krista's smile in the face of an older woman in jeans and a ruffled yellow apron painted with a cartoon cow.

Putting his eyes back on the photo, he cleared his throat. "Who are they?"

"We're not sure. The clothing dates it to after the

1880s, but they look too young to be Jonah and Mary Skye, who built the original homestead, and too old to be the next generation. Employees, maybe, or extended family." She sighed. "It's a shame, isn't it, to lose the stories?"

"When you've got a history like this it is." He looked out the window, imagining the ghost of a covered wagon. "Impressive."

She dimpled up at him. "We're going through all the old photos now, trying to match faces and get their stories written down. It's not easy, though. Some of the pictures have names but no dates, or first names without last. Some don't have anything at all, like this one." She tapped the museum-quality glass, expression softening. "Maybe one of these days we'll figure out who they are. But"—her voice sharpened and her eyes gained a new glint—"enough about yesterday. You must be the new wrangler! Welcome!" She held out her hand. "You'll call me Gran. Everyone does."

Which answered one question: She had no idea who he was.

Wyatt shook, getting a surprisingly strong grip in return. "Thank you, ma'am. Is Krista around?"

"She should be out behind the main barn with Jupiter. You'll bring her a cup of coffee. That'll get things started off right." She patted his arm. "We're happy to have you."

"Begging your pardon, ma'am, but you don't know me."

"No, but the guest ranch is Krista's baby. If she

thinks you're good enough for it, then that's enough for us."

Squelching the urge to tell her that maybe it shouldn't be, he said, "Coffee would be great."

A few minutes later, loaded down with two steaming mugs and a couple of fluffy corn muffins that smelled like heaven, plus a day-old biscuit for Klepto, he rounded the back corner of the steel-span barn, where Dutch doors led from the stalls to a series of small individual paddocks. Beyond that, inside a fenced-in arena flanked on two sides by grandstands and a judges' box, a round pen made of eight-foot-high pipe panels stood empty, save for a sparkling-clean water trough and a pile of fresh hay.

"We seem to be missing something," he told Klepto, scanning the horizon. "Where do you think— Ah. There."

On the spine of the ridgeline, a horse and rider stood beside a three-stone marker that looked like it had been there for generations. The scene could've come from a hundred years ago, two hundred, but he knew who it was even across the distance. Feeling her eyes on him, Wyatt raised a hand in greeting, and after a moment, the horse started down the slope.

Krista knew her stuff, that was for sure. It was evident in the horse she had picked, and even more so in what he was seeing now, as the pair loped down off the ridgeline, with the gray mare looking like she had been working under saddle for the past eight months rather than the past eight days. She carried her neck with a natural arch and wore her ears to the front, looking re-laxed and interested as Krista slowed her to a walk. A couple of whinnies came from the barn, and the mare answered right back with a happy rumble, as if to say, *Yeah, that's right. I'm a rock star.*

Krista grinned and leaned down to stroke the mare's neck and whisper something in her ear. And damned if time didn't suddenly collapse in on itself, turning her twenty again, him twenty-four and struck stupid by the sight of the beautiful blonde on a big gray horse, the two of them moving as one. His body tightened and his hands twitched away from his body, wanting to reach, to touch.

Reining in the urge, he swallowed hard, trying to wet a throat gone suddenly dry. And as Klepto looked up at him and whined, he said aloud, "Maybe this wasn't such a good idea." It didn't seem to matter that she wasn't the girl he used to know, because his body seemed to like the woman she had become just fine.

Don't telegraph, Krista told herself as Jupiter entered the arena. *Seat loose, body easy.* Because if there was one thing you didn't want to do when riding a barely broke horse, it was clamp down. She hadn't been braced to see Wyatt this early, though. Wasn't sure she wanted to see him at all.

"I'm impressed," he called. "You two look ready for the ride-off."

"Thanks. So far, so good."

Hello, understatement. She wasn't quite ready to label Jupiter a wunderkind, but the mare had soaked up her ground training in a few sessions and had taken to the saddle and bridle like she had worn them before. Krista didn't think the mare was an escaped riding horse, though—it was more that every now and then a mustang came down off the range ready to learn. They watched the other horses being handled and ridden, absorbing the information by equine osmosis, and offering the behavior back without the usual *people are scary* and *ooh, don't touch me there* reflexes of the typical wild mustang. Knock on wood, Krista was starting to think she had one of those horses on her hands, making her think the possibility of winning the competition wasn't that farfetched after all. But at the same time, she knew that those savant-stangs could be like pressure cookers, going along at a nice boil until a bad training move turned up the heat too far and *bam!* Meltdown.

It was up to her to make sure that didn't happen, which was another reason she needed a top-notch horse trainer on her side. Foster would have been a perfect match for the mare. As for Wyatt . . . She patted the mare's neck and murmured, "I hope you like him, girlfriend. Don't get too attached, though. Odds are, he's already looking for his pickup rider." If he stayed the day, she'd be surprised. Eight weeks? No way. If he had really wanted to make things right, he would've done it before now.

Note to self, she thought as she guided Jupiter into

the arena, *keep looking for a new cowboy.* She had to replace Ty anyway. But as she got closer to where Wyatt leaned against the arena fence, watching them from beneath his tipped-down hat, a quiver took root in her stomach and worked its way outward. Because dang, he looked good standing there, surrounded by all the things that were important to her. More, wearing his trademark brown hat, sturdy jeans, good boots, and a work shirt that had seen some miles, he was one hundred percent cowboy. And she'd been programmed from birth to want herself a cowboy.

Too bad this one came with an expiration date.

He touched the brim of his hat. "Morning."

"You made it." *Paging Dr. Obvious.* But what else was she supposed to say? It wasn't like this was a big happy-happy reunion or some "welcome to Mustang Ridge" fanfare. It was business. Not to mention that she'd be darned if she thought about how she used to picture him making a grand entrance at Mustang Ridge, with them riding double on her favorite horse, complete with a brilliant sunset and the theme from *Chariots of Fire* playing in the background. Which was totally cheesy, sure, but she had been young and dumb.

And now she was totally thinking about it. *Drat, drat, drat!* Trying not to scowl, she shoved the memories away.

She could still see them in his eyes, though, hear them in his voice when he said, "This is a fine place you've got here, Krista. It's everything you said it would be. Everything you wanted back then."

"Not everything," she said, the words coming out level despite the twinge of knowing that her five-year plan of a husband and kids had stretched to seven, then faded to "one of these days." Dreams changed, though. Goals changed. And she wasn't going to settle for anything less than what her parents and grandparents had found in their marriages. Not perfection, but longevity, family, teamwork, and the kind of love that helped two people tough it out through the not-so-perfect times. Which she had come to find was a tall order for someone like her. "But thanks. It's good land, and business is booming. So I appreciate you being willing to consider the position. Did you talk to Foster?"

He nodded. "He gave me the basics on the guests and the competition. Sounded pretty keen on winning, said it would be good PR."

"That, and he's won a few buckles in his day." Leaving it at that, she patted the mare's neck. "This is Jupiter, and so far she's on the fast track."

"I'll say. I figured you'd still be sacking her out, maybe ground driving."

"She skipped a few grades. Granted, we may have to go back later and fill in the gaps." She was tempted to keep the higher ground, but Jupiter was starting to fidget. Stepping down from the saddle, she added, "Right now I'm working on the basics—gas, brakes, and steering. Assuming you sign on, I'm going to need you to put some trick training on her."

"What sort of tricks?"

"You should check out the online videos of other

mustang competitions. We're not just talking about a pretty reining pattern or taking off the bridle halfway through anymore." Talking about the makeover, she could almost ignore the fact that he dwarfed her, his broad shoulders darn near blocking out the sun. "Some of the winning teams have their horses towing cars into the arena, chasing radio-controlled gizmos around like they're cutting cows, and even sitting *in* the car while the cowboy drives them out! We're talking plots and production values here, with horses that only have a couple of months under saddle." And she needed to deliver.

He eyed her. "Do you have a plan?"

"More or less. My dad is handling the props, and the script needs work." At least it did now, because there was no way she was doing the original skit with him. "How about you start by teaching her 'sit,' and 'shake,' and we'll go from there?"

A low "whuff" drew her attention to Wyatt's feet, where a scruffy gray dog—medium-size, with a Brillo coat, a schnauzer's face, and old-man eyebrows—sat holding up a paw.

Krista crouched down, lips shaping a reluctant curve as she found she could be charmed by the dog while wishing wholeheartedly that she didn't need his master on her property. "Well, hello there. I guess you know *sit* and *shake*, don't you?" She shook the proffered paw.

"Along with a few other things," Wyatt said wryly. "This is Klepto."

"Oh?"

"He has a habit of borrowing things. Don't worry.
I'll keep him entertained enough—and tired enough—
to behave."

Great, she thought, knowing the dog wouldn't be
nearly so cute if he was traipsing around with stolen
Ray-Bans or a just-out-of-the-box Justin boot. Or, in the
case of this week's guests, dentures and pill bottles,
along with the Ray-Bans and boots. But she needed the
cowboy, and a good working dog could be a huge asset
on the trail.

She ruffled the wiry gray fur. "Keep your paws to
yourself, young man. We're on to you." Straightening,
she said to Wyatt, "You'll be responsible for any losses,
and he'll need to be tied if things get bad."

"Agreed." He held out a mug. "Coffee? I've got a
muffin for you, too."

She took a step back before she could stop herself. It
shouldn't have felt like worlds colliding to see him
holding the familiar mug. "I take it you met Gran."

"Nice lady. She seemed happy to see me. Then again,
I didn't give her my name."

"I figured we'd see how today goes before I tell
them." She didn't like keeping things from her parents
and grandparents, but she hadn't even been sure he
would show up. And now that he had . . . well, they
would see how it went. The part of her that knew the
ranch needed him was deadlocked with the part of her
that said this was a bad idea.

"Your family, your call."

Steeling herself, she reached for the mug. The coffee had cooled off some, but his fingers were warm where they brushed against hers, and there was that *zzzap* again, like she had grabbed on to an electric fence. She sucked in a breath and snatched the mug, sloshing coffee and sending Jupiter back a snorting step.

"Dang it." She shook the liquid off her hand, careful not to look at him as her mind shuddered. She wanted to blame the sizzle on after burn from last night's chili, but couldn't. Wanted to pretend she wasn't entirely aware of his darkening eyes and the way his shoulders and biceps strained his work shirt, but couldn't do that, either. There was something else going on here, something she hadn't expected, hadn't been braced for.

Sparks. Damn it. She shouldn't be attracted to him, couldn't possibly be.

Staring at her with eyes gone suddenly intense, with his nostrils flaring like a mustang stallion scenting his mare, he said only, "Did you burn yourself?"

"No. I'm fine." Only she wasn't fine. Her blood thudded very close to the surface of her skin. Because his expression said that it wasn't just her feeling the sudden heat. *Oh, no. Heck, no.* This so wasn't happening. She took another involuntary step back, because suddenly there was a big gray thing standing there with them, and it wasn't Jupiter. *Hello, elephant in the arena.*

He held his hands away from his sides. "It was just coffee. I'm not going to jump you."

She flushed. "You don't need to be crude."

"I'm not. I'm being honest."

Taking a deep breath, she said, "This isn't going to be a problem, right? You and me? This . . . whatever we suddenly seem to have going on here? Which is stupid, right? You agree that it's stupid?" Why was she even asking?

"How about we go with ill-advised?"

"Stupid by any other name is just as dumb." As was feeling even the slightest hint of disappointment. Not because she wanted to start anything with him, but because she wanted him to want it, so she could throw it back at him, preferably with some heel grinding involved.

So much for being a grown-up. *Gah.*

"How about this?" he said. "The two of us together wouldn't work these days. I make it a point to keep things uncomplicated."

There was no reason for that to irritate her. But it most certainly did. "For all you know, I'm the most uncomplicated cowgirl in all of Wyoming."

"I'm going to be working for you and your family, and the two of us have a past. That's about as complicated as it gets."

"Then why were you looking at me a minute ago like you wanted to . . . well, you know?"

One corner of his mouth kicked up, though there wasn't any humor in his eyes. "I'm a guy, Krista, and we're pretty basic when it comes to a beautiful woman. And when two people have got the sort of history we do, there are bound to be leftovers."

"Leftovers!" Shelby's screech vibrated down the line later that evening. "He actually said *leftovers*?"

Her indignation went a long way to soothing Krista's pique. Hunkering down in her desk chair, she nodded into the phone. "Yep. Leftovers. Like I was a piece of day-old broccoli or something."

"While undressing you with his eyes."

The memory shouldn't have kicked an echo of heat through her system. "That might be overstating it a bit. But he definitely looked like he wanted to take a nibble." She shot a look out the door as she said it, hoping that hadn't carried to the main room.

"Why are you whispering?" Shelby hissed. "Is he there?"

"No. But my mom and dad are in the other room."

"Do they know who he is yet?"

"I told them a little while ago. Mom fussed and threatened to go 'have a talk with him'—shudder—but I think I convinced her not to. Dad muttered a couple of things I don't think he'd appreciate me repeating, but said he'd respect my decision. Big Skye said Wyatt sounded like an idiot, which I appreciated. As for Gran . . . she didn't say much, really." Which had been the hardest to take. Krista didn't want to disappoint her gran, didn't want her to worry. "I hope I don't look back on this and think, *Boy, that was dumb.*"

"How was he with the guests?"

"Amazing." Which shouldn't have made her want to slam her head in the filing cabinet.

"What week is it, anyway?"

"Golden Singles." That had been a lucky break, as it was one of their less dramatic themes. The older singles had plenty of opinions and needed to be watched carefully with the horses, but they tended to keep the ups and downs of their romances a little more private than the younger crowd.

"Foster said he sounded legit when they talked. And you said he's gone to get his stuff and move into the bunkhouse, so I take it that you guys came to an agreement?"

Krista's sigh felt like it came all the way up from her toes. "He's the right guy for the job. We got everybody in the saddle by eleven, nobody fell off, and even Junior—who wanted the job even though he's totally not ready for it—admitted that Wyatt rocked Riding 101 and the guided ride. Not to mention that the guests adored him." On the trail, Wyatt had worked his way up and down the line of horses, turning the ladies into eyelash-fluttering cowgirls and making the guys puff up their chests. "And when we got home, he ducked an offer from a couple of librarians, but managed to do it so they walked off smiling."

"And you just happened to overhear this?" Shelby's voice dropped. "Krista Skye, were you stalking the cougars that were stalking him? What else happened? C'mon. Dish!"

"I . . . Oh, shut up. I'm not ready to laugh at myself yet. It's been a long day. Leftovers my butt. I just want to curl up in the peace and quiet of my room, and *not* think about the fact that my ex is moving into my bunkhouse." Suddenly, feeling all of the hours of sleep she had missed over the past week, she sighed. "In fact, I think I'm going to turn in. Catch you later?"

"Anytime, girlfriend."

After disconnecting, Krista pushed away from the desk, stood, and reached up her arms in a spine-cracking stretch. Yeah, bed would feel good. Maybe a full night's sleep would reboot the part of her that had spent the day noticing how deftly Wyatt had handled Brutus, one of the trickiest horses in the wranglers' string, and how his jean-clad thighs had worked to control the beast with shifts of pressure and balance. *Yeah. Bed. Oblivion. Deal with it tomorrow.* Pretty sure she was on the verge of losing her mind—or at least the logical, rational part of it that she relied on—Krista turned for the doorway. And found it already occupied.

"There you are!" Gran said, looking expectant.

"Was I missing?"

"Oh, you. Here, I want you to take this." She held out one of the picnic baskets the guests used for romantic one-on-one getaways and short fishing trips down the river. Woven from local reeds and lined with blue-and-white checkered cloth, the baskets were sweet and homey, and had recently been added to the gift line.

Krista eyed it. "Is this a hint that I'm not eating enough?" Sure, she forgot a meal now and then, but her sweet tooth usually made up for it.

"No, silly, it's for Wyatt. He didn't come up for dinner with the guests, and you didn't give me enough warning to stock the fridge in the bunkhouse. I want you to run this over to him."

Suddenly, the basket got a whole lot less cute. "Gran—"

"You told us to trust your decision in hiring him, and the job includes room and board."

"He went to get his stuff. I'm sure he'll grab something while he's out." But it sounded weak, even to Krista, and she knew that the more she argued, the more Gran would fuss. Or, worse, start getting ideas about her and Wyatt. She held out her hand. "Fine. I'll take it."

Besides, she could always put it on the porch, ring the bell, and run away. If she was lucky, he wouldn't even be home yet.

8

After everything Wyatt had seen so far at Mustang Ridge, the bunkhouse shouldn't have surprised the stuffing out of him. But unless cowboying had changed a whole lot in the last few years, this was way more than the usual "room" part of "room and board."

The long, narrow log cabin might've been a lowly bunkhouse during an earlier incarnation, but now it sported a modern-day cistern, solar panels, and its own driveway a couple of miles from the main house—though it was closer if you hiked the trail that went over the hill.

Inside, the ongoing reno had opened things up with fifteen-foot ceilings and a spiral staircase leading to an enclosed loft. There was a high-end stainless-steel kitchen, a big flat screen over a stone-hearth fireplace, surround-sound speakers tucked into planters that bloomed with greens and purples, and framed landscapes on the walls. The only unfinished bit was the indoor hot tub, which was built into a platform opposite the fireplace, and was surrounded by boxes of tiles and buckets of grout.

"All the comforts of home, and then some," Wyatt announced, coming back into the main room with a towel around his hips and another looped over his neck.

Klepto, snoozing on his bed by the fat leather couch, condescended to lift his head and shoot Wyatt a look of *Do I need to react to that?* Then, apparently deciding that was a *no*, he lay back down with a sigh.

Wyatt grinned. "And thus we prove the old saying: A tired dog is a good dog." Klepto had surprised him by working up and down the line of riders like a pro, helping keep the horses in their double line. Even better, the dog had been drooping pretty good by the time they got back to the barn, and there hadn't been any calls of "Hey, has anyone seen my whatever?"

After collecting his things from Sam's house, Wyatt had dumped his tools—which hadn't seen the light of day since he crossed the Wyoming border—in the steel-span building behind the bunkhouse, and hit the no-expenses-spared shower for a hot, steamy soak that left him feeling human again. Now he padded into the kitchen for one of the beers he had bummed off Sam, humming under his breath.

After a rough start, the rest of the day had turned out okay.

The horses were a nice bunch, mostly gentled mustangs with decent heads on their shoulders; the assistant wranglers, Junior and Stace, knew their stuff; and the guests were a hoot. Trixie and Tracy—a pair of part-time librarians from Long Island—had attached themselves to him firmly but politely, and had proven to have some horse smarts. Some of the other golden singles seemed to be leaning toward pairing up, including Joe the botanist and Bebe the florist, who had been talking tomatoes the last he'd heard. After the horses were put away for the night, he had spent some time with Jupiter, who had picked up on the idea of targeting with ridiculous ease, almost immediately making the connection that bumping the proffered ball-on-a-stick with her nose would be rewarded by a noise from his handheld clicker followed by a couple of pellets of grain. By the fifth time through, she was looking at him like, *Yeah, yeah. Bump, click, treat. Got it. What's next?*

As for Krista, well, at least things hadn't gotten any worse than they started. He hadn't meant to be a jerk earlier—the kick of attraction had caught him off guard almost as much as her asking about it point-blank, and the truth had been out there before he could think to soften it. He had a feeling that had been for the best, though, because it had put some frost in the air between them for the rest of the day. And, when they met up after his training session with Jupiter, there hadn't been any sizzle to their exchange—just a *The job is yours if you want it* from her and a *Then I guess I'll go get my stuff* from him. Moreover, if today was anything to go by, with her riding drag and disappearing into the house as soon as they got home, he had a feeling he wouldn't be seeing her that much over the next couple of months.

"Whuff!" Klepto's head came up and his ears cocked toward the front door.

"Need to use the boys' tree?" Wyatt asked, having given the dog a "don't you even think of piddling in here" lecture earlier. But then headlight beams cut through the windows and a car rolled up beside Old Blue in the darkness, and he nodded. "Ah. Early warning system. Thanks, buddy." Not that the dog had given him much lead time, as he heard the car door open and shut almost immediately, followed by boots on gravel.

He glanced down at the towel he was wearing around his waist, then shrugged. It was probably Sam taking him up on the offer of a beer and a chance to scope out his new digs, or maybe bitch some more about his missing this, that, or the other. So Wyatt hitched up his towel and opened the door just as his visitor hit the porch. "Hey! I was just telling Klepto—" He froze, the words locking in his throat at the sight of a picnic basket and a pair of big blue eyes that flew wide.

It was Krista. And he was damn near naked.

Oh, help. It was all she could think as she was confronted by an acre of tan skin and rippling muscle, and surrounded by the scent of freshly showered male and a hint of spicy aftershave. Her boots nailed themselves to the porch and the picnic basket threatened to slip from fingers that were suddenly itching to touch the line of sparse hair that began at his nipples, met in the center and traveled down, thickening as it went. *Don't you dare,* she warned her libido, wishing desperately for a flash flood, a lightning strike, or for the couch behind him to spontaneously combust. Something—anything—to send her running. She had seen his body before, granted. But it hadn't looked anything like this. *Pull yourself together,* she chastised, trying to channel her inner Shelby. *He called you leftovers.*

"Here." She shoved the basket at him. "Gran didn't want you to starve. I told them who you are, and they're trusting my judgment on hiring you."

"Good to know." Expression shuttered, he took the basket and set it aside, then looked over his shoulder to where two leather duffels sat on the couch, open and partway unpacked. Nearby, a sleek little laptop rested beside a half-finished beer. "Come in. Or wait here, whichever. I'll put on some clothes."

"I'm not staying." She didn't move, though, and neither did he. And after a nanosecond pause, with her brain clamoring *no-no-no-don't-do-it* and feminine insult cheering her on, she added, "But before I go, there's one more thing."

"What's that?"

Pretty sure that this was one of the stupidest things she had ever done but unable to fight the urge to make her point, she grabbed the ends of the towel he wore around his neck, went up on her toes, and announced, "I'm nobody's old broccoli." And she kissed him.

*   *   *

Wyatt would've rocked back in his boots if he'd been wearing any. He didn't know what this had to do with old broccoli, but that fleeting thought was his last rational one as his brain short-circuited and his body reacted to the kiss.

His hands came up to grip her hips and take in the feel of denim and a concho-studded belt. His mouth parted her lips, his tongue found its mate, and his senses filled with a light scent that reminded him of riding through a field of wildflowers right after the rain. She tasted sweet and fresh, yet there was a spicy undertone as she moved restlessly against his body, wringing a groan from his throat.

But at the sound, something kicked back on in his brain like a blown fuse resetting itself.

What was he doing? This wasn't the plan. Exactly the opposite.

Hands off, moron. Remember?

He yanked away, peeling his body from hers and then grabbing the towel at his waist when it threatened to head south, all of it feeling like a mad scramble for sanity. But with his pulse pounding in his ears and the taste and feel of her imprinted on his neurons, he didn't think sanity was coming anytime soon. "Sorry about that," he rasped, because it seemed like he should say something.

"Don't be sorry because I kissed you." Her eyes blazed and twin spots of color rode high on her cheeks. "Be sorry for trying to pretend that this"—she poked a finger from her to him and back again—"was left over from before. Because, news flash, it's not."

Left over. Leftovers. Broccoli. Right. Which wasn't the point. But what was? "Krista—"

"I have every reason to have zero interest in you, but I can't pull it off." She glared. "I'm attracted to you, and it pisses me off."

He should probably pretend that he wasn't interested, but that would be tough to pull off when he could've hung the towel off his johnson. Not to mention that ever since that wretched night eight years ago, he'd made it a point to be honest from the very start—both in business and pleasure—rather than letting things slide until it was too late and people got hurt. "Okay, fine," he said. "We've got some killer chemistry going on, and it's not just because we've got a history. Is that what you want to hear? But we both know that sparks aren't enough when two people are headed in different directions. And I don't want to hurt you again."

Her eyes flashed. "I don't intend to let you."

Which sounded great, but experience said that stuff like this always circled back around on a guy. He would've stuffed his hands in his pockets, but his pants were across the room. "So now what?"

"So now nothing. Enjoy your dinner and I'll see you tomorrow." She swept down off the porch like she was exiting stage left, and slammed the car door for emphasis.

The noise brought Klepto to the door. He stood at

the threshold, head cocked, while Krista whipped the vehicle around and headed up the drive.

As the taillights dwindled, taking the engine noise with them, Wyatt glanced down. "Well. That was interesting." And by "interesting" he meant he needed to go take another shower, this one cold. Because, damn. Rather than cooling his jets, the exchange had blown any chance of him pretending he wasn't attracted to her. He'd always had a thing for blond cowgirls in general, and this one in particular. To find that she'd gotten feisty with age and experience, and was ready to go toe to toe with him despite their history . . . Yeah. He was in trouble.

By the time Krista got back home, she had calmed down enough to decide she should probably chalk up the past hour—maybe even the past forty-eight—to temporary insanity. That would explain why she hadn't fled the moment Wyatt answered the door in a towel. And why she had kissed him.

"Great job," she muttered as she let herself in through the front door. "Way to prove that you're not over him." Or, rather, that she couldn't resist the big, capable cowboy he had grown into. Without meaning to, she called up that first sight of him at the door—a centerfold moment of wet hair, bare chest, and white towel. As her blood heated at the memory of feeling his body against hers, though, something brushed at the edge of her mind, a discordant twinge, like she was missing something.

"Is that you, sweetie?" her mom caroled from the sitting area, where she was camped out on the couch with her feet up and her e-reader in her lap. "I didn't know you went out."

Krista paused at the bottom of the stairs. "I was just delivering supplies to the bunkhouse." *Ogling my new wrangler. Kissing him. Please don't ask.*

"Oh?" There was a wealth of meaning in the word.

"It's fine, Mom. I'm fine."

Rose set the reader aside. "I just worry about you, sweetie. I want you to be happy."

"I *am* happy. I've got everything I want right here." She set her foot on the bottom step. "Including, thanks to you, the world's comfiest bedroom. Which is calling my name." *Please don't start the "you're putting too much of yourself into the business and if you want a family you can't wait forever" thing, I'm begging you.*

Okay, so maybe her mom had given her that sit-down only once. But even a year later, it hadn't scabbed all the way over. It wasn't like Krista didn't *want* to meet someone. And of course there were kids involved when she pictured herself down the line—what was a family ranch without the next generation? But there wouldn't be any kids without a husband—not in the Skye family, anyway—and it wasn't like she had candidates beating down her door.

"You're not thinking you and he will—"

"Wyatt is just filling in while he's between jobs," Krista said firmly. "That's it. Period. End of story."

"Maybe this will be good for you," her mom said,

not looking entirely convinced. "Having him around for a few weeks might help you get him out of your system so you can move on, find someone else. Have you thought about online dating?"

Krista barely heard her, though, because all of a sudden the twinge was stronger, the discord louder. She frowned, thinking back. And it clicked.

If Wyatt was between wrangler jobs, why didn't he have a horse, or even a saddle? And how many unemployed cowboys traveled with high-end leather bags and a top-notch laptop?

Then again, he hadn't actually said he was between wrangler jobs, had he? Just that he was between jobs. She had assumed. *And you know what they say about that.*

Doing a U-turn, she said, "Can I . . . Let me get back to you on that, okay, Mom?"

Rose frowned. "I thought you were going to bed."

"I am. I will. I just need to check on something first."

Once she was behind her desk, though, staring at the computer screen, she hesitated, feeling like Pandora getting ready to pop the top on her pretty box. Or like she was holding a party-popper can and wasn't sure she wanted to be wearing worms.

With any other potential hire, she would have plugged his name into Google first thing, looking for horse-related mentions and wacko social media rants. With Wyatt, though, she hadn't done any of that. Partly because it had felt like she'd be e-stalking an ex, which was pretty much the definition of *not over him* . . . but mostly because she didn't want to know what he'd been doing since he disappeared on her.

Which was also pretty high up there on the "signs you're not over him" list, come to think of it.

Groaning, she buried her face in her hands. "This is stupid." She had to do it, especially now that things weren't lining up. And especially since she had kissed him, and they had . . . whatever they had going on between them. So she blew out a breath and steeled herself. "Here goes nothing," she said, and she typed CHARLES WYATT WEBB into the box, and hit ENTER.

It took a second for her mind to process the images that popped up on the screen, another for her jaw to drop.

Wyatt?

She had been expecting rodeo photos, maybe a ranch Web site offering trick training or turnaround of problem horses. Or, after seeing his personal stuff, maybe links to a horse-related white-collar job of some sort. What she got, though . . .

Wow.

The tiny thumbnail images at the top of the screen showed horses, all right, but they weren't training projects or rodeo remounts. The life-size metal sculptures were made of gears and pistons, frozen images that reared, galloped, and fought, seeming to come alive even in miniature.

"What the . . ." Her eyes went to the top Web site hit, GearHorseGallery.com, and the short description below. *Unique, one-of-a-kind Western pieces by award-winning artists working in reclaimed metal. The only source for pieces by the renowned C. Wyatt Webb.*

There was a Denver address, but it could have been a cross street on Mars for all the sense it made to Krista. She wouldn't even have believed it was the same Wyatt Webb if it hadn't been for the thumbnail picture. He was wearing a white button-down shirt that was open at the throat and popped against a background as dark as his eyes. And while his hair might be shorter, his tan less evident, there was no question it was the same man who was living in her bunkhouse.

The one she had kissed half an hour ago, and who had kissed her back. And who was clearly more than just an out-of-work cowboy.

She leaned back. Blinked. Rubbed her eyes until they blurred and cleared again. But none of it changed what she was looking at on the screen.

"That's . . ." *Impossible,* she wanted to say, but obviously it wasn't. A lot could change in eight years.

The room took a long, slow spin around her as she clicked to open the Web site, then hit the prominent link to his name. And whatever breath she'd been hanging on to vanished from her lungs in an instant. Not because of the three-quarter picture of Wyatt with his Stetson low on his brow and his sleeves rolled up over his muscular forearms.

No, it was the showcased statue that had her brain vapor-locking.

The metal mustang was caught midgallop, not in the

legs-neatly-tucked nanosecond of suspension that so many artists used, but in the spraddle-legged moment when two feet make contact and the other two claw the air for more speed. The horse's head was twisted to the side, its ears flat and its mouth open as if snapping at an unseen threat, and every line of its body was perfect, maybe not anatomically—though that was darn close— but in sprit. There was movement in the motionless image, making inaudible hoofbeat sounds in the viewer's mind.

It would have been impressive had it been carved from stone or cast in bronze. It was even more so because it had been constructed of barnyard scraps— gears, tractor parts, old horseshoes—making it seem like a mustang's ghost had walked out of a junkyard and glared around as if to say, *Yeah? Come over here and say that, why don't you?*

And Wyatt had made it.

That wasn't even the craziest part, though, wasn't the thing that had her shaking her head and brushing her fingers across the screen. Because she knew that horse. She had seen it in person. On a date.

Holy cow.

Two winters ago, she had visited California for a short course in modern dude ranching—four weeks doing intensive course work and two interning at a luxury horse resort. There, she had hit it off with Ballard, an assistant wrangler who liked his coffee black, his horses fast, and his relationships short and sweet. That had sounded just fine to her—she was on vacation, away from her friends, family, and her usual responsibilities, and sick of having only a single notch on her proverbial bedpost.

They had flirted and shared a couple of drinks, and on her day off he had surprised her with tickets to a dinner-and-dress-up museum gala, celebrating a traveling exhibit of Western-themed art. The mustang sculpture had been the centerpiece of the section devoted to modern pieces. And it had grabbed her instantly. She might have stood staring at it for hours if Ballard hadn't nudged her along. It had been that good, that powerful.

She hadn't gotten the artist's name, though. What would she have done if she had seen WYATT WEBB on a nearby plaque?

She flushed, remembering that she'd gotten her second bedpost notch that night. A week later, she and Ballard had parted with a whole lot of "keep in touch" that neither of them had meant. And she'd never had to reassure herself that she was over him.

Scanning the tabs at the top of the Web site, she hesitated over the one that said BIO. Clicked it.

The same galloping horse from the main page was set atop this one, suggesting it was a favorite, or one of his better-known pieces. Below it, she read:

A lifelong horseman, Wyatt Webb grew up wanting to be a rodeo star, a stunt rider, or Indiana Jones. After having some success with the first two, he turned his attention to learning how to hot-forge horseshoes, intending to go into therapeutic shoeing. When master farrier Ryan Dillon agreed to take him on as an apprentice, he had no idea his life was about to change.

An embedded picture showed Wyatt with a grizzled barrel of a man, both of them wearing heavy suede shoeing chaps and bent over the upturned foot of a bay horse. Krista's heart squeezed at seeing a younger and leaner Wyatt who was more like the guy she remembered. At the same time, it was strange knowing that this had come after they were both out of each other's lives. The bio continued:

While learning to create precisely balanced shoes from blank stock, Wyatt became interested in decorative forging. Ryan taught him a blend of old and new techniques, and the two teamed up in forging competitions.

A photo montage showed the two men standing with a series of sculptures made from bent and welded metal bars—everything from a tabletop model of Denver's Rainbow Arch bridge to a life-size mermaid. As the pictures progressed, the pieces increased in their size and intricacy and the prizes went from ribbons to trophies, and from there to oversize checks.

Soon, Wyatt struck out on his own, using agricultural scrap metal to create life-size representations of Western scenes from yesterday and today.

The bio went on to list a bunch of awards, along with several museums and state buildings that displayed his work. But it was the line of photos along the bottom that caught Krista's attention. There were half a dozen horses—all caught midmotion and no two the same—plus a bucking bull with a cowboy coming off the side, and an annoyed-looking cow being hassled by a bristling dog made from pieces of a combine. Each was made up of cleverly combined metal parts—a whole junkyard come alive.

She stared, baffled, her mind buzzing with a strange mix of pride and discomfort. Why had he come to Three Ridges? Why was he still in town? And most of all, why was he working for her?

She didn't have a clue. But first thing tomorrow, she was going to find out.

9

Krista headed for the barn early to get ahead of Wyatt, only to find that he and Jupiter were already gone. She told herself to let it go, catch him later, use the time to chip away at her to-do mountain. Instead, she pulled out her saddle and called, "Hey, Lucky-boy. You up for a morning ride?"

A glossy black horse in a nearby stall nickered, arching his neck and pressing the perfect diamond in the center of his forehead against the bars of the sliding door.

She grinned as she put him on the cross ties. "I'll take that as a yes."

Admittedly, taking Lucky out to look for Wyatt and Jupiter was the cowgirl equivalent of taking a Lamborghini down the street for a gallon of milk. But it wasn't every day that a girl discovered that the guy who broke her heart had gone on to become a famous artist.

Once she was mounted, Lucky's smooth paces ate the distance, putting them at the marker stones in no time flat. Reining in, she scanned the undulating hills. "I don't see—"

Lucky pricked his ears and bugled at the sight of the horse and rider two valleys over.

"Thanks, buddy. Off you go." She nudged him into motion, barely needing the cue with him eager to stretch his legs. He flowed down the ridge and settled into a rocking-chair rhythm that would get them to the others in a few minutes.

Hopefully by then she would have figured out what she wanted to say.

Wyatt saw her a ways away, cued by Jupiter's quick shift of attention and the sudden fine tension running through her body. Or maybe the tension was in his body, sparked by the sight of Krista astride the elegant black gelding, with her hair in cowgirl braids and a sassy red bandanna knotted around her neck like she was planning to rob the eleven o'clock stage.

It made him want to stop and stare, as that kiss played back through his mind like it had been trying to do all morning.

She's not for you, he reminded himself. There were sparks there, sure—damn near fireworks. But they were traveling on two different roads these days, and he had sworn off hurting people.

He rode up to meet her, letting Jupiter pick her way along a prairie surface that looked smooth from a distance, but had proved to be a minefield of gopher holes and shifting rocks up close. As they closed the distance, he saw that the black horse was as fine a specimen as he'd seen in a long while, and Krista's narrowed eyes were aimed full bore at him.

Jupiter did a little dance beneath him, warning that he'd tensed up.

As Krista came up opposite him and the horses touched noses, trading scent, he said, "Morning, boss. Nice horse."

"Don't you *nice horse* me, Wyatt."

"You're mad." Was it about the kiss?

"Why didn't you tell me that you're famous?"

Oh. That. "Only according to my agent and the PR people." Seeing her glare narrow further, he added, "I figured you'd look me up if you wanted to know what I'd been doing with my life. And I like being back around people who care about things like crops and calves rather than visual metaphors and social commentary." He paused. "It's not that I'm ungrateful. I'm lucky that Damien saw some of my pieces and threw the weight of GearHorse Gallery behind me, lucky that people lined up to buy, talking about the clash between tradition, industrialization, and the green revolution." He shrugged. "The thing is, I just like making horses out of metal." At least he used to.

It was probably the most he'd said about it to anybody since coming to Wyoming—the most he'd said to her about anything.

She didn't seem impressed—more like she was ready to kick him. Was it bad that he found he preferred that over the usual *ooh, ahh* reaction he got from women?

"Okay, fine," she said. "You're on your vacation, getting back to your roots, or whatnot, and it's my responsibility to background check my hires. But why are you *here*? Why take a job you don't need? I'm having a hard time believing it's all about making amends when you let it go eight years without a word."

The girl she had been would've taken it all at face value. The woman she had grown into knew better, and she kept her eyes on his as she waited for an answer. News flash: She hadn't just gotten feisty; she had gotten tough, too. Tough enough that she would walk away from him if he ducked her question. Which would probably be better for both of them—he didn't want her inside his head any more than she already was, hadn't expected to feel anything when he stood near her, caught her scent.

Let it go. Isn't it enough that I'm here? That was what he should say. Or, better yet, *Lady, I'm just here to do a job.* Instead, he grated, "I wish I could tell you that I came here with you in mind, but the truth is, I came to Three Ridges because I'm blocked, and I was hoping to hell that spending some time in the backcountry would loosen things up."

Saying it aloud put a fist of self-directed anger in his gut, a punch that came from admitting he didn't have his head screwed on tight enough, didn't have control of his process, such as it was.

"Blocked." She said it levelly, carefully. "Like writer's block?"

"Something like that. Used to be that I could look at

a pile of junk and see a bucking bull, or picture a mustang and know where to go for the parts. I didn't think about it, didn't worry about it, the right answers were just *there*. After a while, though, it started getting harder to go from the pictures in my head to the actual build." He had told himself it was because he was getting distracted by the business side of things, and hired people to handle the shows, the e-mails, all of it. That had just made it worse. "I got through my last show and promised myself I would take a break and clear my head . . . but the American Pioneer Museum asked me to do a piece for their post-reno relaunch next summer. It's a career-maker, and they're open to whatever I want to do. When I sit down to actually start the work, though . . ." He shook his head. "Nothing." Like his prospects if he didn't get his ass in gear.

A single blink was Krista's only outward response. "And you think leading dude-level trail rides and teaching a mustang to do a bellhop skit is going to fix that?"

"We're doing a bellhop skit?"

"Wyatt." The word was a warning. One that said he could either be honest with her or brush her off, but he had to make a choice.

Trying to find the right words when he had already said far more than he normally would, he answered, "I didn't really have an agenda. I hope you'll believe that. It was more that things fell into place in a way that made sense—you needed help and I was getting bored at Sam's place, and I figured I owed you one. And, yeah, I'm hoping that getting back in the saddle full-time will help with the block."

"Has it?"

"It's only been a couple of days."

"Which means no."

"It means I'm not sure." Thinking he knew what she was getting at, he nudged Jupiter forward so the horses were parallel and Krista was less than an arm's length away. He didn't reach for her, though. Didn't figure he had the right, even though she had kissed him. "You've got me until the end of the season. And I'm sorry I didn't tell you about what I do. I guess I just wanted to go back to being a cowboy for a couple of months."

"I didn't ask."

"I'm telling you anyway." He reached out and gripped her thigh—not a move a guy would make in the normal day-to-day, but not that unusual in the saddle, when it was an easy reach. "I'm not going to bail on you this time, Krista. That's a promise."

She hesitated, eyes darkening. "I don't—"

Her gelding jerked his head up and gave a piercing whinny, the kind that said, *Hey! I see a horse!*

Wyatt swiveled around to see a lone rider up on the ridge, standing beside the marker stones and scanning his land with a pair of binoculars. And watching them get up close and personal.

"Big Skye caught you and Wyatt *kissing*?" Stace's eyes went big and round, and the chestnut mare she was riding tossed her head.

"Shh," Krista hissed. "Keep it down." They were at the back of the double line of riders as the group started up the last set of hills toward home, with Wyatt in front and Junior keeping an eye on the middle of the pack. But just because she and Stace were eating dust didn't mean she wanted to broadcast things. "And he didn't kiss me that time. He just had his hand on my leg." Which didn't sound much better, did it?

"There was another time?" The assistant wrangler—and soon to be fully accredited child psychologist—was practically bouncing in her saddle. "Tell me, tell me!"

"It doesn't matter," Krista said firmly. "It's not going to happen again."

"The way he's been sneaking looks at you all day? I'm not buying it."

Krista didn't let herself ask, didn't let herself glance in his direction. Not when she had peeked far too many times already today, trying to reconcile the cowboy at the head of the line with the man who wore tuxes and worked with steel and iron, or the one who had walked out on her without a word. It was one thing to realize they were both different people now, another to know what to do about it. Her cautious self said the answer was *nothing* . . . but it wasn't easy to ignore the way everything around her seemed sharper and more inter-esting suddenly, her body more in tune with the sway of the saddle and the way a subtle arch of her back pushed her breasts up and out beneath her shirt. She had told Gran and Dory that it took her longer than a week to get interested in a guy, but there was no doubt she was interested now, despite everything. It was like part of her was programmed to want this particular cowboy even when her better sense knew it was stupid.

Stace nudged her with a boot. "You're totally thinking about it. I can tell."

"I don't want to be. I'd rather be—" Krista broke off as the double line of horses ahead of them wavered and broke. "Whoops! Can you grab Bramble?"

"On it!" Stace urged her horse up the line to where Bernie Trigg—a former investment banker who was shaping up to be this week's "I rode a horse once" know-it-all—had gotten tangled up in his reins again, sending his saintly mustang mare into a slow, disorganized spin. Stace bumped her horse into Bramble and unhooked his left rein with a cheerful, "Bernie, are you showing off for the ladies again?"

"What? Oh, right!" Bernie—stout, florid, and flushed—jumped on the excuse, puffing up his chest. "Absolutely. I was showing them a reining pattern. The horse I used to ride spun on a dime, you know."

As Stace got Bernie sorted out, Krista filed her thoughts of Wyatt under *chemistry alone isn't enough* and followed Bernie's so-called "ladies"—a former nurse who had turned her knitting hobby into a cottage industry and looked more amused than impressed by him, and a Manhattanite who seemed to be buying his bluster—through the outer perimeter fence and along the single-lane dirt road to the parking lot.

The guests dismounted with the help of several barn

staffers, who surreptitiously propped them up while their saddle-locked joints loosened and the pins and needles disappeared. There were far more smiles than groans, though, and signs of growing confidence as the greenhorns gathered their reins and led their mounts into the barn. Wyatt was right in the thick of it all, helping a couple of the guys with their cinches, nudging two horses apart when they started making pissy faces at each other, and directing the steady flow into the barn. As he led Brutus after the guests, he looked over, found Krista watching him, and winked.

Heat washed over her—at the wink, at getting caught staring—but she gave him a thumbs-up for a job well done. Then, shaking her head at herself, she swung down and headed into the barn along with the last couple of stragglers.

One of them waited for her. "It's lovely, isn't it?" Tall and ballerina-elegant, she wore a happy smile and a smudge on one cheek.

Bebe the florist, Krista's memory banks supplied, along with the thought that Bebe and Botanist Joe made a good match, but lived on opposite sides of the country. "The backcountry you mean? Gosh, yes, especially on a day like today, when the sky is clear and looks like it goes on forever."

"That, too. But I was talking about the flirting. Me and Joe. You and Wyatt." The older woman gave a happy sigh as they passed through the doors into the shadowy cool of the barn. "Even if it doesn't turn into anything, it's lovely to feel those sparkles again."

Krista should probably set Bebe straight and defuse the gossip. Lord knew she was going to have to do the same with her family after what Big Skye had seen earlier. She and Wyatt hadn't been kissing, hadn't been doing anything, really—but a ranch boss wouldn't let a wrangler put his hand on her thigh unless she wanted it there.

As Wyatt's deep, resonant voice rolled through the barn, though, chiding Tracy and Trixie for underselling their horse experience and getting trilled laughter in return, Krista found herself nodding. "You know what, Bebe? You're right. Sparkles are very nice."

If nothing else, it was nice to know she still had them inside her, and that passion—at least the way she did it—didn't belong solely to her younger self.

Over the next half hour, the guests untacked and groomed their horses, then filtered back to their cabins to shower and get ready for dinner. As the barn quieted down, Krista slipped into Lucky's stall and methodically ran her hands over his body and down his legs to his hooves. Straightening, she patted his shoulder. "Looking good. Do me a favor and keep it that way, okay?"

"Does he need the reminder?" Wyatt asked.

She turned to find him standing in the doorway with his shoulder propped and his thumbs hitched in his pockets, making a picture that she could imagine getting shared around on the Internet with all sorts of *Save a horse, ride a cowboy* captions.

Reminding herself it was one thing to feel the sizzle,

another to act on it, she brushed Lucky's forelock away from the white diamond in the center of his forehead. "I threaten to bubble wrap him some days. It's hard to see now because scar hair comes in white, but he tried to lobotomize himself at eighteen months. He was playing with his buddies, lost his footing and fell on the fence. Three months later, he stepped on himself and nearly tore off one heel. A week after that, he got hold of a two-pound bag of individually wrapped peppermints and ate the whole thing, wrappers and all." She sighed. "And that's not even counting the two hoof abscesses and a summer cold." Except she was totally counting them. It was one thing to deal with her retirees' many issues, another when her favorite baby horse seemed bent on self-destruction. "Anyway." She gave the gelding a final pat and left the stall, waiting for Wyatt to get out of the way so their bodies wouldn't brush. "Good job today," she said as she closed the door. "The guests love you."

He fell in beside her as they headed up the barn aisle with Klepto trailing behind. "You've got a top-notch setup and they're making it easy."

"This is a good group." She rolled open the sliding doors wide enough for them to slip through. "Not every week is going to be this— Oh!" She stopped dead at the sight of her parents and grandparents standing in the parking lot, shoulder to shoulder and looking braced for a shoot-out.

Her stomach headed for her toes. She loved her family, she did—loved the way they fit together, laughed together, worked together, especially these days. And there had been times in her life that she had been incredibly grateful to have her parents and grandparents backing her up, letting her lean on them, or giving her a needed kick in the butt. Unfortunately, this wasn't one of those times. In fact, it was times like this that she thought longingly of a one-bedroom apartment or a little cabin in the woods, someplace where she didn't have a well-meaning committee weighing in on her every move. What had happened to "We trust your judgment, honey"? *Gah!*

She stepped in front of Wyatt. "Hang on. It wasn't what it looked like. We were just—"

Without warning, a hand clamped over her mouth from behind, bringing a quick impression of warm skin and rough calluses. Then she was set firmly aside as Wyatt moved up to face the others. "I've got this."

10

As a rule, Wyatt didn't do complicated, he didn't do long-term, and he sure as heck didn't do meet-the-parents. He didn't know exactly how he had wound up one-for-three on that, but he'd meant it when he said he wasn't going to bail on her this time. More, he wasn't going to bail on himself, or the better man he had tried to be in the years since he'd walked out on her.

Squaring off opposite her family, he held still as big, grizzled Ed Skye gave him a long up-and-down, and said, "We'd like a word with you, Webb."

"I'd say you're due several. First, though, I owe you folk an apology for a meal I missed eight years ago."

Beside him, Krista sucked in a breath. "Wyatt, you don't have to—"

"Yeah, I do." At first he'd been relieved that she hadn't asked him about that night. Now he felt like it needed to be said, not just to her, but to all of them. "I panicked. I'm not proud, but that's the short and long of it."

Ed Skye's eyes narrowed. "Go on."

He tried to get it right. "I was twenty-four, and I'd been out on my own since after high school, rodeoing to help support my ma and my sister because my old man couldn't be bothered. So you'd think I'd be mature for a college kid. Maybe I was, in some ways. Not where it came to Krista, though." He glanced over, saw that she had backed off a few steps, face pale. "I fell hard for her, and I fell fast, and suddenly I wasn't just thinking about getting a job and saving for my own place anymore. There was Krista, Mustang Ridge, her plans to start a dude ranch. . . . It was incredible, *she* was incredible, and there was this whole new life opening up in front of me. But then . . ." He faced her fully, because telling the others was taking the easy way out. "I wish I could say there was something big, a defining moment when I knew I couldn't do it. But there wasn't. It was more that in those last couple of weeks before graduation, that big wide world you were offering me started feeling smaller and smaller, like I was a bull caught in a squeeze chute. I kept checking out job listings that weren't anywhere near Wyoming. Then, when that wasn't enough, I called on a couple." When he got the offer, it was like a gate had opened up at the far end of the chute and he had glimpsed brilliant green grass beyond. "That night, when it came down to meeting your family, taking the next step . . . I just couldn't. I wanted to be with you, but I wanted everything to stay the way it was at school, with all of us looking forward to whatever came next. I couldn't"—*commit, box myself in, lock myself down*—"be the guy you needed."

She didn't say a word. He didn't know if that was a good sign or bad. The others, too, were silent. Watching him. Listening. Judging. Finding him as lacking as he found himself when it came to those last few weeks of school.

"That night, I was getting dressed to head to the restaurant, when . . . I don't know. I just blanked." Standing frozen in front of the mirror, seeing a stranger in the glass and feeling like the tie she'd bought him for the occasion was cutting off his air. So he'd hacked off the tie with his pocket knife, pulled his bags out of the closet, and started stuffing them full. His face had been wet, his heart sick, but that hadn't stopped him. "I drove straight through to Texas, where there was a job waiting for me."

He had lasted eight months there, seven at the next place, then bounced around until he hooked up with Ryan and learned that mixing metal with fire and an eight-pound hammer could forge a quiet place in a man's brain.

Nearing the end, wanting to get it over with, he said, "I'm sorry for embarrassing you in front of your family and ruining graduation. Most of all, I'm sorry I didn't tell you all of it sooner, and in person, the way I should have. That was about as wrong a thing as I've ever done, and one of my biggest regrets." When Krista didn't say anything, just stood there staring at him with a blankness he hoped to hell covered anger rather than pain, he turned to the others and said, "I was old enough to know better and handle it like a man, and I didn't. If any of you want to take a swing at me for it, then go ahead."

For a second he thought Krista's grandfather was going to take him up on the offer. Instead, he harrumphed and said, "It's one thing to own what you did wrong, another to not do it again. And the two of you looked pretty close this morning."

"We were just talking." Which was the truth, but not really an answer. Wyatt wasn't even sure he *had* an answer, because the more he was around her, the more he remembered why he had fallen so hard in the first place. Krista was unique. Special. She saw the best in everyone but wasn't a pushover. She was a caretaker, a nurturer, and sat a horse in a way that made a man want to write a bad country song. None of which he was going to say to her parents or grandparents, especially when he was just passing through. So instead, he said, "With all due respect to each one of you, what happened this morning is between me and Krista. I'm going to leave it up to her when and if she wants to discuss it." He turned to her. "That work for you?"

He didn't get an answer, though, because she was gone.

Down by the lake, on the far side of the boathouse where nobody would see her unless they came looking, Krista pressed her face against the rough wall, shaking with the force of her sobs. The tears burned her eyes, her skin, and the place where she had bitten her lower lip hard enough to draw blood as she forced herself not to react to his story, not to let him embarrass her all over again in front of her family.

Damn him. *Damn* him. Why couldn't he have left it alone? She hadn't asked, hadn't wanted to know. She just wanted to move on.

The tears hurt. Everything hurt—her head pounded, and her heart felt gaping and raw. She didn't want to feel this way, hated that he still had power over her.

She didn't want to be twenty again, didn't want to remember the restaurant, the mad rush to the apartment, the walls collapsing in on her as she read his letter out loud to her family. Which hadn't been the worst of it. The worst had been waking up the next morning with her eyes and throat raw, then turning to find Jenny asleep beside her, and having it come crashing down on her all over again—that he had lied to her, left her, hadn't loved her enough.

Her dreams of having a family and a forever-after with Wyatt had died hard over tear-soaked weeks and months. Yet somehow there were more tears now, more grief, and the new panic-sting of knowing she was in danger of doing it all over again.

God, this sucked. Why did it still hurt like this? And why was he the only one who made her *feel*?

"Ah, hell, Krista," Wyatt's voice said suddenly from right behind her. "I'm sorry."

She jerked and spun toward him, galvanized by horror—that he had come after her, that he had seen her like this—and her hands came up against his chest as he put his arms around her. His pecs were warm and firm beneath the material of his work shirt, his body solid.

She tried to shove away, but he held on tight. Furious, she smacked his chest and glared up at him. "Let go of me!"

Eyes dark, he shook his head. "I can't do that. Not when you're this upset."

"Leave me alone!"

"It seems I can't do that, either." The regret in his voice made her heart shudder, as did the feeling of his body pressed against hers.

He would let her go if she struggled, she knew, leave if she insisted. But she was weak, darn it, and he was solid and strong, and offering a shoulder. Against all her better judgment she sagged against him as the tears broke free once more. Burrowing into his chest and finding that her head didn't hurt so much when the lights went out, she wailed, "Why did you say all those things?"

He didn't pretend to misunderstand. "I thought you and your family should know what happened back then."

"I didn't want to know!" It hurt to cry, hurt to hold him, hurt to let herself be held.

He tightened his arms around her, like he was afraid she would pull away when he said, "I'm sorry I took off on you, Krista. I'm sorry I left that letter. I was afraid if I told you in person, I'd never make the break."

Let it go. It doesn't matter anymore. But the words came unbidden, feeling like they were being ripped from her chest. "You said I was different, that the way you felt about me was different!"

"You are. It was."

"Don't!" She beat at his arms. "Don't tell me what you think I want to hear. Tell me the *truth*, damn you!"

He was holding her so close that she could feel his pulse. "That *is* the truth, always was. I never had the same feelings for anyone else, before or since. But it turned out that I wasn't wired for forever. I wanted to be. I tried to be. But I didn't have it in me back then. Still don't now, but at least I know better than to try." His voice went hollow. "I was a stupid kid and I pulled a crappy stunt taking off like that, but whether it happened then or a few months later, the end result would've been the same. We were too young to get in that deep so fast."

She wanted to argue, but wept instead, sobbing like she had that night.

Stupid to cry, stupid to feel anything. Stupid, stupid, stupid.

"Shh," he said against her temple, rocking her. "Any boy who treats you like that doesn't deserve you crying over him."

She sniffled. "That's what my father said."

"Smart man. You should listen to him."

She pushed at him. "Let me go."

"Not yet." He tightened his grip on her. "Give yourself another few minutes."

But as the tears drained to an empty ache, she was too aware of how their bodies lined up, hard to soft, and how badly she wanted to nestle in close. Which so wasn't happening.

Forcing her voice level, she said, "I need to get cleaned up for dinner. You should come. We're playing strip Bingo. I'm sure Trixie and Tracy would let you sit with them."

He chuckled obediently and finally let go and eased away from her, but his eyes were serious on hers. "You sure you're okay?"

"I'm fine." She used the tail of her shirt to swipe her face dry, aware that his eyes followed the motion as he waited for a real response. She gripped his wrists, then stepped back, breaking his hold on her. "I'll be fine. Honest. It just hit me harder than I would have expected." She would think about what that meant later.

When she released his wrists, he let his hands fall to his sides as he studied her. "How about us?" he asked with a new note in his voice. "Are we okay?"

She hesitated, then said, "Not yet. But I think we're getting there."

Later that evening, after the sun dropped behind the mountains in a fiery ball that turned the cloud-feathered sky to salmon and purple, Wyatt dragged out his sketch pad and a fountain pen, on the theory that maybe vintage would spark vintage in his stubborn brain. Heck, he'd sketch with a quill if that was what it took, or use a charred stick.

"And it's a bad sign when a change of writing implements is as creative as I get," he grumbled.

Klepto's head came up from his doggy bed, his ears angled forward. "Whuff?" *You missing something?*

"Yeah, my spark." Except that wasn't really true—he had plenty of sparks going on in other parts of his life all of a sudden. But when it came to the piece for the pioneer museum, he had *nada*.

The furry gray face tilted in inquiry. *You want me to find the pretty lady again? I'm good at finding the pretty lady.* Which was true. Klepto had tracked Krista to the boathouse, giving Wyatt the opportunity to see firsthand the damage he had done by following the grand Webb tradition of loving and leaving.

He had known it before, but now it was burned into him like a brand. He had quit on her, bolted on her, taken the easy way out. Not that it had been easy for him—he wore his own scars from that night. But he'd spared himself the big, messy scene . . . until today. He wasn't sure if he'd helped or hurt by telling her the truth about that night, or if it didn't matter one way or the other now. All he knew was that he'd made her cry, and he never wanted to do that again—which meant staying away from her and keeping his hands to himself. He needed to forget the sparks, forget the way the sunlight turned her hair to gold, and do the jobs he'd been hired to do.

Like be her head wrangler. Train her mustang. And design the biggest sculpture of his career when he totally wasn't feeling it.

Muttering under his breath, he flipped open his sketch pad. It fell to the page of notes he'd jotted down during his meeting with the museum board—snippets like *go beyond the wagon train*, *embrace the vaquero tradition*, and something indecipherable that probably didn't say *rampant rubber mice* but sure looked like it.

Not that he needed the notes—he knew what the museum folk were after, knew he could deliver if he could just get his blasted brain back in the game. But that was the thing, wasn't it? He had hung out at the museum, done a boatload of research, and had even taken a wagon train ride near Jackson Hole. More, he had scoured his usual sources—a mix of repair shops, junkyards, auctions, and falling-down barns where decades of farm equipment had gone to die—for scraps that would put themselves together in his mind and make his fingers itch for a torch. He had even called Ryan for help, and on his mentor's advice had ordered some raw bar stock so he could get back to basics.

None of it had worked though, forcing him all the way back to paper and pencil, hoping that the sketches would shake something loose.

Muttering under his breath, he flipped the page. Then kept flipping, past several variations on the same theme—a cowboy hunkered over a fire, making coffee while a scruffy mechanical dog begged for scraps. "Hm." He stared at the least lame of them, getting a glimmer as the last bit of pink bled from the sky and darkness closed in.

Maybe he was overcomplicating things.

Swapping out his pen for a worn pencil, he scrubbed the eraser over the dog, wiping it out and leaving the cowboy alone. There. That was better.

11

"Okay." Krista opened up a blank page on her lap-top. "We need a new script for Jupiter's free-style. Ideas?" She, Jenny, and Shelby had sneaked in a rare midafternoon meeting, and were celebrating the hour off with fresh fruit, wine, and cheese. Since it was Friday—farewell barbecue night for the golden singles—Gran and Dory were manning the big grills out by the gazebo, leaving the kitchen free.

"Are you sure the old skit is a no-go?" Shelby asked. "You were fine doing it with Foster."

"I never slept with your husband."

"Good to know."

Krista made a face. "It's one thing to play honey-mooners with a guy friend. It's another to do it with your ex." Especially when she wasn't nearly as over him as she had thought when she got the bright idea to hire him. "Besides, have you looked at the script lately? I don't know what we were drinking when we wrote it, but there's a whole lot of naughty in there."

"Sex sells," Jenny said. "Why do you think the singles weeks are the first ones to fill up?"

"Followed by the reunion weeks in close second," Krista countered. "Hello, irony."

"Everything in the script is PG," Shelby put in. "It's more innuendo than anything."

Not exactly. The skit cast the two humans as gown-and-tux-wearing honeymooners who first arrived together on horseback, with Jupiter trailing tied-on cans and noisemakers—a sure test of any horse's nerves and training—and wearing a JUST MARRIED sign on her rump. A quick costume change put the horse in a huge cowboy hat, standing behind a prop reception desk, checking in the oblivious honeymooners, and ringing for a luggage cart. Next, wearing a bellhop's uniform, Jupiter would push and then pull a giant, overflowing luggage cart with a couple of interruptions to round up the honeymooners, who kept stalling to kiss. Finally, in the honeymoon suite—a big prop bed with a whole lot of reinforcement—the mare would pour champagne into two glasses, look at the humans, and shake her head at seeing them kissing again. Then, she would climb into bed and curl up to sleep.

It was cute. It was funny. It was manageable, given how well Jupiter's clicker training was coming along. Most of all, it would be a killer advertisement for Mustang Ridge: luxury, romance, and well-trained remounts. What could be better?

And Krista couldn't do it. "Why are you guys pushing it, anyway? You're supposed to be on my side."

"Do you want us to hate him?" Jenny asked. "We can do that if you want. Thing is, we're pretty sure you don't hate him at this point, and if you don't, why should we?"

"I . . ." Krista bit into a strawberry. "I'm *trying* to hate him. Life would be a whole lot easier if I did."

"It's hard to hate somebody who's doing the right thing now," Shelby said, "and who probably did the right thing back then, too, even if his delivery sucked."

"Oh, shut up." But Shelby was right, darn it. Krista sighed. "Okay, fine. Maybe that's part of it." In the four days since her and Wyatt's blowout, a busy week had kept them from spending any real time together except for trail riding at opposite ends of the line and exchanging quick "Jupe was a rock star today!" progress reports on their training project. He hadn't been out of her head for more than a few minutes at a time, though. And, yeah, maybe it was time to admit that they had been on completely different trajectories when they knew each other before, even if she hadn't realized it. "It's just . . . I don't know. I think I got it in my head that I was going to be like Gran and Big Skye, or Mom and Dad—you know, meeting The One before twenty-one, getting married and starting a family right away. When it didn't happen, it was more than just a breakup. It was a failure." Saying it out loud put a catch in her throat.

"Oh, sweetie." Jenny pulled her in for a one-armed hug. "No. Never think that."

"Too late." Krista returned the hug, then straightened, squaring her shoulders. "But having figured that out, I can walk away from it. I *am* walking away from it." Working on it, anyway. "As for the other stuff, we were young and clearly dumber than I want to admit, and he probably did us both a favor." She narrowed her eyes at the other two. "But that doesn't mean I want to play newlywed with him."

"It's just for a few minutes," Shelby pointed out, "and it's not like you're supposed to really kiss each other. Unless there's something you and Foster want to tell me?"

"Nope." Krista pinched the bridge of her nose, not sure if she was on the verge of a headache or a wine buzz. "Okay, how about this? We keep the bones of the skit the same, but lose the kissy-touchy parts. Our honeymooners could be all wide-eyed about the pretend mountain views instead of each other. That would still have them wandering off during the luggage bit, and then oblivious once they're in the pretend honeymoon suite."

"That might work," Jenny said, tipping her head to one side as she pictured it. "I think we need more, though."

"I agree." Shelby snagged a raspberry off Krista's plate and popped it into her mouth. "What about—"

"There are my girls!" Gran trilled, coming up the stairs to the side door and using her hip to bump through. Her arms were stacked with barbecue-sauce-streaked bowls. "How goes the brainstorming?"

Shelby popped up. "Let me get those."

"Oh, poosh, I've got them. You stay right where you are and tell me what you've come up with."

"We mostly know what we're *not* going to be doing," Krista said, "but here's what we've got so far." She sketched out the skit and the four of them bounced some ideas around while Gran washed the bowls and threw together a salad with fat tomatoes providing pops of red against the fluffy green.

Struck by the visual, Krista said, "What about room service?"

Gran blinked at her. "What about it?"

"Maybe we could switch out the luggage bit for a room service gag. It'd be mostly the same tricks—Jupiter could push the cart, take the cover off the food and—"

The front door slammed, startling her, and heavy footsteps crossed the main room with slightly arthritic unevenness.

"We're in here, Arthur!" Gran called. There was no answer, though, and the footsteps continued through to the back of the house.

"Guess he didn't hear you," Shelby said.

Gran pursed her lips. "Maybe."

"Everything okay?" Krista asked, not liking the sudden hint of hurt in her grandmother's eyes. "Is he being Grumpy Gramps again?"

Gran gave the salad an unnecessary fluff with the tongs. "He's . . . I don't know what he is these days." Her eyebrows drew together. "I love the man, but some days I just want to thump him upside the head."

"Is he feeling okay?" Krista asked. She hadn't seen much of Big Skye over the past couple of weeks, but that wasn't unusual. He may have gotten resigned to the dude-ification of Mustang Ridge, but he still avoided her as much as possible.

"He had a checkup a couple of weeks ago," Gran said, "and the doctor said he was good to go for another sixty thousand miles, at least."

"Let's go see what he's up to." Krista nudged Jenny. "He'll get a kick out of visiting with his favorite granddaughter."

Jenny poked her back. "I'm only his favorite when I've got my camera."

"Want us to wait while you run out to the car and get it?"

"Ha!" Jenny sailed past her. "Last one to the sitting room is a rotten egg!"

Krista hung back as Jenny and Shelby headed for the main room. To Gran, she said, "You coming?"

"I've got the barbecue to see to."

"Do you need help?"

"No, you go on. If anybody can jolly Arthur out of his mood, it'll be you three girls." Gran concentrated on setting the last of the bowls in the drying rack, banging them together with more volume than usual.

"Hey." Krista crossed to her, wrapped her arms around her gran's waist, and put her chin on her shoulder, as she'd been doing ever since she grew tall enough to pull it off. Rocking them both, she said, "Talk to me. What's going on with you two?"

Gran covered Krista's hands with her own and gave a little pat. "Nothing we haven't gotten through before, and nothing we won't get through this time. But if we agree that all men are stubborn, I'd say your grandfather is worse than most."

"Amen." Krista kissed her cheek. "But he loves you."

"That's not what I'm worried about."

"Then what is?"

"When I figure it out, I'll let you know. Now go on. See if you can get him to smile. I'll even settle for not stomping around like he's a Clydesdale with a fly on its belly." Gran squeezed her hands, then stepped away. "I'm going to see how Dory is doing with the smoker."

Krista hesitated, tempted to press but not wanting to overstep. With three generations living and working together, there had to be some boundaries—and "I don't want to talk about it right now" was a biggie. "I could make you a batch of cookies. They might make you feel better."

Gran's expression lightened. "Don't you dare, young lady. It took four coats of paint to cover the soot marks from the last time."

"Hey! I was fourteen. I'm not sure it's fair to still be holding that one over my head." But at least it had made Gran smile. "Okay," Krista said, pretending to settle a suit of armor on her shoulders. "Cover me. I'm going in."

"Oh, poosh. He's not that bad!" Gran's laughter warmed Krista as she headed out of the kitchen.

The main room was empty, but in the brightly lit dining room beyond, she found Big Skye, Jenny, and Shelby sitting around the big table with an archival box open, old photos spread out in slippery piles, and their heads together as they studied a picture.

"Whoa, Gramps," Jenny said. "What's with the lapels?"

He harrumphed and scowled, but there was a thread of amusement beneath the bluster.

"Cut him some slack," Shelby said. "It was the seventies."

"What have you guys got there?" Krista asked, coming around to stand behind Jenny and Big Skye. "I'm guessing this isn't a box of eighteen-whatever, guess-who's-in-the-tintype mystery photos?"

"Better." Jenny held up a five-by-seven. "Big Skye doing *Saturday Night Fever*."

Krista snicker-snorted at the sight of her gramps wearing a light blue tux and a wide-collared shirt with way too many buttons open at the top, looking so young, yet somehow exactly the same. He had his arm around a younger Gran, who was wearing a shiny sequined dress that clung to her slight body and ended well above her knees. Behind them, a dessert buffet sagged under its load and dancers filled the floor. The grainy color snapshot had probably been state-of-the-art in its day . . . but then again, the clothes probably had been, too.

"It wasn't anybody's fever," he grumped. "It was the Cattleman's Ball."

"You don't say?" Krista marveled, and got a dirty look in return. At Shelby's raised eyebrow, she said, "The local stockmen's association is plenty progressive when it comes to computerized databases, cattle genetics, and using the latest and best veterinary tech, but when it comes to the annual ball . . . well, let's just say that big hair and plaid may come and go, but the party swag, big-ass steaks, and playlist are set in stone."

"Who's that?" Jenny pointed to the dark-haired dancer in the background. "He looks familiar."

"That's . . ." Big Skye frowned, making a humming noise. "It's . . ."

"He looks like a Lemp," Krista noted.

Her grandfather scowled at her. "Of course it's a Lemp. Anyone can see that. Maybe Max? Humph. I know it starts with an 'M.'"

"Martini?" Jenny suggested. "Or Melba?"

Shelby studied the picture. "He looks like a Manfred to me."

"Nope," Krista said decisively. "That's the family rebel. He goes by Bob."

"Ask your grandmother," Big Skye said, flicking the picture away. "She'll remember who it is. Probably his whole life story, too." He snagged another from a nearby pile. "Now *this* is a good one."

As he and Jenny put their heads together over a Polaroid from some rodeo or another, Krista pulled out a chair and sat on the other side of her grandfather, relieved that he seemed like his usual self. "Who's got a pen? Remember, we're supposed to be documenting this stuff, not just flipping through for crimes against fashion." And, as they settled in for an hour of "hey, remember this?" and the unutterable disconnect that came from a photo of Big Skye water skiing in a Speedo, she felt some of the tension drain away.

Maybe her five-year plan had gone off the rails, and maybe Jenny's marriage had put more green in her eyes than she wanted to admit, but if scraping the surface of the family photos had proven anything, it was that the Skyes always found love eventually—and once they did, it was forever.

"Come on, don't be shy." Trixie looped an arm through Wyatt's and urged him along the gravel pathway to the gazebo, where the farewell barbecue was already in full swing, with mouthwatering smoke coming from the pit, happy-looking guests scattered at picnic tables, and chirpy fiddle music coming from hidden speakers.

"*Shy* isn't usually the first word people think of when it comes to me," he drawled, knowing it would make her laugh.

It did. She patted his arm with her free hand. "Fine, then. Circumspect. Don't tell me you're antisocial, because I don't buy it, which means there's another reason you've been avoiding the dining hall. And don't think we haven't seen what's going on between you and Krista. I've got ten bucks on a spring wedding."

He coughed as a lungful of air somehow got caught sideways. "A suggestion? Put another fifty on *just friends*." And even that was pushing it. Ever since that night down by the boathouse, they had been giving each other a wide berth.

"Nonsense," she said as they reached the party. "I've seen how you two look at each other."

He wouldn't ask, because it didn't matter. There was no arguing the attraction, only what he and Krista were—or, more accurately, *weren't*—going to do about it. Even if he wanted to go there on her turf, surrounded by her family, he kept remembering those tears. "You should get those glasses checked, Trix. I think you're seeing things."

"Ha! You know what I think? I think you're smart enough to know there might be something real there, and it's got you spooked."

He nudged her toward the buffet line. "Go on, get yourself a plate before it's all gone."

"Like Gran would let that happen!" But she moved off, tossing a wink over her shoulder, and calling, "You just think about what I said, cowboy. You don't want to let things like this slide, or pretty soon you'll turn around and find that it's already too late."

He watched her go, shaking his head. Not because she was all that far off base, but because part of him wished it was that simple.

"Dare I ask?" Krista said behind him. "Or do I not want to know?"

He sucked in a breath, and the scent of wildflowers and rain hit him in the gut. Steeling himself—to not stare at her, not react to her, not let her know that the man he was today wanted the woman she had grown into, despite everything—he turned. "Let's call it an inside joke," he said, and then fell silent.

She had left her hair down and dressed up for the farewell barbecue, in a flowing red-and-blue patchwork skirt that showed the tops of her flower-tooled brown leather boots, and a stretchy red shirt that bared just a hint of cleavage, making a man want to take a second look.

"An inside joke. I like that." Her lips curved, but her smile went wistful as she scanned the crowd. "I can't believe they'll all be gone tomorrow."

"If you ask me, you'll see some of them again." He nodded to Terry M. and Terry P., an auto mechanic and a children's book editor who had bonded over sharing the same first name and now sat close together.

"I hope everyone got something out of the week, with or without a hookup."

"I think I can guarantee that. You do good work here, Krista. Real good work." It still felt strange to say her name, like he was riding on an eyebrow trail on a horse that might stumble any second.

"You did your part this week. I'm grateful." She paused, then slid him a sidelong look. Started to say something, but didn't. His pulse kicked up a notch for no good reason, and he stuck his hands in his pockets to keep from doing something he'd already decided he wasn't going to do. In the end, though, all she said was, "Have a nice day off tomorrow. I'll see you Sunday morning for Riding 101."

She moved off with a swing of golden hair and a

swish of red and blue skirt that left him staring at the patches of color on the back that seemed to say "put your hands here." Which he so wasn't going to do.

"You should come to the bonfire tonight," said Trixie's voice behind him, "and ask her to dance."

"What I should do," he said as he turned, "is put my back against the wall so nobody can sneak up on me."

She hooted with laughter and turned away, calling, "Patrick! Yoo-hoo, Patrick. You're going to save me a dance, right? Krista's taking requests for tonight's playlist. What do you think about that song from *Dirty Dancing*?"

Taking the opportunity to escape, Wyatt whistled for Klepto. "Come on, buddy. Let's head home."

He got a "whuff" in response, and a wiry gray body emerged from under a nearby picnic table. With it came a pink-flowered shirt clamped in happy jaws.

Wyatt sighed, but there was some relief, too. Long after the summer ended and he left Mustang Ridge, Klepto would still be with him, still be "borrowing" things and bringing them to him with that goofy expression of *Look what I found! Isn't it cool?*

"What did I tell you . . ." he began, but then gave it up because there was no real point. It wasn't like complaining was going to make a dent, and it was his fault for not keeping a better eye on the dog. "You're lucky I find you entertaining. Drop it." He snagged the shirt, shook it out, and draped it at the end of a picnic table, figuring it'd be reunited with its owner when things wound down.

Then, whistling his unrepentant mutt to heel, he headed out along the trail to the bunkhouse.

The party noises faded as they crested the first hill, leaving them surrounded by a whole lot of grass and fresh air, all of it turned red-gold by the first few hints of dusk.

This, he thought, filling his lungs with air that he didn't have to share with anybody else. This was why he'd needed to get out of Denver, away from crowds, Wi-Fi and coffee shops on every corner. Away from Damien and the rest of the people who, when they said, "How's it going?" were really asking when he'd have a new piece to show. He could breathe out here. He could hear himself *think* out here. Especially when he was away from the clamor. Once upon a time, he had pictured himself surrounded by family and ranch guests . . . but he was learning that it could close in on a man real fast.

Klepto sniffed his way to and fro, zigzagging along Wyatt's track as they topped the second hill and started down into the shallow valley that held the bunkhouse. When they reached level ground, Wyatt turned for the steel building where he'd stashed his tools. Stopping with his hand on the lock, he looked into the distance at the rippling hills and darkening mountains, and imagined there was a small, rough-hewn cabin behind him, maybe a revolver on his hip and a hungry ache in his belly.

Still nothing. *Damn it.*

Turning away, he said to Klepto, "What do you say we take a look at that hot tub instead?"

He had a blowtorch and some know-how, after all. And if he kept busy—even if he wasn't working on what he was supposed to be doing—he wouldn't give in to the temptation and go down to the lake, where Krista would be dancing in that ruffled skirt and low-cut shirt, and a man could easily get himself in trouble.

"I had the perfect idea for your grandparents' anniversary," Rose said brightly late that night, pitching her voice to carry over the music and the chatter of the dozen or so guests who were still gathered around the bonfire. "Skydiving!"

Krista, who had been trying to decide if she should add more wood or let the fire burn down, took a second to process that one. "What, like having an aerial display team come down over the ranch with a HAPPY ANNIVERSARY banner or something?"

"No, silly." Rose waved that off. "I mean we should send *them* skydiving. You know how much your grandfather loves those old aerial photos of the ranch."

How that translated to "we should totally send them skydiving," Krista didn't know. "Gran doesn't like heights," she pointed out, "and their anniversary is in December. They'll freeze."

"So we'll give them some sort of presentation at the party, and schedule the jump for later." Her mom's eyes lit. "How about next year's Harvest Fair? They could parachute onto the track and then wave the flag to start the big stock car race!"

Stifling the sudden image of Gran dangling from a

Ferris wheel by a tangled-up parachute, Krista said, "I was more thinking we should send them to Paris for lunch." Or was it breakfast in Paris and lunch somewhere else? Full of good food and warm from the fire, she couldn't remember.

"Why Paris? She doesn't like French cooking."

Actually, she did. Just not how Rose did it. "It's just a thought."

"Anyway, I'm pretty sure your grandfather is thinking along those lines. He asked me the other day about travel agencies and those discount Web sites that do the all-inclusive packages to Europe."

Way to go, Gramps. "So you're helping him out with the planning?"

"You betcha. I hate to think what he might end up with otherwise." Rose shuddered. "A bus tour of student hostels, or paying for a hotel that only renovated the one room they photographed for the Web site. If they rented a room in a bad part of the city and got mugged, I'd never forgive myself."

"This from the woman who wants to send them skydiving."

A couple of years ago, her mom would've dug in for the battle. Now, she sent Krista a sidelong look. "You think it's too much."

Remembering the pictures of Big Skye on water skis, she said, "Maybe not, but they're getting up there, you know. Speaking of which . . . how does Gramps seem to you?"

Instead of the immediate "Fine, sweetie, why do you

ask?" that Krista was expecting—and admittedly hoping for—there was a pause that dragged on long enough for the fire to pop a few times and her to notice that the party was down to six—her and her mom plus two diehard couples hunkered together, talking in low voices as the flames burned low.

Then, finally, Rose said, "Any marriage has its bumps along the way, even one that's coming up on fifty years."

Gran had said something similar, but she hadn't been working so hard to pick the right words. "You know something, don't you? Tell me. I want to help."

But her mom shook her head. "I'm just guessing, sweetie, based on having been married to your father for as long as I have. Don't worry. It'll pass. These things always do."

Reunion Week said otherwise, but Krista didn't want to think along those lines when it came to her grandparents. "You'll tell me if I can do anything to help?"

"Just the usual. Love them. Tell Gran her cookies are the best and make Big Skye feel like he's indispensable."

"They are. He is, even though he's a grouchy pain in the you-know-what sometimes. I just worry about them."

"They'll be fine." Her mom patted her hand. Then, seeming to think that wasn't enough, she squeezed Krista's fingers, then held on. "Speaking of relationships."

"Don't tell me you and Dad are having problems. Or Jenny and Nick. My worldview couldn't take it."

"No, dear. Haven't you heard? Us Skyes mate for life, like wolves."

Krista let out a relieved breath. "I think the wolf thing is a myth."

"Swans, then. Or fruit flies. Whatever species does *for better or worse*. But that's not what—or, rather, *who*— I wanted to talk to you about."

So much for relief. "Wyatt, you mean." A quick glance showed that the others were happily oblivious, but it still felt like his name had come out too loud.

"Of course I mean Wyatt. Unless you started something this week I wasn't aware of? With Bernie, maybe, or Patrick?"

"Ha. No. And, anyway, I thought you wanted grandkids? I think this weeks' guests are beyond that phase."

"I do want grandbabies, but not—" Again, Krista's mom picked her words. "I hope you're being careful, that's all."

Stifling a condom joke—not going there, especially when the subject was Wyatt and she was talking to her mom—Krista shifted in her chair as a log hissed and popped. "I thought you guys were okay with him now, after his apology and all." Even her father had agreed to give him a chance.

"Okay with him working here, sure. As for anything more than that"—Rose tightened her grip on Krista's hand—"I just don't want to see you get hurt again, baby.

He's a handsome, charming man with a good smile, and he's an artist, to boot. I can see the attraction."

Krista shook her head. "There's nothing going on between me and Wyatt. Nothing. Nada. *Nyet. Capisce?*" She hoped that didn't fall under the category of the lady doth protest too much, but she wanted to get the point across. "Seriously, Mom. There's no way Wyatt and I are picking up where we left off. That's over and done with. Finished. Buh-bye." And she was stopping now.

"There hasn't been anybody else for you, baby, and you're not getting any younger."

Ouch. "I'm twenty-eight, Mom, not ninety. And I've dated other guys."

"Not seriously."

"So . . . what? Do you want me to start back up with him, see if he was supposed to be my one-and-only after all? Because, trust me, he's not." If he had been, they would've been inseparable from college on, just like her mom and dad.

But Rose said gently, "No, sweetheart. I want you to use this time to get over him. Then you'll be free to look for your wolf."

"Swan," Krista said automatically.

"I don't care if it's a monogamous bedbug, as long as he—or she—makes you happy."

And, dang it, she didn't have a comeback for that. Especially since it had struck a chord—not the bedbug thing, but taking the opportunity to get over Wyatt. All these years she thought she had moved on . . . but she hadn't had a relationship other than her fling with Ballard, had she? And there were still sparks—big ones—with Wyatt. "I *am* happy, Mom." She swept a hand at the landscape that was lost in the darkness beyond the flames. "How could I not be?"

"In other words, butt out."

Krista grinned. "I didn't say that."

"Sure you did, but I can take it." Her mom dusted the crumbs off her fingers and stood. "Just think about it, okay?"

"I will." Krista stood and kissed her cheek. "Thanks. Sleep well."

As the darkness swallowed Rose's tall figure and her footsteps receded in the distance, Krista crossed to the fire, where the crowd had dwindled to a single couple snuggled near the blaze. "Do you guys want me to throw on some more wood?"

"Not on our account." Joe stood, brushed himself off, and helped Bebe to her feet. "Thanks for the bonfire. It was the perfect finale for one of the best weeks of my life."

Bebe tipped her head against his shoulder. "We're going to stay in touch with each other, see where it leads. Maybe we'll see you next year for a different theme week."

Krista smiled. "I'll look forward to it."

"Would you like help cleaning up?"

"No, you guys go on. I'll take care of it."

But once they were gone, Krista turned the music down low, snagged a nearly empty bag of marshmallows, and leaned back on a log facing the lake, where the blue-white light from the half-moon and the red-orange of the bonfire made the water sparkle like it was coated with jewels. She didn't bother toasting the marshmallows, instead nibbling straight from the bag as the night quieted around her.

The snack didn't fill the hollow in her belly, though, because it wasn't the hungry kind of emptiness. It wasn't that she was worried about Big Skye, either. At least not entirely. No . . . here in the darkness, in a rare moment of privacy, she had to admit that her mom was right about one thing—she wasn't all the way over Wyatt. If she had been, she wouldn't be disappointed that he'd been a no-show for the bonfire.

Which was stupid. It wasn't in the job description, and the guests had partied to their hearts' content. . . . Yet she had wanted him there, more than she had admitted even to herself when she had traded her jeans for a long skirt, switched her work shirt out for a red number that showed some cleavage, and left her hair down. Sure, she had gotten plenty of compliments at dinner and hadn't lacked for a dance partner when the bonfire kicked into high gear, but the one man she had hoped to dance with hadn't shown.

She didn't know why she had thought he might. Didn't know what it really meant that she had wished for him. But maybe that was her mom's point. Did she want to waste time wishing for him to show up?

That would be a no. Standing, she crumpled the empty marshmallow bag and stuck it in her pocket. "Well, that's that, then. Might as well clean up and call it a night."

"Whuff." The quiet canine greeting came from the darkness, sending heat careening through her at a rate far greater than warranted by the bonfire.

She turned just as Klepto padded into the pool of firelight, followed a moment later by Wyatt. The dog zigzagged with his nose down, hunting graham cracker crumbs, while his human master hooked his thumbs in the pockets of his worn jeans. He was bareheaded, wearing a denim work shirt unbuttoned over a white tee, and looked like everything she shouldn't still want.

"I didn't think you were coming," she said, going for a noncommittal tone that ruined itself with a quiver.

His eyes searched hers. "I told myself not to. Yet here I am."

"Here you are," Krista echoed, suddenly very aware of the fire's warmth on her front, the lake's chill at her back, and the darkened windows of the cabins and main house. "Why is that, exactly?"

"I can only erase the same dog so many times before it gets stuck on the page."

"That sounds strangely profound."

"Wasn't meant to. I'm sketching concepts—at least I'm trying to." In a low, mellow drawl that threatened to wrap around her and paint pictures in her mind, he told her his idea of building a cowboy and his horse camped alone at the edge of the frontier. "It's not working for me, though, any more than it did before. It's gotten so bad that I even started playing with the idea of switching it around, so the horse was making coffee and the cowboy was standing off to the side, wearing the saddle and bridle."

"Which would be . . . interesting."

His teeth flashed. "Admit it. You're thinking it would be fifty-fifty whether it would creep the heck out of the museum patrons or make them think of poker-playing dogs."

"Actually, I was thinking it's really weird to be out here with you, talking like this."

"Like what?"

"Like we're friends." She faced him fully, so it felt like they were a couple of gunslingers squaring off outside a long-ago saloon. "What do you really want, Wyatt? Why are you really out here?" Because her gut said there was more to it than him needing to stretch his legs, frustrated that his work wasn't going well.

12

"I'm . . ." Wyatt paused, needing to get this right. Because some time after erasing the dog for the sixth time, he had found himself looking down at a whole new sketch. And, staring at it, he had known what he needed to do. "How much do you remember me telling you about my old man?"

Her expression tightened. "It doesn't matter anymore."

"I'm not so sure about that." He closed the distance between them, so he could smell rain-soaked wildflowers and see the wariness in her eyes. Even without their bodies touching, he could feel the stir of energy between them, could see the change in her expression that said she felt it, too. "Work with me here."

After an endless moment that lasted from one pulse thud to the next, she said, "I knew he was a bull rider, like you, and that he wasn't around much when you were growing up. And that after Ashley was born, he stopped coming around at all, leaving you to pick up the slack."

He wished he could say the bull riding was where the similarities stopped. "I'd like to tell you more of it, if you're willing to listen."

She hesitated so long he thought she was going to tell him to jump in the nearby lake. But then she gestured to a couple of chairs near the fire. "Want to sit? Toast a marshmallow?"

He sat, accepted a stick, and stuck on a couple of the Stay Pufts she offered, not because he was hungry, but because he figured it wouldn't hurt to have a reason to stare into the fire. When Krista loaded a stick and took the chair beside him so they were shoulder to shoulder, studying their toasting marshmallows, he figured they looked like a couple of fishing buddies waiting for a bite. Except that they weren't fishing, and the buddy thing was debatable.

After a moment, she said, "So? I'm listening."

The fire hissed and popped. After a moment, he began. "My old man wasn't just a bull rider. He rode broncs, worked the gates, did setup and teardown . . . pretty much anything it took to keep him on the rodeo circuit year-round. California, Texas, Mexico, he didn't care as long as he wasn't stuck at home with me and Ma." In the single-wide that was all she could afford on a cashier's salary. "When I was little, he'd visit every month or so. Ma would set out her grandma's dishes, scrub extra hard behind my ears, and put on her best dress and fancy perfume. And while we waited, she'd tell me about all the bulls he'd ridden the full eight seconds while he was away, all the prizes he'd won and all the important people he'd met." Later, he'd heard her tell Ashley the same stories, pretending that they were new and Daddy would visit as soon as he could.

"I think your marshmallows are done," Krista said. "Unless you're a fan of charcoal."

"Thanks." He pulled his stick out of the fire and rested it on his knee so the toasted blobs could cool. "Back then, it was like Christmas, my birthday, and the Fourth of July, all rolled into one when he came through the door. We'd all hug and kiss, and he'd spin me over his head, telling me how big I'd gotten, and how much I looked like him." He had worshipped his old man, felt like he was being tossed around by a giant. "We'd have a big celebration dinner that night, then go somewhere special the next day, and the day after that . . . but after a week or so he would start inviting friends over, staying out later, drinking more. Getting bored." With the trailer, the town, and his family. "Then, eventually, he would leave. And every time, when he was on his way out the door, he'd turn back and say, 'You're in charge, Wyatt. Take good care of your mother, you hear? You're the man of the house while I'm gone.'"

"That's a lot for them to put on a kid," she said, staring into the fire.

"He put it on me."

"Your mother let him."

"She let him do a whole lot of things. That was the least of it."

Her sidelong look said she didn't agree, but she didn't say anything.

After a moment, he continued. "Ashley came along when I was twelve. By then, he was down to one or two visits a year, and he'd stopped telling Ma that they would get married as soon as he saved enough for a ring and a proper ceremony." He paused, then figured *what the hell*. "Did she get pregnant again thinking it would bring him back to her? I don't know. Maybe. He visited the hospital right after Ash was born, and gave Ma all the *oohs* and *ahhs* she needed, and I could see she thought everything was going to be okay. But then he pulled me out in the hall, gave me a hundred bucks, and said, 'Take good care of your mother and little sister, you hear? You're the man of the house now.'"

Krista's eyes went wide. "Was that the last time you saw him?"

"No. But it was the last time I asked him to stay." He pulled one of the marshmallows off his stick and took a bite, the flavor bringing back childhood campfires with his friends' fathers. "It was also pretty much the end of me being a kid. When money got tight—which happened fast—I hired on at a neighbor's place to bale hay and help move cows through the summer and fall, then worked another ranch through the winter, feeding in the morning before school and cleaning after. When I wasn't working or at school, I watched Ash so Ma could work."

Her fingers splayed, like she was stopping herself from making a fist. "I'll say it again. That was a lot to put on a kid. It's to your credit that you stepped up the way you did."

"A couple of neighbors helped now and then, but they weren't family. And Ashley made it easy. She was"—a happy, pink little thing that had reached for him, smiled at him, called him *Wy-wy* and held his hand when she took her first few wobbly steps—"a good baby, grew into a good kid. But kids need more stuff than babies do, and by the time she started school, Ma was having trouble getting hours at the store where she worked. I had been rodeoing for a bit and was starting to make some money. So the day before my high school graduation, I loaded up my saddle, kissed her and Ash good-bye, and hit the road."

Like father, like son. At least he had felt bad that his Ma was crying when he left. And he'd sent almost every penny home.

"So young." Krista's throat worked.

"No younger than you were when you decided to turn Mustang Ridge into a dude ranch," he pointed out. "We both grew up early, though we took different paths to do it." Throat gone dry from the air, the talking, he said, "I had been rodeoing for a couple of years when Ma met Jack. She was still seeing my old man when he bothered to come around, still telling herself that he was going to change. Thank God Jack wouldn't take no for an answer. He eventually wore her down enough to get a ring on her finger, and moved her and Ashley into his house in the 'burbs. And suddenly I wasn't the man of the house anymore, wasn't responsible for any bills but my own."

It had been like cutting loose from a rank bull—an

endless few seconds of free fall, followed by a jarring thud and a whole lot of *How the hell did I get here?* Except that there hadn't been a loose bull behind him, looking to get in a shot or two with his horns before the bullfighters ran him off. It had taken him a while to believe that, longer still to figure out who he was without that bull chasing him.

"So you went back to school, where you developed your eight-week buzzer." Krista tossed her marshmallows to Klepto, who snapped them out of the air with uncanny precision. "Or had that been part of you all along?"

She would remember that, wouldn't she? *Damn it, Sam.* But although Sam had given the pattern its name, it hadn't been a new behavior. "The rodeo circuit wasn't exactly designed for anything long term—more like lips passing in the night. And after, in college . . ." He shook his head. "I'd last a month, maybe two, and be ready to move on." First, he'd want to hang out with friends instead of catching a movie with his girl; then he'd have trouble getting places on time for their dates. Until, finally, he would start looking for an out. "Then I met you and everything changed."

Her head whipped up; her glare cut into him. "*Don't.* Don't you *dare* say that. Not when we ended exactly the same as the others."

"I missed graduation, bailed on my job and bolted. I wouldn't call that business as usual."

"Is that supposed to make me feel better?" The firelight caught the sudden glint of tears. Or was that anger? He wasn't sure, but either way, it made him feel lower than dirt.

"I should've broken it off with you before things got serious, should've been honest with you when the walls started closing in. I know it probably doesn't help, but it just about killed me to leave." Though that hadn't been enough to make him turn around when the wide open was calling.

Her expression hardened. "Why are you telling me this now, Wyatt?"

Don't do it, he told himself. *Leave it alone.* But he couldn't leave it alone—couldn't leave *her* alone—so he pulled the folded page from his pocket and handed it over. "Because of this . . . And because the way I feel about you right here, right now, is about as far from leftovers as these things can get."

Krista's fingers trembled as she unfolded the piece of sketch paper—from fury, she told herself, not the almost painful need to weep at guessing that this was a breakthrough sketch, the missing piece he needed to move forward with his sculpture. "Damn it, Wyatt. You don't get to come out here, say things like that, and then . . ." She trailed off. Stared.

It wasn't an idea for the pioneer museum. It was a sketch of her.

Arcs of soft charcoal hinted at her cheeks, jaw, and throat, while lighter lines suggested her Stetson and the braids she wore out riding. Her lips were curved in a small, secretive smile she didn't recognize, and her eyes . . . Heat kicked through her, because if that was how she'd been looking at him over the past week, no wonder Bebe had assumed she was flirting.

"That's not me seeing the girl you used to be and wishing things had turned out different." His voice had gone rough, his eyes dark. "It's me looking at the woman you are today and wanting to do this." He shifted in his chair, and suddenly their faces were very close.

Krista stiffened as heat bloomed beneath her skin and she was trapped suddenly in place, not by the broad shoulders that all but blocked her view of the fire or the powerful legs that bracketed hers, but by the churn in her belly and the part of her that said *yes-yes-yes* as he leaned in.

And kissed her.

Wyatt. That was all she could think as his lips closed on hers, just his name. The man kissing her now wasn't a memory and he wasn't the brash young cowboy who had told her she was different and tried to mean it.

Far from it. He was a man now, and knew himself well.

And his kiss. Oh, his kiss. Where before in the bunkhouse he had held himself back, now he dove straight in, leaving her to hang on for the ride. His lips were firm, his tongue masterful as he traced her mouth and then dipped inside. His stubble rasped gently across her lips and cheek, an unexpected sensation that stirred her and made her want to touch him, explore him, learn the shapes and textures that were uniquely his, and—

She jerked back so hard that her chair shifted in the lakeshore sand, then batted away the hand he put out to steady her. "Don't," she said too sharply, then, softer, "Please. Just give me a second here."

A second to get a grip, to pull herself together. To level off her breathing, and keep her voice steady as she said, "What do you want from me, Wyatt?"

His eyes were dark in the firelight, his breath warm on her skin. "I think that's pretty obvious at this point. Even knowing I should keep my hands off you, I can't do it. I can't walk away, and I can't stay away."

The rough declaration shouldn't have sent a new kick of heat into her bloodstream, especially when he'd done both of those things before. "I may not be the same girl, but I still want pretty much the same things." She waved toward the main house, pleased that her hand stayed steadier than her thundering heartbeat. "A home, a family, a future."

He touched her lower lip with his thumb. Lingered there. "Seems to me you're not giving yourself near enough credit. You've created a whole fantasy world here for your guests—a living, breathing paradise they can escape to. You become their best friend while they're here, and they're better for it when they leave." His thumb cruised across her lip, then caught her chin as he dropped his voice low to say, "You don't just sell the adventure, Krista. You live it one week at a time. Don't you think you deserve to take some of it for yourself?"

And darn him for knowing her too well, even after all these years. *Adventure.* She yearned for it some days, just like she wished at times she could be like the rest of her family—creative, artistic, inventive, and more than the sum of their parts. And while she loved the smaller, quieter niche she had carved for herself . . . it was too quiet some days, too much like she was surrounded by friends and family, yet still alone. But what kind of adventure was he talking about? "So . . . what is this, Wyatt? Are you asking me out?"

His eyes were steady on hers. "Name the day, and tell me whether to saddle a horse or clean out Old Blue."

But it was more than that, she knew. Because there was no way they could be together and not want to take it all the way. "A no-strings fling. Is that what you're offering? A few weeks of fun and then done, no regrets?"

He nodded, expression guarded, maybe even a little regretful. But there was no regret in his voice when he said, "I'm here for six more weeks, until the end of the season, and I want to spend them with you."

Why don't we forget about the calendar and just see what happens? she wanted to say. She didn't, though, because she'd be darned if she tried to talk him—or herself—out of the familiar pattern. Been there, done that, and it hadn't ended well. Besides, she might be a soft touch for aged mustangs, dried-up cows, and three-legged barn cats, but she wasn't in the market for a project when it came to men. No, she wanted someone who wanted her enough to make a grand gesture to win her, like Foster offering to give up the Double-Bar H and move to Boston with Shelby, and like Nick taking on a partner so he could travel with Jenny. More, she wanted to be romanced, wanted the slow step-by-step buildup, the foundation that could be turned into something lasting and important.

One of these days she would make the time to find the guy who could give her all those things. She would love him, adore him, and trust him utterly. In the meantime, though, she had a gorgeous cowboy sitting with his knees bumping hers, the pulse at his throat still working from their kiss, making her want to kiss him again.

"Say yes," he urged, "but only if it's what you want."

"I don't know what I want anymore," she said, shocked to realize that she was seriously considering it. "So for tonight, let's just say I'll think about it." It wasn't like she was going to be able to think about anything else.

13

The next morning, Krista woke late and hit the ground running, pitching in to help her mom and Gran with more than the usual number of "did anyone turn in a left boot to lost and found?" and "have you seen my pink sweater?" calls to the front desk, with a bonus round of "I think the maid threw out my dentures. They were in a water glass next to my bed."

A veteran of far odder Saturday morning calls, Krista didn't miss a beat at that one. "The cabins haven't been cleaned yet this morning, Sukie. Have you checked the bathroom and the floor under the bed?"

"Of course I did!" the Manhattanite said with twice her normal level of starch. "I'm old, not dead." That last bit came out with a hint of pride, like she'd done something recently to prove it.

Aha, Krista thought. *Gotcha.* "I don't suppose there's any chance you might have left them on someone else's nightstand?" *Bernie's, perhaps?*

"Young lady! What are you..." The indignation

trailed off and was followed by a chastened, "Never mind. Thank you," and the click of a disconnect.

Krista pantomimed dusting off her hands. "Mystery solved."

"She left them at Bernie's?" her mom asked.

"Yep."

Gran sighed happily. "It's just like that movie, only they didn't spend the whole weekend in his cabin together. Just Friday night."

"I'm pretty sure *Weekend at Bernie's* wasn't a romance, Gran."

"Still, it's got a ring to it, don't you think?"

"So does *It's almost time to load up the shuttle and get Junior on the road*. You want some help carrying out the snacks?"

Gran blinked at her. "Since when do you get all excited about guests leaving? Usually it's the other way around."

Krista went with a casual shrug. "It's not that. I'm just tired, I guess." Tired from too little sleep and too much buzzing in her brain. She hadn't settled until well after midnight, and even then she'd found herself staring into the darkness, thinking about what Wyatt had said.

It hadn't all been news to her, of course. She had known his father wasn't part of his life, and that he'd helped raise his sister until his mom remarried. But she hadn't known about his father's drive-through visits or how early Wyatt had started working to help pay the bills. How much time he had spent taking care of his sister. It explained some things, she supposed. Maybe it didn't excuse them, but it explained them.

"Krista?" her mom said, with enough concern to suggest that she had missed something. "Are you okay, sweetie?"

"Yes, I'm fine. Sorry. Did you ask me a question?" Wanting to ease their suddenly worried expressions, she tacked on, "Please don't tell me that Sukie called to say that Bernie's wearing her dentures, and could we please get them back for her."

"Actually," Gran said, "the question was: Do you want us to handle the good-byes, so you can go take a nap? But I think we should upgrade that to an order." She pointed to the stairs. "Go on. Shoo!"

"But I need to—"

"Take a few hours off," her mother finished for her. "Nap. Read a book. Take Lucky for a ride. Do something for yourself for a change, will you? We can hold down the fort."

She wanted to argue but was afraid she might win, and the thought of an extra hour or two of free time beckoned like green grass on the other side of a fence line. "You're sure you guys don't mind?"

"Go, already!"

Krista went. First, though, she made a circuit of the cabins to say individual good-byes. Most of them were of the usual "thanks so much for coming, I hope to see you again" variety. Except for Sukie, who complained about the maid using her makeup and didn't get the joke when Krista said she didn't think it was Fernando's color, and Bebe, who pulled Krista in for an extra-long hug and whispered in her ear, "Just remember, sparks don't come around every day, and neither does a good man."

Which was true, she thought as she headed for the barn. Question was: What was she going to do about it? Wyatt had said something last night about it being time for her to have some fun, and her mom and Gran had echoed that just now. And darned if it wasn't starting to resonate.

She worked her butt off to make sure the guests were having the time of their lives. When was it going to be her turn?

Lucky nickered from his run as she came around the corner, bobbing his head as if to say, *Are we doing something cool? Are we, are we, huh, huh?* But Krista's attention went to the middle of the arena, where a tall, muscular cowboy in jeans, a work shirt, and a brown hat stood with a gray mustang mare. The sight reminded her of the moment she first saw him, two weeks earlier at the mustang lottery, and the buzz that suddenly ran beneath her skin wasn't sparks so much as a sense of inevitability, like they had been heading toward this moment ever since.

As she crossed to the arena fence, he backed away from Jupiter and offered a long, flexible stick with a wad of rag tied to the end. The mare stood stock-still, her ears pricked so far forward that their curving tips nearly touched. Then, when he gave a low-voiced command, she raised one forefoot to touch the end of the stick, then alternated to touch it with the other, then bump it with her nose. Each behavior was rewarded with a click, and when she finished the routine, Wyatt praised her and patted her neck.

Then, as if he had known all along that she was there—which he probably had—he glanced at Krista. "Well, boss lady? What do you think?"

The tingle that ran through her suggested he wasn't just asking about Jupiter's training, but she wasn't ready to talk about last night just yet. Focusing on Jupiter, she said, "Not bad, cowboy. Any problems so far?"

He moved to hitch a boot on the rail and prop his elbows beside hers, so they mirrored each other, one on either side of the fence. "Nothing serious. The one thing I'm noticing is that she doesn't like being crowded."

Like you're crowding me? But, darn it, she liked having him right there, liked the prickle-heat that skimmed through her. "By other horses, you mean?"

"By man-made stuff, actually. Gates, stall doors, that sort of thing. She wants to plant her feet and give it a good look, sometimes a snort, like she's afraid it'll slam shut on her."

"Hm." She reached out to stroke the velvety nose. "We're going to need you to be braver than that, big mare. The ride-off has three phases, and I guarantee there'll be a gate or two in the obstacle course." Glancing at Wyatt, she said, "We're going to need to be near perfect on the first two phases if we want to have a shot at winning."

His eyes were steady on hers. "And winning is important to you?"

She hesitated. Then, figuring *what the heck*, she said, "The prize money is important. I want to start a mustang sanctuary here at the ranch." Saying it out loud gave her a buzz—part excitement, part *ohmigosh, am I really going to do this?*

He cocked an eyebrow. "Oh?"

"I want a whole herd, a family unit." She waved a hand toward the foothills. "I'll section off a few hundred acres, maybe a thousand, and see about driving a herd straight from government land. We'd geld the colts—no point in adding more to the overpopulation—and turn them loose."

One corner of his mouth kicked up. "The guests would enjoy seeing wild horses roaming the high pastures."

"So would Big Skye. He hates how the rangeland is shrinking and the mustangs are getting squeezed out."

"Which is why it matters to you."

He would see that, wouldn't he? "Not the only reason. But, yeah, that's part of it." She looked past the fencing to where the grasslands stretched all the way to the foothills. "I want him to have something he can get excited about. Maybe even something the two of us could share." She wished she hadn't said that last part, but once it was out there, she didn't take it back. And, when he raised an eyebrow, she added, "Growing up, I was always his little girl, the heir apparent. He bragged that I could ride before I could walk, and my first four words were *horse* and *that darn cow*. He always said that the ranch would be mine one day, and that it would be my responsibility to make sure it stayed in the family."

"I remember you worrying how he would take your big proposal."

It didn't hurt nearly so much now to remember those long-ago, so serious discussions about her dreams. The balance had changed between them, making the present seem more important than the past. "The family has equal shares, but Gramps was counting on me to preserve our heritage. For the longest time, he didn't believe that the changeover was my way of doing that and felt like the dude ranch was a betrayal. It's gotten better in the last year or so, but"—she shook her head—"he's not happy. I'm hoping that putting him in charge of the sanctuary will help, but I need the prize money to get it off the ground." She doubted that it would fix everything between her and Big Skye, but it might be a start.

He caught a fistful of Jupiter's long mane and gave it a gentle tug. "You hear that, maresy? You'd better man up where it comes to gates."

"Wouldn't that be 'mare up'?"

"That, too." He looked at her. "It's a nice idea and a good cause. I'll do what I can to help."

Her throat tightened. "Thanks." After a moment, she said, "When Big Skye was a boy, he used to sneak up on the herds, belly crawling until he was practically underneath them. Then he'd watch them interact—

their body language and pecking order, and how the stallion might show off but the alpha mare really ran things." Her lips curved. "I think that's one reason he and Gran do so well together—she might be small and quiet, but she's fierce when you get on the wrong side of her."

Jupiter bobbed her head—no doubt from dust or bugs, but it was like she was weighing in with an *Alpha mares, unite!*

Wyatt chuckled at her, but then sobered and said, "I used to think we came from different worlds, as much as two people could when they grew up around cattle and horses." He glanced around at the homestead. "Now I'm sure of it. You've got your own little piece of heaven here."

Something shifted inside her, but she kept it light. "Says the famous C. W. Webb. How many countries have you visited?"

He shook his head. "Places are just places. This is something else. And the next time I sit down with my sketches, I'm going to picture your gramps belly crawling up on a herd of wild horses. That's the mind-set I need to put myself in, the kind of image I need for the statue. Something that embodies the pioneer spirit." He tipped his head toward the top of the ridge. "Those marker stones are close—I can picture your long-ago ancestors busting their asses to stack them, so the riders of Mustang Ridge would always be able to find their way home. But I need something else. Something more."

The cave, Krista thought, a sizzle running through her as she realized she knew exactly the place, complete with a history that ran all the way back to the wagon trains, maybe even earlier. But it was *her* place—hers and Jenny's—and she wasn't sure she wanted him in it, wasn't sure she wanted the memories of him to linger there once he was gone. *Show him*, said the part of her that reveled in the heat of his body next to hers. *Don't you dare*, said the part that knew better.

Pulse racing as she made the decision, she said, "How about you saddle up and meet me up at the marker stones in fifteen? There's something I want to show you."

Ten minutes later, Wyatt swung aboard Jupiter, settled his hat on his brow, whistled for Klepto, and headed out. Was this a bad idea? Maybe. Probably. But right now he didn't give a rat's patootie. It was his day off, and he wanted to go riding with Krista. Besides, Jupiter needed the miles. Now that he knew what they were competing for—how could a guy not get behind re-homing an entire herd and setting them free on land like this?—he was even more determined to put some polish on the gray mare, and have her ready to kick some serious butt in six weeks' time.

Krista was waiting up on the ridge astride her classy black gelding, who stood beside the marker stones with his neck arched and his ears pricked. As Jupiter drew near, Wyatt called, "The two of you make a heck of a pair. I feel like I should take a picture." Or sketch them with the fewest lines possible, just the outline of the horse and a few more details of the rider—the way the curves of her straw hat were echoed in the soft hollows of her throat, and how her twin braids turned back the clock and made her look like a teenager, even though her eyes said she wasn't a green girl anymore.

"Thanks to Jenny, I've got plenty of pictures." She touched a rein to Lucky's neck, wheeling him with the barest hint of pressure. "Come on—we've got some ground to cover and I want to be back before the new guests arrive."

"Lead on, boss lady."

She flashed him a grin and they set off, alternating between an easy jog and a ground-covering lope that carried them from ridge to valley, and over the rolling hills beyond. They didn't talk much, instead falling into the sign-language shorthand of the trail, with gestures like *Check out the hawk up there* and silent whistles when they came upon the tracks of a huge wolf.

He had missed this, he admitted as Jupiter picked her way down one side of a dry gulch and scrambled up the other, her head up and her ears always on the move. Missed the inner calm that came from the noisy silence of a couple of horses and no conversation, the feeling that they could be the only two people for hundreds of miles, the only two who had passed this way in decades, centuries. Maybe ever. And how cool was that?

On the guest trail rides, they had gone mostly west from the homestead. Now they headed north, out of the grasslands and into rougher terrain, where the trees were bigger and the horses had to mind their footing. Eventually, Krista zeroed in on a ragged patch of forest at the top of a rocky incline. Jupiter followed the gelding up the hill and into the pines, and soon the air grew heavy with mist and the sound of rushing water.

"Watch the branches," she called, flattening herself against Lucky's neck as the trees closed in around them. "Just keep coming. It opens up pretty fast."

Wyatt sank into the saddle. "Go on," he told the tensed-up mare. "They won't get you."

Jupiter hesitated, then gathered herself and plunged forward. The trees whipped past, dragging at his clothes, and then they were through, squirting out like a seed from a squeezed lemon.

Krista raised a cheer. "Brave mare!"

"She sure is." He fished in a pocket for the clicker and some treats, and looked around the clearing as the mare munched. The pretty little grotto was edged with greenery and pink flowers, and echoed with the sound of a nearby waterfall. Knowing there was no point in bringing up another, long-ago waterfall, he said only, "Do you bring guests out here?"

"It's more of a family deal." She looped Lucky's reins over a branch. "Will Jupiter be okay standing tied for a few minutes?"

"Should be. We've practiced it." Deciding to go with the flow rather than analyzing either of their motives— hers for bringing him to a private spot, his for chasing a woman who didn't seem to be fully interested in being caught—he tied the mare and whistled for Klepto. When the mutt zipped into the clearing, he pointed to a safe spot. "Keep an eye on these two, will you?"

The dog flopped down and glared at the horses.

"He's a funny one, isn't he?" Krista said with a small smile. "Not exactly your typical cattle dog."

"He was a city stray."

Interest sparked in her expression. "I bet there's a story."

"There's always a story when it comes to Klepto," he said drily. "This is a good one, though. It was the night of my first show for Damien. There was lots of money, lots of pretense, and after an hour or so it really started getting to me. I stepped out back for a break, and this ugly gray dog came out from underneath a Dumpster and mugged me for my cocktail wieners." The woman he'd been seeing, Desiree, had been horrified by the filthy, smelly creature, but he'd felt more than a little kinship. "When I said I was keeping him, Damien took pictures and splashed the story, and the show sold out on the second night." He ruffled the dog's upturned head. "I wouldn't say he made my career, but he sure kick-started my popularity. Now it's up to me not to torpedo things by flaming out on the pioneer piece."

"I think I might be able to help with that." She gestured him to where a trail led into the scrub. "Come on, but watch your step."

Wyatt followed her along a corridor of rocks and trees while the waterfall noise went from a whisper to a roar and the air turned damp. Up ahead, two stone slabs leaned against each other, forming a tunnel. He followed Krista through . . . and found himself in a slice of the backcountry at its very best. On one side of the wide ledge, char marks on the cliff face attested to decades—maybe centuries—of campfires. On the other, a plume of green-and-white water plunged past and down to crash in a boiling pool that carved deep into the stone and fed a winding river. The valley beyond was pure Wyoming, all greens and browns, and bounded by high canyon walls.

Krista didn't stop, though. She kept going along the ledge, shot him a sassy smile, and ducked right through the cannonading waterfall. There was a splash and then she was gone. But a moment later, her voice carried back over the sound of the rushing water. "Come on. There's room for both of us."

Adrenaline zinged through him as he followed. Had he told her she needed more adventure in her life? Suddenly, it seemed like she had plenty without him. The rocks were slippery, the mountain-cold water a shock when he plunged through the falls. Beyond, he found himself in a cavern that was lit with an eerie dance of dark and light. It took a moment for his eyes to adjust, but when they did, the hairs on his nape prickled at the sight confronting him. "Whoa."

Krista hadn't been sure about bringing him here, but as she watched him cross to the back wall of the cave and trail his fingers reverently over the words and drawings that had been carved there, she was glad she had. His face was intent in the flickering half-light, his lips parting as he scanned the intricate carvings. Names, dates, and pictures—the marks of dozens of people who had visited the cave, maybe hundreds over the years.

"I'll be danged," he rasped. "You've got your own little Independence Rock here." He drew his fingers across a foot-tall inscription: WILLIAM T 1897.

He got it, she realized. Of course he did. "This was the Skyes' version of it, anyway—not so much land-mark for the wagon trains, like Independence Rock down south, but more a way for the cowboys of Mus-tang Ridge to leave something of themselves behind." She moved up to stand next to him, eyes tracing the familiar names carved in everything from bold block letters to illegible scratches, beside dates ranging from the mid–eighteen hundreds through nineteen-sixty, with a few modern ones carved at the edges. There were pictures, too. Female silhouettes beckoned from rock formations that suggested their curves, and stick mustangs galloped among anatomically improbable cartoon bulls and hump-shouldered bison, the lines working together like city graffiti to create a whole that exceeded its parts. She reached up and trailed her fin-gers across the letters ROP, which sat alone near the top.

"Roper?" he guessed.

"Maybe. Or Robert, and he didn't get to finish the B. When I was a little girl, I pictured him coming up here every time he brought the herd through, and chiseling away a little bit each visit. Whenever Big Skye brought me and Jenny up here, I would race see if he had gotten more of it done. Eventually, I figured out that he lived a long time ago and never got to finish." She shrugged. "I like to think he met a girl, started a family, and moved on from cowboying."

"Nothing wrong with giving his story a happy ending."

Trying not to let his approval warm her more than it should, she crouched down and pointed. "This is one of my favorites. Jeremiah Skye. He was Jonah and Mary's son, the first generation born at Mustang Ridge. And then there's this." She brushed her fingertips over a collection of thinner scratched lines, so light that they were nearly invisible. Two names together inside a heart. *Jenny and Krista.*

A corner of his mouth kicked up. "How old were you?"

"Eight. Big Skye gave us matching pocket knives for our birthday, and the first thing we wanted to do was come up here." She touched a nick in the stone. "I broke mine, and we finished it using hers." She straightened away and stuck her hands in her pockets. "Anyway, some of it is pioneer era. I thought it might give you some ideas." And maybe she had wanted to bring him here to prove she could.

"There's a whole lot of history here." He spread his palm on the wall, covering a name, a date. "A whole lot of continuity."

"I feel centered here," she said, "like I can feel the

ground more clearly beneath my boots. The carvings remind me that Mustang Ridge has been through its ups and downs—floods, fires, sickness, robbery, you name it. Yet we're still hanging on."

Studying the carvings, he said, "I used to wish for a big family. Someone to take the pressure off me and Ma."

It wasn't what she had expected him to say, so it was a moment before she replied. "You turned out okay. Ashley, too, right?" She wasn't sure she expected an answer—despite what he'd told her about his father, he'd never been much for talking about his family.

He surprised her by shaking his head. "She's got no degree, no plan, and a deadbeat boyfriend who keeps circling back around to her when he doesn't have a better option." He made a disgusted noise. "She's just like Ma. Guess one of us had to be."

She told herself to leave it alone but couldn't ignore the tense set of his shoulders, the echo of grief in his voice. Resisting the urge to touch him, she said, "You're not your father, Wyatt."

He shot her a look. "Near enough. When I stay long enough with anything—a job, a place, a person—the switch eventually goes off in my brain. Good old Sam's eight-week buzzer. Maybe it's not eight weeks anymore, but eventually the walls start closing in and it's time to go."

And suddenly things got far more serious than she thought either of them had intended. *Don't,* she told herself. *It doesn't matter anymore.* But it did. "Have you ever tried to fight through it and stick with something long term?"

He hesitated. "Twice. No, three times." A glance over at her. "Once with you, and then a few years ago with a woman named Desiree. She was the one who ended it, but only because I refused to."

"And the third time?" Was that her voice? It sounded so much steadier than she felt.

"Is now, with the sculptures." He strode to the front of the shallow cave, where the rock ledge dropped off forty feet and the waterfall sheeted past. "I'm not going to give up on it. I can't."

Leave it alone, she told herself. *Leave* him *alone*. She had brought him out here hoping that the setting would help. That didn't mean *she* had to help. He wasn't her problem, wasn't even really her friend—she should go back through the waterfall and give him some time with the inscriptions. But the same part of her that was never able to turn down a creaky old cow or a one-eyed cat couldn't walk away from him now. "Tell me."

The waterfall seemed suddenly loud in the silence that followed. It went on so long that she thought she had her answer, told herself to just go.

But then, voice low, Wyatt said, "When I'm working on a piece, it's like I'm inside it. The bull is bucking to beat the cowboy on its back, to prove that he's bigger and faster, and that no measly human is going to tame him. The rearing stallion is fighting off a rival, and the cowboy sitting by the fire is so lonely that he pretends his horse is a saloon girl named Matilda and talks to her for hours, yet when he goes into town he usually leaves before his money runs out, because he can't breathe around so many people."

Her heart gave a long, slow roll, both because he was talking to her—really talking to her—and because of what he was revealing. "The sculptures connect you to something bigger than yourself." She got that, even if she didn't have an artistic bone in her body.

He nodded. "When I built the first metal horse, I didn't do it to help Ma or Ash, to pass a class or make a client happy. I didn't even do it thinking I would make money. I did, though. Enough that I didn't have to worry about a boss or a schedule, and so I could keep moving, keep things fresh. Except that doesn't seem to be enough anymore." Expression flattening, he said, "Which just goes to show that I'm so much my old man's son that I can't even make myself stick when I want to. With you. With Desiree. And now with the sculptures."

"You haven't quit on the sculptures," she pointed out.

"I don't plan on it." He turned to her, lifted a hand to brush his knuckles across her cheek. Voice softening to regret, he said, "Don't take that to mean I've got a serious relationship in me, though. I spent a chunk of my growing-up years raising Ashley and worrying about Ma. The last thing I want to do is tie myself down like that again."

There it was, Krista realized as the waterfall sounded

suddenly loud in her ears. He wasn't just following an old pattern or his father's footsteps, wasn't just a short-term guy because that was all he knew how to be. He had already raised a child, supported a family, been the man of the house—and he didn't want to press REWIND. And she couldn't blame him.

She hadn't meant to hold out hope, but her stomach still sank as it hit her once and for all: She had to either take him as he was and enjoy him for the next six weeks, or decide that it wasn't enough.

On the long ride back to the homestead, Wyatt had to work not to fill the silence.

Sure, she had said they were good as they left the waterfall. She had even suggested he come back another time and try sketching beside the fire pit, sitting where generations of vaqueros had watched over their herds from the high ground. But her voice had been different, and now she rode ahead of him on her big, black gelding with her spine ramrod-straight and her eyes fixed on the marker stones that said they were nearly back to the ranch.

Last night at the bonfire, he had thought there might be a chance for the two of them—to have some good times, to see where the sparks would take them. Now, though, that seemed about as likely as Jupiter rising up on her hind legs and doing a tap dance. It wasn't the first time that brutal honesty had cost him a chance with a woman, but he had never before been so tempted to keep talking and see if they couldn't meet on his side of the fence. He didn't do that, though, just like he didn't ride up beside her and try for a kiss that would remind her that there was something special between them that didn't come along every day. *Let her alone. She's made her decision.* She hadn't said as much, but he could tell.

When they reached the marker stones, she reined in and waited for him to join her at the edge of the ridge, where the land fell away to the homestead valley and they could see little people-dots gathered around the big white shuttle bus.

"Looks like we're a few minutes late," he said. "I can put Lucky away for you, if you'd like to get right down to the guests."

"Thanks. There's something I want to ask you before we head in, though."

He braced himself. "What's that?"

"Do you have any plans for tomorrow night? Because if not, you can pick me up at eight."

14

The shock on Wyatt's face brought laughter bubbling up even as the heat in his expression kicked an answering buzz through Krista's system.

"You mean it?" His voice was a rasp, his eyes suddenly avid.

"I mean it. You were right when you said I sell adventures. Well, you know what? I've decided it's time for me to have one of my own." There was such joy in saying it. When was the last time she had let herself be reckless and wild, let herself throw out her usual rules to take something she really wanted? Had she ever? "Oh, and heads up? If you ask me whether I'm sure or try to talk me out of it, I'll kick you in the shin."

"Trust me," he said with a wicked curve to his lips. "That wasn't my first impulse."

Her pulse kicked into overdrive. "Oh? What was?"

"This." He leaned across, from horse to horse, and kissed her.

And, oh, his kiss.

She had forgotten what it was like to have a man look at her like he was starving, how it felt to be wrapped in his arms like she was his anchor in the middle of a stampede. His tongue slid along hers, and she felt his leashed strength as she drew a hand up his muscled arm, conscious of the saddle beneath her and the restless shifts of the horses. Heat seared through her; desire overruled everything, overwhelming her with the need to knock his hat to the ground, bury her fingers in his hair, and hold on tight.

Instead she eased away, knowing they were in plain sight and she had guests waiting. And knowing there would be plenty of time for them to enjoy each other, starting tomorrow night, after she got the new guests settled in. "So," she said in a voice that came out huskier than she had intended. "How about it, cowboy? You up for a moonlight ride?"

"Not tomorrow." His eyes were dark, his pupils dilated.

"Oh? You'd rather stay in?" The idea shouldn't have sounded like genius.

"That's good, too," he agreed in a voice that sent shivers through her. "But tomorrow we're going out." He straightened, gathered his reins, and settled his hat, looking very much like a cowboy—*her* cowboy, at least for now. "This time we're going to do it right," he said firmly. "And that means a real first date. Drinks, dinner, fancy napkins, the works. Eight o'clock. I'll pick you up and we'll take it from there."

*   *   *

Early the next morning, Wyatt gave Jupiter a good rub-down and put her in the run-in stall next to Lucky. "Be-have," he said as he rolled the door shut. "If you two get along with a fence between you, the next step is a few acres of grass."

Leaving the horses to work it out—though keeping an ear out for noises that would suggest they were do-ing more than making nasty faces at each other—he headed for the guests' tack room. With Krista doing an extended version of Riding 101 after breakfast—this was First Timers Week, geared toward rank greenhorns with zero riding experience—he had a little time before the guests made it to the barn for the hands-on stuff. He shifted a couple of brush boxes, made sure there was a curry per, and swapped out the rub rags for fresh. Then he grabbed the half-full laundry hamper, figuring to get a jump on the wash.

He stopped. He stared. He cursed.

Then he raised his voice, "Klepto! Get your furry butt in here!"

Behind the hamper, piled up against the wall, was a careful arrangement of two toilet paper tubes, several dog biscuits, a copy of last week's schedule, the deer-hide roping glove he'd been looking for since Wednes-day, and a high-end contractor's level.

He had thought he was paying close enough atten-tion. Clearly not.

Grateful that most of it was trash—at least in human terms—he cleaned out the stash, tossing the garbage, and reuniting the glove with its mate. Which left the level, and he had a pretty good idea who it belonged to. "Think you're so smart, don't you?" he said, seeing one hairy eye peering around the edge of the door frame. "Well, nuts to you. I was headed there anyway."

He hadn't asked a father's permission to date a girl since ever, and didn't intend to start now. But he also didn't want to meet up with the business end of a shotgun when he went to pick her up, so he figured it was time for a little one-on-one with Ed Skye.

Complicated? Yeah, but she was worth it.

With Klepto taking a time-out in an empty stall, he headed out past the back barn, to the long, narrow workshop located about halfway up the ridge. As he drew near, he heard the rumble-thud of classic rock and the buzz of a circular saw.

Ed Skye was supposedly the peacemaker of the family, a quiet-spoken man who had run cattle for most of his life because he'd been born a Skye but was a handyman, tinkerer, and inventor at heart. Wyatt thought they might have enjoyed each other if they had met as strangers. *Too bad.*

When the saw noise paused, he banged on the door and stuck his head through. "Morning. Can I interrupt?"

Wearing a plaid button-down with the sleeves cut off to show biceps that said *tough old guy*, Ed had a dusting of sawdust on his face and goggles covering his eyes, giving Wyatt no clue what he thought of the drop-in.

"Webb." The goggles got pushed up, revealing eyes

the same blue as Krista's, but hard and uncompromising.

Wyatt held out the level. "I'm guessing my dog stole this from you." When the other man didn't make a move, he set it on a nearby workbench. "Sorry about that. I'll keep better tabs on him."

"That it?"

"You tell me."

Ed pulled his goggles all the way off and ran a hand through his hair, knocking loose some of the sawdust. Expression taking on an edge of frustration, he said, "Krista told us to leave that part of things alone, and when it comes to the business, she's the boss."

"This isn't business. It's between you and me."

"The way I see it, we don't have anything to say to each other."

"Then I'll say my piece and get out of your space." Wyatt waited for a nod, didn't get one, so he kept going. "I've got a little sister, Ashley. She's not much older now than Krista was when she and I were together. Growing up, I was more of a father to Ashley than our old man ever was, and these days she's hooked up with a boyfriend who doesn't treat her right. So I get wanting to pound on the guy who hurts one of your own. In fact, if you want to take a swing at me, I'll stand for it."

The other man seemed to consider that for a moment, but then shook his head. "I don't need to hit you. I just need your word that you'll stay away from her."

"I'm taking her out tonight."

The lake blue of those eyes darkened to storms. "Then we've got a problem."

"Things are different this time."

"How so?"

"With all due respect, that's between Krista and me, and we're adults now, with a right to our privacy." Even in a place like this. "But if I hurt her again, you won't need to take a swing at me. I'll do it myself."

Ed studied him, giving him a long up-and-down. Then he reached for the radio, and cranked up the tunes. Over the racket, he said, "Close the door on your way out. And keep your mutt away from my shop."

"Going out?" The question, coming from the main room in her father's voice that evening, stopped Krista in her tracks.

She closed her eyes, tempted to mutter something she'd probably regret, and then felt guilty for the impulse. But ever since she had asked her mom to cover the late shift with the guests—and explained why—she had been dealing with a whole lot of "I hope you know what you're doing" from her family. Gran had plied her with chocolate chip cookies and offered to brainstorm dating-site user names, starting with Reverse-Cowgirl and going downhill from there; her mom had hit her with "this wasn't what I meant when I told you to get him out of your system"; and Jenny had sent her a couple of asterisk-laden texts and left a voice mail. Now it seemed it was her dad's turn. She had figured him for Switzerland on this one, but apparently not.

Pasting on a bright smile, she turned back. "Yep, I'm out of here for a few hours." *Which you already knew.* "Mom is on call tonight for guest requests."

Her father rose from the overstuffed recliner and crossed to her, wearing an expression that made her want to tug up the scooped neckline of the not-quite-slinky blue shirt she had paired with a long denim skirt and her going-dancing boots. He searched her face. "You're sure about this." It wasn't exactly a question.

"It's just a date." Actually, she was hoping it would turn into more than that, but she wasn't going to tell him that.

"With the only guy I've ever seen you cry over."

"That was a long time ago." She went up on her tip-toes and kissed his cheek. "I love you for worrying, but I'll be fine."

"You always say that."

"That's because I know how to handle myself. You guys taught me well." She patted the place she had just kissed, feeling the roughness of a two-day stubble and seeing more salt than pepper. "I'll see you later. And I promise that no matter what happens, I won't cry this time." That was what ground rules and grown-up conversations were for.

He grumbled something as she headed for the door, but didn't call her back. And a moment later, she was out on the porch with the door shut between them, breathing a sigh of relief. She loved her family, wouldn't change them for the world, but every now and then it got old doing things by committee.

Wyatt pulled in as she reached the parking lot, stepping down from his pickup to come around and get the passenger door for her. He was wearing dark jeans and a crisp new snap-studded shirt in a forest green that emphasized the russet streaks in his dark hair. His boots gleamed, his belt rode low on his hips, and for a second he looked so much like his younger self that her footsteps faltered and something inside her said, *This isn't really happening. It's all some crazy dream.*

Two weeks ago, she had never expected to see him again. Now they were going on a date.

He gave her an up-and-down as she crossed to him. "Hey, boss lady. Looking good."

She resisted the urge to fuss with her shirt, her hair, the strap of the little purse she rarely used. "Thanks. You, too." Which was a major understatement. Up close, she could smell the freshness of his shower and see the comb marks in his hair. Which shouldn't have made her feel so unutterably tender toward him, yet churned up at the same time. "You ready to hit the road?"

"In a minute. I've got one thing I need to do first."

"What's that?"

"This," he said. And, in front of any guests who might be watching from their windows, and her father, who was definitely watching from the house, Wyatt leaned in and kissed her for all the world to see.

15

For a first date that wasn't really a first date, Wyatt went upscale, Three Ridges style. The Fancy Place—that was its name, even—had cloth napkins, a decent wine list, and a low-key atmosphere that conveyed "around here, a nice night out still involves denim." Damien's crowd would've been split on whether the post-and-beam décor and faux oil lamps were kitschy enough to circle back around to cool, and Wyatt would've preferred the watering hole down the street, but the way Krista's face lit when they walked in and the hostess greeted her by name told him he'd called it right.

"You come here much?" he asked as the hostess led them to a small table tucked in a little alcove, where an arched window overlooked the red-and-gold sunset.

"Now and then. Birthdays, big announcements, that sort of thing." She pinkened. "Never before on a date, though."

With another woman, he would've quipped something about being her first. With Krista, he pulled out her chair and let his fingers linger on her nape, not entire sure of his moves. His usual dates, whether buckle bunny, artist, or connoisseur, were with him to see and be seen, with an expectation of some fun at the end of the night. Seeing and being seen meant something very different in a place like this, though, and Krista was nothing like his usual. She rode like a lithe blond centaur, juggled a big family and an even bigger business like it was nothing, and made room for animals—and, he suspected, people—that needed her. She humbled him, amazed him, made him want to step up and do what he could—with Jupiter, with the guests, with her. But the thing was, while she might be different, he was his same old self. And he didn't want to screw this up.

As if he'd said that last part out loud, she looked up at him, squeezed his hand where it rested on her shoulder, and said, "Sit down, cowboy. As long as we keep talking and stay honest this time, we won't get ourselves in trouble."

And, just like that, everything was okay. Grinning, he moved around to take the chair opposite her, so their knees bumped intimately beneath the table. "When did you get so smart?"

"Rumor has it I was born that way." She flipped open the menu. "Now. Where do you stand on red wine? I could use a glass after today's ride."

He chuckled. "I'm up for a bottle. I give our first timers an A for effort, though." When it came to guided trail rides, there was nothing quite as hairy as two dozen rank beginners, several of whom—including a couple of firefighter brothers from Yonkers—thought they already knew everything because they had watched both *City Slickers* movies. So when the waitress came around, Wyatt ordered a bottle of decent red and he and Krista shared a grin. And damned if his chest didn't tighten at the sight of her smiling opposite him, with the fading sunset beyond the window casting her face in copper and gold. Suddenly, he wanted to sketch her smile, sculpt her laughter, capture the moment so it would always be like this—new and fresh. Instead, he leaned back and cleared his throat. "So, are you ready to give me some details about Jupiter's freestyle? How's the script coming along?"

When the waitress came back with the wine and took their orders, he went for a steak and potatoes, while Krista ordered a fussy-sounding pasta dish and asparagus mousse. Grinning, she said, "Don't tell anyone back home what I ordered. Gran will talk trash about capers, Mom will pull out her Italian cookbooks, and one or both of them will try to make a mousse out of something that really shouldn't be moussed. Like short ribs, or maybe popcorn."

"Your secret is safe with me." He poured with a flourish, then held up his glass. "To a night out on the town."

"I'll toast to that!"

They kept it light, laughing over his stories of Klepto ambushing Sam during his in-home business meetings and hers of dude mishaps ranging from poison ivy cases dubbed "how exactly did he get it *there*?" to the little boy who, earlier in the year, had smuggled a barn cat home in his luggage. Now named Frequent Flier—Freak for short—the cat was living the life of luxury in New Jersey.

Dessert was more mousse—chocolate for him, berries for her, and a debate on whether the kitchen staff's apparent fascination for whipping things extended to other parts of their lives. The conversation quieted on the drive home, but not in an awkward *we've run out of things to say* way. It was more that the undercurrents were suddenly doing the talking. Their eyes met and his body tightened with edgy anticipation; he brushed his fingertips over the back of her hand where it rested on the seat between them, and her breath caught, then quickened.

When he reached the twin pillars that marked the main entrance to Mustang Ridge, he rolled to a stop and looked over at her. "You ready to call it a night?"

She met his eyes, her lips curving. "Only if you are."

"Not even close," he said, and hit the gas.

Over drinks one night back in Denver, Damien had asked about Wyatt's definition of a perfect date. At the time, he had said something about a smart, witty woman in a little black dress who wanted him but didn't need him. Now, he thought it would be more along the lines of a beautiful blonde who knew that he could offer her only so much, yet still turned her hand over beneath his and twined their fingers together. He didn't know where tonight was headed, exactly, and that was just fine with him. Because right now, he was exactly where he wanted to be.

He parked in front of the bunkhouse, grinning at the sight of a fuzzy gray mug in the window. Figuring he should really give her some sort of formal invitation, he said, "You want to come in? I've been doing some work on the hot tub."

Amusement lit her eyes. "Was that a 'hey, baby, do you want to see my grout'?"

"Something like that."

"How about you show me your setup out back?"

That brought a twinge. "There's not much to see." Just a few tools, a pile of scrap, and a whole lot of bad ideas.

"Indulge me."

With anybody else, even Damien—especially Damien—he would've found a distraction, even if it meant getting creative. Instead, he came around and opened Krista's door, then held out a hand. "You'll have to use your imagination."

"I can do that."

He helped her down, then kept her hand as he let them into the steel building and flipped on the lights. Somehow the darkness made it look better than it usually did—the tools seemed mysterious rather than stark, and his junk pile suddenly looked like a halfway interesting mix of dark and light shapes. "I've just got a small forge and a welder with me," he said, "and some stuff I salvaged from Sam's neighbors."

"Oh!" Her eyes warmed. "You've been working!" She

tugged him to the makeshift workbench he'd cobbled together out of leftovers from the bunkhouse reno.

At the time he'd knocked it together, he had feared that the ugly waist-high table might be it for his creative urges at Mustang Ridge. Now, though, it held a foot-tall structure made of curved metal pieces he had salvaged from the latches of old stall doors, topped with two ornate door knobs—one engraved brass, the other cut crystal.

"It's just something I was fiddling with this morning." After his face-to-face with her father, Wyatt had thrown open the steel doors, fired up his torch, and given himself permission to fool around for an hour. At first, he had been jazzed about the piece, which was the first thing he'd started from scratch in months. Now, though, he eyed it with zero enthusiasm. "I thought it was starting to turn into something cool, but it had other ideas. Now I think it wants to be bad hotel décor, or possibly a mutant jellyfish." Or a total waste of time that reminded him why he should stick to sketches until he knew where he was headed.

"Not a jellyfish," she said, studying it with an adorable intensity that did away with his frustration between one pulse-thud and the next, and put him in a very different mood.

"No?" He leaned in so his eyes were level with hers and her hair brushed his jaw, filling his senses with her flowery scent. "What, then? A daffodil?"

"Nope. It's a man and a woman kissing. Don't you see?"

"Not in a million . . ." But he trailed off, because suddenly he *did* see it, or at least a glimmer of it in the way the doorknobs bent together, nearly touching, one catching the light and the other blocking it off.

"But it's not finished yet, is it?" She leaned in. "What comes next?"

He could almost see that, too, how the figures needed to be fleshed out, intertwined. Were they dancing? Kissing? As he stood there beside Krista, looking at the piece and seeing it through her eyes, he could almost remember what it felt like to be good at his job. But almost wasn't good enough and over the past few years he'd learned that women and work didn't mix, at least for him. So he said, "Next, we go in the house for a drink or something. Neither of us is dressed for welding."

She poked him in the ribs. "I own a guest ranch. Everything I own is one plumbing emergency away from being barn clothes."

"Oh, really? You do much riding in a skirt?"

"Well, there was that one Halloween. . . ." She didn't push him on it, but a challenge glinted in her eyes.

Danged if he didn't feel a stir of the same urge that had driven him into the workshop earlier that day. Not to mention that she was offering him an excuse to put his hands all over her, the way he'd been dying to for the past couple of hours. Days. Weeks. He let go of her hand to rummage a moment, grabbing goggles, earplugs, gloves, and a heavy apron. "Here. Put these on."

Her face blanked in surprise, then she backed off,

holding up her hands. "Hang on. Wait a minute. This is your gig. I'm just cheerleading."

"No way. This was your idea." He advanced with the protective gear. "Put it on, or I'll put it on for you." He feinted, then made a grab.

She squeaked and dodged, laughing as her skirt flared around her ankles. "Okay, okay. Give it here."

"Tuck your hair back. Sparks are going to fly." *In more ways than one*, he thought as she donned the oversize gear, looking adorable and out of place.

When they both had their gear on, he guided her to the workbench and put his arms around her, so they were aligned with her back to his front and their bodies were snug together. She felt small against him, delicate, making him very aware that this was a first for him. Not just that he was letting her into his creative process—such as it was—but that he wanted her there.

Then again, Krista was different. She always had been.

Over the next hour, Krista went from warm to overheated to blazing, and not just because of the waves of heat radiating from the tabletop forge. There was hot, and then there was *hot*—in the snap and spark of molten metal, in the sharp taint of mask-filtered air, in the clang-bang of the heavy hammer against a waist-high anvil. And, most of all, in the way his arms wrapped around her, making her feel safe and vulnerable at the same time as he guided her in welding a joint here, adding a line of flux there.

And, as they moved together, with her hands wrapped in his, she had to lock her knees to keep from sagging. She had gone into tonight thinking she knew what she was getting. But she hadn't expected anything like this.

"Beautiful." Wyatt's approving growl, coming from just beside her jaw, could have been directed at the sinuous twine of metal he held with a pair of tongs, but it went straight to her core, resonating with the greedy heat that surged there, stringing her tight with anticipation. And she wasn't alone in that, she knew, because he said it again, closer to her throat, and then kissed her where the word landed. *Beautiful.*

Shifting away from her, he grabbed a hammer and set the glowing metal on the curved anvil. The apron, goggles, and gloves protected her from the sparks, the earplugs from the onslaught of noise as she watched the play of his massive muscles. She had seen blacksmiths make shoes out of raw metal stock, had seen branding irons heated to that intense orange-red that almost seemed alive. But she had never felt the hammer blows in her core before, hadn't ever been dry-mouthed as the metal came to life beneath gauntleted hands.

The sculpture didn't just hint at a kiss anymore—it shouted in passion, from the curves of the intertwining metal limbs to the angles of the wrought-iron bodies.

"Here," he said, coming back to her with a smaller soldering iron and a roll of flux that gleamed in the overhead lights. "They need faces." He bracketed her, guided her, making her feel vulnerable yet so powerful as together they touched lines of molten metal to the cooling surfaces, hinting at closed lids and curving lips. Until, finally, he whispered against her skin, "I think we're done."

"It's amazing," she said, knowing that wasn't nearly enough. "Incredible. I'm blown away."

He turned her to face him, gently lifted her goggles off and stripped her gloves and apron away, tossing them aside, then doing the same to his own. "I was thinking of you when I started it," he rasped, "but I didn't see what it was meant to be until I had you here with me." And, bending his head to hers, he kissed her with all of the pent-up passion that had been building between them.

Yes. Oh, yes. She gripped double handfuls of his shirt to anchor her when the world went white-hot around her, the heat of a thousand forges blasted through her, and she let him sweep her away. Because this was now, and now was very, very good.

Wyatt didn't care that it was too crazy, too fast, too everything. In that moment, all he cared about was getting his hands on her. He was playing with fire, and wanted the burn.

He was done talking.

He cupped her waist and felt the play of long, lean muscles; tangled his tongue with hers and felt like he'd stood too long in front of the furnace. Without breaking the kiss, he scooped her off her feet and into the cradle of his arms. His long strides carried them out of the steel building, across the moonlit yard, and up the porch steps two at a time.

The door was an effort when his entire focus was on the play of his mouth on hers and the drag of her fingers through his hair, but he got them inside, covered the distance to the sitting area, lowered her to the huge leather sofa and followed her down. The room was lit only by the digital displays in the kitchen and the blue-white moon outside, and the darkness heightened his senses, making him very aware of her soft, feminine body beneath him, the hitch of her breathing as he splayed a hand along her ribs, and the way her scent had deepened, going earthy and urgent.

A skitter of claws on wood and tile had him waving a hand. "Not now, Klepto. Go play."

Her body vibrated with amusement. "Are you sure that's a good idea?"

"Don't care," he said, kissing along her jaw, the soft spot beneath her ear. "I'll replace whatever he demolishes. Just don't tell me to stop."

She curled her fingers into his shirt, tugging it up to find her way beneath. "Don't you dare stop."

He groaned at the sensation of her fingers across his abdomen and the softness of her breast beneath his palm. He kissed her, touched her, explored her, finding sensitive spots that made her sigh and move restlessly against him, ticklish spots that made her squirm, and hot buttons that made her moan and reach for him. Dying for her, needing to be inside her, he shifted, giving her access to his belt buckle. When she eased back, he sucked in a breath, but one look at her face let him know that she wasn't putting on the brakes. Far from it.

Breathless and excited, she said, "I don't have . . . You know."

"I do. In my bags." Protection was usually front and center for him. Now, he had to think about it. "Somewhere. Upstairs, I think?"

She leaned back in and nipped his chin. "I'll race you."

"I'll give you a head start." He scooped her up once more, tossing her high enough to elicit a gasp and a grab, then carried her laughing up the stairs and through the door with her in front. "You win." He tossed her lightly to the bed, where she sank into the luxurious mattress and disheveled bedclothes. "What do you want for your prize?"

She crooked a finger. "You."

"Hold that thought." He beat it into the bathroom, unearthed the unopened box of condoms, and let out a relieved breath at the expiration date. Bearing them like a trophy, he came back out into the bedroom.

And stopped dead.

The rumpled sheet and spread were on the floor, the bed a wide expanse of dark blue cotton and pillows, with Krista in the center, completely naked.

Wyatt stared. He couldn't *not* stare. In the warm light coming from the hallway, her skin was like honey and shadows, and her eyes were alight with anticipation and a faint challenge. "Problem?" she asked archly.

"No. No problem at all." He tossed the box onto the bed beside her, then followed it down, taking his weight on his arms while he skimmed his lips along her throat and the curve of her collarbone. "I just couldn't breathe there for a minute. Still can't."

This was important. *She* was important. And that was okay with him.

She worked the buttons of his shirt, the snaps popping in sequence. "How about now?"

"I'm pretty sure I don't need to breathe, as long as I can kiss you." He found her lips and sank into her mouth, skimming a hand down the smooth skin of her rib cage, her hip, her thigh. She quivered as he followed his hands with his lips, kissing his way down her body while working at his clothes.

She arched against him, hands fisting in the sheets. "I can't . . ." she whispered.

"What?"

"Breathe, either."

He came back to her lips, sliding up her body with the rest of his clothes gone and the condom in place. "Does it matter?"

"Yes. No. *Oh!*" She curled her legs around him as he settled against her, and her eyes fluttered shut on a soft moan. "Who needs to breathe?" she asked softly, and pressed herself up against him.

His pulse hammered. His vision hazed. "Krissy." The nickname came from deep within him, feeling very right as, with a roll of his hips and an answering arch of her body, he slid home.

Warm. Wet. Pleasure.

Incredible.

He gritted his teeth against the surge that threatened to send him racing ahead of her. Heat surrounded him, poured from him to her and back again, and it was all he could do not to bury his face in the curve of her neck and cut loose. He held on, though, concentrating on the gentle bite of her fingernails on his back and the low, broken moan that said they were in this together.

When he had some thin thread of control, he began to move—one stroke, then two. But then Krista surged against him and whispered his name, new heat cannonaded through him, and any hope of a slow build vanished.

Rearing back, he seated himself to the hilt and reveled in her moan, backed off and thrust again, aware that she was meeting him move for move. He lowered himself so they were face-to-face, belly-to-belly, and dragged his lips across hers as the tempo increased.

She moaned and his body tightened; she dragged her fingernails along his ribs and down, and he bucked against her. Aware that he was teetering on the edge, he worked a hand between them and stroked her with the rhythm of his thrusts. She cried out and pushed against his hand, her fingers digging into his hips as she sucked in a breath, held it, and then came in a rush, whispering his name. And that shuddering, wondering voice sent him over the edge. He thrust home and let out a raw groan as his release pounded through him, leaving him locked above her, around her, inside her.

It went on forever but ended too soon, draining to a deep, drugging lassitude that made him want to stay put for the next couple of lifetimes. Rolling to his side, he gathered her close, so her head nestled beneath his jaw and her hair brushed his cheek. "Sweet Krissy," he rumbled. "Thank you."

Then he closed his eyes and let the lassitude have him, not asleep but not really awake, either. And plenty happy to be exactly where he was.

Lying curled against Wyatt, Krista blinked into the half-light while the world came back into focus around her. She saw the rubbed-wood columns of the four-poster bed, the pale overhang of the homespun canopy, and the curved porch rocker in the corner, loaded with soft pillows and flanked by a reading table on one side and a silver champagne bucket on the other. Which meant she was upstairs in the bunkhouse loft. That, along with the tug of unfamiliar muscles and the warm bulk beside her, left zero room for doubt.

She and Wyatt were lovers. Again.

Her heart went *tappity-tap* and her stomach knotted with excitement, anxiety, and pride. She knew what she was getting into this time, knew how to keep herself whole and come out of it in one piece. She smiled into the darkness, imagining herself running up onto the ridgeline naked, beating her chest, and giving a Tarzan scream with a chaser of *I am woman, hear me roar*.

Then she pictured Jenny there, filming it, and chuckled.

Wyatt's arm tightened around her. "Something funny?"

He hadn't tensed, but she thought the potential was there. She wasn't going to censor herself to avoid his twitches, though. He could take her as she was, or not take her at all. "I'm happy. Really, truly happy. And don't worry, it's not because I think my life just changed forever and ever. I'm not going to go get your name tattooed on my fanny or anything. It's more that I got what *I* wanted for a change—not for the business or the family or anyone else. Just me."

"Glad I could be of service." He patted her rear end. "But about that tattoo . . ."

"Ha. Keep dreaming." She danced her fingers across his ribs. "That is, unless you're planning on reciprocating. The ranch logo would do nicely."

"Free advertising?"

"I guess that depends on where you put it." She grinned up at him. "Middle of your forehead? Now that's a billboard."

"With some of Damien's crowd, that'd be tame." He kissed the top of her head. "Want a drink? I've got water and iced tea, and I should check on Klepto."

"I'm good." She levered away from him. "In fact, I should go."

"You could stay." He didn't hesitate. Apparently, he didn't have a no-overnights rule.

She thought she might, though. "Not this time." Not with her father potentially asleep in the downstairs recliner, waiting for her to come home. She didn't want to think about the time—the minutes had flown in the workshop, but she suspected it had been hours. Like the wee hours of the morning.

Wyatt exhaled and stretched. "I'll drive you." But his eyes were half-lidded, his words drowsy.

"Sleep." She kissed his cheek. "This is my home turf. And you look whupped." Which she should have been. She didn't know where the jittery, jumpy energy was coming from, only that she couldn't stay put.

"Take my truck. I don't want you walking that far alone in the dark."

Which should have made her want to roll her eyes, but was actually kind of nice. "Fine. Where are your keys?"

"Pants. Somewhere." He was already drifting off. And, damn, he looked good doing it—like a sleepy, well-fed mountain lion, all tawny skin and big, loose muscles.

Given what they had just done together, it shouldn't have felt weird to go through his tossed jeans for the keys, and it shouldn't have put a quiver in her belly to climb in his truck and breathe in his scent. It was no big deal—she was just borrowing his wheels for the quick trip home. Still, she found herself grinning like a fool as she rolled away from the bunkhouse. And when she reached the house and found it midnight-quiet, she did a little tap dance up the stairs to her bedroom, where she flopped down on her bed and shot off a quick text to Jenny: *Girl Zone?*

The phone rang almost immediately. Krista answered with: "I take it you and Doc Hottie weren't sleeping—or, you know, otherwise occupied?"

"Why? You want a blow-by-blow?"

"Dear God, no."

Jenny's laugh carried on the airwaves. "Didn't think so. It wouldn't be all that interesting, anyway—Nick is at the Plunkett place for an emergency call and I'm fiddling with one of the ads I'm doing for Mayor Teapot."

"What's the slogan? *Come blow off some steam in Three Ridges*?"

"Ha! So tempting. In fact, I'm writing that down for Shelby." Her keyboard went *clicka-clicka* in the background. "But enough about me—you're the one who invoked the sacred Girl Zone. So start talking, *chica*! Good date? Bad date?"

"We had sex."

That got her a moment of startled silence. Then, "Well . . . Good sex? Bad sex?"

Krista laughed, then sighed. "I love you, sis. You always say the right thing."

"Except when I don't, but even then you know I meant well." A pause. "I'm guessing good sex. Do you want to talk about it? Come over? Dial Shelby in?"

"No, it's late."

"Yet you called me."

"I texted. There's a difference." Now that they were on the phone, Krista didn't really want to postmortem the date. Which was strange, really. When she first got home, she had been dying to tell someone that her long dry spell was finally over, and she was in control of the situation. Now, she just wanted to curl up in bed and hug the memories to herself. Tonight was hers. The next six weeks were hers—she was giving herself this present, this vacation from the everyday.

"When do Shelby and I get to meet him?"

"I don't know—"

"I do. Pick a day and we'll triple date." And when she used that tone of voice, Jenny was unshakable.

16

The next morning, Wyatt was out in the arena early, more because he wanted to get Jupiter worked than because he'd awakened and reached for the empty spot in the bed, though there was some of that, too. He and Krista hadn't planned to meet for the morning's training session, but he'd just swung into the saddle when she appeared around the corner of the barn, carrying a couple of steaming mugs and a napkin-wrapped bundle that said "muffin" or maybe—pretty please—"homemade doughnuts."

She was dressed for the workday, in jeans and a dark green logo'd shirt, and as she got closer and his pulse picked up a notch at her warm smile, it felt like the sight of those cowgirl braids and the dusting of freckles across her nose were being burned into his brain.

"Morning, cowboy." She set his coffee on the flattened-off top of a fence post, and lifted the wrapped bundle. "Beignets."

He nearly moaned. "With sugar and cinnamon sprinkled on top?"

"Of course."

"Since when?"

"Mom took the breakfast shift so Gran could go to a doctor's appointment."

"She okay?"

"Routine stuff, as far as I know. How's our girl this morning?"

Since when was he tempted to turn a question like that back on a woman he was seeing? He wanted to ask how she was, tell her how much he'd enjoyed last night. Instead, he said, "She seems good so far. I was going to warm her up with some gate work, then maybe start getting her used to pulling weight, like she'll need to do for the freestyle. She drags a tarp just fine, so we'll see how she does with a tire next."

"Mind if I watch?"

"I'd mind if you didn't." He nudged Jupiter closer to the fence so he could grab a couple of swigs of coffee, then lean in for a kiss. Krista came up on the bottom rail, bringing their faces level, and brushed her lips across his, bringing a hint of coffee and kicking the heat level up a notch or two. When his horse shifted and stomped a forefoot, he eased away. "I missed you this morning."

After the briefest of hesitations, Krista dimpled. "You can see more of me later."

"Tonight?"

This time, the hesitation was longer. "Actually, Jenny wants to meet you. She thought we could all get together—you and me, her and Nick, and Shelby and Foster."

Remembering the lottery, and being glared at by a dark-haired version of Krista wearing a T-shirt that read I'M STARRING IN MY OWN REALITY SHOW, it was his turn to pause. But he had known going into this that Krista's family was woven into the fabric of her life. "Sounds good. When do you want to leave?"

He left it too long, though. "It doesn't have to be tonight," she said with a small smile that said she understood. "In fact, it doesn't need to happen at all. She'll cope. She's just—"

"Feeling protective," he finished for her. "And I can't say I blame her. I wish I had taken the time to get to know Kenny when he and Ash first started seeing each other. Not that it would've changed anything. She's stubborn."

"So am I. I'm also old enough to know what—and who—I'm doing." She wiggled her eyebrows. "So . . . a couple of drinks with my meddling sister, then back to your place?"

He grinned. "I'm not cheap, but I can be bought."

"Beignet?" She held them out.

"Sold." Chuckling, he snagged a couple, then reined Jupiter around. "Come on, hoss. Let's show the pretty lady how brave you can be when those scary gates come swinging at you."

Thanks to the training he'd done over the past week, the gray mare stepped up to the challenge, pivoting on command so he could unlatch the round pen gate and swing it open. When it swung back and bumped her haunches, she flattened her ears and tucked her butt, but held her ground.

"Good mare!" Krista cheered as he nudged the horse through and turned back to refasten the gate, then again when he reversed the process. "She's so much better already."

He clicked and patted the mare—he had started mixing praise with food treats—and said, "Better, yes. Ready for the trail course? Not yet. She still has trouble when things get narrow. I was thinking the next step is to—"

"Heads UP!" a voice bellowed from the barn, followed by a loud crash, several clatter-bangs and Klepto's frenzied barking. Another voice hollered, "Close the door! Don't let her get out front!"

"Someone's loose!" Krista said, and started to run.

Adrenaline zinging—a thousand pounds worth of panic could do serious damage in seconds—he urged Jupiter up beside her and held down a hand. "Come on!"

She grabbed his wrist and swung up on the saddle skirt behind him while Jupiter danced in place, unnerved by the extra weight and the noises coming from the barn. But the gray mare had heart. At his urging, she ran toward the chaos rather than away, while Krista gripped Wyatt's waist.

They galloped out of the arena and down the short path, whipping around the front of the barn just as a brown-and-white blur shouldered through the narrowing gap of the rolling doors with a barn worker pursuing on foot, optimistically waving a lead rope and shouting, "Come back!"

"Don't let her get to the main house!" Krista cried. "She'll destroy the kitchen!"

Wyatt wheeled Jupiter and clapped his heels into the game gray mare. *"Git!"*

She flattened out and flew after the spotted cow as it dodged between a couple of parked cars and accelerated across the parking lot. With no lasso to work with, he cut Jupiter to the left, forcing the cow to swerve toward a three-sided equipment shed with an empty bay.

At the sight of the dark opening, the cow slammed on the brakes. Jupiter—a few hundred pounds heavier and not used to balancing under one rider, never mind two—overshot.

"Whoa!" Wyatt sank into his saddle and the mare sat down on her haunches in a perfect figure-eleven stop that gouged parallel furrows in the gravel drive. Wheeling the horse, he sent her lunging back toward the cow, who was darting glances between the shed and the path leading to the main house, where Gwen and Charm—a pair of yoga instructors from Florida—were standing making *ooh, look at the cow!* gestures, oblivious to the danger.

"Go in, Betty Crocker!" Krista urged. "Go in, go in, go in—"

Suddenly, channeling however many escaped cow horses had found their way into her family tree, Jupiter closed on the cow, snaking her lowered head and dancing on her pointed toes, ready to spin on a dime if her target tried to break away.

Eyes bugging, Betty Crocker gave a startled "Mooo," then wheeled and plunged into the tractor shed.

"Block her in!" Krista cried, but Jupiter didn't need the urging—she surged forward to plant herself in the opening and give Betty Crocker a *don't even think it* glare. Swinging down, Krista caroled, "Good mare!" Looking up at Wyatt, she gripped his knee and voiced a low, fervent, *"Thank you."*

Then, whirling away, she went into damage-control mode as a couple of the barn guys came running up from one direction, the yoga instructors from the other, and a babble of voices arose from the direction of the dining hall.

"You heard her," Wyatt said, stroking the mare's tense, sweaty neck. "You're a good mare." Which was one of the biggest understatements of his career in the saddle. Kind of like him saying that he'd enjoyed last night. Both statements true, neither one nearly enough.

The horse was something special. Just like the woman who'd picked her from the herd.

Trying not to let the others see she was shaking, Krista fisted her hands on her hips and said sternly, "Betty Crocker, you naughty cow! Why aren't you with your friends?" As Gwen and Charm reached her, clearly dying to be part of the excitement, she grinned at them. "Did you see that? We just had ourselves a one-cow stampede!"

"Is everyone okay?" Charm asked, eyes darting like she was afraid she might miss something.

"Absolutely!" Krista assured her. "It's all in a day's work when you're dealing with horses and cattle."

"Oh." She seemed disappointed.

Gwen went up on her tiptoes, craning to see into the shed. "That's a bull, right?"

"Actually, she's a former milk cow whose owner turned her loose on state land when she stopped producing. She's one of the rescues we have here at Mustang Ridge." As she did her darnedest to divert the yoga instructors, Krista watched out of the corner of her eye as Wyatt—thank God for him and Jupiter—blocked the shed door while Deke got a halter and lead on a disgusted-looking Betty Crocker.

"Poor thing!" Gwen said. "But she sure got lucky with you, didn't she?" She pouted. "I can't believe someone would toss her out like that. She's sooo cute. Just look at that sweet, innocent little face!"

She's a massive pain in my ass, Krista thought as the cow planted her cloven hooves and dug in for a round of tug-of-war with Deke, who had a nice touch with the horses and guests, but zero experience with cattle. "She's—" Krista broke off at a clatter of hoofbeats behind her, wheeling around just as Big Skye and Bueno rounded the corner at a gallop, fast enough that the gelding's shoes struck sparks. "Whoa!" Krista jumped in front of Gwen and Charm, waving her hands. "Slow down! It's fine, she's right here!"

The burly, age-roaned bay slid to a stop, and Big Skye glared down at Krista. With his hat askew and his face red, she wasn't sure if he was embarrassed or angry. "That cow should be shot," he announced. "She's a menace."

Make that angry. And, based on the gasps coming from behind her, really not helping the situation.

"Like I said," she repeated pleasantly, "everything's fine. No harm done." To the ladies, she said, "We have an extensive herd of rescued or retired horses and cattle, and my grandfather here sees to their special needs."

"Ayup," he agreed, eyeing Betty Crocker with zero affection. "We've all been put out to pasture."

"Hey, Gwen and Charm," Wyatt said, nudging his horse up beside the two greenhorns. "Could you guys help me put Jupiter away?"

"Really?" Charm's eyes lit at the prospect of handling the mare, who was normally off-limits to the guests. "Come on, Gwennie."

"But breakfast—"

"Won't run out. And the Brothers Studly will be totally impressed that we got to help with Jupiter."

As they left, Krista made a mental note to remind the others—especially the firefighter brothers, who unfortunately might take it as a dare—about the barn rules and the off-limits horses. Wyatt had saved the moment, though—it would take him three times as long as usual to untack and groom Jupiter with the greenhorns' help, but he'd given them something better to talk about than a loose cow on an almost-rampage.

She would thank him properly for that later. In the meantime . . .

Tucking her hands in her pockets and turning to look off toward the hills—Big Skye didn't do well with a direct confrontation unless he started it—she said, "What happened up there?"

He harrumphed. "Nothing you need to worry about."

Maybe not—livestock got loose all the time on a ranch, and it got dealt with. And, more, the Over the Hill Gang was his bailiwick, and he didn't take to meddling, especially coming from her. But Betty Crocker was different, and Mustang Ridge didn't need videos of her on a rampage to hit YouTube with catchy titles like *Cow In Da House* and *Udder Chaos*. Knowing she was treading on unsteady ground, she said, "Could you use an extra set of hands up there? Maybe we should hire on an assistant."

"Leave it," Big Skye ordered, leveling his hat on his head. "My herd, my problem. I'll tighten up the fence, maybe add a second line and another gate."

"Like an airlock." She nodded. "Feel free to grab Deke or one of the others if you need help."

"I said I'll handle it," he said sharply. "You want me to run the herd, then let me do it. Either that, or fire me and put me out there with them."

"I was just—"

He wheeled Bueno and rode off in a clatter of hooves and a spray of gravel. Which left her standing there staring after him, not sure whether to be mad or sad for him . . . and feeling it for herself, instead. Because no matter how many times she told herself it was okay that she wasn't his little cowgirl anymore, it still sucked eggs.

"He's wrong," Wyatt said from behind her.

"It's fine," she said. It was nothing she hadn't heard from her grandfather before, after all, along with so many variations on the theme. "And it's still better than it used to be."

"That doesn't make it right."

She turned as he approached. "Seriously. I'm fine." And he hadn't signed on for the messy stuff. "I'm used to dealing with Grumpy Gramps."

"Okay, then let's say that I need a hug after the stress of dealing with your rogue milk cow." He wrapped his arms around her. "Just let me lean on you for a minute, okay? Then we'll get back to work."

Her resistance melted as his warmth and scent enfolded her. She burrowed in, rested her cheek against his chest, and sighed. "I'm sorry Betty Crocker stressed you out. She's a very naughty cow."

"Lucky for me, I was on a heck of a horse."

Her lips curved. "Jupiter is that. Can you believe how far she's come?"

"I almost can't. I even checked her over the other day, seeing if I could find signs that she was someone's escaped saddle horse."

"Great minds—been there, done that. I didn't find anything. You?"

"Nope. I think we just lucked out."

It was a nice thought, and one that she needed right

now. *Lucky me.* "You didn't leave Gwen and Charm alone with her, did you?"

"No, ma'am. Deke is overseeing things, and under orders to give them five minutes and escort them back to breakfast. I wanted to get back here and make sure things went okay with your grandfather."

"Which they did."

He didn't argue, but he didn't agree, either. He just dropped his chin onto the top of her head, in a gesture that made her feel small and safe, and reminded her of being in the workshop with him last night. After a moment, he said, "There's one more thing. About tonight."

Disappointment thumped, but she covered it with a shrug. "Don't worry about it—it's no big deal. I'll tell Jenny that you're not up for the inquisition, and we're going to keep this to ourselves." He had been there when she needed him, after all. She could give him a pass on this one.

He gave her a little shake. "That's not what I was going to say. I was thinking we should turn those drinks into dinner. Take our time. Enjoy ourselves."

Her heart bumped in her chest. She didn't look up at him, didn't dare let him see that it really was a big deal to her. "Are you sure? You really don't have to—"

"I'm sure." He tightened his arms around her. "I've already done the meet-the-parents thing. How bad can your sister and best friend be?"

17

Between schedules and guest stuff, it was Saturday night before the triple date actually happened, which meant that the parking lot of the Rope Burn—a cowboy bar with all the trimmings, from the neon beer signs to the hitching rail out front—was jam-packed full. With a whole lot of blue collar spilling out onto the front porch with beers in hand and Aerosmith pumping through the open door, it was just the sort of place Wyatt would be happy kicking back with a brew to do some unwinding. In fact, he and Sam had done just that once or twice.

Tonight wasn't about unwinding, though—it was about Krista. Meeting her sharp-edged twin wasn't exactly tops on Wyatt's wish list, but it was important to her. And for all that her family loved her and vice versa, he had noticed that nobody really did much for her at Mustang Ridge. Sure, her gran did the food-is-love thing, and any of them would pitch in to help with the chores and the guests when Krista asked, but she always had to ask. Which made him think it might be lonely at the top of Mustang Ridge some days.

At the moment, though, she looked far from lonely. Wearing a ruffled blue skirt and a calico button down shirt with a subtle fringe, with her hair down and a layer of pale pink lipstick that made him want to home in and take a nibble, she grinned at him as he parked Old Blue in the far corner of the dirt lot, between two other equally disreputable farm trucks. "They'll behave, I promise."

"Why? Did you threaten to interrupt the cookie pipeline?"

"That only works on Jenny. But I told Foster that if he gave you any grief, I would book back-to-back Singles Weeks next year and then take a vacation and leave him in charge of everything."

"Evil," he observed as he came around and got her door for her, handing her down from the cab. "I like it." Taking her hands, he drew her in for a kiss that she returned with interest. They had spent time outside of work every day that week, riding out together, working on the hot tub, and just enjoying each other. They had even played around in the workshop, though the *Doorknob Kiss*, as they had dubbed the piece they had made together, was the only thing that was even vaguely worthwhile so far. The rest had just been tinkering. And each night, she spent an hour or so in his bed and then slipped home—no fuss, no drama, no expectations beyond what they had already agreed to.

Now, determined to give her a nice night out, he eased the kiss, tucked her fingers into the crook of his arm, and said, "Shall we?"

She patted his hand. "Thanks for this. You're a good sport."

"Remember that when it comes time for my quarterly job review."

"Your performance gets an A-plus from me, cowboy. Especially that thing with the chocolate sauce the other night." She blinked innocently up at him. "Or wasn't that the performance you meant?"

"Sassy. I like it." He dropped a kiss on her nose, and they headed for the Rope Burn.

The place was Saturday-night loud and crowded, with bodies piled two and three deep at the bar, a bearded DJ on the stage transitioning from Aerosmith to George Strait, and a two-step happening on the dance floor.

"Come on!" Krista yelled over the din. "We usually grab a booth in the back."

Sure enough, in the relative peace and quiet of the far back room—which was still pretty loud—a couple of tables had been pulled together to accommodate a crowd. There was a tough-looking guy on the end with his leg encased from crotch-to-ankle in a hospital brace, and propped up on a chair. Beside him was a pretty, dark-haired woman in a vivid red shirt, with buttery black leather thrown over the back of her chair. Next came a lean, tanned guy with shaggy hair and a capable air that suggested he'd be equally at home doing intricate surgery on a house cat in a sterile clinic or a water buffalo out in the field. And beside him was Jenny, who might not be glaring daggers at Wyatt like she had at the lottery, but didn't look all that welcoming, either.

"Coo-kies," Krista singsonged, dropping into the chair beside her twin. Then, as Wyatt took the last empty seat, she said to him, "You've probably put it all together, but the guy in the soft cast is Foster, and the bombshell beside him is Shelby. That's Nick, who's our go-to guy when the horses do what horses do and try to kill themselves in the most expensive ways possible, and you know Jenny."

"Hey," her sister protested. "I'm a bombshell, too!"

"Of course you are, but saying it feels weird, because that's the same as saying it about myself."

"Not even, blondie." Jenny tugged Krista's hair.

"Anyway," Krista continued, "that's everyone. And everyone, this is Wyatt. Be good."

Bull by the horns, he thought, and said, "Nice to meet you all, but I figure there's no point in playing games." Looking at Jenny, he added, "You got something to say, go ahead and say it. I care about Krista, and she cares about you, and I don't want her caught in the middle of anything if I can help it."

There was a moment of surprised silence. Then the waitress bopped over, wearing a checkered shortie apron over an even shorter pair of cutoffs, and said brightly, "Welcome to the Rope Burn! What are we drinking tonight? And can I recommend our Tie Me Up, Tie Me Down appetizer special?"

"That depends." Wyatt nodded to Jenny. "What do you say?"

Her lips twitched. "I came in thinking I might want the He's Not Worth It nachos, but now I'm not so sure. Give me a Corona Lite and an order of chicken fingers."

"They don't have a cutesy name?" he asked.

"Yeah," Nick said drily, "the I Wouldn't Push Your Luck nuggets."

The waitress frowned. "I'm not sure we have those. Do you want me to ask the cook?"

When everybody laughed and Krista squeezed his fingers under the table, Wyatt decided that might've been the right way to go, after all. After some "I'll get that if you split yours" negotiations, he ordered nachos for him and Krista to share, along with a Coke.

"Not much of a drinker?" Jenny asked as the waitress skipped off with a jingle from the pair of roweled spurs she wore on a pair of low-cut boots that probably hadn't ever made it near a horse for anything more than a calendar shoot.

"Now and then. Figure on keeping my wits about me tonight, at least for starters." He slung his arm over the back of Krista's chair, grateful that she was looking more amused than annoyed by the back-and-forth.

Jenny leaned in. "I went to school with Kai Vitelli."

On a scale of one to what-he-was-expecting, that scored pretty low. He searched his memory banks. "Multimedia artist-slash-ski bum. I did some welding for him last winter."

"That's the one. I asked him about you."

That was the downside of Damien's PR machine. Enough Web searching and the degrees of separation plummeted. On the upside, he didn't think there was much Kai could say about him that went beyond the stuff in his official bio. "And?"

"He said you're one of the most down-to-earth people he's met in the Denver scene. Honest. Hardworking. Reliable."

"Coming from him, I'm not sure that's a compliment. As far as he's concerned, an artist isn't the real deal unless he's on the edge."

"Maybe not, but when you're dating my sister, it's a good thing. Especially given the history."

"Jen-ny," Krista said in warning.

"No," he said. "It's cool. I'd rather get it out there." This was something he could give Krista. Something she would never ask for. To Jenny, he said, "You ever do something that you thought about long and hard at the time, and were sure you were making the right call, only to look back later and realize you'd been a hundred percent wrong?" When Krista shifted beside him, he squeezed her shoulder in what he hoped was reassurance that this would be over soon, and the rest of the night—and going forward—would be better for it. "I was a jerk to leave the way I did—no argument there. But that was a long time ago. I'd like to think we've all learned some lessons since then."

"And this is you making up for it?" Jenny wagged a finger between them.

"No. Me filling in for Foster was, in part. Krista and me getting involved has been something else entirely."

"Which would be what?"

"Our business. I hope you'll respect our privacy and let me leave it at that."

She grumbled but dropped it. Wyatt was tempted to look under the table and see if Nick's foot was atop hers, bearing down. Figuring they might as well go around the table at this point, he asked, "Anyone else?" To Foster, he said, "How about it? I know you and Krista have been friends a long time. You want to take a swing at me?"

The wrangler—who seemed the quiet, thoughtful sort—said, "That depends. How's the gray mare coming along?"

"She's good. Smart as a whip and taking to the tricks like nobody's business. She keeps going this way and we'll have a chance at the finals."

Foster nodded. "Just don't push things too far, too fast. You do that, and the two of us are going to have a problem."

And suddenly they weren't talking about the horse anymore. "I don't intend to push," Wyatt said. "Not like that."

"We're good, then."

The waitress appeared, her bounce diminished by a loaded drink tray. A server trailed behind her bearing appetizers. "So," she said brightly, "who ordered the Let's Move On Already fries?"

* * *

By eight that night, Krista was wrapped in a warm glow that came partly from a couple of beers with dinner, but mostly from good food, good friends, and a lively conversation that bounced from horses to advertising to TV and back again. By nine she was giddy, watching Wyatt and Jenny go head-to-head in a game of nine-ball that she suspected he was keeping closer than it needed to be. And by ten, after the others had called it a night and Wyatt claimed a slow dance before they left, she was floating.

The dance floor was still full, but it was no hardship to snuggle up against him, with her head on his shoulder and his arms forming a protective barrier between her and the rest of the jostling dancers. His scent seeped into her pores, his heat into her bones, and her belly tugged with the knowledge that they'd be heading back to his place soon.

"Thank you," she said against his throat.

His arms tightened around her, pressing her close in a full-body hug, and his wonderful voice rumbled in her ear. "I don't mind dancing, especially with a beautiful woman in a long, swishy skirt."

"Not for the dance. For dealing with Jenny the way you did. It made tonight a thousand times better than it would have been if we were all trying to avoid the elephant in the middle of the room."

"I'm pretty sure it's a mechanical bull." But he kissed her temple. "They're good people, and they love you. A guy's got to respect that."

Not all of them would, though, she knew. And very

few of them would have handled the situation the way he had. "Still. Thanks. You ready to get out of here?"

"I thought you'd never ask." But he kept holding her close, swaying to the music. After a few beats, he said, "Will you stay the night?"

She thought about her guests and her family, and said. "Why not? I don't think I've ever officially done the walk of shame before."

"There's a first time for everything," he said solemnly.

Yes, there was. For the first time, she was in a relationship for the pure fun of it—not because she was thinking about a ring and a baby, or because she was trying to prove a point, but because she was exactly where she wanted to be. And how awesome was that? Grinning up at him, she patted his cheek. "Come on, cowboy. Let's take this dance horizontal." She didn't have to ask him twice.

18

Rustlers Week galloped past with a Singles Week on its heels, and suddenly they were down to three weeks before the finale, when the contestants were invited to show off their horses in the annual Summer's End Parade. First thing that morning, Wyatt loaded Jupiter and Lucky into the trailer, and he and Krista hit the road for Three Ridges.

She looked pretty as a sunrise in green chaps that were studded in silver and edged with an iridescent fringe, paired with a big, flashy belt buckle she had won at a long-ago rodeo, and a gleaming white shirt that was fringed in green and silver, and had the ranch's name and logo splashed on the back. With her hair in braids and her snow white hat dressed up with a tooled leather band and a peacock feather, she looked bright and vivid, and like she was ready to take on the world. She grinned over at him as they drove. "The others are going to eat their hearts out when they get a load of Jupiter."

"Not to mention that she's going to be some darned

good advertising. I saw the saddle pads you had made up for today." White edged with emerald green and embroidered with the ranch's name and logo. "You'd better hope she behaves."

"We'll bail if things get too hairy."

"I'm going to hold you to that." He was mostly teasing, though. When he first heard about the parade, he just shook his head at the thought of a bunch of half-broke mustangs sandwiched between a marching band and some fire trucks, and quickly losing their furry little minds. He had to admit, though, that it could be a good way to prep Jupiter for the chaos of the Harvest Fair. And putting her in close quarters with the other horses would be a good test of the desensitizing he and Krista had been doing over the past couple of weeks, working the mare through narrower and narrower chutes with gates at odd angles, trying to get her to trust that the rider would always find a way out.

Back in his regular, everyday life, he probably would've found it ironic, given that he was a pro when it came to not letting himself get boxed in. But Mustang Ridge had a different feel to it, a different flow, making all that seem less important. Each week was different, and there were so many moving parts to the guest ranch business that every day brought surprises, good and bad. Like the Rustlers Week guests who turned out to be tech geeks for a drone-camera startup company, and had wound up teaming up with Jenny and Shelby to get aerial footage of the overnight roundup. Or when two of the singles turned out to have been best friends back in grade school before one moved away, and rediscovered the old spark—times a hundred—twenty years later.

Wyatt sure wasn't bored with the work. And he wasn't looking to get away from Krista anytime soon, either. Their lives at the ranch fit together so naturally that the weeks had stopped counting down in his brain and he'd found himself thinking it wouldn't be half bad to still be living in the bunkhouse when the snow started to fall. Until he really buckled down to the pioneer piece, which was still doing a slow boil in his brain, he could work anywhere he pleased. And for the moment, he was plenty happy at Mustang Ridge.

"Here we are," she said, turning in to the strip-mall parking lot that was being used as a staging area for the mustangs. "Let the chaos begin."

The trailers were parked in parallel rows with enough space between them that the horses could be tied. Right now, though, most of the fresh, overstimulated mustangs were being led in wide circles as they danced on their toes like racehorses headed for the post parade.

"Hope you brought your crash helmet," he said as Krista killed the engine.

To his surprise, though, Jupiter and Lucky came off the trailer without too much fuss and stood for their riders to mount up as the speakers atop the Mayor Mobile—a half-ton silver pickup draped with banners advertising the Harvest Fair Mustang Makeover—gave a *crackle-whine* that sent a couple of the teams scattering.

Standing in the back of the pickup, wearing a suit that already looked too hot, the mayor lifted her microphone, beamed around at the shifting sea of horses, and said, "Welcome to the Summer's End Parade! With eight scratches and several teams electing to keep their horses in their trailers, we have twenty-two competitors marching today, and I'd like to personally thank you for putting yourselves out here to support the competition and our efforts to draw attention to Three Ridges!" She went on to describe the parade route, safety precautions, and bail-out options for the horses and riders.

"What do you think, Lucky?" Krista stroked the gelding's arched neck. "Do you want to babysit Jupiter here so we can march in the scary parade?"

The big black horse didn't answer, but he sure looked businesslike.

"Let's do it," Wyatt said.

She tapped her toe against his. "You got your seat belt on?"

He settled deep in the saddle and pulled the brim of his hat down, like a bull rider ready to give the gate crew the nod. "Good to go."

The Mayor Mobile moved out with the mayor standing in the back, followed by the jittering, mincing mob of mustangs and their escorts. Seeing most of the others hanging toward the rear of the pack, Wyatt and Krista moved up to the front by unspoken consent.

Glancing back, she said, "Do you think the others know there are baton twirlers coming in behind us?"

"They will soon," he predicted.

But darned if the horses didn't handle the crazy just fine, moving out of the staging area and onto Main Street. There, locals and tourists of all ages cheered from behind ropes and sawhorses, while Mayor Teapot did her rah-rah thing, pimping the Harvest Fair and the Mustang Makeover on the loudspeaker, and tossing peppermints into the crowd.

Beaming, Krista waved at a pair of little boys in the front row. Wearing straw souvenir hats and clutching fat wands of blue cotton candy, they stared up at her, round eyed with awe as the horses passed.

Wyatt grinned at them and tipped his hat. *I know how you feel, guys.* He found himself staring at her like that now and then, and getting that caught-staring-at-the-sun head spin. In his case, though, there was also the chest-puffing knowledge that when the sun rose in the morning, she'd be in his bed and greeting him with a kiss.

"There they are!" Krista waved up ahead. "Hey, gang! Woo-hoo, go Team Mustang Ridge!"

Her parents and Gran leaned over a sawhorse, cheering. Beside them, Nick stood with Jenny, who was panning the scene with an expensive-looking camera, and Shelby had her arms around a dark-haired, happy-looking kid who had to be her daughter, Lizzie.

Krista gestured to Jupiter with an expression of *get a load of our girl!* and her family whooped. Lucky puffed up his neck and pranced, not being naughty so much as reacting to his rider's enthusiasm. Still, Wyatt could tell that Krista was bothered by her grandfather's absence—early that morning, Big Skye had muttered something about finishing the new fencing up in the high pasture, and rode off with Deke and a couple of the other guys behind him, like the work couldn't have waited the few hours that the rest of them had carved out to make the parade. Not for the first time, Wyatt was tempted to give the old man a piece of his mind. Couldn't he see how much the distance between them bothered Krista? Didn't he care?

Not your family, better to leave it alone, he told himself. They had warmed to him somewhat, but there were limits.

"Yo, Wyatt!" The shout pulled his attention to the other side of the street, and there was Sam, with his arm around a gorgeous blond giggler and a footlong in his free hand.

Krista grinned. "Sam has changed, hasn't he? I remember when we first met, he could barely look me in the eye, never mind carry on a conversation."

"He still lives on strawberry Pop-Tarts, though."

"You're kidding."

Wyatt grinned. "Would I kid about Pop-Tarts?"

They waved to the onlookers—many of whom knew Krista on sight and vice versa—and traded quips as the parade carried on, through several traffic lights and past a sea of faces, with the marching band still going strong behind them, though the mayor's voice was starting to sound ragged. Then, finally, they came around a corner and the horses' heads came up, and Lucky let out a little "whee-ho-ho-ho" of greeting.

Krista patted his sleek neck. "Can you smell the trailers, buddy?"

As promised, the Lemps had moved all of the rigs to the parade's end point. To Wyatt's relief, the horses loaded without issue, lured by the stuffed-full hay bags and relative quiet of the trailer.

He was double-checking the door latches when he heard the sound of high heels *tap-tap-tapping* behind him, followed by a woman's voice. "Mr. Webb? Could we have a word?"

He turned to find the mayor standing there, along with a younger version with honey-colored hair and a friendly smile. Where Mayor Tepitt looked overheated, wilted and in serious need of a cold drink, her counterpart looked fresh and cool as she held out a hand. "Mr. Webb, I'm Constance Dewitt. It's a real pleasure to find a man of your stature here in Three Ridges."

As Krista joined them, wearing a look of *what's going on?* he wiped his hand on his jeans, and shook. "Pleased to meet you, I'm sure. But after today I wouldn't say I'm much out of the ordinary around here when it comes to trainers."

"But not sculptors." The woman turned to Krista. "Ms. Skye, I'm a fan of yours as well. You've done some really impressive things at Mustang Ridge, both in terms of infrastructure and PR. Not to mention your excellent use of local businesses to implement your guest services."

Krista shook her hand, putting on a polite, dimple-free smile. "Thank you, Miz . . ."

"Constance Dewitt. But Connie is fine. I'm heading up the Harvest Fair Committee, which is why I wanted to talk to your Mr. Webb here." To Wyatt, she said, "We met once, during a show at the GearHorse Gallery."

"Oh?" He had long ago learned not to pretend to remember people—it just led to confusion. He had also learned to wait for the pitch in situations like this. There always was one.

"Yes. It was very impressive, but I'm sure I don't need to tell you that. The critics either loved it or hated it, both of which are a win in my book, and you sold out within, what, three hours?"

"Nice to hear you enjoyed it. What can I do for you?"

"I was hoping . . ." The coolness cracked a little, letting hope shine through as she said in a rush, "Wouldyoubewillingtojudgethechainsawcarvings?"

That so wasn't what he had been braced for—he'd been expecting her to ask for a demonstration or a big-ass sculpture for city hall—that he didn't get all of it. "Excuse me?"

She took a breath, got the cool back in place, and said, "My apologies. It was such a shock to recognize you riding in the parade, that . . . Well, anyway. I'd like to invite you, on behalf of the Harvest Fair Committee, to judge our chainsaw sculpture competition."

He relaxed. "Oh, sure. Yeah. I can do that." Couldn't think of a reason not to, and after hearing the mayor harangue Sam over donations, he'd rather just say yes and be done with it.

"You . . . Really?" Connie looked like he'd just

handed her the reins of a top-notch cutting horse on the eve of the championships.

"As long as it doesn't conflict with the Mustang Makeover."

She nodded and whipped out her phone and made a couple of notes. "Where can I reach you to firm things up?"

"It's a done deal on my end. Just leave a message at Mustang Ridge telling me the day, the time, and where to meet you."

"Can I get a bio? Maybe some photos? And we'd love to show one of your pieces. . . ."

Yeah. That was more along the lines of what he'd been expecting. But while a few weeks ago he would have ducked having his name connected to Three Ridges, now he thought, *Why not?* "Call Damien at GearHorse. He'll hook you up and help get the word out. Now, if you'll excuse us, we need to get our horses home in time to welcome the new crop of guests."

He got another round of *I love your work* from Connie, which he fielded as genuinely as he could, and then he and Krista beat it for the truck and hit the road.

Surveying the traffic, Wyatt grumbled, "Thanks to them, we're going to get to sit with five thousand of our nearest and dearest. I should've pretended I didn't hear the mayor."

"I don't think that would have gotten you out of it," Krista said tartly. "That Connie seemed pretty intent on nabbing you."

Her tone had him shooting a look across the cab. "Are you mad about that?"

"No. Why would I be?"

"I don't know, but I'm getting a vibe." And it wasn't like her to play games. "I was just being friendly, you know."

"That's your first shot? That I'm *jealous*? After spending the last few weeks watching you fend off dudettes and getting to be all smug because I'm the one who gets to wake up next to you? I think not." But at least she looked amused. And after a moment, she sighed and shook her head. "No, it's stupid, and it's not you."

"I'm not stupid?"

"Well, you're not, but that's not what I meant. *I'm* being stupid, my reaction back there was stupid. It's just . . . I've gotten used to having you to myself. Sounds dumb, because at the ranch there's always someone around, always people coming and going. But there's a weird sort of privacy, too."

"No, I get what you mean," he said, relaxing a degree. "We've got our own thing going on there, and then the real world intrudes."

"Mustang Ridge *is* my real world," she said with a bit of an edge. "But I think I let myself forget that it's not yours. Seeing you get all professional and schedule-y with Connie, it hit me all over again that this"—she pointed between the two of them—"is an interlude. And the clock is ticking."

"Krissy," he began.

"I'm not trying to start a deep and meaningful discussion, promise. In fact, I'd rather just leave it like this. I'm not mad or jealous, I swear. It just hit me that you're more than my fill-in wrangler as far as the rest of the world is concerned, and that's my problem, not yours."

How could a man not react to that? Especially when she was trying to get it right this time—they both were, by being open with each other, honest. Part of him wanted to tell her that he'd started imagining himself in Three Ridges a few months from now, a few years. But he'd gotten caught in that trap before, and gnawed through both of their souls to get free. So instead he said, "Give me until eight tonight before you come over, okay? I've got a surprise for you."

19

That night at two past eight, Krista pulled into her spot beside Old Blue in the bunkhouse parking lot, killed the engine, and sat for a moment as Klepto appeared in the nearest window, head cocked as if to say, *What's with the car?* She had driven over, figuring she would celebrate Jupiter's success at the parade and Wyatt's promise of a surprise with a flirty skirt and a pair of high-heeled boots that really weren't designed for hiking.

Anticipation and desire skimmed through her as she got out of the car and headed up the steps, hearing Klepto bark to announce her arrival. She raised a hand to knock, not wanting to spoil the promised surprise if he wasn't yet ready, but before her fist made contact the door swung inward. And there he was, with his dark hair shower-damp, his plain white T-shirt and worn jeans molded to his body, and his feet bare, revealing the crooked toe that had been broken twice by the same horse.

Smiling, she stepped across the threshold. "The

guests are tucked in for the night and Mom is on call, so here I am."

"So you are. And you look amazing." He spun her around so the skirt flared away from her ankles, her heels tapped on the polished wood, and Klepto danced like his legs had turned to springs. Then Wyatt drew her in for a kiss and murmured against her lips, "It seems almost a shame to get you naked."

Heat thrummed through her. "Right now?"

"Well, that's up to you." He nudged the door shut and flipped off the overhead lights illuminating the main room. "Come see what you think."

"What I think about— Oh." Her mouth fell open at the sight of a dozen fat white candles lighting the tiles surrounding of the hot tub, which had been high and dry yesterday, but now was full and steaming, with bubbles and swirls making the surface dance while ghostly mist turned the air soft and humid. "Oh, wow." She tightened her grip on Wyatt's hand as she took in the gleam of mosaic tile, the perfect lines of sealed grout, and the polished wood door that protected the controls and electrical circuits. "You finished it! When . . . how . . ."

He grinned. "Last night. I know you'll need to get someone to sign off on it for guest use, but I figured we could take it for a test drive."

As her eyes adjusted to the shock, she saw that the surface was dotted with familiar pink flowers that made her think of the waterfall, with more of their petals scattered on the surround, leading to a bottle of her favorite red wine, open to breathe beside a pair of glasses. Emotion lumping in her throat, she managed, "You set all of this up for me?"

"I didn't do it for Klepto." Wyatt came around behind her, dropped his head, and nuzzled her neck. "You smell better than he does when you're wet."

A laugh bubbled up alongside a dizzy rush that made her feel like she had stood up too fast. "Thank you."

"Well, he's a dog. They're supposed to smell like dirty sheep when they're wet."

She turned in his arms and found his lips with hers. "I meant thank you for the flowers and the wine. Which you knew perfectly well."

He kissed her long and deep, sliding his hands down her body, and gathering a double handful of her skirt. "Yeah, but I like making you smile."

"Is that what the Reddi-wip is for?" She said, tipping her head to where a familiar canister sat next to the drugstore bag she suspected contained a new box of condoms to replace the one they had burned through last night.

"Technically, the whipped cream is for the brownies and strawberries I've got in the fridge. I was going to put them on a plate with the wine, but . . . You know."

"Klepto."

At the sound of his name, the dog thumped his butt on the floor and cocked his head.

"Yeah, right," Wyatt said. "We're so on to you."

"Don't listen to him," Krista whispered. "I'll share."

"Later," Wyatt said, pulling her into him for a kiss. "After."

"After what?" she said, as if his hands weren't busy on the buttons of her shirt.

"After I get you out of these clothes and into the water." He eased back to give her a boyish smile that made her heart shudder in her chest. "What do you say, Krissy? Will you come hot-tubbing with me?"

"I thought you'd never ask." She shimmied out of her skirt and tossed it on a nearby chair. That left her standing in her open shirt and the skimpy panty and bra set she had bought in town on her last supply run, imagining his face as Kitty bagged her purchase. Now, in the flickering candlelight, his expression was everything she had imagined, and then some. Eyes gone black with desire, he trailed a finger along one of her collarbones, down between her breasts, and across to toy with one sensitized nipple through the lace-edged fabric of her bra.

The air hung heavy with the scent of flowers and passion, but no matter how deeply she filled her lungs, she couldn't catch her breath. Then he knelt in front of her and pressed his lips to her stomach, and she dug her fingers into the heavy muscles of his shoulders through the heated material of his T-shirt. And she decided that breathing was overrated. Who needed oxygen when there was so much to *feel*?

His smooth-shaven jaw contrasted with the thick

fullness of his hair and the slide of skin on skin when he worked his way up her body and kissed her lips, drawing her shirt off and letting it fall.

"Boots," he rasped against her lips, "unless you want them getting wet."

She toed them off and kicked them aside, and the second they thudded to the floor he swept her up in his arms and carried her to the raised platform. She didn't have a chance to admire the finished surround, the wine, or the candles, because without pausing for an instant, he stepped straight into the hot tub and started down the shallow staircase.

"Wyatt!" She pushed at his arms. "You're still wearing your—"

He sank down, carrying her with him. She gasped as the water closed around her, then murmured in pleasure as she found it warm rather than hot, so it energized her rather than sapping her strength. "Jeans," she finished on a breathy moan as he settled her against him face-to-face, spreading her legs around him so she was riding the hard, jutting ridge behind his fly.

"I know." He kissed her throat, her ear, the upslope of one breast. "They're the only reason I'm not already inside you."

"So what are you waiting for?"

"Wine," he muttered, hands splaying to cup her buttocks beneath the water. "Brownies. Slow seduction."

"Later," she said, going to work on his fly. Reaching up, she snagged the bag, found the condoms, and soaked the box getting it open. When she had one of the packets free, she reached beneath the water to press it into his palm. "Right now—I don't want to wait."

His eyes fired and his lips curved, a cocky boy's smile in a face that was all man. "Good. Because neither do I."

Wyatt had known they were good together, but before tonight, he hadn't known how far "good" could go. Hadn't had a clue.

In the warm languor following their first hard, fast encounter in the hot tub, they sipped wine and fed each other strawberries dabbed with whipped cream, and talked about a long-ago picnic when they had ridden up into the hills and picked wild berries. By unspoken consent, they left the brownies for later and turned to each other instead, twining together in the hot tub, only to emerge an hour later, waterlogged and laughing, to towel each other off between kisses and caresses. Then, as had become his newest favorite habit, he swept her up, cradled her against his chest, and carried her up the stairs to the bedroom.

As he started up the short hallway, she danced her nails across his chest and kissed his throat until he groaned and rasped, "You keep doing that and I may drop you. I won't mean it, and I'll feel really bad afterward, but I'll do it."

"No, you won't," she purred, tugging on his earlobe with her teeth. "I trust you not to let me fall."

"Don't," he said, tossing her on the bed, "speak too soon!"

She squealed as she landed and bounced, damp, na-ked and pink-skinned, and so glorious that part of him wanted to stand there and stare, and wonder how he'd gotten so damn lucky. He dropped down to the bed beside her, instead, and covered her with his body, in-tensely aware of how perfectly she wrapped around him, welcomed him home, and then took him some-place else entirely.

In the aftermath, lying with her tucked against his side, with her hand on his chest and his cheek resting on the top of her head as usual, he dozed, not really ready to sleep when sleeping would mean the end of an incredible night. Mind drifting, he listened to the now-familiar sounds of the bunkhouse. The hot tub was off and cooling, but the passive vent system whirred, powered by the heat still coming off the water. The re-frigerator kicked on now and then, as did the solar-charged battery that fed to an exterior generator. And under all of that, counterpointing the sounds of their breathing and the occasional *click-click-click* of Klepto's nails on the floor downstairs, was the rare *creak-pop* of the logs settling for the night.

Of all the sounds, it was strange to think that those *creak-pops* were the only ones that the long-ago inhabi-tants of the bunkhouse would have heard.

He imagined the place as it would have been back then, a single-story, single-room dormitory with a card table at one end, bunks at the other, and saddles stacked by each bed. Because a cowboy could borrow a horse, but he couldn't call himself a cowboy without a saddle.

The bunkhouse would've held a dozen men, maybe more—they would ride together, eat together, even blow off steam in town together come payday. And when it came time to round up the herds and drive them down to the railhead several hundred miles away, they would have one another's backs for the duration.

He pictured them scattered around the fire—some tending to the horses and cattle, others seeing to the camp, while the Cookie whipped up biscuits and gravy and brewed coffee the consistency of hydraulic fluid. Maybe they didn't all like one another, but they needed one another. Their sum was far greater than its parts, but it was never static because they were the kind of men who didn't stay in one place very long before their feet started itching, telling them it was time to move on.

And damned if he didn't see it all of a sudden, a tantalizing glimpse of what could be: a fire of metal strips that spun in the breeze; a coffeepot that bubbled with recycled oil; a backdrop of hammered-flat car hoods etched with lines that suggested saddle horses on a picket line and a massive herd of cattle being held by the watering hole; and a dozen mechanical men in ten-gallon hats made of flywheels and air filters.

It was fresh, different, exciting. He hadn't done anything like it before. Didn't know if anyone had. And where a few minutes ago he'd thought he might not ever move again, now his blood hummed with a different sort of urgency—diffuse and not fully formed yet, but still more than he'd felt in too long. *I could build that. It could be good.*

Giving in to the gloriously sudden urge, even knowing that tomorrow was going to suck if he didn't get any sleep, he eased out from beneath Krista.

She snuggled up with his pillow, frowning in her sleep as he bent down and kissed her cheek. "Wyatt," she whispered, reaching for him.

"I'll just be down in the workshop," he said, knowing she wouldn't remember the conversation. "Klepto will keep an eye on you."

At the sound of his name, the dog poked his head through the door.

Wyatt pointed to the floor near the bed. "Stay here," he said. "Keep her company." He didn't know how many words Klepto actually understood, but the mutt did a couple of turns and lay down on the throw rug, facing the bed. The sight of her in his bed, with his dog on the floor nearby, put a curl of warmth in his chest and a sense that everything was where it was supposed to be. For right now, anyway. Careful not to look at it too close, he headed downstairs and out into the darkness, suddenly itching for his tools.

Krista awoke to a pink-tinged darkness and stared at the wood-beamed ceiling while the last of her dream—something about giant corn muffins with foam-rubber tentacles battling a flash flood, and she really didn't want to run *that* through a dream analyzer—drained away and her pulse slowed.

"Well," she said. "That was crazy." Then, realizing

the space beside her was empty, the sheets cool, she called, "Wyatt?"

"Whuff?" A gray-whiskered face appeared over the side of the bed.

She tousled Klepto's head. "Hey, buddy. Where's the big guy?" Wide awake despite the early hour, she crawled out of the big, soft bed and pulled on the yoga pants and T-shirt that had migrated from her place to his. Sticking her feet into a pair of canary yellow flip-flops—more migrants—she said, "Come on. Let's go see what's up."

Hoping it wouldn't be tentacles and flash floods—or their real-world equivalents, whatever those might be—she headed down the stairs and swung open the front door. Klepto flung himself down the stairs with canine abandon, barking as if to say, "Hello, world, here I am!"

Clang-bang! The noise brought Krista's attention around, and she grinned. "Well, what do you know? Seems like the hot tub is already paying dividends. Who needs the Fountain of Youth when you've got the Hot Tub of Creativity? We'll have to put that in the brochure."

Ignoring the pang that came at the thought of renting the place out next season, she rolled open the sliding steel door and slipped into the shop, where she found the workbench covered with drawing paper and Wyatt standing over a collection of metal scraps that had been laid out in an indecipherable outline, like some mechanical fossil.

"Whuff!" Klepto barged past her, jogged into the shop, and dropped a flamingo-pink hairbrush at his master's feet.

"What—" Wyatt looked at the dog, blinked at her, and then seemed to come out of whatever fugue he'd been in. "Hey!" Expression clearing, he crossed to her, tugged her into the shop. "Come in. Here." Snagging a work shirt off the welder, he shook it out and draped it around her shoulders, then drew her in for a kiss. "You look cold."

"You don't," she said, flattening her hands on his T-shirt and going up on her tiptoes for a second, more lingering kiss. "You look like you've been working. How's it going?"

"I've finally got it, I think," he said, drawing her to the workbench.

The three drawings showed a campfire scene that could have come straight out of her childhood, with a whiskered, dour-looking Cookie crouched over the fire, a young whip of a cowboy hauling wood, and a cattle dog eyeing the supplies like he was looking for an opening to snag a piece of bacon. Her lips curved. "I see the dog made it back in."

"Can't seem to get rid of him. There's more." He brushed his fingers across the other sketches, which showed other little scenes—cowboys tending their horses and tack, with herds and mountains in the background, while notes and arrows suggested materials and fabrication techniques. "It's just a start, but"—he gestured to the fossil pile—"it's what I was looking for without even realizing it—something new and different, and not like anything I've done before."

That struck a chord, but not in a good way. She pushed the twinge away, though—she was happy for him—she *was*. "Congratulations." She wrapped her fingers around his wrists, holding him close. "It's going to be amazing."

"It's just a few lines on a piece of paper at the moment. But, yeah, I think I can get to work for real now." Looking down at the sketches, he added, "In fact, I need to head south. I've got some pistons back home that I can use with the stuff I have here. I figured I could cut out after the ride on Friday, be back by Saturday night." She didn't know what he saw in her face, but his expression softened. He pulled her in, kissed her forehead, and then held her close, saying against her temple, "This doesn't change anything, Krissy, except that I won't be able to dance with you at the bonfire Friday night, and I'll miss waking up beside you Saturday morning."

"And I'll be sleeping in my own bed." The prospect bothered her more than she would have expected, more than she wanted to analyze right then.

"You could stay here while I'm gone," he said.

"Alone? No, thanks."

"Invite the girls over. Use the hot tub. Call it a spa night."

"No, that's . . . Hm. Tempting."

"Good." He gave her a smacking kiss on the lips. "That's settled. Now, what do you say we get dressed and head up to breakfast? Rumor has it there's a new crop of greenhorns in town, waiting for us to teach them which end kicks, which end bites, and why it's a good idea to set the saddle so the horn goes in front. And, Krista? I'll be back Saturday afternoon. That's a promise."

20

"To Wyatt," Jenny proclaimed, lifting her wine. "For finishing the Jacuzzi." Submerged to her collarbones, with frothy bubbles camouflaging her strapless bathing suit, she could've been naked.

Krista was tempted to snap a phone picture for future blackmail, except that Jenny's ideas of revenge tended to be both public and creative.

"Hear, hear!" Shelby pantomimed a toast across the tub. Sitting with the water just below her breasts, she wore a killer red bathing suit with all sorts of cutouts and push-ups that made Krista feel flat and boring in her blue one-piece. But she had long ago decided that it was okay for her to envy Shelby's body and wardrobe, on the theory that if you couldn't fake-hate your best friend, who could you fake-hate?

Sitting between them, Krista clinked her wine with one and then the other. "To girls' night in."

Jenny nodded. "May it be the first of many, because why have a luxury guest cabin if you can't sneak it for yourself now and then? You'll have to block it out for a week or two next summer so we can still have access once this place is being rented out."

Shelby studied Krista. "This *is* a guest cabin, right? Or are you thinking of turning it back into a bunkhouse for your head wrangler?"

"Foster is my head wrangler."

"Your second-in-command wrangler, then. That's not what I'm asking, and you know it."

"I don't . . . I'm not . . ." Krista took a sip of her wine, buying herself a few seconds. It wasn't like she hadn't thought about it—this was the Girl Zone, after all, and she knew the questions would be coming. But now, sitting between her twin and her best friend, she didn't want to talk about Wyatt's lack of interest in anything long-term when the others were married to men who had loved them enough to make it work. "Wyatt and I have an agreement."

Jenny waved that off. "So did Nick and I. We renegotiated."

"That's not on the table."

"Why not? You're falling for him, aren't you?"

"*No!*" Krista said, so quickly that the panic didn't have time to take root. "That would be"—stupid, suicidal, contrary to everything she'd worked so hard to do right—"ridiculous."

"You're in a relationship, aren't you?"

"It's not a relationship. We're just lovers."

"There's a difference?"

"Lovers enjoy each other. A relationship implies a future. Can we change the subject? Please?"

"I don't mean to nag." Jenny even managed to look contrite. "It's just—"

"You're one of those annoying happily married people who think everybody around them should get married, too," Krista finished for her.

"Yes, I am. And I want you to be one, too. Is that so much to ask for my favorite sister? Remember how you used to plan your wedding? You wanted Great-grandma Abby's ring and even had your kids' names picked out. What were they again? Abby, Edith, Rose, and . . ."

"Edward Arthur," Krista filled in, "after Dad and Big Skye. Too bad it sounds like a knight of the Round Table. Sir Edward Arthur, at your service." She mocked a bow, refusing to feel sorry for herself. "And for the record, we were eight. We also thought that oatmeal cookies could cure a case of the cooties and that babies were made using a special sourdough recipe. Otherwise known as the facts of life, à la Gran."

Shelby buried a snicker in her wine. "I should've sicced her on Lizzie rather than going with the *Dummy's Guide to Talking to Your Kids About Sex*. Though Foster and I got some good giggles out of the diagrams."

"Did you follow the instructions to make sure they got it right?" Jenny asked, deadpan.

"Why, do you want to borrow it, see if you and Nick are missing any steps?"

"Ha! We graduated to the *Idiot's Guide to the Kama Sutra* a while back." Jenny stuck out her tongue. "So there."

"Oh? Have you tried page eighty-seven yet?"

"Why, do you need pointers?"

Relieved that the conversation had moved past her and Wyatt, Krista settled lower in the water and sipped her wine.

Maybe she had imagined her wedding and named her children-to-be when she was too young to know what it all really meant, and maybe deep down inside, she had always figured she would get married and have kids before Jenny. But she had let go of those fantasies a while back, along with her five- and ten-year plans. Plus, she refused to put Wyatt in the picture, knowing that when the season ended, so would they.

When the thought brought a stab of anguish she wasn't interested in dealing with—why mope for the last couple of weeks when she could enjoy herself instead?—she skipped ahead, her mind going to the next project, the next business plan, the next fun thing on the guest list. The things that had kept her happily busy all these years.

Into a lull in the conversation, she said, "Now that the bunkhouse is pretty much done, can you guys put your creative brains together and come up with some ideas for advertising? I was thinking maybe we could offer it for long weekends this fall and winter, as a romantic getaway." There, she had even said it without a twinge. More or less.

"Hot tub, catered meals, and a big bed far away from the hustle and bustle." Shelby gestured with her wine. "It sells itself. What do you need me for?"

"A slogan with a little more punch than *A hot tub, catered meals, and a big bed*?" Though she had to admit, it had potential. "And for you and Jenny to get together on the visuals. I was thinking pictures of the interior, maybe get some models for some romantic shots, and—"

"Pictures!" Jenny shot up from the hot tub, creating a mini tsunami that slopped over the mosaic tile as she grabbed a big, fluffy towel and scampered for her bag.

"I didn't mean—" Krista began.

"Don't bother," Shelby advised. "You've already un-leashed the beast."

"Ye gad, I know. Jenny, don't—" *Clicka-click* went the camera, no doubt catching Krista with her mouth flap-ping, as usual. *Speaking of blackmail.* "I said *models*," she protested. "I wasn't talking about me and Shelby!"

"You're just as hot as the local talent," Jenny coun-tered. "Well, at least Shelby is."

Krista gaped. "You did *not* just say that about me."

"About us, really. Smile!"

Shelby slung an arm around her shoulders, lifted her wine, and said, "*Sex for Dummies!*"

Krista was laughing when the camera clicked, then whooped when Shelby got a hand on her head and dunked her beneath the warm suds. The world went wet and loud for a moment, as the sound of the under-water jets drowned out everything else. Then she broke the surface and lunged for Shelby. "I am *so* going to get you for that!"

She heard the camera doing its *click-whirr* thing but

didn't care as Shelby feinted and dodged, eluding her in the small, slippery space, then doubled back and dunked her again, shouting, "City girls fight dirty!"

When Krista came back up, she was laughing. "That wasn't the sort of slogan I was thinking of." But at the same time, this was exactly what she needed—the camera, the wrestling match, laughing so hard her lungs burned and her ribs ached . . . and the reminder that love might come and go, but friends and family were forever.

Late Saturday afternoon, Wyatt turned off the main road and rolled through the stone pillars of Mustang Ridge, wincing when Old Blue bottomed out from all the weight he'd loaded in the back.

"Think she'll like it?" he asked as Klepto did a whole-body wag, excited to be back at the ranch. "Yeah." Wyatt patted the wiry back end. "I think so, too."

It took him an hour to offload his gift, another to install it. Then he stood back and nodded, well satisfied. "Okay, that'll do it. Let's go pick up our girl."

He had called ahead, so she was waiting for him when he rolled in, standing on the bunkhouse porch wearing her patchwork skirt, a denim shirt rolled up past her elbows, and a broad smile of welcome. And his danged heart skipped a beat.

Always before, he'd thought that was just a saying. Now he knew better.

He parked and opened the door, releasing Klepto to

bounce around, barking his fool head off while Wyatt crossed to Krista, caught her by the waist and spun her around, surprising a laugh out of her. When he let her down, he felt her skirt brush his legs as he lowered his head to claim the kiss he'd been thinking about for eight hundred miles, give or take.

Her lips parted; her breath mingled with his. And he felt more of a homecoming in this moment than he had when he pulled up in front of his cabin outside of Denver, or even when he stepped back into the workshop he had built himself from steel, stone, and wood. Burying his hands in her soft, loose hair, he drank in her flavor and surrounded himself with flowers and rain. Then he eased away to feather kisses along her mouth, her cheek, across her jaw to her ear. There, he whispered, "I have a surprise for you."

"Really?" She craned to look in the back of the truck, which was still half full of pistons and tractor parts.

"It's not in there. Want to go for a little ride?"

She looked down at her skirt. "Should I change?"

"In the truck," he clarified. "Just a short drive." He pulled a blue bandanna out of his back pocket, shook it out. "Oh, and did I mention the part about the blindfold?"

With Wyatt's bandanna tied over her eyes, Krista could see some lights and darks, but nothing more. She could feel the bumps as the truck turned onto the road, the pressure of Wyatt's fingers where they held hands on the bench seat, and the warmth of the late-day sun on her skin. Her heart drummed lightly in anticipation—of the gift, of having him back, of the night ahead. The week ahead. "Are we there yet?"

He chuckled. "Almost."

The truck slowed, then turned. "We're going to the ranch?" she asked. "Did you bring something for the horses?"

"No and no." The truck rolled to a stop and the engine cut out. "We're here."

"At the end of the driveway?"

"You're not very good at playing along with surprises, are you?" There was a chuckle in his voice. He came around the truck, opened the door, unclipped her seat belt, and took her hand. "Come on out. I've got you."

"You know I'm not allowed to play in traffic, right?"

"Would you hush already?" He clapped a hand across her mouth and marched her over a section of grass, then onto the driveway. Moments later, the blindfold tugged and fell free, and he said softly into her ear, "Surprise."

"What—" she began, but then broke off at the sight of twin twisted arches of new metal supporting the old sign. The missing horseshoes had been replaced, welded back into place, so the arch was unbroken, the sentiment unquestionable.

WELCOME TO MUSTANG RIDGE.

"Oh, Wyatt." It came out as a whisper. "You fixed our sign."

He hooked an arm around her waist, and snugged her back against his body. "I did. Do you like it?"

"I love it." Her voice broke slightly. "You didn't just fix what was there, you made it look even better. More modern. But you kept the bones."

"That's the story of Mustang Ridge, isn't it?" He kissed the top of her head. "Every generation takes what's already there, preserves the best parts of the past and brings the rest up to date."

Tears prickled. "I wish Big Skye could see that."

"Maybe he doesn't, but I do." He looked up at the sign. "This is important, Krista. What you do here is important. You make Mustang Ridge a home, not just for your family and employees, but for the guests, too. And that matters."

She closed her eyes and felt a tear break free. "Thank you. For understanding me, for making the sign so much better than it used to be." *And for coming back,* she managed not to say. Swallowing past the lump in her throat, she went up on her tiptoes to kiss him, whispering against his lips. "Now I owe you one."

"Not even close."

"What if I said I was going to repay you by . . ." She whispered it in his ear.

"Annnd, we're headed back to the bunkhouse!"

She laughed as he practically dragged her to the truck, boosted her in, and slammed the door, getting them back down the road in no time flat. They barely made it through the door before he was kissing her, holding her, overbalancing her onto the couch in a tangle of limbs and half-attached clothing. Then they were rolling, tugging, stripping each other naked in a flurry of kisses and happy sighs until, finally, Krista arched her body, took him inside her, and let the heat carry her away.

21

Early the next morning, with her system still humming from last night and a happy tune playing in her head—something along the lines of *Welcome to Mustang Ridge. There's wine and cake in the fridge, dum diddly ump de dum*—Krista danced into the kitchen of the main house. And stopped dead, mouth dropping open. "What the . . . ?"

There were cupcakes *everywhere*.

Hundreds of the prettily frosted desserts were crammed onto every available flat surface and stacked in the cooling racks like rainbow-colored chicks in a brooder, wearing fluted paper cups and topped with sprinkles and saucy little decorations in every possible color, making it look like someone had blasted a bazooka full of Skittles into the normally neatly ordered space. The air was so sweet it made Krista's molars ache; the ovens were going full blast, counting down six more batches, even though there wasn't any place to put them; and the big mixers were running, their arms whirling in synchrony, like the Sorcerer's Apprentice had taken up baking rather than brooms. That, combined with the three overhead fans running at top speed, made the place look like a culinary funhouse gone mad.

Pulse bumping—what was going on here?—Krista stepped into the room, calling, "Gran?"

"In the pantry, sweetie," came the muffled answer. "Could you help? I need more flour."

Hastening in that direction, Krista found her grandmother climbing down from a step stool, lugging a ten-pound bag of King Arthur. "I would have gotten it for you!"

"Not this one. I need the other one, too. It's toward the back, and I can't quite reach it." Which would make twenty pounds of flour to go along with the liter of vanilla, two bags of sugar, and three packages of chocolate chips that sat by the pantry door.

Looking from the pile to Gran and back again, Krista said, "Are you going for the Guinness Book record for the most cupcakes produced by a single human being in a twelve-hour period?"

"Poosh." Gran waved her off. "The Helping Paws for Veterans bake sale is today."

"Are they expecting an army?"

"Never mind. I'll get it myself." On a mission, Gran elbowed past and started up the stepladder, only then realizing she was still carrying the first bag. She stalled on the top step, wobbling.

Krista reached out. "Let me—"

"I've got it!" Drawing back, Gran heaved the bag into the kitchen . . . and it missed the counter entirely, hit the floor, and detonated with a *whump* of powdery white. Krista's jaw dropped as the cloud whirled in the updraft of the ceiling fans, coating everything in a twenty-foot radius, including most of the cupcakes.

Gran scrambled down off the step stool and charged into the kitchen, making sneaker prints in the white. "Quick! Turn off the fans." She picked up one of the white-dusted cupcakes and shook it, sending more sprinkles flying than flour. "We can fix this, but we have to hurry."

"Gran, you've got plenty."

"Not of the pink ones," she said, voice going panicky. "Oohhhh. How are we going to clean these off?"

"Garden hose?" Krista suggested. She didn't know what was going on, but the Willy Wonka factor was increasing by the second. "Shop vac?"

"Krista May, be serious! This is—"

"Yes. What is it?"

"It's . . ." Gran trailed off. Blinked. Then her shoulders sagged, and she said, "Ridiculous. That's what it is. It's ridiculous, just like your grandfather."

Uh-oh. Amusement draining, Krista closed the distance between them, her boots slipping a little in the spilled flour. "What did he do?"

"He called me old."

Krista smothered a wince. *Oh, Gramps. How could you?* "I'm sure he didn't mean it the way it came out."

"Yes, he did." Gran jerked up her chin, eyes flashing. "I am, of course. I'm old, old, old. It doesn't bother me to say it. But that's not the same as hearing *him* say it."

There was no arguing that one. To Big Skye, *old* was a curse word. "Oh, Gran." Krista put her chin on her grandmother's shoulder and wrapped her arms around her thin waist. "Do you want to tell me about it?"

"Not really. And don't worry, I pinned his ears back for it." She huffed. "I love the man, but when he gets in a mood, he's enough to drive a sane woman to drink."

"Or bake."

That got a watery laugh out of Gran. "Or bake," she agreed. "In my defense, there really is a charity thing today. I just got a little carried away." She patted Krista's hands where they linked across the front of her flour-dusted apron. "Don't fret, sweetie. We'll be fine. We always are, eventually."

What would it be like to have that sort of confidence in a relationship? "Is there anything I can do?"

"Could you check on him? I know the doctor said he's fine, but I worry."

They all did, especially since he rode out alone every day. "Of course. If I don't catch him at the barn, I'll ride out after him. Want me to bring him a cupcake?"

"Ha! Stubborn old goat will be lucky if I don't feed him sprouts and tofu for the rest of the week."

When Krista reached the barn, she found Deke and a couple of the guys finishing up cleaning the stalls. "Morning," she called as she came through the sliders. "Any drama to report?"

"Nothing yet." Deke did the knock-on-wood thing with a nearby stall door. "You?"

"Not that you guys need to worry about. Is my grandfather around?"

"Haven't seen him, but we cleaned the back barn first. He could've gone the long way around."

"Thanks." She tipped her hat. "Carry on."

The short covered walkway that connected the new and old barns had been intended to make things easier in the winter, but got stuffy in the summer, especially since Big Skye kept the doors closed at each end, the EMPLOYEES ONLY signs prominent. When Krista pushed through, though, the air freshened back up, bringing the scents of horses, sawdust, and hay. The back barn was narrower, the ceiling lower, with six stalls on one side, tack, grain, and grooming areas on the other, and a trophy case on one wall that held a mix of silver buckles, trophy cups, and framed photos—her and Jenny mugging for the camera at the old Harvest Fair Rodeo; their parents riding hand in hand in a long-ago Summer's End Parade; Big Skye making the eight-second buzzer on a saddle bronc back in the day.

"Gramps?" she called, but didn't get any answer. The stalls were empty and a glance in the tack stall showed no sign of his favorite saddle. But as she turned back for the main barn, hoofbeats sounded outside the open double doors.

They didn't sound good, though. The normal four-beat cadence of a flat-footed walk had taken on the syncopation that said the horse was hurting.

Krista hurried outside just as Bueno shambled through the back gate. The old mustang had his head down and his back humped under the saddle, not because he was trying to buck, but because he was trying to keep his weight off his front feet. Which wasn't easy when he was balancing a rider who sat square in the saddle, seeming oblivious.

"Gramps!" She rushed to Bueno's head. "What happened? Are you okay?"

He scowled down at her. "Of course. What kind of a question is that?"

"But Bueno—"

"It's a loose shoe, for Pete's sake. I brought him back down rather than riding it off and busting up his foot, didn't I?"

She gaped. "This is more than a loose shoe!"

"Arthritis, then. He hasn't warmed all the way up yet." He said it like it was the most obvious thing in the world. Which made something else all too obvious.

"Oh, Gramps." Her chest tightened and sudden tears prickled—at the horse's pain, at her grandfather's confusion, at the realization that everything was about to change, and not in a good way. "Get down." Her voice broke.

He flushed. "Now you listen here—"

"Please!" Something in her tone must have gotten through, because he grumbled and stepped stiffly down from the saddle, leaning hard on his stirrup and thudding to the ground.

Bueno swayed unsteadily, flinching as the weight forced him to balance on his front feet. But the tough mustang didn't even flatten his ears. He just rocked back onto his hind feet, like a dog stretching its spine, and looked at his longtime partner with stoic resignation, as if to say, *If this is what you want from me, you've got it.*

Big Skye scowled as the horse's discomfort finally seemed to register. "Nick must have quicked him when he reset that shoe. Serves me right for letting a vet set nails." He patted the sweaty bay neck. "Sorry, hoss. I'll pull that shoe for you. Set you back to rights."

But when Krista crouched and ran her hands down the animal's legs to his blazing-hot hooves, she knew it was far worse than a bad nail. Guilt stung—how long had this been going on? How had they all missed it? Rising, she bracketed her mouth with her hands, and bellowed, "Deke! I need you!"

Seconds later, his head popped out of a stall window in the main barn. "Yo!"

"Call Nick. Tell him to get here ASAP. Bueno is foundering, bad."

Deke cursed—the horseman's universal response to the word *founder*—and disappeared.

Big Skye spluttered. "What are you talking about, founder? That's crazy talk. He's just a little stiff, and we sure as blazes don't need the vet!"

He didn't see it. How did he not see it? She couldn't swallow, could barely breathe, but she forced her voice level and met her grandfather's faded, angry blue eyes as she said, very clearly and distinctly, "Bueno doesn't have a hot nail, Gramps. He's got laminitis."

The condition was a bad one, with the hoof wall separating and sloughing off while the bony structures of the front feet rotated and dropped, sometimes so badly that they came through the bottom of the horse's soles. It was incredibly painful and often fatal. And the earlier it was treated, the better the horse's chance.

Hoping to hell they weren't already too late, Krista whipped out her phone. It didn't have enough bars to call out, but it had enough juice to connect to the in-ranch network they had set up last summer. Gran picked up on the second ring. "Did you tell him about the sprouts and tofu?"

"We didn't get that far. Bueno's foundering."

"*No!* How bad is it?"

"Bad. Can you fill two of those big tubs with ice and have Dad bring them down here in the cart? And keep the icemaker going. We're going to need it."

When she rang off, Big Skye put himself in front of Krista with his arms folded and his eyes blazing. "You're getting mighty big for your britches these days, Missy, and I don't like it one gosh-darned bit."

"I'm sorry," she said, even as her heart tore cleanly in two. "You don't have to agree with me, or even like me, but I'm not letting you torture this horse for one more second. And, news flash? You'd better start being nicer to Gran, too."

"Ahem." Deke stood in a nearby doorway, looking like he wished he could retreat and do the whole *I just got here, didn't overhear anything* routine. When Krista gave him a "go ahead" wave, he said, "Ruth is going to do her best to get someone out here ASAP, but she says there are emergencies across the board this morning. Best case scenario, Nick will be here in two or three hours. Worst, case, late this afternoon."

Damn, damn, damn. But there was nothing they could do about it—Nick's practice covered a huge area; the other large-animal vet was strictly a cow guy; and the nearest equine hospital was a long, hard drive away. "Okay. Let's get some Banamine into him and some cold water on those feet. Clear the broodmare stall and bed it deep enough to swim in. If nothing else, we can get him more comfortable than he is right now."

Bracing herself for a knockdown, drag-out, she turned back to Big Skye.

He was cradling Bueno's head against his chest, with tears running down his weathered cheeks and a lost look in his eyes, like a cowboy who'd gotten launched off a bull and hit the dirt hard, and wasn't sure how he'd gotten into the middle of a big arena with a scoreboard that had two-point-five seconds on the clock.

Except in this case, she was afraid it was more that the clock had gone past the eight-second mark and the buzzer had sounded. Or maybe it had been more gradual than that—a gentle slide, like when an old dog started to show its age and you didn't consciously notice it until you came across a picture from years ago and saw the difference.

She didn't want to give it a name, even in her mind. But, oh, the ache.

When their eyes met, he said, "Save him." On the

surface it was an order, but there was grief and guilt in the way his big-knuckled hands stroked the grizzled muzzle, and Big Skye's eyes held a shattered sort of understanding.

She wanted to wrap her arms around him like she had done with Gran, but she didn't know how to anymore. So instead, she dialed another number, hoping it had the bars to go through.

Wyatt picked up on the fourth ring. "Hey! Sorry, I got caught up working in the shop." Led Zeppelin was playing in the background, with Robert Plant singing about rambling on.

Heart tugging—that he was there, that he sounded happy—she said, "You're not late. But we've got a situation up here, and I need your help."

"Name it."

"Bueno is foundering and Nick is tied up. Can you get his feet stabilized?"

"I'm on my way."

It took Wyatt two sweaty, backbreaking hours to pull the ailing horse's shoes and build makeshift stabilizers from the materials he had on hand, but by the time he killed the forge and stripped off his gloves, the gelding had a glimmer of life in his eyes as he picked at the hay Krista's grandfather was holding up for him, a handful at a time.

That didn't mean they were out of the woods, though.

"Thank you." Krista tipped her head against his shoulder. "He looks much better."

"Once we've got some X-rays to look at, we can see how much his coffin bones have rotated, and work on leveling them off. Or, at a minimum, keeping them from sinking any further."

"Fingers crossed," she said, because they both knew they might not need a treatment plan. "At least we should be able to move him into the main barn now." A glance at her phone brought a wince. "And you and I have a ride to lead—there's no way Junior can manage this week's crowd by himself." The twenty guests were all executives, friends from a big IT company who vacationed together every other year and seemed to exist solely to one-up one another with little regard for collateral damage.

It was the first time he'd seen her sigh at the thought of riding out with her guests, like it was a chore rather than a pleasure. She was worried, not just about the horse, but about her grandfather and the decisions she and her family were going to have to make. Even standing there, Big Skye looked drawn and deflated, like someone had let out a few pounds of air.

"Junior and I can handle them," Wyatt said, nudging her toward her grandfather. "I'll take Deke to ride sweep. You stay here."

It was a sign of just how bad things were that she didn't argue. She just reached up on her tiptoes and brushed her lips across his. "Thank you. Good luck with them, and I'll see you tonight."

Those last four words were ones a man could get used to, he thought.

*   *   *

Wyatt was done with the guests and back waiting with the others by the time Nick showed up near dinnertime, harried, exhausted-looking, and deeply apologetic. Jenny was there along with Krista and their parents and grandparents, all of whom wore the game faces of longtime ranchers—the ones that said *whatever comes next, we'll deal with it.* When Bueno hobbled out of the oversize stall, looking like a cyborg in his cobbled-together therapeutic shoes, Nick gave a low whistle. "That's a heck of a MacGyver, Webb."

"Want me to take them off for the X-rays?"

"Please." Nick stood back while Wyatt got to work unbolting the cuffs and working them off. "Any idea what brought this on? Did he get into the grain or some unusually lush grass?"

"No grain, no grass," Krista said. "Big Skye and I have gone through it and we can't think of anything that could've triggered this."

"When did you first notice the problem?"

There was a pause, then Big Skye said, "A few days, maybe a week. I . . . er, harrumph . . . I thought he was just getting older." His voice sounded rusty, like it was the first thing he had said in a while.

Nick jotted it down. "He's got some age on him, it's true, but he's fit and healthy. We'll run some blood tests and see if his thyroid is slowing down. If so, we can medicate to keep this from happening again. In the meantime"—he pushed away from the wall—"let's get a look at what's going on inside these feet of yours, old man."

As he got to work, Wyatt leaned back against the wall next to Krista, very aware of when she took his hand and twined their fingers together.

It was the first time he'd been around all of the Skyes at once, the first time he'd really been face-to-face with her father since he and Krista started sleeping together. And, even though he'd gotten some very sincere thanks for his work on the welcome sign, he still wasn't sure where he stood with the Skye family. It wasn't easy to keep his distance when their lives were so intertwined with Krista's, and when the things that hurt them took a crack at her, too.

Like the bay mustang that sagged on the crossties, and the old cowboy standing there, stroking the droopy muzzle as Nick studied the digital X-rays on his laptop.

"Well?" Big Skye demanded with a hint of his usual tone.

"His coffin bones have rotated and dropped," Nick reported, "more on the right than the left. He's got good sole depth to work with, though. If we can stop the progression right where it is, he's got a good chance to be pasture sound, maybe even go back under saddle with the right shoeing job."

Big Skye let out a long, gusty sigh. "Thanks, Doc. Appreciate it."

"Thank Wyatt, here. He's the one that got the rotation stopped. The way you guys described it, I have a feeling this would be a very different conversation if he hadn't been here."

Wyatt suddenly found himself at the center of a whole lot of attention, ranging from Krista's proud smile to her father's *oh, hell* look of resignation. Holding up both hands, he said, "I did what anybody would. He's a nice horse."

But Ed straightened reluctantly and said, "Not everybody would've had the skills to help like you did." He held out a hand. "Thanks. Mustang Ridge owes you one, Webb."

"You don't owe me—" Wyatt broke off at the determined look in the other man's eyes, the wistful one in Krista's. Knowing that it would matter to her, and that she'd already had a hell of a day when it came to her family, he shook her father's hand. "Appreciate it. And you're welcome."

And what do you know? Instead of closing in on him, the barn walls stayed right where they were.

22

That evening, with Bueno resting as comfortably as they could manage and Krista putting in some time with the guests, Wyatt gave Klepto the usual "don't even think about misbehaving" lecture—which was starting to feel overkill, given that the dog hadn't put a paw wrong in the past few weeks—and headed out to meet Sam at the Rope Burn.

The place was weeknight quiet, with the DJ booth empty, the mechanical bull doing a mechanical snooze, a small crowd at the bar and maybe half of the tables occupied. The bartender lifted a hand when Wyatt came in. "Howdy, Webb. What can I get you?"

He'd never been big on having a regular dive before—once the servers knew his name, it started feeling like a routine—but the options were pretty limited in Three Ridges. And, besides, the way this place changed depending on the night and the entertainment, it hadn't started feeling stale yet. "Hey, J.J. How about a longneck and some loaded nachos? And let Sam know

I'm in the back room when he gets here. There's a dart-board calling my name."

"Will do."

Ten minutes later, Wyatt was seeing how many darts he could bury in the bull's-eye—he was up to three, with a couple of others scattered in the inner ring—when Sam came through the door, carrying the nachos and a couple of longnecks.

Wyatt held up the darts. "Bull's-eye baseball?" It had been their college go-to.

"I dunno. It's been a while, and it looks like you've been practicing."

Without admitting that he had a dartboard over the sink in his shop, Wyatt said, "I'll give you a handicap. You can start with the third inning."

"Deal." Sam waited while Wyatt cleared the chalk-board and set up the scoring grid. Then he took the proffered darts and, without missing a beat, sank two in the thin outer ring of number three, two in the mid-dle ring, and one in the bull's-eye, all within a ten-count: *thwack, thwack, thwack, thwack, thwack.*

Wyatt groaned. "I did not just let you hustle me."

"Hey, I didn't wrangle you into making a stupid bet first, did I? Say, five hundred bucks that I couldn't pick up that barrel-racing brunette? You know, the one I later found out you knew darn well had a boyfriend who moonlighted as a bouncer?"

"Ah, good times." Wyatt got his bull's-eye, but only racked up three runs in the number one slice of the dartboard. "You should move on. I know I have."

Taking his place, Sam sighted along his first dart. "Speaking of moving on—or in this case, circling back—how's Krista?"

"She's good." He propped an elbow and dug into the nachos. "We're good. Had some excitement at the ranch today, though." He told Sam about Bueno, skimming over the family stuff.

"Sounds like you saved the day." Sam nailed the bull's-eye along with some real estate in number four. "Also sounds like you're settling in up there on the ridge. You thinking about extending your stay? It's real pretty up there in the winter."

"There's no heat in the workshop, and I'm not interested in freezing my balls off. Besides, we said all along that it was only for a couple of months." And he wasn't ready to admit he'd been thinking otherwise. He took the darts. Missed the bull's-eye. "Crap."

"We said or you said?"

Wyatt handed over the darts. "What's that supposed to mean?"

Sam leaned back against a nearby pool table. "It just seems to me that you've got a pattern. Remember Tricia? And what was her name, Desiree? Seems to me you were a whole lot more on board with the 'keep it short and simple' than they were."

"Desiree didn't like dogs."

"Which is why you got a dog."

"I like my dog."

"He's a menace. But weirdly brilliant, I'll admit. I found my stuff stacked in a circle in the sun room. It was like Stonehenge or something, only made of unopened condom boxes, water bottles, and four left sneakers."

"Send me a picture."

"I will. And you're changing the subject."

"For the record, Klepto seems to have put his thieving behind him. Most days he's so tired from riding out with me that all he does is thump down and sleep. I'm even thinking of changing his name. To Brillo, maybe, or Unibrow."

Sam chuckled and took his turn with the darts. "Sounds like he's right at home. How about you? Because I gotta tell you, bro, I'm not getting a really strong 'I'm outa here in ten more days' vibe."

Ten days? Seriously? Wyatt did the math in his head, caught himself frowning. "Is there any particular reason why you're busting on me when there's a steady stream of women in and out of the mansion?"

"Because I think you've got it bad for her. And I'm kind of having fun watching you squirm on the hook— sort of a *better you than me* deal."

Wyatt's dart went *thunk* and stuck, quivering, in the wood paneling beside the board. He shot Sam a disgusted look. "You've been watching the Lifetime channel again, haven't you? Or is this your version of trash talking?"

"Just calling it how I see it." Eight more darts and Sam had run the board and the game was over. He toasted Wyatt with his beer. "You lose."

"Bite me." But as they set up for another game and

the conversation moved on to the newest *Aliens vs. Lunchmeat* or whatever the hell game Sam was into this week, Wyatt found himself thinking maybe his friend wasn't all that wrong. Not that he was squirming on anybody's hook, but he wasn't counting down the days, either, and the grass on the other side of the fence didn't look any greener than the stuff he was munching. So to speak.

Which meant . . . what? He didn't know, and he sure as hell wasn't going to talk to Mr. Lunchmeat about it. But as he took his spot for game two, he couldn't help thinking that the buzzer still felt a long ways off, and wondering what Krista would think about extending their ride past the Harvest Fair.

Early the next morning, Krista slipped out of bed before dawn.

Wyatt stirred and said thickly, "Hang on a minute. Klepto and I will walk you over."

"I know the way. Get some more sleep. You earned it last night." She dredged up a wink, though it was tough to feel sexy when she was staring down the barrel of a family meeting.

He snapped on the light and scrubbed a hand through his hair, leaving it adorably hedgehogged. "I thought I would work with Jupiter for a bit this morning."

Knowing that meant he wanted to drop her off at the family meeting, wanted to be nearby when it was over, she leaned in and kissed him. "Last one in the shower is a rotten egg."

Half an hour later, more waterlogged—and water-loved—than showered, but far more relaxed than she had been when she awakened, Krista let herself into the main house and headed for the dining room. There, the photos had been piled on the sideboard, and her parents, Gran, and Jenny were already at the table, sipping coffee and nibbling on cupcakes.

Jenny toasted her with pink-and-sprinkles. "Morning. Have a frosted sugar muffin."

Krista took the empty chair beside her. "Is that what we're calling them?"

"Yep. It sounds more breakfast-y than cupcakes worthy of a Barbie-themed birthday party, don't you think?" Despite the quip, though, Jenny looked tired. They all did, especially Gran. And Krista had seen the stress-circles under her own eyes in the steamed-up bathroom mirror.

Taking a cupcake and peeling away the paper, she looked across the table at Gran. "How did he seem last night?"

"Quiet. He apologized for being an ass yesterday morning."

"Anything else?"

"Said he was tired and he was going to bed." She blew across her coffee, but didn't take a sip. "I still can't believe he was riding Bueno in that condition. If you hadn't seen them . . ." She shook her head, expression hollow. "Being cranky with us is one thing—we're family, we can either take it or tell him to stuff it. But the animals can't. They won't. Which means that it's up to us to make sure that things like this—or the Betty Crocker incident the other week—won't happen again."

"But how?" Jenny said.

"He needs to see another doctor," Rose said firmly. "A specialist, someone who'll be able to tell the difference between dementia, senility, Alzheimer's, and just plain getting older and slowing down."

And there they were—the words Krista hadn't let herself think. The futures she didn't want to consider. Swallowing a sudden surge of nausea, she set her cupcake aside. "Do you think he'll go?"

"If we sit him down as a family, yes. Which is what we're going to have to do anyway." Rose hesitated. "I'm not sure he should ride out alone anymore. If he's missed something as obvious as founder, who's to say he wouldn't walk right under a tree that's got a wildcat in it? Or worse?"

Krista didn't want to know what would qualify as worse in her mom's book, any more than she wanted to think that she was once again going to be taking things away—his horses, his job, his sense of freedom . . . God. Was it really better this way?

"What if we assign him an assistant?" she suggested. "Somebody who'll follow his orders, but also keep a good eye on things. Deke, maybe."

"We can work out the details later," Gran said. "For now, he needs to know that we don't want him riding out alone until after he's been to the doctor. Once we know what we're up against, we'll have a better idea how to deal with it." But while her voice was steady, her hand shook slightly as she lifted her mug and took a sip.

The sight nearly broke Krista's heart. Abandoning her seat, she came around behind Gran and wrapped her in a hug, followed moments later by Jenny, so the three of them rocked together in sympathy. "It'll be okay," Krista said against the soft white hair at her gran's temple. "We'll get through this. We always do. We just need to sit him down and lay it out, and then we'll go from there."

But Jenny said, "Are you sure that's such a good idea?"

"Why? What do you have in mind?"

"I don't know, but it seems to me he doesn't do well with the whole *hey, Gramps, we voted and you lost* thing. Maybe instead of a family meeting, he should hear it from just one of us."

"From who, you?" Krista shook her head. "Don't, Jenny. He loves making movies with you, and I'd hate to see that go away, too." And not Gran, either, because they already had their own issues to work through, or her parents. Which left them with—

"I'll do it."

Krista looked at her father in surprise. "Dad?"

He nodded. "He won't like hearing it from me, but he'll listen. And the way I see it, a heart-to-heart is overdue. I should've told him a long time ago to ease up on you, that he should be grateful you care so much about this place that you're not just thinking about how to keep it going for the next five or ten years—you're thinking about the next five or ten generations." He tipped his head toward the stacked pictures. "That's what the Skyes are really about. Not the cattle, but the land, and the people who live on it."

Her emotions rose even higher, making it hard to breathe through a closed-down throat. "Don't apologize. You didn't do anything wrong."

"Yes, I did. But I can fix it." He climbed to his feet, dropped a kiss on the top of her head. "I'll go find him, talk to him. Wish me luck."

"You don't need any," Big Skye's voice growled from the doorway. "Because I'm right here."

He looked like hell. He was haggard and hollow-eyed, and wearing a smear of white paste on his sleeve, suggesting that Bueno had been feeling good enough to wrestle over his morning dose of drugs. Krista surged to her feet. "You should sit, Gramps. Here. Let me get you some coffee."

He waved her off. "You sit, girlie, because I have something to say to you." Those faded blue eyes locked on her, then swept the room. "I've got something to say to all of you."

"It better not be that we're too damn old," Gran said with some asperity.

"No. It's that I am."

Krista sank into her chair, legs going shaky because here it was. She had thought they would have time to talk it through, plan it out, get a doctor involved. She wasn't ready for this, didn't want to hear it.

Really, though, this wasn't about her.

"I've been forgetting things," he said heavily. "Names, details, what I walked into a room to get. Even trails. The other day I almost didn't make it back. Might not have if it hadn't been for Bueno. And then yesterday I near killed him. Best horse I ever owned, and that's the thanks I give him."

Ed came around the table and touched his shoulder. "Sit down, Pops. We'll figure this out together."

But Big Skye shook him off. "I'm not done. Because you were right—you should've kicked my hiney a long time ago for how I was treating your girl. My granddaughter."

"Gramps—" Krista began.

"Hush." He stumped over, turned an empty chair to face hers, and then dropped heavily into it. Leaning forward, he searched her face, eyes so intense that she had the sudden urge to squirm. Voice cracking, he said, "I'm sorry, Krista. You were right about—about the cattle, the guests, the business. All of it."

Throat lumping, she managed, "It's okay."

"Not even close. I wanted everything to stay the same, and when it didn't, I took it out on you. I should've told you how amazing you are, and how proud I am of what you've made this place into." He squeezed her fingers. "Mustang Ridge is alive because of you. It's something wonderful because of you."

Krista couldn't breathe. Why couldn't she breathe?

He leaned in and kissed her brow, bringing the scents of cinnamon and neat's-foot oil, and making her feel like she was eight again, and he was giving her that first short-lived pocket knife. "Thank you, Krissy," he said gruffly. "Mustang Ridge is lucky to have you. And so am I."

A sob buried itself in her throat, and she launched herself into his arms. "Oh, Gramps!"

His arms closed around her; his scent enfolded her. And suddenly it didn't matter that his arms were thinner and his middle was softer—he was just Gramps. And she was his cowgirl. Tears broke free and tracked down—for him, for herself, for all the things that had already changed and all the things that were soon going to.

He patted her shoulder. "I'm sorry, little girl. So sorry. I'll do better from now on." He said it over and over again, until the quick burst of tears dried up and she drew a shuddering breath.

Easing away, she swiped at her face. "It's out there now," she said with a watery smile. "No takesies backsies."

"No takesies backsies," he said solemnly, and offered her a gnarled, twisted, and oft-broken pinkie.

She linked with him and they pinkie swore, like they had when she was little. Then she turned to her sister. "You want in on this?"

"Nope. This one's yours." But Jenny slung an arm around her neck and gave her a hug and a smacking kiss on the top of her head. "You earned it."

Big Skye patted her knee, then rose creakily and moved around the table. "There's one more thing that needs saying."

Gran looked up when he stopped by her chair, and

her eyes softened. "I don't need the words, Arthur. I know your heart."

"Yes, you do. But I'm going to give you the words anyway." He crouched down, knees popping, so his eyes were level with hers. Taking her hands, he said, "I'm sorry I've been a beast lately. I get mad when I forget things, and I've been taking that out on you. That stops now. I swear it. We're a team, Biscuit. You and me against the world."

Gran's eyes filled. "Oh, Arthur." And she flung her arms around him and pressed her lips to his.

And, darn it, there went Krista's tears again. But this time she didn't wipe them away, because this was good. It was right. She didn't know exactly what next month was going to look like for her grandparents, or next year. But whatever they were facing, they would do it together.

From high up on the hill beside the marker stones, Wyatt watched as Krista's grandparents came down the front porch steps hand in hand, and Gran did a light-footed little shuffle of a dance while Big Skye guided her around in a wide circle.

"Well, what do you know?" He patted Jupiter's neck. "That's got to be a good sign. Now, where's our girl?" He hadn't seen Krista leave the house, but he'd been on the ridge for only a couple of minutes. "Ah," he said when Lucky emerged from the barn with a bridle but no saddle, and a lithe blond figure boosted herself nimbly onto his back. "There she is."

He didn't know if she saw him or he'd guessed right that she would come up to the marker stones for some quiet time after the meeting, but she guided Lucky through an open gate and straight for the dirt track leading up to where he and Jupiter stood. Wyatt held his ground, heart bumping at the sight of her astride the big black gelding, moving with his motion, like the two of them were one.

What a woman, he thought. And felt himself fall a little deeper in the hole that he was already farther down than he'd meant to go. But Sam was right—he was hooked, at least as far as he ever let himself get. And at the moment, he wasn't struggling to get away.

"Hey, cowboy." She rode up beside him, controlling Lucky with a shift of weight and a touch of the reins. "Fancy meeting you here."

"I had a feeling you might come up here." He nudged Jupiter closer and reached over to draw his knuckles across her cheek, seeing where the tears had been. "How'd it go?"

"It went . . ." She blew out a soft breath. "It went. Mom said the words. Alzheimer's. Dementia. Senility. The things none of us want to think about."

"Ah, baby." He slid his hand down her arm, linking their fingers. "I'm sorry."

"No, it's okay. It's . . . Well, it'll be what it is, right? He'll see the doctors, they'll give it a name if they can, and we'll deal with it. Him and Gran and the rest of us, we'll deal with it. And he apologized." Her lips curved softly. "He said he was proud of me, of what I've done here."

A strange pressure shifted in his chest—there and gone so quickly that he might've thought he imagined it, except for the fullness left behind. "Good." It came out in a husky rasp. "That's good."

Something must have come through in his voice, because Lucky's head came up and her eyes sharpened on his. "Wyatt, are you okay? You look . . . odd."

He felt odd, with that edge-of-a-cliff feeling that used to come when he'd gotten the last twist of the bull rope wrapped around his gloved hand, then tucked his chin to his chest and gave the ground crew the nod that said, *Go ahead, open the gate and start the clock.* Except he wasn't starting a clock now. Exactly the opposite. "I've been thinking."

"About?"

"Us."

Her expression flattened, went wary. "Oh?"

"Actually, I was thinking about how you'll still be running guests through here even after the end of the official season. And especially now, with things up in the air with your grandfather . . . I was thinking I could stay on for a while longer. If you wanted me to, that is."

23

Krista blinked at Wyatt while her brain did its best to catch up. Because a couple of weeks ago—heck, even a couple of days ago—she would've said the only thing less likely than her grandfather apologizing to her would be Wyatt wanting to stay on past the Mustang Makeover. But the look in his eyes and his grip on her hand said he meant it.

This was real. It was happening.

"How much past?" Were they talking about a couple of weeks, or did he have something else in mind?

"I don't know. A while. Eventually, I'll have to go back down to Denver to do the heavy lifting on the APM piece. But maybe by then the guest season will be over for real, and you can come visit." One corner of his mouth kicked up. "I'm sure Klepto would be happy to see you."

"Just Klepto?"

"And me, too." He leaned in and brushed his lips across hers in the lightest of kisses, one that reminded her of their very first, back at that long-ago waterfall.

Leaning his forehead against hers, he said, "What do you think? Are you willing to throw out the expiration date and see what happens?"

Her heart took a long, slow roll in her chest—one that reminded her of being twenty and stupid in love again. Except she wasn't either of those things now. She was older and wiser, and she knew better than to assume she knew what he was offering. "We're still talking about a good time here, right? No strings, no promises, just two grown-ups enjoying each other."

His grin widened. "Is that a yes?"

It shouldn't be, she knew. But if she had learned anything that morning, it was that nothing stayed the same, even if you wanted it to. And if right now was pretty darn good—the best she'd ever had—why not let it go on a little longer?

Because it'll hurt when it ends, she told herself. But that was already guaranteed, wasn't it? She might not love him, but she was as close as she could get without going over that line. He challenged her, excited her, impressed her, occasionally infuriated her, made love to her, made her laugh, made her sigh . . .

And she wasn't ready to give that up yet. Not even close.

So, not sure whether she was being a coward or the bravest she'd ever been, she nodded. "That's a yes, cowboy. Let's throw out the clock and stay on this bull as long as we're still having fun!"

"Yee-haw! Come here, cowgirl!" He pulled her toward him for a deep and thorough kiss.

Senses firing, she leaned in and twined her arms around his neck, then gave a whoop when he straightened and scooped her up, sliding her off Lucky's warm, slippery back and into his lap. "Beast!" She drummed on his chest. "You did that on purpose!"

"Do you blame me? Seems to me this is an occasion, and an occasion calls for a grand entrance." With that, he sent Jupiter rocking down the hill in a showy, toe-flipping canter while Lucky ran alongside, tossing his head and humping his back in a series of crowhops that looked like the equine version of *wheee*!

Sunday morning of the last official week of the season—where had the second half of the summer *gone*?—Krista took the stage at the back of the dining hall, powered up the microphone, and gave the twenty-five break-fasting guests a big, "Hello, everybody, and welcome once again to Makeover Week!"

That got some whoops and scattered applause, and she smiled as she scanned the crowd. Joan and Sabra, sitting together in the back, were breast cancer survivors who had met in a chemo clinic and were celebrating a disease-free milestone. At a middle table, Bob had lost almost two hundred pounds over the past three years, and had always wanted to rope a cow. And in the front, sitting beside her mother, birthday-girl Claire gave a shy, gap-toothed smile and pointed to the ribbon bracelet she wore on her wrist.

Winking at the little girl, Krista continued. "Remember yesterday how I said we're going to have some special guests joining us throughout the week? Well, hang on to your hats—or, rather, get ready to give them up—because after our ride today, we're offering a field trip to Bootsy's Saddlery and Western Apparel, where Bootsy herself is going to give us some shopping tips."

She ran down the rest of the week's nonriding plans—an in-house spa day, hair and makeup consults, and two-step lessons, all leading up to the Mustang Makeover on Saturday, followed by an after party back at the ranch. With the usual schedule extended by a day there was room to fit in the extras, though just barely. And with the last of Big Skye's tests coming back negative for the scary stuff and his new doctor talking about some small dietary changes that she thought would bump his energy levels and help with his spells of confusion, it was easy for her to be upbeat.

"But enough about what's happening later, right? Let's talk about the horses!" That got a second, louder cheer and a couple of whistles. As Krista launched into her Sunday-morning spiel about barn safety, boots rang on the porch and the saloon-style doors swung to let Wyatt through.

Her heart probably didn't actually skip a beat. But after last night it sure felt like it did—they had ridden out to the waterfall by moonlight, built a fire on the ledge, fed each other strawberries and wine, and made love in the cave. Doing her darnedest not to blush, she raised a hand in greeting.

He touched the brim of his hat and mouthed, *We're all set.*

When heads started swiveling, she said, "Speaking of the horses, I'd like to introduce our head wrangler, Wyatt Webb. He's a rodeo star, a stellar horseman, and an old friend, and together we're going to do our very best to make sure each and every one of you has a fabulous week in the saddle. But first, we need your help with something. We'd like you to be our audience as we—and the fabulous Jupiter—run through our first dress rehearsal of the freestyle we'll be doing at the fair this weekend. Are you guys game to sit in the stands and make a little noise? Then follow Wyatt out to the arena, and I'll see you in a minute!"

The guests made plenty of good-natured noise as they came to their feet. Most of them followed him out, but Vicki and Claire hung back.

"Hey, you two." Krista grinned down at the child. "And happy birthday, kiddo! A little birdie told me today is the day." The same little birdie had arranged for there to be cake for everyone later, along with a couple of surprises that would be delivered to their cabin later this afternoon.

Claire tucked herself behind her mom, but peered out, eyes alight.

"All these new people have her feeling shy," Vicky confided.

"I'm not new people, am I?" But Krista didn't push. It was usually better to give a spooky horse—or child—room to get curious. "It seems to me there's someone in the barn who's looking forward to seeing you."

"Marshmallow?" It was barely a whisper, but four

days sooner than Krista had heard anything out of the little girl the last time.

"Yep. He can't wait to hang out with you this week."

Claire held up her bracelet with an expression that made it into a question.

"Does he still have his ribbon? I don't know. You'll have to see for yourself." Okay, that wasn't entirely true—Krista had plaited the pink polka-dotted ribbon into the gray pony's mane yesterday morning and double-checked it half an hour ago. But she figured the universe would forgive her for the fib. To Vicki, she said, "How have you guys been?" They hadn't had a chance to catch up yesterday.

"Good! Things are good. Work is work, but Claire and I have been looking at barns near the house, and we may have found one that checks all the boxes on the list you gave us, so we're hoping to start lessons for her soon. What's new with you? Besides the new wrangler, that is. An old friend, you said?"

"College boyfriend."

That got her an elbow nudge. "And current one, too, I take it."

Krista took a quick glance around. "Mayyybe."

Vicki hooted. "I knew it! That look he shot you." She fanned herself. "Hoo, baby! And hot! Wow, I won't mind watching that backside on the trail."

"Annnd I think I hear the horses calling us," Krista said, laughing as she herded them toward the door with a bounce in her step. She had been looking forward to Makeover Week even before the summer began. Now she had a top-notch horse to ride in the big event, a skit that was shaping up to be a real showstopper, and a drop-dead gorgeous cowboy to wake up with every morning, without an expiration date in sight. What could be better?

In his workshop, Wyatt was so deep in the creative process—or in this case the *uncreative* process, as the dog was the only thing that looked anything like the picture in his head so far—that it took a minute for the ring of his cell phone to penetrate, another for his eyes to adjust to the unexpected name on the screen.

He hesitated, then answered. "Hey, Ash. Happy belated birthday. Did Ma forward my card?"

"Is that your way of asking if I'm still in LA?"

Sigh. "No, it was my way of asking if you had fun with the hundred bucks I sent you. But, hey, since you brought it up . . . Are you still in LA?"

"Yeah, I am." Sullen. "And thanks for the money. It paid for some gas."

No doubt for Kenny's skanky van. "How are you guys doing?"

There was a beat of silence. Then Ashley said, "What, no dig about Kenny's skanky van?"

He chuckled. "Would it have done anything other than annoy you?"

"No."

"Then why bother? Besides, I don't want to dig at you. I'd rather hear what you've been up to."

There was another pause, then she said, "Well, we

went to see the tar pits the other day. Have you ever been there?"

"Mammoths and stuff? Sure. Pretty cool."

"I thought so. Some of the skeletons reminded me of your sculptures. It was like they were moving without actually moving, you know?"

"Yeah." He tucked the phone tighter against his ear, suddenly hearing an echo of the little girl who'd had a question for everything and an eye for the beauty in ordinary life. Back then, he'd thought she would do something artsy with her life. Funny that it had wound up being the other way around. "I liked the fishbowl thing they've got in the tar pit museum. You know, where you can watch the archaeologists working?"

"They weren't there when we were, but I'd like to go back and see them on my next day off." She hesitated. "I'm, um, working in an art supply store. It's just part-time, and I don't make much . . ."

Did she always sound so hesitant, or was it only with him? He hoped not. "Do you like the people?"

"They're pretty cool. The boss is obsessed with cleaning the coffeemaker and making sure all our lunches have our names and dates on them if we use the fridge, but other than that everyone seems nice. I've only been there a few weeks, but I made a display the other day and Carrie—that's the boss—really liked it. She said maybe I could do others."

"Send me a picture, okay?"

"You want to see it?"

"I asked, didn't I?" And it had made her voice stronger, even put a hint of pleasure in her tone. Not to mention that this was probably the longest they had been on the phone in forever. "And take a picture of the coffeemaker, too. You've got me curious."

Her laugh was a light, tinkling noise he hadn't heard nearly enough of lately. "What's up with you? Is the new sculpture going awesome or something?"

"Actually, it's complete crap at the moment."

"Then why do you sound happy?"

"Because I am." It was out before he knew what hit him, startling in its simplicity. "I'm happy."

"I didn't think you did happy. Brooding and artistic, maybe, but not happy. What gives? Are you in Denver?"

"Wyoming. I'm working at a dude ranch."

"Really?" She sounded thrilled. "You're back riding?"

"I'm even competing this weekend." He filled her in on the Mustang Makeover, making her laugh with his description of the bellhop skit.

Something must have come through in his voice, though, because hers went teasing. "So . . . tell me about this boss of yours. Is she pretty?"

She's an angel, only better, because she's mine to touch. Grinning at the almost-poetry that had found its way into his head—and thinking the world should be grateful he'd gone the sculpture route instead of free verse— he said, "She's something special, that's for sure. We knew each other back in college."

"Really?" Her voice went up a couple of notches. "She's the one?"

"Huh?" He hadn't told her about Krista back in the day. Hadn't told anyone.

"The one who broke your heart and sent you bouncing around after school."

"You've got that backward. I broke her heart, and I'm the one who bounced. Remember? It's in the DNA."

She made a *pfft* noise. "Not even close. Dad bounced because he wanted to pretend he was eternally twenty years old—which, by the way, stops looking cool after thirty-five or so, and really looks janky now that he's over fifty. But you've been bouncing because you haven't had any reason to stay in one place. Maybe now you do."

A cool breeze touched the back of his neck, coming through the open shop door. "You've been listening to Mom again. You know that can be dangerous."

That got a giggle. "She isn't always wrong. She always said one of these days you'd find a woman who makes you want to stick around."

"I'm not really a stick-with-it sort of guy."

"You've stuck with the horses all your life."

"Only because that's what I grew up knowing. That made it easy."

Again with the *pfft*. "Admit it. You love them, and part of you wishes you were born back when it was enough to have a good saddle and some skills, without all the PR and Internet crap."

"I . . . Hm." It was tough to argue that one when he was staring at a campfire scene that gave a shout-out to exactly that. "When did you get so smart?"

"When you weren't looking," she said tartly, but he had a feeling she was enjoying the opportunity to give him grief, rather than the other way around.

"Well, I'm looking now, and I like what I see. Or hear. Whatever." He paused, wondering how he could bring things back around to Kenny and stuff like *Is he paying his share yet?* or *Is he treating you right?*

"Don't say it," she warned.

"Say what?"

"Whatever you were thinking. This is going so well, you're just dying to do something to set me off. Well, guess what? I'm hanging up before this perfectly lovely conversation goes off the rails. There's one more thing, though."

He grinned, appreciating her in a way he hadn't done for a long time. "What's that, sis?"

"Welcome back, Wyatt."

"Huh? I didn't go anywhere."

"If you say so. Love you, big brother. Maybe I'll even visit you one of these days." She hung up before he could answer one way or the other.

Shaking his head, he set the phone aside and said to Klepto, "Well, that was interesting." When was the last time they had talked like that? Years, he thought, pretty much since she bagged out on college and he had blasted her for it, seeing her setting up to make so many of the same mistakes that Ma had.

He had missed talking to her, he realized. They had come from the same place, had some of the same experiences. There was continuity there, and maybe he hadn't given it enough credit, hadn't given *her* enough credit.

Besides, if he'd learned anything from being around the Skyes, it was that family mattered. So maybe he should find a way to think of his as something other than a chore. "Now there's a thought."

"Whuff?" Klepto tilted his head in inquiry, or maybe to see if Wyatt was going to fork over a biscuit.

"Nothing. Just talking to myself." And staring at the mess-in-progress, where the cowboy in the middle suddenly looked okay, with his thumbs hooked in his pockets and his hat tipped down low, but the dog looked wrong again. Stepping back, Wyatt frowned at the metal skeletons, at the sketches, and felt something nibble at the edges of his mind—an aha moment that wouldn't quite gel. After a moment, though, he shook his head. "Nope. Not seeing it."

Oh, well. He would figure it out—at least the ideas were flowing now, and the pictures were there in his head. And if worse came to worst, he could always tear things down and start over. He was good at that.

Bootsy's Saddlery was a local fixture, from the two-story tall fiberglass boot out front to the faux-log exterior and the scent of expensive leather coming from the back rooms. And from the way the greenhorns' eyes lit when they walked in and looked around at the walls of hats and boots, the spinning racks of colorful clothes, and the towering displays of blinged-out belts and glittering buckles, Krista could tell it had been the perfect choice for the "pick your outfit for the Harvest Fair" portion of Makeover Week.

"Dibs!" Bob beelined for a display of horse blankets, and held one up against his chest. "It's my color, don't you think?"

"I don't know." Sabra pretended to consider the question. "Do you really think Black Watch plaid says *country fair*?"

"So you'd go with the solid blue, instead?"

"Hello, everyone!" Bootsy called from the back of the main room, where she stood on a short flight of stairs that led up to a tack-filled loft. A lithe, dark-haired fiftysomething, she wore a flamingo pink cowboy hat with a peacock feather stuck in the band, along with tight jeans and a flirty, jewel green top that showed off cleavage and rhinestones, and somehow stopped short of making her look like a disco ball. She gave a little wave and came down the stairs, angling her body to show off her generous curves and the high-heeled boots that made tapping noises on the way down.

The lady knew how to make an entrance, that was for sure, and Krista wasn't surprised to see Peter's jaw drop. The recently divorced dentist was determined to get on with his life—ergo, Makeover Week—and appeared to have "vacation hookup" pretty high on his to-do list. He had struck out with Joan and Vicki, but as Bootsy sauntered through the front room of the shop with an extra wiggle in her walk, she gave him an up-and-down, as if she liked what she was seeing.

Or else Bootsy was just being Bootsy and Krista was

doing the same annoying "I'm getting some, so you should be, too" thing she had accused Jenny of just the other week.

"I thought you said you were bringing me city folk," Bootsy said cheerfully to Krista. "This crew looks like it's ready to hit the roundup trail."

"They can hold their own in the saddle," Krista agreed. "But we need to get them ready for a night of square dancing, cotton candy, and good old country fun."

"We can do that!" Bootsy cupped her hands around her mouth and called, "Come on, girls. We're going to need reinforcements!"

Four more employees, all in feather-topped hats—which wasn't the norm, and Krista appreciated that they had gone the extra mile—came out of the back rooms and descended on the greenhorns, splitting the herd and driving the smaller groups through the racks.

"My group is doing hats first!" Bootsy announced. "The perfect party outfit starts with the right lid!" She held out a hand to Claire. "What do you say, kiddo? You want to try on an awesome hat like mine?"

Krista started toward them, wanting to intervene before it got too awkward—Bootsy was big and loud, and Claire had only just started talking to the other guests. "How about we—"

She broke off as Claire put her tiny hand in Bootsy's manicured one, and said, quite clearly, "Can I have a feather like yours?"

Vicki's face blossomed into a smile. She met Krista's

eyes over her daughter's head, and gave a little air-punch of victory, mouthing, *Score!*

Seeing it, Bootsy grinned at Krista. "How about you, Krista? You in for a hat party?"

"Heck, yes," Krista said, joining the group. "You know what they say—a girl can never have too many hats or too many friends."

The guests spent a raucous hour selecting their outfits and then regrouped for try-ons. There were only two fitting rooms, so it turned into a fashion show of sorts, with Joan and Sabra kicking things off by coming out together in matching fringed shirts—breast cancer pink, of course—and body-hugging jeans, and swinging each other around in an impromptu square dance while the others laughed and applauded.

Peter and Bob were next up. Peter came out to strut his stuff in his same jeans, but with upgrades on the boots and shirt that transformed him into a real cowboy—albeit one fresh off the rack and in need of some scuffing.

"Hot dang!" Bootsy gave him a twirl, followed by a pat on the rear. "You'll do." Then, spinning away, she knocked gently on the door of the other fitting room. "Bob, honey? You doing okay in there? Need a different size?"

There was a low murmur from inside.

Bootsy gave a little nod. "I'm coming in, okay? Trust me, there's room for two, and I can help."

A brief pause, then the door cracked open.

Vicki came up beside Krista and said in an undertone, "He was worried about all the extra skin. He doesn't want to do surgery, but he hates when it shows."

Bootsy emerged a moment later, did a quick tour of the racks, and disappeared back into the dressing room.

"Who's next?" Krista asked brightly. "Allison? How about it? I'd love to see that skirt on you."

The plump, pretty brunette dimpled at being singled out—she was going to nursing school by day and waiting tables at a chain restaurant by night while working on not disappearing into the crowd of identical uniforms—and headed for the empty fitting room.

Just as her door closed, Bob's swung open and Bootsy stepped out. With a flourish of her arms, she intoned, "I'd like to introduce you all to . . . Cowboy Bob."

A man moved into the doorway, and logic said it had to be the same person that had gone in a few minutes ago—a cheerful guy who liked to tell jokes on himself, and whose personality was far bigger than the body inside his saggy, low-slung jeans and the too-big shirt that puffed out above his belt. But the sagging and puffing were gone now, and his body made an impact of its own in a pair of Wranglers and a dark green snap-studded shirt, unsnapped and hanging loose to show a narrow strip of plain white T-shirt and a studded black belt that matched the chunky biker-style boots on his feet.

With a black Stetson pulled low on his forehead, and wearing a layer of stubble Krista hadn't noticed before, he was unexpectedly sexy. "Wow!" she said. "You look awesome!"

The others chimed in seconds later, with hoots and

wolf whistles. And rather than brushing it off with a joke, he grinned and sketched a bow, then gave Bootsy a quick hug and whispered something in her ear before he rejoined the group, looking more at home with himself than he had all week. He was just in time to lead the applause when Allison came out with a vivid blue skirt swishing around the ankles of her sparkly boots, and wearing a smile that nobody in their right mind could lose in a crowd.

Grinning so hard that her cheeks hurt, Krista worked her way around to where Bootsy was sitting on the edge of a display riser. Crouching down, she leaned in to say, "Thank you. This is everything I hoped it would be, and more."

"They're wonderful. And they're making it easy on us. Did you see Bob's face when everyone started whistling?" Bootsy nodded. "That was a moment, sure enough."

"Thanks to you."

"He just needed someone to tell him how to make the shapes work together. It's not about hiding the soft spots, or sucking them in; it's about fooling the eye into looking somewhere else."

"Hopefully, he'll take that to heart." Krista looked over at where Bob was down on his heels, letting Claire check out the patterned leather band on his hat. "He's a good guy and he's done some amazing things, but he doesn't think it's enough."

"It doesn't matter what anybody else says," Bootsy pointed out, with an air of *been there, done that*. "It takes a long time to stop seeing the bad stuff that used to be in the mirror."

"Amen to that. And thanks again." Krista stood, intending to get Vicki and Claire heading into the fitting rooms. She stood up too fast, though, and the room turned suddenly gray and spinny. Sagging, she grabbed for Bootsy's shoulder. "Whoa."

"You okay?" Bootsy shot up, concerned. "Here, sit down."

"No, I'm okay." Krista took a couple of deep breaths and her vision cleared. "Just a head rush." And the last thing she wanted to do was mess with the makeover mojo.

"Are you sure?"

"I'm fine, really. Probably a little low on blood sugar, that's all." She'd gotten busy with Jupiter that morning, and hadn't really eaten much. Even the usual *snag a muffin on the way out the door* routine hadn't sounded all that appealing.

"Go grab something in the break room. We've got this under control."

Krista hesitated. "Are you sure?"

"Positive. Go. Help yourself to whatever looks good in there. We're not territorial."

But once Krista was in the small kitchenette, the smell of coffee and microwaved soup made her wrinkle her nose, and the brief burst of appetite fled.

Knowing she needed to eat something, she scrounged some leftover soup crackers and filled a mug with tap water, and alternated little sips and bites until she stopped feeling like she was going to fall down, pass out, or puke. Which was totally not her usual style, even when she was hungry, making her think she was more nervous about the ride-off than she had realized. That was the only thing she could think, unless . . .

Oh, no. Hell, no.

Heart pounding, she frantically scrambled to do the math, counting weeks that wanted to blend into one another. And then, legs turning to rubber, she sank back against the counter as a round of applause from out in the main room said that someone else had come out to do a twirl. "No. It can't be." Was she *pregnant*?

24

"We used protection." Sitting at the edge of the plush couch in Nick and Jenny's TV room later that evening, Krista rocked back and forth. "Every single time. Condoms, condoms and more condoms. We've gone through cases of the things."

"Now you're bragging," Jenny said, but she kept a steady grip on Krista's knee, and her eyes were full of understanding. "And, well, they're not a hundred percent."

"But they're ninety-nine-point-nine-nine whatever! And . . ." Throat locking, she buried her face in her hands. "I can't believe it. This is . . ." She didn't have the words, didn't know what to think about the three tests she had taken, which had yielded two little pink lines, a blue plus sign, and the digital word that made it a done deal.

Pregnant.

"Hey." Jenny shook her. "Hey! It's okay. Everything's going to be okay."

"Dad is going to kill me." Worse, he would be disappointed. They all would, because Skyes didn't have babies out of wedlock any more than they fell in love with the wrong men.

"Of course he won't," Jenny reassured her, but then added, "He might go after Wyatt, though."

"Aaaaah!" Krista screamed into her hands. "Don't say that! It's not his fault."

"But it's his baby."

"Don't say that, either."

"That it's his?"

"No. *Baby*. I'm still wrapping my head around *pregnant*."

"One follows the other." Jenny scooted closer and hugged Krista. "And you're starting to sound pretty nuts. You know that, right? This isn't the end of the world." She tightened the hug. "You're going to be a *mommy*!"

"Don't say that, either. I'm not ready."

"Sweetie, you've been ready since you were eight." Jenny paused. "Okay, that sounded weird, but you know what I mean. You're the most nurturing, patient person I know. And, come on"—she gave Krista a little shake—"Mom managed it, didn't she? And she didn't have the nurturing or patient parts going for her."

"But she had Dad."

"And you've got Wyatt."

"No," Krista said sadly. "I don't." Because that was the worst part of the shock—not just knowing that he absolutely didn't want a family, but knowing that whatever happened next, the good times they had shared over the past couple of months were over.

"Give him a chance," Jenny urged. "He's in deeper than you think. I bet he'll surprise you."

"And do what? The last thing I want him to do is propose because he knocked me up!" Krista launched to her feet and paced the wide room, needing to move. "If being in a relationship for more than a couple of months makes him feel like he's suffocating, what do you think this will do?"

"Make him man up?" Jenny suggested with a bit of an edge. "It seems to me that he's pretty darn good at taking the path of least resistance, at least when it comes to relationships. You need to make him care enough to dig in his heels and fight for what he wants—like he's doing with the sculpting." A corner of her mouth kicked up. "And this is coming from the *it takes one to know one* department. For the longest time, it was more fun for me to keep moving than to stay put. Then I met Nick, and staying put became the fun part."

"But you and Nick love each other."

"So do you and Wyatt."

"No." Krista's eyes were so dry they burned. "That wasn't our deal."

"So change the deal. Seems to me, you don't have a choice. It's not like you're going to keep this a secret from him." An eyebrow lifted. "Right?"

"No. I'll tell him. I just . . . I need to think things through first." Krista pressed a hand to her stomach, as nerves and nausea mixed with the discomfiting knowledge that she wasn't alone in her body anymore. There was something growing in there that was going to change her life. More, it was depending on her to make the very best choices she ever had, starting now.

"Tell him," Jenny urged. "Now. Tonight."

"Maybe." *Not.*

"I'm pushing. I'm sorry, I'll back off. I'm just . . ." Her lips curved and her eyes went all soft. "You're going to have a *baby*, Krissy. This is a good thing. Such a good thing."

Something loosened inside Krista, letting her finally take a breath. "I know. It's just . . ." Her voice climbed to a wail. "Why can't anything except the business go according to *plan*? This isn't the way it was supposed to happen! Mustang Ridge doesn't *do* single parenting. And where the hell is my perfect guy? He should have *been* here by now!"

Jenny sat back. Blinked. "You had a plan?" Then she shook her head. "Of course you had a plan. What was I thinking?"

Krista pinched the bridge of her nose. "It's stupid. I'm being stupid."

"Maybe a little unrealistic. But you've had a pretty crazy day, so I'd say you can be excused. Maybe you should go home and turn your brain off for a while, if you can manage it. Or do you want to stay here? Nick should be home in a bit. We could watch a movie or two, and the pullout in the guest room doesn't suck."

"Don't talk to me about pullouts," Krista grumped. "Maybe we should've used that instead of condoms."

Jenny snorted. "Science suggests otherwise, but I'm glad to see you've still got your sense of humor."

"I'm going to head home," Krista decided. "It feels too wimpy to hide out here."

"What are you going to do?"

"Maybe I'll make a plan. That seems to be a good way to ensure that the exact opposite happens."

"Let me know if I can do anything." Jenny hugged her tight. "I love you, kiddo. And remember, you've got a lot of people on your team."

"I love you, too, sis." But as Krista burrowed into Jenny's embrace, the hollow ache inside her said she didn't want a team—she wanted Wyatt. Problem was, she didn't know how to make that happen without trapping him . . . and if she did that, sooner or later, he would hate her.

Wyatt had just treated himself to a beer and Klepto to a couple of slices of turkey from his small stash in the bunkhouse fridge when his phone rang. Thinking that the cell was getting a workout today, he checked the ID and grinned as he answered, "Hey, stranger. How did everything go at Bootsy's this afternoon?"

"Good. Everything was . . . good. I think the guests had fun." Krista's voice was blurry.

"You okay? You sound tired."

"It was a long day."

"There's a hot tub here, calling your name."

"Can I have a rain check? I think I'm going to crash here tonight."

He did a double take. "Are you sure you're okay?"

"I'm fine, really. Just need some down time."

"Want me to come over and make you soup, or tea or something?" Which was stupid, given that she lived with her parents, and her grandparents' cottage was just down the hill. But she didn't sound like herself.

"I'm good. Just tired. See you in the morning?"

"Sure," he said, doing his damnedest not to be disappointed. She wasn't obligated to spend every night in his bed, after all. "Sweet dreams, cowgirl."

"Thanks, Wyatt. You, too."

"Call me if there's anything I can do. And if you change your mind, the door's always open."

After ringing off, he stood for a minute, dangling his beer and trying to laugh at himself for suddenly being all *now what?* about having a night to himself. "Looks like it's just us guys," he told Klepto. "You want a beer?"

He doled out more turkey, instead, and then they headed for the workshop, where the cowboys sitting around the fire had stalled out and he'd gone back to the drawing board. He kept coming back to the *Doorknob Kiss*, the piece he and Krista had made together. It didn't say "Wild West," of course, or "pioneer spirit," but something about it kept tugging at him, the same way he kept looking at the main cowboy and the dog together and thinking that it was almost there, but still missing something major.

Staring at the doorknob statue, he could picture a whole line of the tabletop sculptures, each of them different, always with a man and a woman, and sometimes a horse or two, made from household scrap metal. But that didn't solve his more immediate problem—the APM was doing its post-reno relaunch in the spring, and expected him to have something more than a couple of half-finished cowboys and a dog that really ought to be something else.

But what?

"What do you think?" he asked Klepto. "A calf, maybe?" That could work—maybe there was a tame dogie with the cowboys, an orphan that tagged along with the Cookie. Possibly named Mini-burger. Or Slider. "Okay, forget the calf."

He needed movement in the foreground, though, something to draw the eye up to the main cowboy's face. Flipping to a fresh sheet of paper, he grabbed a Sharpie because he was suddenly jonesing for bold, black lines that he couldn't erase. Looking from the doorknob piece to the cowboy and back again, he blocked in the man's figure, but then paired it with an obviously feminine shape.

He didn't know what the woman was doing out on the roundup or why she was holding the cowboy's hand and looking down at the dog, but the shapes sent a shiver down the back of his neck. Like maybe he was finally on to something.

Krista sat alone at the dining table, flipping through a box of old pictures and not really seeing the faces. Instead, she was hearing the concern in Wyatt's voice when he offered to brave the main house to make her a cup of tea.

She hadn't told him. Why hadn't she told him? It was just three little words: *Wyatt, I'm pregnant.* Except those three words had such power, maybe even more than *I love you.* Because suddenly there was another life involved in the conversation.

It was strange, really, to think that all of the people in these pictures had started that same way, in one form or another. *Honey, I'm pregnant. We're going to have a baby. Knocked up. A bun in the oven.*

Stopping at a black-and-white of a dozen or so people posed in front of the big fireplace, circa the forties, she picked out her great-grandparents and a blanket-wrapped bundle that, based on the two older kids standing with them, had to be Big Skye. Who, at some point, had been a *Honey, I'm pregnant.*

At least she could think the word now without hyperventilating. She was still sneaking up on *baby.*

"Find anything good?"

She looked up, startled to see her dad standing in the wide entryway. He was wearing a battered old T-shirt, his lucky fishing hat, and the old denim overalls that went under his waders.

"Going fishing?"

"Sure am. You want to come?"

It was more tempting than she would have expected—the tug of the current against her legs, the feel of rocks rolling beneath her boots, and the rushing sound of the river as she and her father cast the light fly lines over and over again, not really caring if the trout latched on or not.

She shook her head, though. "Thanks, but I think I'll stay in tonight."

"Everything okay with Wyatt?"

"Sure. Why?"

"Your bed hasn't seen much of you lately. Seems strange to find you here now."

Ack. Fighting not to squirm, she said, "I've got everything under control." *Sort of. Not really.*

"Maybe that's the problem."

"I didn't say there was a problem." But she wrinkled her nose at him. "What do you mean?"

"In my experience, the minute you think you've got a relationship figured out or going according to plan . . . well, that's when you get yourself in trouble, because you're not the only one in the equation. It's like working with a mustang—you can train in all the buttons you want, but you're still dealing with a wild creature that's got a mind of its own."

She frowned. "So I should click and treat him until he does what I want?"

He chuckled. "I was thinking more along the lines of asking for what you want, but not getting too caught up in how you get there. But what do I know? I'm just an old man who's headed out for a wild night on the river with his fishing pole."

She rose, crossed the room, and wrapped her arms around his waist. "Thanks, Dad. And thanks for giving Wyatt a chance."

He kissed the top of her head. "He's a good man, in

his own way. But if he messes with your head again, he'll have to deal with me."

I think this time it's going to be me *messing with* his *head.* But maybe Jenny and her father were right. Maybe it was time for her to ask for what she really wanted, and see whether he wanted her enough to make a change.

And if not . . . well, she would deal with it.

"Good luck." She kissed her father's cheek and nudged him toward the front door. "And keep your hat higher than your feet, okay?" It was what she usually said to the greenhorns, but she figured it applied equally well here, too.

When the door swung shut behind him and the house quieted around her once more, she returned to the table and shuffled the photos she had been poking through, sticking them back in their bins to await official cataloging. Because, really, all she had been doing was flipping through and thinking: *face, face, two faces, baby, face, face—*

Two faces with a baby. And not just faces. Familiar faces in washed-out sepia tones, with a swaddled baby and chickens pecking around the edges of the woman's skirt.

Krista froze, pulse bumping as she realized that it wasn't exactly the same picture they had hanging in the dining hall. The chickens were in different spots and the man's arm was around the woman, his hat tipped down as he looked at her and the baby, as if to say: *Mine.* She didn't know why the photographer had taken two of the same picture—maybe because this one was so washed out, or maybe for some reason she would never know. But her hand shook as she lifted this one. Turned it over. And saw faded writing in a spidery, angular hand.

Patience Smith (younger sister to Mary Skye), her husband Seamus, and their adopted daughter, Blessing. A church foundling, Blessing later married Jeremiah Skye. The local pastor refused to recognize the union, believing them cousins (though not of blood), so they had a native ceremony. They died in old age within hours of each other, and were survived by five children.

Krista traced the writing and let out a soft breath. If this wasn't a sign from the universe, a Big Foam Finger saying *yes, you know what you have to do*, then she didn't know what was. Because the situations weren't identical, but the message was clear, at least to her.

Family was what you made it, as was love. And sometimes that meant breaking the rules.

Pocketing the photo, she stuffed her feet in her boots and struck out along the trail, needing the air and the wide open. When she crested the hill and saw the bunkhouse, though, the air went thin and the wide open suddenly felt like it was crowding in. She made herself keep going, pushing herself up onto the porch and forcing herself to knock, even though he'd said he would leave the door open.

There was a scuffle and a "whuff," then the sound of boots on the floor. Moments later, the door swung inward to reveal Wyatt, still dressed for the workday.

"Hey!" His face brightened. "You changed your mind!" He tugged her in for a kiss that started soft and gentle but heated quickly, until she was pressed up against him with her arms twined around his neck and a voice inside her saying, *You don't have to do it tonight. You can wait. Enjoy the end of the season. Get through the ride-off. Get used to the idea yourself.*

But she couldn't, she knew. It would be too much like what he had done to her, back in the day.

"Are you feeling better?" he asked against her lips, then pressed a kiss to her cheek, her temple. "Or did you come for that cup of tea?"

"Actually, I came because there's something I want to show you." Then, God help her, something she wanted to tell him. And after that? Well, they would see. Because this was about to become either one of the best days of her life, or a complete train wreck.

25

"You found them!" Wyatt grinned at the picture that Krista had laid on the breakfast bar, then flipped it over and read the inscription on the back again. "I can't believe you actually found them. What are the chances? We should ride up to the waterfall in the morning and see if we can find their names. Seamus, at least, should be up there."

"I think he might be," she said, surprised that her voice sounded so normal when part of her was standing aside and looking at him, thinking, *This is the father of my unborn child.*

"You guys had it right all along, didn't you?" he enthused. "Gran said you figured they were a few years younger than Jonah and Mary, but not Jeremiah's generation. Except for the baby, of course." His lips curved. "Blessing. That's a nice name. I wonder what her story was, how she ended up left at the church? Seems like she got lucky, winding up here."

"She lived here her whole life, with Jeremiah." Her one and only. When had Blessing finally realized she loved him? Or had it been part of her all her life, like the shape of her nose and the color of her eyes?

Something must have come through in her voice, because he glanced over. "How about that tea?"

"I don't need tea."

"Wine, then. Or cookies. You're pale."

"I need to ask you something."

"Anything." He turned to face her and slid the photo aside, then pulled out the barstools at the kitchen counter. "Sit. I'll get some wine."

"Water's fine." It seemed like some sort of cruel cosmic joke that alcohol was off limits at a time like this.

The ice maker's buzz was loud; the sound of water going into the glasses reminded her of the waterfall. And by the time he set her glass in front of her and took the other seat, with their knees bumping and his hand stretching across to the arm of her chair, his expression had gone serious, his eyes wary. "You can ask me anything, Krissy, you know that."

She did. Just like she knew he would tell her the truth now, even if it wasn't what she wanted to hear. "If you close your eyes and look five years into your future, what do you see?"

To her surprise, he closed his eyes and thought about it for a few seconds, giving her a moment to watch him. A moment for her heart to shudder in her chest.

She didn't want to do this. But what other choice did she have?

His eyes opened and found hers, and in them she saw regret. "You want me to tell you that you're in the picture, but I can't say that. I can't say much, really. I see myself still sculpting, maybe dancing with Ashley at her wedding—hopefully not to Kenny, but if that's what she wants . . ." He lifted his hand from the back of her chair to touch Krista's cheek. "I thought we were having fun. Can't this be enough?"

She would've given anything to be able to say yes, but that second little pink line had changed everything. "I've tried to tell myself it's enough." She caught his hand and flattened his palm against her cheek, held it there. "It's more than I've had before, and I don't regret a second of the time we've spent together. I need you to know that. I need you to know that I"—*love you*—"care deeply for you. That's not going to change, and neither will the memories we've made this summer."

He was pale now, the stubble turned to a dark line on his tense jaw. "But you need the words, the promises."

"I need to know there's some potential for a future. I want a husband, Wyatt. Children. I'd give anything for you to be that husband, for those children to be yours." Guilt stung as she skirted the edge of honesty, but she'd be damned if she trapped him. She would give him this one chance, and if he didn't want her for her own sake, she would cut him loose. Then, later, she would tell him about the baby and they would make the necessary arrangements.

Arrangements. Gawd, what a terrible word. And how she hated knowing that she'd be bringing her child into the world already saddled with things like visitation and custodial agreements. *Don't cry. Hold it together. You can do this.*

"Krista . . ."

Her heart sank as she heard the answer in his voice, saw it in his eyes. "It's okay. We had a deal."

"It's *not* okay." He took her hands, gripped them hard. "I don't want to promise you something I can't deliver."

"The future or the children?"

"Both." He shook his head. "I'm not in the right place for this. Maybe in a few years. . . . If we could just keep bumping on the way we are for a while, and see how things go . . ."

She wanted to. Oh, how she wanted to. But that wasn't an option anymore. Voice cracking, she said, "I can't. I'm sorry. I can't be with you, loving you like I do, and know that you're not on the same page."

Love. The word registered in his eyes.

She nodded. "I love you. Please don't say it back, even if you think you might feel it. Please don't say anything about it. Please, just . . ." She swallowed a sob, knowing tears would make it worse for both of them. "Say thank you or something."

"Thank you." He leaned in and kissed her, long and hard, and with a desperate edge that sparked the same greedy need inside her.

But that would only make things worse, she knew. So she put a hand on his chest and eased him away.

His eyes met hers, searching for something she didn't think she could give him. "What happens now?"

"Now . . ." She swallowed hard, feeling her heart rip raggedly in her chest. "I think you should leave."

Wyatt sat stunned—by the words *you should leave*, by the way they cut into him, and by the part of him that bellowed like a wounded bull, even though he usually lived his life with one foot out the door. She had told him she loved him. Now she was kicking him out.

He wished he could say he didn't deserve it, that there wasn't anything he could've done different, but they both knew the truth. "Can I stay through the ride-off?" Was that his voice? It sounded like hell.

She wanted to tell him no; he could see it in her eyes. But she said, "If you want. Don't feel like you have to, though. I can get someone to fill in for the freestyle."

The walls were very close, pressing in on him and making it hard to breathe. "So that's it, then." Anger edged his voice. "Thanks for the help, Wyatt, now buzz off?"

She paled. "I'm sticking to our original agreement, just ending it a little early. Don't worry. You'll get your full pay."

He almost told her where she could stick his pay. "This isn't about the money. It was *never* about the money."

"No," she agreed. "It was about bringing things full circle. I think we've done that, only this time I'm cutting you loose rather than waiting around for you to bail. Can you really blame me?" But his heart turned over at the catch in her voice.

What the hell was he doing? She had given him the choice, told him what he needed to do to stay. It wasn't her fault he couldn't commit, even to the one woman who made him wish he could. "No," he said. "I don't blame you." He pushed his chair back with a wood-on-wood screech. "I'll be gone by morning."

Krista didn't know how she made it out of the bunkhouse when all she wanted to do was stay, didn't know how she took the path when her eyes were drenched with tears. Somehow, though, she found herself back at the ranch, standing in the parking lot and staring up at the stars.

Most of the time, she could tip her head back, think of the generations of Skyes that had looked up at the same stars, and remember that her problems were small in the grand scheme. Not tonight, though. Tonight, the sky just looked bleak and cold, and the stars looked very far away. Even the main house seemed big and black in the darkness, like a fortress, her bedroom cool and empty. The barn was the only place that seemed alive, with rustles and thumps echoing as the horses picked at their hay and shifted in their stalls.

She dragged her feet down the aisle, trying not to think that she wouldn't hear Wyatt's voice coming from the tack room tomorrow morning, wouldn't see him at the head of the line when they rode out. Wouldn't wake up beside him, feel him moving over her, inside her.

Ever. Again.

That stopped her in her tracks, made her fight for breath. She struggled for control, hearing a strange, wounded-animal noise and knowing on some level that she was the one making it.

Staggering, stumbling, she bypassed Lucky and Jupiter and made for the second stall from the end, where the knee-high stall guard contained the barn's smallest occupant. Fresh tears gathered as she said, "Hey, Marshmallow. Can I hang with you for a while? I could use a friend." One that wouldn't ask questions or make suggestions, wouldn't ask what had gone wrong.

Gathering a couple of flakes of hay, she spread it in the corner and lay down on the nest it made. And, curling up in a tight ball, she put her face in her hands and let go.

The sobs that tore from her throat, raw and feral, sent the pony scampering to the other side of his stall. Krista couldn't stop them, though. They poured out of her in a ragged, hurting wave that crashed over her, held her under, and left her helpless to do anything but remember.

She wept for the moment she added up the symptoms and realized that her life would never be the same, for the flash of panic on Wyatt's face when she said *love*, the sharp grief when she told him to go. She cried knowing that she would be getting huge and awkward, and doing it alone, going into labor alone, learning how to be a mom alone. Surrounded by family, yes, but still very alone.

The hay rustled nearby and a soft muzzle touched her hand, blowing warm breath on her skin. Then, spurred by the same instinct that made him move so slowly around the scared or physically challenged kids, the one that spurred him to nuzzle the ones who needed him the most, little Marshmallow gave a sigh, folded his stubby legs, and collapsed into the bedding beside her.

"Oh." Fresh tears scalded her eyes—at the gesture, at the knowledge that this was her best option for cuddling, starting now—she wrapped her arms around the sturdy neck, buried her face in the pony's thick mane, and wept while the man she loved packed up his bags and drove away. Again.

It felt wrong, how little time it took Wyatt to clear his things out of the bunkhouse and load Old Blue with his tools and scrap. Forty-five minutes from start to finish, and he had his bags in the cab and Klepto standing near the couch where his bed used to be, looking up at Wyatt with a canine expression of *what gives?*

"We're hitting the road." At least he wasn't leaving a note this time. But the hollow ache in his chest and the burning in his eyes were the same. Worse, even. Because this time he wasn't just leaving behind a college relationship built on a whole lot of what-ifs and future stuff. He was leaving behind a beautiful, brilliant woman who impressed the hell out of him on so many levels. She challenged him, went toe-to-toe with him, made him want to be a better man.

He wasn't though. He was the same guy he'd always been.

"Come on." He whistled for Klepto. "Get in the truck."

He hated closing the door, knowing he'd never again open it and hear her voice. Never again soak in the hot tub with her, or sit on the porch and watch the sun go down. And he'd never again carry her up the stairs to the loft and toss her on the big bed and follow her down, or wake up to her kiss and a round of lazy lovemaking before getting started with their days. He would miss the work, miss the horses—especially Jupiter—miss the ever-changing parade of personalities that came through the swinging doors of the dining hall wearing their starchy new shirts and unscuffed boots.

"Damn it." Now the burn had turned to moisture, wetting his cheeks and making him feel like a fool. For coming. For staying. For leaving.

All of it.

Turning on his heel, he strode down the porch steps and got in Old Blue. Firing the engine, he drove off, doing his damnedest not to look back at a long, narrow log cabin that hadn't ever been his to keep. And, as he turned onto the road and rolled past the main entrance, where big solar lights illuminated the stone pillars and threw slivers of light on the metal archway, he found himself thinking he should've made it two-sided, so the people on this side would see a different message. NOW LEAVING MUSTANG RIDGE. Which he'd always meant to do, after all.

Klepto, curled in a ball on the passenger side, packed in with the bags, gave a low, anxious whine.

"It's back to just you and me, buddy. How does home sound?" Even as he said it, he knew it sounded wrong—Denver wasn't home any more than his and Sam's apartment during college, or any of the other spots he'd put down his shallow excuse for roots over the years. Just places, a set of GPS coordinates he could call his own until it came time to move on again. "Maybe it's time," he said. "How does California sound to you? Not LA, of course. Maybe the desert."

The dog didn't answer, just sighed and plopped his head back down.

Traffic was light and Wyatt's foot was heavy on the gas, and he did the four-hour drive in two and a half despite the heavy load in the back of the truck. When he pulled in, the motion-activated lights did their thing, illuminating the cabin and adjoining workshop. He hit the garage door remote and the big door accordioned up, giving him plenty of room to pull the truck inside.

The door rolled back down as he got out of the truck, leaving Klepto to sleep, and when the panel sealed shut, it was like he'd just closed out the rest of the world. The insulated walls blocked the sounds of the nighttime forest and the blowers came on automatically, stirring the air and adding a neutral white noise he usually found soothing.

Now, it set his teeth on edge. So did the overhead lights, with their cool fluorescents and almost complete lack of shadows. And the way it was too damn easy to swing the block and tackle over his truck and unload the heavy pieces.

It was all smooth and calibrated, exactly as he'd built it to be. It shouldn't have felt soulless, like it was the exact opposite of the pioneer spirit, with none of the danger and adventure that came from making something out of nothing.

Feeling the walls edge in on him—sterile and white, dang them—he pulled on his protective gear. It didn't matter that he hadn't been in the house yet, didn't matter that it was three in the morning. He wasn't hungry and sleep was a long ways off. And if he stopped moving long enough for all the things he wasn't thinking about to catch up, he might do something stupid. Like drive back to Wyoming and tell Krista he wanted to be with her, for better or worse, whatever the hell it took.

Which would be a really bad idea.

So instead, he would erase another really bad idea. Lighting his biggest torch, he got to work on the crap sculpture he'd built up on the ridge.

And, as the first cowboy's head hit the deck with a satisfying rattle-clang and rolled off under a workbench, Wyatt felt a manic-sounding laugh tear at his throat. "You know what they say." He pitched his voice to echo off the insulated walls. "If at first you don't succeed . . . it's time to start the hell over."

26

The next morning, Krista told herself not to go down to the bunkhouse. Then she went anyway, driving under the archway and letting out a low moan when she found Old Blue missing and the workshop door closed tight.

She parked in the lot. And stalled, staring at the front door.

You can do this, she told herself. *You can. Just do it.* Was it only two months ago that she'd told herself the same things when it came to calling him about the wrangler job? It seemed impossible.

"Just go in, grab your stuff, and get out." She wanted her flip-flops and the inscribed picture of Seamus, Patience, and Blessing. The errand got her out of the car and up the steps, and she even managed not to think—at least not too much—that it was less than twelve hours ago that she had knocked and he'd opened the door and kissed her. Less than twenty-four hours ago that everything had still been normal.

Well, this was her new normal.

Steeling herself, she pushed through into the main room of the bunkhouse, which looked the same as it had last night. At first, anyway. But then she saw that Klepto's bed was missing. The coffee table was clear of books and sketches. And there was no brown Stetson sitting on the breakfast bar.

He was really gone.

Krista's breath thinned in her lungs, and although she wanted to think she had cried herself dry last night, new tears flooded her sore eyes. "Damn it." She swiped at her red, raw cheeks as her stomach churned, heading toward nausea.

Thunk, thunk, thunk. The sudden sound of boots on the porch wrung a gasp from her. She spun, heart leaping into her throat . . . and then sinking to her toes when Jenny stepped through the door.

"Oh," she put a hand to her throat, holding in the disappointment. "Hey." Not that she wanted to see him. Not that she had hoped, even for a second, that he had changed his mind.

Except she totally had.

Jenny came in, took a look around, and gave Krista's hand a squeeze. "I guess he's gone."

"Thanks for not saying *again*."

"It's not the same."

"No." There was no note this time. She already knew why he was gone.

"Did you tell the others?"

"About the breakup? First thing this morning." She had called Jenny at midnight, sitting alone on her bed with hay in her hair. Now, she leaned her head on her sister's shoulder and sighed. "This sucks. Makeover Week was supposed to be the high point of the season."

"Five years from now, when you look back, what are you going to remember most?"

Krista knew what answer she wanted. "Finding out I was pregnant."

"There you go." Jenny squeezed her in a one-armed hug. "Maybe try to focus on that for now. Or if that's too big and scary, then take it one day at a time. Today, we're going to ship Jupiter over to the fairgrounds to let her get acclimated. In fact, we're due there in an hour."

"Okay." Krista took a deep breath that didn't do much to settle her stomach. "First, let's get my stuff out of here." She took a long look in the direction of the hot tub. "It'll be a while before I come back." And longer still before she could stand in this room and not think of Wyatt.

Wyatt didn't know what time it was when he finally set his torch aside and came up for air. He was pretty sure he had missed a meal or two and at least one night's sleep—was that dusk outside, or dawn? He didn't have a clue. But it didn't matter, because finally—*finally*—he had gotten the pioneer piece right. And he knew what it had been trying to tell him all along.

He stared at it and shook his head with disbelief. "It wasn't ever supposed to be a dog. And I'm an idiot."

The sculpture had started with inspiration from the picture of Seamus, Patience, and Blessing, but it had taken on a life of its own, becoming a flow of metal shapes that suggested a wild, harsh landscape behind a hollowed-out Conestoga wagon. A metal man dug with a blunt-ended shovel while his woman stood with a rifle on her shoulder and a baby in her arms. A wolf watched from one of the distant ridges and a herd of horses flowed down another, making the humans look very small against the sweep of the frontier. Up close, though, they were strong and sure, with gears for joints and pistons for limbs. And the infant cradled in the woman's arms stared up at the sky, where a hawk spun on an invisible wire, watching the pioneers break ground for the homestead that would become a ten-generation legacy.

It was raw, yet, but he knew the heart was there. Which was ironic, really, because he'd left his heart behind when he left Wyoming. He'd left his family—or the beginnings of it, at any rate—behind.

He whistled. "Hey, Klepto. You want to go home?"

The dog was bedded down under the workbench, curled in a sweatshirt of Krista's that he had smuggled from the bunkhouse. He barely even twitched.

"I don't mean inside. I mean *home* home. Mustang Ridge? Krista?"

The mutt's head whipped up. "Whuff!"

"Come on, let's go. The competition starts in . . ." He checked his watch. "Whoa. A few hours. We've got to haul ass."

He had a big, huge apology to give, and some promises to make.

That is, if he wasn't already too late.

As he dashed for the house for a change of clothes, he dragged out his phone, punched in the main ranch line, and crossed his fingers that Krista wouldn't answer. He didn't want to do this on the phone.

To his relief, Gran picked up. "It's Wyatt, but please don't hang up," he said quickly. When there was an ominous silence on the line, he said, "Remember when Ed said that Mustang Ridge owes me a favor? Well, I'm calling it in."

Krista did her best to join in on the Makeover Week festivities, but by the time she and Jupiter were on deck to enter the arena for the trail class, a big part of her just wanted it to all be over and done with.

Forty-eight hours from now, the guests would be headed home and she would have four blessed days off to hide out, lick her wounds, see a doctor. *Gack.*

A round of applause indicated that the horse ahead of them had finished the obstacles. Jupiter shifted, her ears flipping back and forth as she tried to track the noise in front of her, the horses behind her, and the *ping-ping-jingaling* noises and cheerful tunes coming from the midway and carnival rides. The mare had settled in better than Krista had any right to expect, and kept all four feet on the ground as the wide gate swung open and a feisty chestnut gelding jogged out of the arena, with his rider collecting high fives and fist bumps on the way out, suggesting a good score.

Krista didn't even look at the number. She just

wanted to give her nice horse a good ride and not embarrass Team Mustang Ridge. She didn't need to win anymore. Not with Big Skye slowing down and her life eight-plus months from being turned upside down.

Leaning down in the saddle, she stroked Jupiter's neck and whispered, "Just do your best, sweetheart."

Once they were in the ring, though, the mare arched her neck, set her ears forward, and strutted her stuff like a runway model, as if she somehow knew she was being judged. Krista barely needed to do anything except point her from one obstacle to the next as they breezed through the weave poles, equine teeter-totter, drag, and cavalletti. The obstacles blurred together, and then suddenly they were at a narrow squeeze chute with an even narrower gate at the far end.

"You can do it," Krista said, and sent her horse into the chute.

And Jupiter, bless her, marched through without flicking an ear. The applause began when they reached the third to last obstacle and swelled from there, with a chant of "Mustang Ridge, Mustang Ridge" that had no doubt started with her family and the guests, but seemed to be spreading.

Jupiter tackled the bridge and loped over the crinkly tarp like it was nothing, then stood like a rock while the score came up and the applause swelled.

"Brave mare!" Krista ruffled the long gray mane.

Big Skye met them at the gate, eyes sharp and excited. "You're in second place, girlie! Only two points behind the leader." He caught Jupiter's reins and guided the horse through the crowd to where the others were waiting, with the family in front and the guests ranged behind, packed two deep and looking sharp in their new outfits.

Brightening her smile, which felt dull and muted, Krista held out her fist for little Claire to bump. "Did you see Jupiter? Wasn't she the best?"

The little girl nodded. "She did the gate perfect!"

"She sure did." Krista swung off the mare. "Time to change into our freestyle outfits. I'll be right back."

As the others clustered around Jupiter—who fortunately seemed to be soaking up the praise and thriving in the Harvest Fair chaos—Krista sank down on a nearby bench and concentrated on breathing. Because if she was breathing, she wasn't puking or crying, both of which were far closer to the surface than she wanted.

"Hey." Jenny dropped down beside her. "How are you holding up?"

"I'm good. I'm fine. I'm . . ." She put her face in her hands and burst into tears.

"Whoa there! Oh, sweetie." Jenny hugged her.

"I'm sorry." Krista sniffed back the tears with a force that made her sinuses bulge and put a headache square between her eyes. "I'm okay. It's just"—*hormones, grief, guilt, regret*—"I should have told him about the baby. I should've given him the chance to make the decision rather than making it for him." She sighed. "Dad was right. You can install all the buttons you want, but there's still another living creature in the equation."

Jenny blinked. "If you say so. Which means . . .

what? That you're going down to Denver to see Wyatt?"

"No. I'm going to call him."

"Face-to-face might be better."

"No kidding." She pawed through her equipment bag for her cell phone. "I mean I'm going to call him right now and tell him I'm coming down as soon as the after party is over." She dialed, cupping a hand around the phone in an effort to hear it ring.

It did, but not in the digital bleat she was expecting in her ear. Instead, the first few bars of "How 'Bout Them Cowgirls" rang out behind her.

Krista's. Heart. Stopped.

Jenny whipped around, and her mouth fell open. "Well, I'll be . . ."

Working against legs that didn't want to hold her up, Krista rose shakily and turned around, suddenly aware that she was the focus of a whole lot of eyes. Not just from her family or the rest of Team Mustang Ridge, but also from the nearby grandstands.

But it didn't matter, because Wyatt was standing there, wearing a devastating, form-fitting tux that made him look like someone had dropped James Bond into a country fair. More, he was regarding her with an expression she'd never seen on him before. One that brought the blood buzzing through her system and had her pulse drumming in her ears. "What are you doing here?" she demanded. "Why are you dressed like that?"

He held up his phone. "You called me, remember?"

But then he dropped the cell in his pocket and crossed to her. "I'm glad you did. It makes me think that maybe it's not too late, after all." He searched her eyes. "Is it? Because I've got some things to say to you."

She was dimly aware that the others had pulled off Jupiter's saddle and bridle, and were hanging the JUST MARRIED sign on her haunches. They had been the last to go in the trail class, and were up third in the freestyle. There wasn't much time.

Catching his sleeve, startled by the feel of expensive cloth, she said urgently, "Before you do, I need to tell you—"

"Please." He covered her hand with his own. "Let me. I'm the one who screwed up. I should have seen it sooner."

"Seen what?"

"That you're my open prairie, my fast horse, and my gorgeous sunset, all wrapped together."

She blinked. "Is that poetry?"

"Never. It's something that Ashley said to me the other day, sort of." He shifted to clasp both of her hands in his, his eyes dark and intense. "I keep seeing myself as someone who moves on rather than sticking it out, but she pointed out that the horses have always been part of my life. Maybe I ease away from them now and then, but I always come circling back around to having them in my life, one way or another." He squeezed her hands. "That's you and me, Krissy. We keep circling back to each other. Only this time I'm not leaving. Because I never want to leave you, ever again."

Her pulse thundered in her ears, and it was a very strange moment when Jenny came racing toward her with a wedding dress and veil. "Wait! What—"

"The number two horse is a scratch, which means you're on deck. Put this on!" She dumped the dress over Krista's head and started doing up the Velcro they had built into the costume. "Do the veil. Quick!"

Wyatt grabbed the headpiece and got it into place, chest vibrating with amusement. Then he flipped the veil back and leaned in to kiss her. Part of her froze while another did a Snoopy dance—that he was kissing her, that he had come for her. But it wasn't enough. It wouldn't be enough until he knew the whole truth.

She pulled back and blurted, "I'm pregnant!" And she said it way louder than she had intended.

Every conversation halted in a forty-foot radius, but she barely noticed. She was entirely focused on Wyatt's jaw dropping and his face going blank.

"Mustang Ridge!" a voice called from the gate. "You're next!"

Suddenly, she knew exactly what he meant about the walls closing in, the air going thin, and the grass on the other side of the gate looking very green. "Coming!" she hollered back. Then, throwing Wyatt a last, panicked look, she sprinted for Jupiter, swung aboard, and kicked the horse toward the gate.

Wyatt spent a three-count frozen in place while the word ping-ponged around in his brain. *Pregnant. Pregnant. Preg-nant.* But as quick as the shock had hit him, it got chased off by a surge of *hell, yes!* Punching a mental fist in the air, he spun to go after her—

And found himself facing off against her family members, who were standing shoulder to shoulder, with a collective look of *if you want to get to her, you're going to have to do it through us* tinged with a sort of wild-eyed shock that said the announcement had been news to most of them, too.

Ed Skye, wearing the costume tux from the bellhop skit, said, "Looks like you've got a decision to make, Webb."

But it was a wonderful no-brainer. "I made my decision before I left Denver. She's mine, if she'll have me. The baby is mine either way." He tipped his head to where Jupiter danced at the in-gate, swinging the JUST MARRIED sign. "That's the woman I love over there, and she's carrying my child. I'd be obliged if you'd get out of my way, so we can kick some ass on the mustang we trained together."

Her father stuck out his chin. "And if we don't?"

"I haven't fought for enough things in my life. From now on, I intend to fight for her."

When the gate swung open and the open chords of the freestyle music began to play, Krista's heart lodged itself in her throat. *Where are you, Dad?* Was she going to have to do this alone?

"*Sssst!*" The gatekeeper gave her a furious wave. "You need to get in the ring."

"I'm waiting for—"

"We're good!" Wyatt said, hopping up behind her. "Go!"

Jupiter didn't need any more urging—she knew the music, knew it was her cue. With her front feet flipping in a high-stepping Spanish walk, she danced into the arena to an explosion of flashbulbs and a bunch of *oohs* and *aahs* from the crowd, followed by laughter when the audience got a load of the sign on her bum.

Under the cover of that noise, Krista hissed, "My dad was supposed to be doing this with me." Wyatt had his arms around her and his chin on her shoulder, and the whole-body press was seriously distracting.

"I'm pretty sure that's illegal in most states," he said against her neck.

"Wyatt!"

"You thought I would cut and run, but I don't blame you." His hand snuck down, then splayed protectively across her belly in a move that darn near melted her heart. "Thing is, Krista . . . the dog wasn't really a dog."

The music changed as Jupiter reached the registration desk, and they dismounted, removed the sign from her rump, and pulled a couple of Velcro tabs to quick-change her from a car to a bellhop.

The crowd roared as the horse nudged Wyatt out of the way to go around behind the registration desk and ring the prop bell, calling the luggage cart, which she proceeded to fill with foam rubber luggage that kept falling out. Every time another piece hit the dirt, the mare shook her head and snorted.

Laughter and applause followed each pratfall on

cue, and Krista and Wyatt met over by the registration desk, where they were supposed to fake a kiss.

Wyatt sold it, bending her over his arm and working it for the crowd, but against his lips, Krista whispered, "What do you mean the dog wasn't a dog? What is he? A little old man in a fur suit?"

"Not Klepto. The dog in the sketch. It was a baby all along. It was my brain's way of saying there was something missing, not just in the sketch, but in my life. A baby, Krista. Our baby."

Jupiter snorted down the back of his neck, and he brought Krista up from the dip so they could follow the luggage cart to the honeymoon suite setup, complete with the reinforced platform bed and huge bottle of fake champagne. There, Jupiter poured while they kissed again.

"Since when do you want kids? I thought raising Ashley burned you out on all that." She wrapped her arms around his neck as he kissed her cheeks, her body beginning to burn while her heart swung between wanting to believe him and being afraid he would yank it all away again in a few weeks.

"I'm an ass," he said against her lips as he cued Jupiter to try to interrupt the kiss, then walk around them, shaking her head in disgust. "Ash is still my sister, always will be, but that's not the same as having my own kid. Our kid." He grinned down at her. "I want the adventure, Krista. I want everything to be new and exciting—not because I'm somewhere different, but because I'm where I'm supposed to be—at

Mustang Ridge, with you and our family. Watching our kids grow. Helping the business grow. Seeing the sun come up over the mountains every day with you, and knowing I'm exactly where I'm supposed to be. Because I love you. Not the way I did before, when I was trying to be the right guy for you, but stronger and harder than anyone will ever love you. Because now I *am* the right guy for you."

Her heart rolled in her chest. "Oh, Wyatt. I love you, too. But how can I be sure this isn't you trying to convince yourself again?"

"You can't." He said it like it was the best thing in the world. "There aren't any guarantees in this life, Krissy-girl, except maybe that it isn't forever. Maybe I die tomorrow, maybe the sun doesn't come up over the mountains . . . or maybe—and this is what I'm banking on—maybe we wake up together in the bunkhouse and go down to breakfast, and see what the day might bring. That's the adventure. That's the pioneer spirit, the forging into the unknown because it's there. I might not know much, but I know that I want to do that forging with you and our baby, and another baby. Maybe one or two more after that." His grin lit her heart. "Because I love you and the future we're going to have together."

There was an amplified whinny-sigh as Jupiter gave up on the humans and went to lie down on the big platform bed, to a wave of laugher from the audience.

"So what do you say, cowgirl?" Wyatt grinned down at Krista, with all the love in the world gleaming from his eyes. "Will you give a cowboy a chance to love you, and damn well never leave you again?"

Her heart swelled to bursting, as if a switch had clicked on inside her, saying, *This*. This was what she had seen glimpses of back in school, this was the love she knew they both had inside them. And this was the future, the adventure she had been craving. Her life with Wyatt might not ever be a safe and peaceful routine, but it would never be boring. And they would live it together.

"Yes!" she said, and the single word lit her with joy. "Yes to all of it, and especially to the forever. I love you, cowboy. More than the sun and the moon, and all the waterfalls put together!"

The music hit its crescendo as Jupiter pulled the bed cover over herself with her teeth, lay her head on the pillow, and stretched out a forefoot to dim the lights. And, as Krista reached up to kiss Wyatt—her friend, lover, partner, and the father of her child—applause rolled through the stadium where they had first seen each other after so long, and the chant rose around them, hundreds of laughing voices shouting in unison, "Mustang Ridge, Mustang Ridge, Mustang Ridge!"

27

Two weeks shy of Christmas, with a pretty layer of snow on the ground, clear roads, and no storm on the horizon, a hundred or so of the Skye family's nearest and dearest gathered at Mustang Ridge to celebrate Gran and Big Skye's golden anniversary.

The heated tent had gone up at daybreak; the caterers had arrived at eleven; and Rose had fussed until the flowers and balloons showed up at noon. The guests arrived on schedule to yell "Happy Anniversary!" when Jenny brought in the happy couple. Gran had blushed and done lots of "Oh, poosh. Go on with you!" while Big Skye gave a couple of pleased *harrumphs* and asked if there was cake.

Now, as the outside world darkened with an early-winter dusk, with the food winding down, the cake getting set up for its big reveal and no major disasters to speak of, Krista was almost ready to consider the party a roaring success . . . And she would, as soon as they got through the presents.

"What do you think, little one?" She brushed her fingers across her stomach, which was starting to round out with more than just the snacks she was wolfing, grateful that the all-day sickness had finally worn off. "Are they going to like what we've done for them?"

There wasn't any answer from inside her—no kicks yet, or any real movement she could feel, which was so strange after seeing the baby the other day on the ultrasound screen, a black-and-gray silhouette rocking out to the beat of her own little internal drum.

Our little girl, Krista thought, smiling as she watched her grandparents on the packed dance floor, swaying to something slow and bluesy. *Imagine that*. It still felt unreal some days, like the image on the screen was special effects and nothing was really all that different. Except that so much was different, wasn't it?

She and Wyatt had taken over the bunkhouse for good, splitting their time between the ranch and his place in Denver, where the statue for the pioneer museum had finally come to life, wearing his face and hers, with a dappled mustang mare in the background to remind them of Jupiter, who was running free now, in a river-fed valley paradise about an hour's ride north of the ranch.

They had named it Blessing Valley, and there hadn't been a dry eye in the group when Wyatt had slipped the rope from the big gray mare's neck and sent her to join the herd of forty-three mustangs that her winnings had bailed out of government holding pens. She had stood there a moment, looking from the humans to the horses and back again. Then, with a huge snort, she had exploded into motion, racing to meet her new band. As she flew down the valley, the horses had bunched together and the newly gelded herd stallion had raced forward to meet her, ears flat and nostrils pinched.

Jupiter had whirled and kicked him in the chest, and that was all it took. The humans could practically see the hearts in the herd leader's eyes as he fell for the big gray mare, hoof, line, and sinker. A minute after the horses met, their necks were twined together. Five minutes later, she had been muscling through the herd, meeting the others and letting them know who was in charge.

Even Big Skye had swiped at his eyes, blaming it on dust. And, better yet, their weekly check-ins said that the horses were flourishing in the sheltered valley.

Even with all of that going on, though, Krista had found it easier than she expected, being away from the ranch. In fact, it had been nice to plow through her office work during the day and spend the nights and weekends with Wyatt, exploring Denver, hanging out with Damien, or just staying in and cuddling by the fire while Klepto dozed nearby.

The ranch was fine without her, at least during the winter months. And she was starting to think that home wasn't a place for her, after all. It was more a state of mind . . . and the man she loved.

"Hey there, cowgirl," Wyatt said from behind her, as if he had known she was thinking of him. "Here. This is for you." A plate appeared in front of her, loaded with grilled chicken, skewered veggies, and the potato salad she had moaned over earlier in the day after sneaking a taste.

She grinned up at her man, drinking in the sight of him, so handsome in his dress-up jeans and a striped button-down, and so utterly easy in his skin, whether he was being the cowboy, the metalworker, or somewhere in between. "More food?" she teased. "Seems to me we just ate."

"The rest of us ate. You orchestrated." He nudged her toward a chair. "Sit. Eat. And after that, we're dancing."

She tipped her head, looking up at him as warmth moved through her, simple as the sunrise. "Bossy much?"

"You take care of the guests. I take care of you and the baby. Seems fair to me."

More than fair, Krista thought, taking the plate and enjoying the feeling of being fussed over—her and the yet-unnamed life-changer that was growing inside her. As he sat beside her, she asked, "Has our special guest arrived yet?"

"She's about ten minutes out. Which is cutting it close, I know, but she'll be here."

She grinned as she forked up a mouthful of the creamy potatoes. "Ten minutes is nothing. It'll take twenty for everyone to ooh and ahh over the cake."

"If you say so. Frosting is frosting to me."

She leaned in to give him a smacking kiss. "You're such a guy." And what a guy. *My guy*, she thought, feeling the rush that came with it. Then, seeing a swirl of activity coming from the direction of the kitchen, she shoveled in a couple more bites as the DJ ended the song and announced, "And now . . . it's cake time!"

There was a round of whoops and applause from the crowd, then another, longer ovation when the caterers set the promised dessert on a round table beneath a golden spotlight.

In deference to Gran's status as Queen of All Baking, they hadn't gone crazy with elaborate flavors, fondant, or piping. Instead, there were layers of chocolate and vanilla cake covered in a good buttercream and decorated with scenes from her and Big Skye's marriage. Not edible copies of pictures from the family albums— Jenny had vetoed that on the grounds that eating their faces would be weird—but little symbols of their five-decade marriage, from a cutout of the prize bull and twenty good cows Big Skye had given her father as her bride price, to caricatures of the whole family ringing the top tier.

"Well, I'll be!" Gran's eyes glowed as she took in the massive dessert. "Arthur, look. There's even a little boat for the cruise we took on our twenty-fifth!"

As Krista had predicted, it took some time for everyone to properly admire the cake and take pictures of her grandparents posing with it, cutting it, and even feeding each other demure little bites. Then there were more toasts as the caterers cut the monster and distributed slices, until finally everyone had a piece and Big Skye commandeered the microphone.

"I, ah . . . *Harrumph.*" He fiddled with the mic for a

second, then looked at Gran with a tender expression that was very unlike his usual scowl. Taking a sip of champagne to clear his throat, he said, "It's hard to believe it's been fifty years, isn't it, darlin'? Seems like just yesterday we were chasing Eddie around in his nappies and putting him on old Dancer for his first ride. But now look at us." His gesture swept the crowd. "I'm such a lucky man. Thank you, sweet Edith. Thank you for making a man out of me, and for making a family out of all of us."

Gran started to wave that off with a pleased "Poosh!" but then stopped herself and beamed back at him. "You're right, Arthur. I did all those things. And you know what? You're welcome. You're not the easiest man some days, but you're the best man I know, and I'm proud to have been married to you all these years." She raised her glass. "Here's to the beginning of another fifty years, my love, in this world and the next."

The crowd started to clap, but Big Skye waved them down. "Hang on, hang on. I'm not done yet!" He grinned, dug into the breast pocket of his sport coat—which rocked suede patches and probably qualified as vintage—and came up with an ivory card made of thick paper, with a spray of pressed wildflowers on the front. Holding it out, he said, "This is for you, Edie. Happy anniversary."

As she flushed, Wyatt whispered in Krista's ear, "Did your mom help him pick out the card?"

She shook her head. "Nope. He made it himself."

"Impressive."

Gran gasped as she read the pretty card. "*Arthur!* Do you mean it? We're going to Paris? *Tonight?*"

His grin went from ear to ear. "Surprised?"

"I'm . . ." Her mouth worked and her hands fluttered at her sides.

"Shocked?" Big Skye offered.

"Oh, you!" She swatted at him, smiling. "I've always wanted to go to Paris!"

With a flourish, he looped an arm around her waist and drew her in for a long kiss that scored good marks on the heat scale and sparked more than a few whoops.

"Awww." Krista leaned back against Wyatt. "Look at them."

"Quite a picture," he agreed, dropping his chin on the top of her head.

Gran and Big Skye's togetherness had been on an uptick since fall. Sure, she grumbled about having him underfoot more, and he had driven everyone nuts trying to micromanage the annual winterizing chores from a folding chair rather than the saddle. But he had also thrown himself into the family photo project, which had evolved into several new video clips for the ranch Web site and a coffee-table book, and he was starting to make noises about writing an actual history of Mustang Ridge.

Speaking of which. "Is Maizey here yet?" Krista asked as her mom and dad presented her grandparents with their gift—a day at Le Cordon Bleu, with cooking classes for Gran and an equal number of elaborate tastings for Big Skye.

"I don't . . . Wait. I think I see her. I'll be right back." Wyatt moved off through the crowd as Gran did a little happy dance and hugged Rose tight enough to strangle.

Under the cover of applause and congratulations, Wyatt returned with Maizey Bascomb in tow. The elegant, silver-haired curator of the American Pioneer Museum was wearing a pale blue dress, an imposing amethyst-and-silver pendant, and an expression of suppressed excitement as she gave Krista a quick hug. "I can't believe I'm here! This place is *gorgeous*." She eased back and gave Krista an up-and-down. "And so are you. What's your secret?"

Krista grinned up at Wyatt. "True love." *And a bun in the oven*, she thought, but didn't say, because today was about Gran and Big Skye. "You should come back in the summer. I know I'm biased, but I swear it's the prettiest place on Earth."

"You'll have to bar the gate to keep me away." Maizey's eyes shifted to the center of the room, where a representative of the cattlemen's association was handing over a gift of steaks on the heels of a medium-funny cow joke. "Do they know that you guys renegotiated the deal for *Blessing*?" That was what Wyatt had named the new statue. Because it was, on so many levels.

Krista shook her head. "Not a clue. Are you ready for the presentation?"

"Whenever you are!"

At Krista's high sign, Jenny commandeered the microphone and used her *hey, listen up, this is the TV voice-over speaking* voice to say, "Before we get back to the dancing and making merry, us grandkids have a little something for the happy couple." She held out the mic. "Krissy? How about you do the honors?"

As Krista stepped forward, Wyatt blew her a kiss and said, "Knock 'em dead, boss lady."

"I intend to," she murmured in return. Because this was family. It was everything.

Taking her place at the center of the dance floor, facing Gran and Big Skye, who looked cheerfully shell-shocked by all the presents and speeches, she took a deep breath to steady the nervous little churn in her belly. She hadn't written up anything formal, so it came straight from her heart when she said, "Most of you here today know me. For those who don't, my name is Krista, and I'm one of Arthur and Edith's granddaughters. I'm also the one who pushed the idea of turning this place into a dude ranch. Gran was behind me all the way on it, I think because she wanted a new kitchen."

That got some chuckles, and a twinkling wave from her grandmother.

Returning the wave, Krista continued. "Gramps wasn't as big a fan of the idea, though, and he and I have butted heads over it through the years. He thought that Mustang Ridge should stay the way it's always been. And you know what? He's got a point."

That got a startled, "Eh?" from Big Skye.

"Yeah, you heard me. I said that you've got a point.

Not that we shouldn't adapt and improve, but that we shouldn't forget where we started from, either. Me? I come from them," she pointed to Gran and Big Skye, "from them," her parents, "from here" she widened her arms to sweep the ranch, "and from the generations of Skyes and married-ins who have made this such a special place." She paused, savoring the moment. "So, to recognize that, and to share Gran and Big Skye's legacy with the world beyond Three Ridges, we have a surprise for you. I'd like to introduce Maizey Bascomb, the director of exhibits at the American Pioneer Museum." She held out the mic.

There was lots of curiosity as Maizey tucked a wrapped package under her elbow, took the mic, and smiled at Gran and Big Skye. "Congratulations on your milestone anniversary. To recognize it, and your family's contribution to shaping pioneer history, we would like to designate Mustang Ridge as a Place of Pioneering Interest." She unwrapped the flat object to reveal a polished metal plaque, which she showed to the audience, and then handed to Gran, amid a swell of applause.

"Well, I'll be . . ." Gran beamed over at Big Skye, holding out the plaque. "Look, Arthur!"

The tips of his ears had gone bright red. "That's fine," he said gruffly. "Mighty fine, indeed."

Maizey continued. "We'd like to include some family memorabilia in an exhibit we call The Way North, about settlers who left the main trail and spread into other parts of Wyoming. And Mrs. Skye, we'd love a contribution from you on old-school cooking techniques. Do I understand that you have a sourdough starter that dates back to the original homestead?"

Gran beamed. "Why, yes! Would you like to try him?"

Maizey blinked. "Him? Who?"

More voices than Krista could count chorused in unison, "Herman!" and then dissolved to laughter.

Grinning, Krista rescued Maizey from the microphone, and said, "To my grandparents. Happy anniversary!"

There was a general shout of, "Hear, hear!" and lots of clinking glasses, and the guests moved in to admire the plaque. From the throng, Big Skye reached out a hand to Krista. "Come here, you." Pulling her into his arms, he hugged her long and hard, like she was eight years old again, whispering in her ear, "Thank you. For everything."

And she had a feeling that if Bueno had been in the tent with them, he would've put her up on the saddle in front of him, and called her his little cowgirl.

Eyes stinging with happy tears, she hugged him back fiercely. "I love you, Gramps. So much."

He patted her shoulder. "You're a good girl, Krissy. The best."

Gran was next, hugging her so tight she couldn't breathe, then setting her away to mock-scold, "I know you told him about lunch in Paris."

Krista blinked innocently. "I don't know what you're talking about." Then she grinned. "But wasn't it breakfast in Paris and lunch somewhere else?"

"Who cares? I'm going to Paris!" Gran threw her hands up in the air and did a twirl that flared her skirt around her legs and got Big Skye's attention as the DJ took his cue and spun the next tune—something jazzy and fun that immediately got toes tapping.

When the dancing started up again, Krista walked into Wyatt's arms. He swung her in a circle, then pulled her close and enfolded her, swaying to the music. "Happy?" he said against her temple.

"Blissful. That was perfect."

"Yeah. It really was." His voice was a low rumble, his hands hypnotic on her body as they danced. When the song wound down and another geared up, he said, "You thirsty?"

"Parched, actually, and I wouldn't mind sitting for a minute. And, you know, enjoying the glow of a party well executed."

"Well executed, indeed. But I've got something else in mind." Twining their fingers together, he led her from the tent, snagging their coats on the way out and draping hers across her shoulders. "Come on."

Little bubbles of pleasure fizzed in her bloodstream. "Where are we going?" she asked, though it didn't really matter, as long as she was with him. It had taken her a while to figure that out. But she got it now. She did.

"You'll see."

He took her to the barn, ushering her into the warm, sweet-smelling interior.

A laugh bubbled up. "You didn't buy a pony, did you?" He had been talking about it, though she had assured him that Marshmallow would love having a little girl of his own.

"Nope. This is all for you." He swung open the door to the tack room, where the heat was on and a blanket was spread on the floor, topped with a bottle of sparkling cider and two glasses.

She lifted a hand to her throat as it closed on a swell of emotion. "Oh, Wyatt. It's perfect. I'm so ready for a few minutes of peace and quiet, with just the two of us." More even than she had realized until just this moment.

"Your wish is my command." He took her hand and lowered her to the blanket, then poured the cider as she fluffed out her skirt and let the party din recede from her brain. For a short while, at least.

Stretching her arms wide, she breathed deeply. "I really don't think we could have found a better way to celebrate. Fifty years. Can you imagine it?"

"Yeah, actually, I can." And something in his voice said it wasn't an offhand comment.

Happy sparks lit in her belly and she leaned into him for a kiss. "Me, too." They had talked about marriage, of course, and agreed it would happen when the time was right. Next fall, maybe, or the spring after. It would happen, though, she knew. She had faith.

More, she had love.

"In fact . . ." Wyatt looked around them, then gave a low whistle. When that didn't produce any results, he whistled again and said, "Yo, Klepto. That's your cue!"

Krista gaped when the scrubby gray dog came bounding through the door, with his tail wagging and his cheeks bulging. "Oh, jeez," she exclaimed. "What have you got there? Tell me it's not expensive."

"Yeah," Wyatt said. "Actually, it is."

The dog stopped at the edge of the blanket and sat down like he was actually trained to sit-stay, and looked at Wyatt for his next cue.

Something suddenly made her think that this was about more than a glass of sparkling cider and a moment for them to be alone.

Wyatt sat beside her, lifted his glass, and said, "To us."

"To us," she responded weakly. "What's going on here?"

One corner of his mouth kicked up. "You'll see. Honestly, I thought about doing this after the presents, in front of everyone, and your parents and grandparents were fine with it. But then I figured we didn't need an audience for this. Just each other."

"My . . ." Her parents knew? And Gran and Big Skye? She lifted a hand to her rapidly tightening throat. "An audience for what, exactly?"

"This." He held out a hand to Klepto. "Drop it."

The dog opened his mouth and spit a cardboard jewelry box into his hand.

Wyatt winced. "You weren't supposed to slobber on it, you fool. Glad I swapped out the original box for something you couldn't swallow."

Krista barely heard him. She was staring at the box. "Is that . . . ?"

"Your Great-grandma Abby's ring?" He opened the box to reveal a yellow-gold ring set with a deep red garnet and crusted with diamonds. "Yeah. It is. And it's my promise to you."

Her breath exited in a rush as the world threatened to spin. This was happening. It was really happening. "What kind of a promise?"

"All of them," he said simply, and held out the ring. "Will you wear this, Krista Skye, as a symbol of my promise to love you, adore you, care for you, and be your partner? Will you travel with me, ride with me, and be my anchor and my wings? And, most of all, Krista Skye, will you marry me?"

"I will," she said softly, feeling like her heart was suddenly too big for her chest, too big for her entire body. "I love you, Wyatt. So much. I'm so lucky you came back into my life."

She held out her hand and he slipped the ring—the one she had loved since she was a little girl—onto her ring finger where it fit, snug and perfect, like it had been intended for her all along.

"I'm the lucky one," he said, cupping the back of her neck and drawing her toward him. "You gave me a second chance," he said against her lips. "And thank God for that."

He kissed her then, in a perfect moment that went on and on, lighting sparks in her body that could easily expand to more. She moved closer, slipped her hand inside his shirt, and—

"Hey, you two," Nick called from the far end of the barn. "If you're about done in there, Big Skye is yelling for you. Jenny's setting up for a family picture, and he wants both of you in it!"

Read on for a special preview of the next
book in the series,

FIRELIGHT AT MUSTANG RIDGE

Available from Signet Eclipse
in February 2015!

Danny Traveler didn't put much stock in luck or fortune-cookie sayings, but as the shuttle bus rolled beneath an archway that spelled out WELCOME TO MUSTANG RIDGE in horseshoes, she was starting to think that the whole "if you're going through hell, keep on going" thing might have some merit. The last year or so had sucked eggs, but now, finally, she thought she might be seeing the light at the end of the tunnel.

Or, rather, the rainbow at the end of the tunnel. Because as the luxury bus followed the winding drive between two grassy fields—horses on one side, cattle on the other—they were headed straight for a perfect rainbow that arched over the valley beyond.

"Would you look at that?" Danny's seatmate plastered her face to the window. "It's a sign!"

Danny made a polite noise of agreement. Kiki-From-Cambridge had been talking in exclamation points the entire three-hour ride, to the point that the heavily made-up—and generously endowed—brunette had seemed to be in danger of popping the snaps of her fringed Western shirt as she babbled on about every-thing from the gum-smacking guy who had sat next to her on the plane to the fact that she hadn't been on a horse since she got bucked off a lead-line pony at the age of six. That made Danny wonder why she had de-cided on a dude ranch for her summer vacation, but she kept the question to herself and gave Kiki props for facing her fears.

Too bad she was doing it at top volume a couple of feet away.

Most of the others on the bus had tuned Kiki out by the thirty-minute mark, leaving Danny wishing she had taken the singleton seat in the far back.

"Can you believe we're finally here?!" Kiki gave a happy sigh. "It feels like I've been waiting for this for-ever. What color horse do you hope you get? I want a yellow one! Pimiento, they call it."

Danny couldn't help herself. "I think it's palomino."

"No, I'm pretty sure it's pimiento. And did you see the cowboys on the Web site?" Kiki made a *yum-yum* noise. "I'd like to take a ride on one of them!"

Trying not to picture a horse made of pimiento loaf, a deli product called palomino loaf, or Kiki riding any-thing two-legged, Danny pointed out the window. "Oh, look! There's the ranch! Isn't it pretty?" Kiki made a happy noise and flattened her nose to the glass once more, making Danny wonder what she looked like from the other side, and then gave herself a mental kick for being bitchy. It wasn't Kiki's fault that Danny was winding down just when everyone else on the bus was gearing up. Hoping her internal eye rolls hadn't made it to the outside, Danny asked, "Do you see any of those cowboys?"

"Not yet," Kiki said, staring raptly as the valley unfolded in front of them. "But I see more horses, and you're right. It's sooo beautiful down there!!"

And, yeah, if Danny hadn't given up the window seat the second time Kiki leaned across her to *ooh-ahh* before they even left the airport loop road, she would have been making a face-print of her own on the glass.

Tucked into a perfect V of sun-toasted valley, the ranch was a mix of old and new, from the log-style main house and matching guest cabins scattered near an almost perfectly circular lake to the big steel-span barn that bumped up against an older wooden structure. Fence lines spidered out from the barns and bordered a dirt track that led through a perimeter fence and up a shallow slope to a ridge. Beyond that somewhere was Blessing Valley. Her valley.

Danny let out a soft sigh. It looked peaceful. Wonderful. And like it was exactly what the doctors had ordered.

"Wow is right!" Kiki said, suggesting that Danny had said the word aloud. "Aren't those just the cutest cabins you've ever seen?"

The noise level increased as the other passengers roused from their travel fugue with exclamations of "There's the pavilion where they have dancing!" and "Do you think we can fish in the lake?" along with lots of "Ohh, look at the horses!"

The rising chatter bounced around Danny as the young cowboy in the driver's seat pulled the shuttle up in front of the barn and killed the engine. Getting on the intercom to project over the noise of two dozen vacationers readying to make a break for it, he said, "Welcome to Mustang Ridge, folks! I'd like to invite you to hop on down, fill your lungs with some fresh Wyoming air, and connect with Krista, Rose, or Gran—they're the ones wearing the green polo shirts and carrying clipboards. They'll get you set up with your cabins and tell you all the cool stuff that comes next." He gave a dramatic pause, then deepened his voice. "So … are you ready to take your first step onto the soil that's been walked by cowboys of the Skye family for more than ten generations?"

As a ragged group shout rose, made up of lots of *Yeah* and *Woo* noises, Kiki scrambled over Danny and leaped into the aisle, where she did a shimmy-shake that set a whole lot of stuff shimmying and shaking, and hollered, "Let's ride 'em, cowboys!"

The driver's eyes went deer-in-headlights wide in the rearview mirror, and, instead of doing the "I can't hear you" thing that was probably next in the script, he popped open the doors. "Watch your step, folks! And welcome to Rustlers Week!"

Danny stayed put while the first wave of guests stampeded off. Then she and the stragglers filed out into a whole lot of sunshine. The minute her hiking boots touched down, she got a quiver in her belly that said, *You're here. You made it. Welcome to the next chapter of your life.* Which was totally the power of suggestion, thanks to the bus driver's rah-rah routine, but still. Moving away from the bus, she filled her lungs with dry, sweet-smelling air that carried the scents of horses and sunbaked grasslands.

"You must be Danielle," a voice said from behind her.

She turned, doing a double take at the sight of a pretty, perky blonde who wore a green polo and a baby sling, and was entirely familiar, yet not. "Krista. Hi! Yes, it's me. But, please, call me Danny." She peeked inside the sling and saw the curve of an infant's head, blond baby-fine hair, and a fat pink bow. "And this must be Abigail Rose."

Krista's lips curved. "Abby to her friends, which includes you. Any friend of Jenny's is a friend of ours."

"Jenny and I really only worked together for a month or so." In a faraway rainforest, where Krista's twin had been filming a reality dating show and Danny had been in charge of the zip-lining, bungee jumping and canyoneering dates.

It felt like another lifetime.

"If she says you're cool, then you're cool," Krista said firmly. Then, to the baby, she said liltingly, "Isn't that right, Abby-gabby? Your Aunt Jenny knows her stuff. And, thanks to her, Danny here is going to hang out with Jupiter's herd up in Blessing Valley for a while. Won't that be fun?"

Throat tightening, Danny managed, "I'm grateful. Really. I don't know how to tell you what this means to me."

Krista patted her shoulder. "Don't stress it—we're happy to help. I get it, though. You're way more used to doing favors than needing them."

Danny eyed her. "Jenny told you that?"

"Nope, but like recognizes like." Krista adjusted the sling as the sleeping baby shifted against her, curving into her body like a small, sleepy shrimp. "Up until a year ago, I had to be in charge of things, no matter what. The ranch, the business, life in general . . . I might have asked for help now and then but always on my terms."

"And then she came along?" Danny nodded to the baby.

"Well, first her father came along." Krista's brilliant blue eyes gained a glint. "Wyatt. We were college sweethearts who crossed paths again at a time when I needed a cowboy, he needed some saddle time, and neither of us was thinking about romance. At least that was what we keep telling ourselves."

"And you're getting married soon." Jenny had passed along that detail while Danny had still been trying to catch up with the idea that her freewheeling, country-hopping photographer friend was married to a veterinarian and living in Wyoming when she used to swear she'd never return home for more than a quick visit.

A pleased flush touched Krista's cheeks. "We've got nine weeks until the wedding. Long enough to feel like I should change everything but not long enough that it's an option, so we're going with the plan we've got—

family and friends under the pavilion." Her expression brightened. "You're invited, of course. Please say you'll come!"

Danny had to stop herself from backpedaling, which was silly. Maybe for a while she had hoped the next wedding she went to would be her own, but it was past time for her to stop flinching over that. "I'd be honored," she said. "Thanks for inviting me."

"Brilliant! Don't stress about dressing up, but if you want to shop, Jenny and I are always up for a girls' night, or afternoon or whatever. And our friend Shelby—she always manages to make the stuff she finds in town look like it came out of a fashion magazine."

"That sounds fun." She couldn't spend the whole summer alone, after all. Besides, she wanted to thank Jenny in person for e-mailing out of the blue to catch up, and then, when Danny gave her the short version of the past couple of years, responding with: *Come to Mustang Ridge. It's the perfect place to get your head screwed back on straight.*

"Sweetie?" a voice called from the other side of the bus. Moments later, a petite, white-haired woman came around the front of the shuttle, eyes lighting when she caught sight of Krista. "There you are! I'm going to fix a few folks up with snacks while your mom and Junior show everyone else to their cabins. Do you need anything?"

"Nope, I'm good for right now, and Miss Abby is conked out." Krista patted the heavy curve of the sling. "Bless her for being a good sleeper, and pretty much the best baby ever—not that I'm biased or anything. But before you go, Gran, I want to introduce you to Danny Traveler."

"Hello, dear! It's so lovely that you're here. How was your flight?"

"It was fine." She had picked a plane that had a single row of seats on one side, then strapped herself in, chased an Ambien with a screw-top micro-bottle of white wine, and practiced her deep breathing exercises. It hadn't been fun, but she had made it through.

Gran's eyes went sympathetic, like she had said the rest of it out loud. "I stocked your camp with supplies, but come see me before you and Krista head out there. I have a little basket put together for you."

"And by *little* she means approximately the size and mass of the average blanket chest," Krista put in.

Danny cleared her throat, suddenly overwhelmed— by the warm welcome, the chaos, all the people around her. To Krista, she said, "Do you need to help show people to their cabins? I don't want to keep you from your guests."

"You're a guest, too."

"I'm not paying nearly what they are." Which was yet another reason to be grateful.

"No, but you're staying far longer, and you're not going to require nearly as much hands-on time. Though for the record, you're welcome to participate in any of the activities you'd like. We've always got a spare horse or three, and there's something incredibly relaxing about a long ride in the great, big wide-open."

"We'll see. I'm planning on spending most of my time in the valley."

"Of course. But please consider it an open invitation." Krista touched her arm—like she wanted to do more but could tell Danny wasn't a hugger. "Come on. Let me hand off Abby to her nana, and then I'll show you to your valley." She laughed. "Now *that's* not something I get to say every day! See? I knew I was going to like having you around." She danced off, humming a happy tune and exchanging a few words with each of the guests she passed, introducing herself and the baby, and welcoming the newcomers to her family's world.

Danny watched her, thinking, *That.* That was what she wanted—not all the people and the hustle-bustle of running a dude ranch, but that sense of loving life and doing exactly what she wanted to do. Too bad she didn't know what, exactly, that was.

Yet.

LOVE
ROMANCE
NOVELS?

For news on all your favorite romance authors,
sneak peeks into the newest releases, book
giveaways, and much more—

"Like" Love Always on Facebook!
f LoveAlwaysBooks